The Forbidden Hills

THE FORBIDDEN HILLS

AL & JoAnna LACY

Multnomah® Publishers

Sisters, Oregon

Lac

THE FORBIDDEN HILLS
published by Multnomah Publishers, Inc.

© 2005 by ALJO PRODUCTIONS, INC.
International Standard Book Number: 1-59052-477-2

Cover design by The DesignWorks Group, Inc.

Unless otherwise indicated, Scripture quotations are from:
The Holy Bible, King James Version

Multnomah is a trademark of Multnomah Publishers, Inc., and is registered in the
U.S. Patent and Trademark Office.

The colophon is a trademark of Multnomah Publishers, Inc.

Printed in the United States of America

For information:
Multnomah Publishers, Inc., 601 N. Larch St., Sisters, Oregon 97759

Library of Congress Cataloging-in-Publication Data

Lacy, Al.
    The forbidden hills / Al and JoAnna Lacy.
        p. cm. — (Dreams of gold trilogy ; bk. 2)
    ISBN 1-59052-477-2
        1. California—History—1846-185—Fiction. 2. Gold mines and mining—
Fiction. I. Lacy, JoAnna. II. Title.
    PS3562.A256F67 2005
    813'.54—dc22

                                                    2005007426

05 06 07 08 09 10 — 10 9 8 7 6 5 4 3 2 1 0

I lovingly dedicate this book to my very special friend
Ruby Kitterman.
Though time and miles have intervened,
you will always be a precious *jewel* in my heart.
Blessings,
JoAnna

PROVERBS 17:17

PROLOGUE

In this trilogy that we call DREAMS OF GOLD, we will tell the stories of three major gold strikes that took place in North America in the nineteenth century and changed this continent forever.

The first is the California gold strike in the late 1840s. The second is the Black Hills gold strike in the mid-1870s. The third is the Yukon gold strike in the late 1890s.

Gold is referred to very early in the Bible:

> And a river went out of Eden to water the garden; and from thence it was parted, and became into four heads. The name of the first is Pison: that is it which compasseth the whole land of Havilah, where there is gold; And the gold of that land is good: there is bdellium and the onyx stone.
>
> Genesis 2:10–12

Many people ask why man has valued gold so highly practically ever since he has been on the earth. There are several reasons. Gold is good and highly prized because it is warmly beautiful. It is enduring, for it never dissolves away. Under all circumstances, it retains its beauty. Strong acids have no effect on it. Gold is the only metal that is unharmed by fire. In fact, each time gold goes through fire, it comes out more refined than it was before. It can be melted without harm, and it is marvelously adapted to shaping. Finally, gold is prized so highly because of its scarcity.

Being relatively rare makes gold extremely valuable and much sought after. Hence, when gold was discovered in California, the Dakota Black Hills, and the Klondike region of Yukon Territory in Canada, multitudes of gold seekers rushed to these places to make their fortunes. In this trilogy we will tell some of their stories.

Gold is also mentioned at the very end of the Bible. In the book of Revelation the most precious of metals is portrayed as constituting the New Jerusalem, with even its street made of gold so pure that it is as transparent as glass. As an angel was giving the apostle John a tour of the city in a beatific vision, he even used a reed of gold to measure the city and its gates and walls.

> And he that talked with me had a golden reed to measure the city, and the gates thereof, and the wall thereof. And the building of the wall of it was of jasper: and the city was pure gold, like unto clear glass. And the twelve gates were twelve pearls: every several gate was of one pearl: and the street of the city was pure gold, as it were transparent glass.
>
> REVELATION 21:15, 18, 21

In between the beginning and the end of the Bible, gold is spoken of so many times that one must use a concordance to find all the references.

So often in the Bible gold and the lesser precious metals are linked with money and other possessions that make men rich, and the pursuit of riches is tied to greed and covetousness, which destroys lives. Riches are also often spoken of in the Bible as deceptive, unsatisfying, hurtful, and uncertain. Repeatedly in history, many of the supercilious wealthy have lost their fortunes in the blink of an eye.

These truths will be shown in this trilogy. Let each of us take note of what the Spirit of God told Paul to write to his son in the faith, Timothy:

> Charge them that are rich in this world, that they be not highminded, nor trust in uncertain riches, but in the living God, who giveth us richly all things to enjoy.
>
> 1 TIMOTHY 6:17

INTRODUCTION

Of all the Sioux chiefs in the nineteenth century, the most outstanding leader and warrior was Chief Sitting Bull. In his teen years he distinguished himself in battle, fighting other Indian tribes who were enemies of the Sioux. At twenty-five years of age he was made leader of the powerful Strong Hearts, an elite Sioux warrior society. His fellow warriors observed that he was well-named. He was indeed like a bull: headstrong, fearless in battle, incapable of surrender—in short, *bull-headed.*

In 1863, at the age of thirty-two, Sitting Bull was designated chief of the Hunkpapa Sioux. By his leadership of the Hunkpapas he soon became revered by the entire Sioux nation as their spiritual leader.

At the very time that Sitting Bull became chief of the Hunkpapas, the greatest issue that the Sioux had ever faced was upon his people. The encroachment of white men on Sioux land was coming to a head. During the middle of the 1860s, some of the finest Sioux buffalo hunting grounds were being disrupted by a heavy traffic of gold miners along the new Bozeman Trail, which led from the Fort Laramie area on the Oregon Trail northwestward to Virginia City and other gold camps in Montana Territory.

Another outstanding Sioux leader was Chief Red Cloud of the

Oglalas. His people resided at that time in the very path of these intruders. He and his warriors attacked the traffic along the trail so ferociously and persistently that by early 1868 the United States government was ready to make peace at a high price. President Andrew Johnson met with Congress, and all agreed with him that the government should offer the Sioux a spacious reservation encompassing the entire western half of what is present-day South Dakota and that "*no white person or persons shall be permitted to settle upon or occupy any portion of the reservation for any reason.*"

Moreover, the proposal—to be known as the Treaty of Laramie—declared that the Powder River Country, immediately to the west of the Black Hills Dakota reservation and reaching as far as the Big Horn Mountains, "shall be considered to be unceded Indian Territory."

Further wording in the treaty pledged the United States government to prohibit all persons except authorized government officers, agents, and employees from entering the lands set aside for the Sioux nation.

In May of 1868, Chief Red Cloud and many other Sioux chiefs signed the agreement with government officials, but Sitting Bull was unimpressed by the terms of the treaty, and, not trusting the white men, he refused to accept the agreement. His opinion was that the treaty, while sounding generous, would considerably diminish the vast ancestral range of the Sioux.

While Red Cloud and the other Sioux chiefs who followed his leadership moved their people onto the reservation in the Black Hills area of southwestern Dakota Territory, Sitting Bull and those in agreement with him remained on their unceded land along the Powder River, west of the Black Hills in Wyoming Territory.

Over the next few years both the reservation Sioux and those who, like Sitting Bull, chose to remain in the unceded area discovered that the Treaty of Laramie was by no means the last word in the disposition of the old Sioux land. The unceded territory suffered the first incursion. In 1872 surveyors for the Northern Pacific Railroad, seeking the most economic route from Duluth, Minnesota, to the Pacific coast, decided that the tracks should follow the south bank of the Yellowstone River, which was in unceded Indian lands.

Officials in Washington—including Ulysses S. Grant, who had become president in 1869—expressed no objections. Grant ordered army troops to accompany the surveyors and protect them as they made their plans to locate tracks where they desired.

During the summer months Chief Sitting Bull led occasional attacks against the survey teams and their army guardians in an attempt to discourage their invasion of Indian territory. Such sporadic combat would have become full-scale war had the railroad survey been followed by actual construction. War was temporarily averted, however, when the United States economy sank into depression in late 1872 and grew even worse in 1873. The Northern Pacific Railroad found itself without funds to lay tracks.

The depression was still on as spring came in 1874, but President Grant and Congress felt that the federal government should help finance the railroad construction because the railroad to the Pacific coast would aid the nation's economy. In mid-June, Grant wired General Philip H. Sheridan, who, as army commander of the Division of the Missouri, with his office in Chicago, was in charge of the army in the West. In the wire, Grant told Sheridan that in order to protect Northern Pacific workers from the Indians when the construction got underway, a new fort should be erected in the Black Hills, a well-watered and heavily timbered region on the western edge of the Sioux reservation.

Sheridan wired the president back, agreeing wholeheartedly. Grant wired in return, telling Sheridan to contact Colonel Daniel Huston, commander of Fort Abraham Lincoln in Dakota Territory, and tell him to send an army reconnaissance team into the Black Hills region to locate a suitable site for the fort. (Fort Abraham Lincoln was located on the right bank of the Missouri

River at the mouth of the Heart River, three miles south of the town of Bismarck.)

Sheridan recalled that in July 1873 he had assigned Lieutenant Colonel George Armstrong Custer to Fort Abraham Lincoln, along with ten companies of the Seventh Cavalry under his command. Several other cavalry units as well as a good number of infantry units were also at the fort. He would wire Colonel Huston and have him send Custer to lead a large reconnaissance team onto the Black Hills Sioux reservation to locate and establish a site for the new army fort.

If riches increase, set not your heart upon them.

PSALM 62:10

So is he that layeth up treasure for himself,
and is not rich toward God.

LUKE 12:21

ONE

At Fort Abraham Lincoln in Dakota Territory, late in the afternoon on Tuesday, June 16, 1874, the sun's heat diminished as it sank low, dipping its fiery, red disk behind the horizon of the rolling plains.

In the tower at the fort's main gate were Sergeant Will Hepler and Corporal Justin Scott, who were regulars in the tower.

Young privates Henry Washburn, Jake Barth, and Neal Kline had just arrived at the fort late that morning from an army training camp in Fort Scott, Kansas, along with some forty other new recruits. The three privates had been assigned to the tower that afternoon by the commandant, Colonel Daniel Huston, who wanted them to learn the job of tower guards.

The new men noticed as the sun dropped below the horizon that Sergeant Hepler and Corporal Scott were standing side by side at the tower's railing posts, looking across the plains as if they expected to see something...or someone.

When the two guards looked at each other worriedly, Private Barth asked, "Is something wrong, Sergeant Hepler?"

The sergeant bit down on his lower lip and nodded. "Yes, there is. You see, there are eight Arikara Indian scouts here as part of the fort staff. Seven of them left at sunrise this morning to go on a buffalo hunt. Ordinarily, they would've been back with the meat and the hides at least two hours ago."

"I see. So you're afraid something is wrong?"

"Yes," said the sergeant. "Definitely."

"The group was led by Howling Wolf," said Corporal Scott. "He is the brother of the fort's chief scout, Bloody Knife. You've heard of him, I'm sure."

All three of the new recruits nodded.

"Bloody Knife is Lieutenant Colonel Custer's personal scout, isn't he?" Kline asked.

Hepler nodded. "That's right."

"I understand Bloody Knife earned his name as a very young warrior. They taught us about him at Fort Scott."

The sergeant grinned slightly. "Well, they taught you right. Bloody Knife is something to see in hand-to-hand combat. He—"

Hepler's words were cut off when he saw an army patrol coming over a distant hill. "Here's Lieutenant Colonel Custer and his patrol now. Colonel Custer and Bloody Knife are going to be upset when they find out that Howling Wolf and his men haven't returned."

Henry Washburn blinked as he set his gaze on the trotting patrol that raised great clouds of dust as they rode toward the fort by the vague light that was still in the western sky. "That's a pretty good-sized patrol unit."

Hepler rubbed his jaw. "Mm-hmm. With the Sioux tribes upset at our government, Colonel Custer is wise to have plenty of men in his patrols."

Corporal Scott looked toward the oncoming patrol and then turned to Hepler. "I'll go down and open the gate, Sergeant."

"I'll go with you," said Hepler. Then he said to the new men, "You fellas come down with us, too. I want you to meet Lieutenant Colonel Custer and Bloody Knife."

The patrol was drawing near as the five men reached the bottom of the tower stairs. Corporal Scott hurried to the gate and swung it open. The riders drew rein, and Lieutenant Colonel George Armstrong Custer, with Bloody Knife riding at his side, moved his mount up to the guards and stopped.

"Colonel Custer," said Hepler, "I want you to meet these young men." He introduced the privates first to Custer and then to Bloody Knife, explaining that they were some of the new soldiers who had arrived late that morning from Fort Scott, Kansas.

Custer, at thirty-five years of age, was slender and rawboned, with cool, pale blue eyes, high cheekbones, a droopy mustache, and long, curly hair that touched his narrow shoulders. Still in the saddle, he smiled at the new privates and welcomed them to Fort Abraham Lincoln.

Bloody Knife nodded with a slight smile and welcomed them also. He had expressive black eyes, a square jaw, and muscular arms and shoulders.

"Colonel," said Sergeant Hepler with an edge to his voice, "Howling Wolf and his men have not yet returned from their buffalo hunt."

Custer frowned. "What? They're always back by three o'clock, and surely no later than four."

"I know, sir. This really has me worried."

Custer rubbed the back of his neck. "Does Colonel Huston know that they're not back?"

"Yes, sir. And he is plenty worried, too. He'll want to see you and Bloody Knife right away, I'm sure."

"We're going to his house immediately." Custer hipped around in the saddle and told his men to go on to the mess hall to eat their supper.

Meanwhile, at the Custer apartment in the officers' building, thirty-two-year-old Libbie Custer was seated in the parlor with all seven of the Arikara squaws whose husbands had gone on the buffalo hunt, as well as their children. Summer Wind, Bloody Knife's squaw, was also with them.

As twilight crept into the room, the squaws placed their sewing into woven baskets and started gathering their babies and youngsters to go to their own quarters. The squaws nervously glanced toward the parlor door.

Libbie was anxious about the Arikaras in the hunting party, but she tried to keep the uneasy squaws from knowing the fear that she was feeling. She left the sofa that she was sitting on, started lighting lanterns, and said, "Please don't let your husbands' being late upset you. Perhaps they have killed so many buffaloes that it's taking them longer to skin them out than they had planned."

Summer Wind moved up beside Libbie and nodded. "Yes, Mrs. Custer, that could very well be the problem. It has happened before, and—"

Summer Wind's words were cut off when they all heard the front door of the apartment open and close. Every eye went to the open parlor door, and seconds later Colonel Custer and Bloody Knife appeared in the hallway and stepped into the room.

A quick sigh of relief escaped Libbie's lips as she rushed into her husband's arms. Summer Wind hurried to Bloody Knife, her face showing the disturbance she was feeling over the tardy hunting party.

Libbie, who was petite in size and wore her long, black hair in a bun, noted the deep lines of distress on her husband's features. "Darling, has the hunting party not returned yet?"

Custer glanced around at the worry-filled eyes of the squaws in the lamplit room. "No, they're not back yet, but it could be that they ran into more buffalo than they had expected to and are late because it's taking a long time to skin them out."

Libbie tried to smile. "That's what I told their wives a few minutes ago."

Some of the Indian women quietly murmured among themselves, trying to encourage each other, while others spoke their fear that the hunting party had run into Sioux warriors.

One of the squaws with a small baby boy in her arms stepped close to the Custers. "Colonel Custer, is Colonel Huston aware that our husbands have not returned?"

"Yes, Pale Sky. Bloody Knife and I went to Colonel Huston's house as soon as we learned that Howling Wolf and his men had not yet returned."

"And what are Colonel Huston's thoughts about this?"

"He…uh…he is worried about them. He said that if they do not return by the time darkness falls, he will send me and a good number of my Seventh Cavalry to search for them. Colonel Huston knows the approximate area where they were going to hunt."

Libby looked at the women and said, "Well, it will be dark in less than half an hour. Why don't you all just stay right here until we know something more? I have a large kettle of rabbit stew simmering on the kitchen stove, and we'll make some corn bread. You can feed your little ones first, and then the rest of us can eat. I think it would be best if we all stayed together."

Howling Wolf's squaw, Little Flower, smiled and said, "This is very gracious of you, Mrs. Custer. I, too, think it would be best if we all stayed together."

The other women spoke their agreement and worked together under Libbie's directions, preparing the meal while staying alert for any sounds of the returning hunting party.

In the tower at the front gate of the fort the five guards were scanning the prairie for any sign of the buffalo hunters when Corporal Justin Scott pointed due south and said, "There's one rider, Sergeant Hepler!"

They could all see the lone rider galloping toward the fort in the fading light. Soon they could make out that it was a pinto carrying an Indian, and Sergeant Hepler lifted binoculars to his eyes and said, "It's Howling Wolf. He's bent over like he's been shot."

Hepler told the three new men to remain in the tower and took Corporal Scott down the stairs with him. When they opened the gate, Howling Wolf was drawing up on his pinto. His upper body was smeared with blood, which was coming from a bullet wound in his left shoulder.

Sergeant Hepler stepped up, lifting his arms, and said, "Here, Howling Wolf, let me help you down."

The wounded Indian let go of the reins and leaned into Hepler's arms, breathing with difficulty.

Hepler cradled Howling Wolf in his arms, the blood staining his uniform, and laid the Indian on the ground.

"I'll go get Dr. Stouffer, Sergeant," said Scott.

"Yes. Quick!"

As Corporal Scott took off running toward the infirmary, Sergeant Hepler told the three men in the tower to come down, saying that he would need a couple of them to carry Howling Wolf to the infirmary. Sergeant Hepler knelt down, used his handkerchief to wipe perspiration from the wounded Indian's brow, and asked, "What happened, Howling Wolf?"

Privates Washburn, Barth, and Kline drew up and stood over the sergeant and the wounded Indian.

Howling Wolf's voice was just above a whisper. "After we had killed ten buffaloes…we had just begun skinning them and cutting the meat…when we were attacked by twelve Sans Arcs Sioux warriors. They were led by a sub-chief I recognized. His name is Wounded Bear."

"Where did this happen?"

Howling Wolf swallowed hard and took a sharp breath. "It was on Huff Creek, where it bends at the big rock that looks like an arrow head."

Hepler nodded. "I know right where it is."

"When the attack came, I…I was hit instantly and fell into the creek. I held my breath while I swam underwater to some brush at the bank of the creek. I stayed hidden with my face out of the water enough to breathe. When the firing stopped, the Sioux looked in the creek for me, but they did not see me."

Howling Wolf swallowed hard again. "While the Sioux were skinning the dead buffaloes, I swam downstream underwater a short distance and crawled up onto the bank and made my way into some bushes. I saw that all the other Arikara men were lying dead in plain sight. Our riding horses and packhorses were still where we had tied them to some small trees nearby. I managed to get to my horse without being seen. I led him into the nearby forest and then struggled onto his back and rode for the fort."

Swift-moving footsteps were heard, and in the light from the moon Sergeant Hepler saw Justin Scott and the fort's physician, Dr. Ward Stouffer, coming on the run. The doctor was carrying a lighted lantern.

When they drew up, the doctor quickly knelt down and examined Howling Wolf's wound while Sergeant Hepler told the doctor and Corporal Scott the story Howling Wolf had just told him.

Dr. Stouffer rose to his feet and looked at the sergeant. "We need to get him to the infirmary quickly."

Hepler gave orders to Washburn and Kline to carefully pick Howling Wolf up and carry him to the infirmary. While they were picking him up, the sergeant told Corporal Scott and Private Barth to stay in the tower. He then told Dr. Stouffer that he was going to go to Colonel Huston's house and take him to the infirmary.

Less than fifteen minutes later, Colonel Huston and Sergeant Hepler arrived at the infirmary, where they found the fort's physician administering chloroform in preparation to remove the rifle slug from Howling Wolf's shoulder. The patient was already under the influence of the chloroform.

Keeping a safe distance from the operating table, Colonel Huston said, "Doctor, is he going to make it?"

Dr. Stouffer glanced at the commandant in the light of the lanterns that burned overhead and nodded. "Yes, sir. I believe that he will live."

"I'm glad for that."

Colonel Huston sent Privates Washburn and Kline back to the tower. Then he turned to Sergeant Hepler. "You stay here at Howling Wolf's side. I'm going to the Custer home to tell the squaws the bad news. It's going to be very difficult, but as the fort's commandant, it's my responsibility to tell them. I'm glad, at least, that I can give Little Flower the good news that, though her husband has been wounded, he is going to live."

Hepler nodded. "Yes, sir."

With his heart pounding, Colonel Huston made his way in the moonlight to the officers' building and knocked on the door of the Custer apartment.

Colonel Custer opened the door, and when he saw the pallid look on the commandant's features, he said, "Come in, Colonel. Bad news?"

Huston stepped in, took a deep breath, let it out slowly, and nodded. "Yes. Bad news. I need to tell everyone here the story at the same time."

"They're all in the parlor, sir. We just finished supper."

Libbie stood in the hall at the open parlor door, listening to the conversation. Her heart sank.

Custer led the commandant into the parlor with Libbie at his side and told the women that Colonel Huston wanted to talk to them.

Colonel Huston explained about Howling Wolf riding into

the fort wounded and alone and then told them the story that Howling Wolf had related. When the squaws heard that their husbands had all been killed, they broke into sobs, as did the children who were old enough to understand.

Colonel Huston stepped to Little Flower and told her that Dr. Stouffer was removing a bullet from Howling Wolf's shoulder and that he had said that Howling Wolf was going to live. Little Flower's eyes were already filled with tears, but she broke into sobs of relief and said shakily, "I must go to Howling Wolf."

Summer Wind left Bloody Knife's side, put an arm around Little Flower, and said, "I'll go with you to the infirmary."

Little Flower drew a shaky breath. "Oh, thank you. Let us go right now."

Summer Wind looked back at her husband, and Bloody Knife nodded his assent. He knew that Colonel Huston would soon send Colonel Custer and a unit of soldiers after the Sioux who had killed the Arikara buffalo hunters, and he wanted to be at the colonel's side. He watched Summer Wind and Little Flower dash out the door.

Libbie Custer lived daily with the fear of her husband being killed while on patrol in Sioux territory. Her heart was heavy as she moved among the weeping women, trying to comfort them. Inside, she breathed a prayer of thanks that her own mate was still alive.

Colonel Huston turned to Lieutenant Colonel Custer and, with his eyes flashing fire, said, "I want you to take four companies of your Seventh Cavalry right now to Huff Creek and wipe out those Sioux murderers!"

Custer nodded. "Gladly, sir. It galls me the way the Sioux continually attack the Arikaras, who are never aggressive toward them. I heard about this when I was attached to Fort Riley before coming here, and now I've seen it for myself."

Less than twenty minutes later, Libbie Custer and the wives of the officers who were riding with her husband stood at the fort gate in the moonlight and watched them ride away. An angry Bloody Knife was in his usual place, riding beside Custer.

At the infirmary, Little Flower stood over the operating table between Dr. Stouffer and Summer Wind, waiting for the chloroform to wear off so that she could talk to her wounded husband.

When Lieutenant Colonel George Armstrong Custer and his large unit drew to within a mile of the spot on Huff Creek where the attack had occurred, Custer signaled for them to pull rein. They were on a slight rise. Under the stars in the pale moonlight, the branches of the trees along the creek bank were wrapped in fleecy banners of mist. Huff Creek looked like a cold scar cutting a pallid, silvery path through the prairie.

Looking through his binoculars, Custer could see three fires burning and could make out the Sioux warriors as they worked on the dead buffaloes by the bright firelight. He described to his men what he saw through the binoculars and then pointed to a ravine just below them and said, "Let's go down there and ground rein the horses. We'll move in silently on foot."

Soon the uniformed men drew close to the spot where the twelve Sioux warriors were skinning out the buffaloes. Smoke from the fires drifted on the night air and mingled with the acrid stench from the piles of bloody buffalo hides and the rank odor of fresh meat.

The Sioux were still using their sharp skinning knives to remove the last remaining buffalo hides and to cut the meat into sections for the Arikaras' packhorses to carry to the Sioux village.

Bending low so as not to be seen, the soldiers looked the situation over. The bodies of the dead Arikaras were piled up beneath a cottonwood tree on the creek bank.

"They will pay," Bloody Knife said in a hushed, heated tone. "I want Wounded Bear for myself."

Custer nodded. "You bet. All right men," he whispered, "let's get down on our bellies. I want a half circle spread out from here to the other side of the spot, so we've got them surrounded. When I fire the first shot, you open up and mow them down. Bloody Knife, you go after Wounded Bear."

Custer's chief scout grinned and nodded.

"Okay, men," whispered Custer, "spread out."

Some four minutes later, Custer opened the attack by firing his revolver and dropping one of the Sioux. Rifles roared, and suddenly it was bedlam in the circle of firelight as the Sioux warriors tried to get to their guns, which were near a cottonwood tree. Outnumbered almost ten to one, less than half of them were able to make it to their guns and start returning fire. Bullets struck rocks along the bank of the creek, ricocheting off into space, whining like angry bees.

While guns were roaring and bullets were flying, Bloody Knife saw sub-chief Wounded Bear firing from behind a tree. He dashed in through the billows of gun smoke unnoticed by Wounded Bear, threw a body blow on him, and knocked him down. Bloody Knife sprang to his feet, quickly grabbed the sub-chief's gun, and threw it into the creek. He then tossed his own rifle aside and whipped out his long-bladed knife from its sheath. Wounded Bear stood up, grinned evilly, and whipped out his own knife.

As the two of them came together, the firing stopped. All the other Sioux were dead. Their sprawled and crumpled bodies lay in the light of the fires. Untouched by what few Sioux bullets had been fired, Custer's men gathered in a circle around the combatants.

Within seconds, the muscular Bloody Knife had Wounded Bear down, disarmed, and helpless, the point of his knife touching Wounded Bear's throat. The soldiers began urging Bloody Knife to kill him.

But Bloody Knife did not drive the blade into his enemy's throat.

Custer stepped close and, looking down at him, asked, "Why don't you get it over with? What are you waiting for?"

Looking up at him, Bloody Knife said, "Colonel, have one of the men bring me a rope. There are some ropes lying over there by those remaining buffalo carcasses."

Custer's eyebrows arched. "A rope? What do you want with a rope?"

"Instead of driving this knife into Wounded Bear's throat, I am going to hang him."

Custer shook his head. "What for?"

"You do not know Indian belief about hanging?"

Wounded Bear's eyes bulged in terror.

Custer shook his head again. "I guess not."

Bloody Knife looked down into the eyes of his enemy and then back at Custer. "Colonel, in red man's religion, the only way an Indian can go to the Sky People is if his spirit can come out of his mouth at death. If he is hanged by the neck with a rope, which chokes him, the spirit will die inside his body and rot away with the body. I am going to hang Wounded Bear so that he is no more."

With assistance from the soldiers, a rope was thrown over the limb of a cottonwood tree beside the creek, and a terrified Wounded Bear was hanged.

The soldiers and Bloody Knife worked on the buffalo carcasses until almost midnight; then they prepared to head for the fort with the bodies of the dead Arikaras on their horses and the buffalo hides and the meat on their packhorses.

The fires had been put out, and as the soldiers and Custer's chief Indian scout headed toward the ravine, leading the Arikara horses so that they could mount their own horses, Bloody Knife paused and looked over his shoulder. He set his satisfied gaze on the lifeless form that hung at the end of the rope in the moonlight, swaying in the night breeze.

TWO

The next morning at Fort Abraham Lincoln's infirmary, Little Flower sat beside the hospital-style bed where her husband lay, talking to him in soft tones. Howling Wolf was quite weak yet, but he was clear-minded.

Dr. Ward Stouffer was outside on the infirmary porch, telling a group of soldiers that Howling Wolf was doing well and would be back on his feet within a couple of weeks, when Colonel Daniel Huston came toward the infirmary building from his office.

When Huston drew up, the soldiers saluted him, and one man asked when the burial service for the Arikara scouts would be conducted. Huston told him that it would be at ten o'clock, just two hours from then.

As the soldiers walked away, the commandant turned to Dr. Stouffer and asked, "Is Howling Wolf still doing all right?"

"Yes, sir, he's doing fine. Little Flower has been with him since sunup, and I'm sure her presence is helping him a great deal."

Huston smiled. "Good. May I see him?"

"Certainly. Come on in."

As the two men entered the room where Little Flower was sitting beside her husband's bed, Colonel Huston said, "It didn't take long for word to spread all over the fort about Colonel Custer and his men wiping out the Sioux warriors at Huff Creek. I understand that it was the big subject at breakfast in the mess hall."

"I can well imagine," said the doctor.

Little Flower looked up and smiled. "Good morning, Colonel Huston."

The commandant drew up close beside the bed. "Good morning, Little Flower." He looked down at the Arikara scout. "And good morning to you, Howling Wolf. Dr. Stouffer tells me you are doing well. I'm very glad to hear it."

Howling Wolf managed a weak smile. "Thank you, sir."

"Of course, Dr. Stouffer tells me that you are doing so well because you have this lovely young lady at your side."

Howling Wolf's smile spread. "I am sure that is true, sir."

Little Flower blushed slightly. "Colonel Huston, when will the burial of the scouts be held?"

"At ten o'clock this morning."

Little Flower glanced at the clock on the wall and then said to her husband, "I want to attend the burial."

"Of course," said Howling Wolf. "I wish I could attend too, but I do not think my doctor would let me."

Dr. Stouffer smiled down at him. "You are right, my friend. You are much too weak for that."

At ten o'clock the entire population of the fort, except for Howling Wolf, gathered at the fort's cemetery, just outside the stockade walls on the north side. Colonel Huston allowed Bloody Knife to conduct the service.

The squaws of the dead men stood close together, some holding infants and others flanked by their youngsters. Only a few of the youngsters grasped the magnitude of the situation. The gallant Arikara women stood tall, their countenances stoic even though their hearts were breaking.

When the bodies, which were wrapped in buffalo hides, had been lowered into the graves and covered with soil, Colonel Huston honored the dead men with medals of valor, which he presented to their squaws.

When Bloody Knife closed the ceremony, the Arikara widows gathered their children and walked away silently. Only then did tears rain unchecked down their faces.

Then the cavalry patrols rode out for the day. Along with them was Colonel Custer, leading two companies of his Seventh Cavalry and with Bloody Knife riding beside him. It was almost 11:30.

When the sun was setting, the patrols returned, gladly reporting to the guards at the main gate that there were no incidents with hostile Indians.

As Colonel Custer was dismounting at the fort's stable, one of Colonel Huston's adjutant corporals approached him and said, "Colonel Custer, sir, Colonel Huston sent me to tell you that he wants to talk to you in his office."

Custer patted his horse as one of the stablemen took the reins to lead him away and said, "Tell Colonel Huston that I'll be there as soon as I let Mrs. Custer know that I'm back safely."

"Yes, sir," said the corporal, saluting. "I'll tell him."

At the Custer apartment, as Libbie Custer was passing by the parlor window with broom and dustpan in her hands, she glanced outside at the setting sun. She was hoping to see the slender figure of her husband approaching the apartment building. There was no sign of him.

Since the killing of the Arikara scouts the day before, Libbie's nerves were very much on edge. She had stayed busy, doing more than her usual household chores, ever since the patrols had ridden out that morning.

Libbie moved up close to the window, sighed, and said aloud, "Being an army wife is no picnic."

Only the family cat was there to hear her.

She sighed again. "But I knew coming into the marriage that George would be gone a lot and in grave danger most of the time."

Libbie fixed her gaze on her vague reflection in the glass of the window. "This is what you chose to do with your life, Libbie girl," she said to the reflection, "so snap out of it and stop your fretting."

She went back to her sweeping while humming a nameless tune, glancing periodically out the window in hopes of seeing her husband.

She was almost done sweeping the parlor when she looked out the window again, and her heart quickened pace. *George was walking hastily across the open ground in the fort toward the apartment!*

When the colonel stepped up on the porch of the apartment, the door swung open, and Libbie lunged at him, her arms open wide. George held her as she began to weep, clinging to him. He squeezed her tight and then held her at arm's length and said, "Honey, what's wrong?"

"Nothing, now," she replied. "It's just that—well, after what happened at Huff Creek yesterday, I've been on edge ever since you rode out."

He kissed her softly and said, "Well, I'm home safe, and not one patrol even saw a Sioux today."

Tears were streaming down her cheeks. "I'm glad of that. And I'm so glad you're home."

"Honey, Colonel Huston sent one of his adjutants to meet me at the stable. He wants to talk to me at his office right away. I told the adjutant to tell the colonel that I'd be there as soon as I had let you know that I was back safely."

Libbie sniffed and managed a slight smile. "Thank you, darling, for thinking of me. I really did need to see you when you got home."

George kissed her again. "You always come first, sweetheart. I'll be back by the time you have supper ready."

When Custer drew up to the commandant's office, the door was open, and he saw Lieutenant Colonel Frederick D. Grant sitting in front of Huston's desk. Grant was the son of President Ulysses S. Grant and leader of the Seventeenth Infantry, which was part of Fort Abraham Lincoln's forces.

Colonel Huston stood up from his desk chair, smiling, and said, "Please come in, Colonel Custer."

Grant rose to his feet, greeted Custer, and said, "Colonel Huston, I appreciate your taking the time to talk to me, but you must have business with Colonel Custer. I'll see you in the morning."

Huston shook his head. "Don't go. You are involved in what I need to discuss with him. I want you to hear it, too."

"All right, sir."

Both Custer and Grant sat down facing the commandant, who eased back into his desk chair.

Huston picked up a telegram from his desk and said, "This wire came at three o'clock this afternoon from General Philip Sheridan in Chicago."

Colonel Huston told them about the contents of the telegram, explaining that President Grant and Congress were in agreement that, in spite of the nation's financial depression, the federal government should finance the railroad construction that Northern Pacific Railroad had planned when it did its surveying in 1872. The actual construction had been put off because of the sluggish economy. The president and Congress believed that a railroad line between Duluth, Minnesota, and the Pacific coast would aid the nation's economy.

Huston went on to explain that General Sheridan said in the

telegram that two days ago he had received a telegram from President Grant in which the president stated that, in order to protect the Northern Pacific Railroad workers from the Indians when the construction got under way, a new fort should be built in the Black Hills of Dakota Territory. Sheridan had wired the president back, agreeing wholeheartedly.

Colonel Huston looked into Custer's pale blue eyes and said, "President Grant wired General Sheridan in return, telling him to contact me by wire and to tell me to send a large army reconnaissance team into the Black Hills to locate a suitable site for the new fort. Colonel Custer, General Sheridan specifically named *you* to lead the reconnaissance team. He wants you to go onto the Black Hills Sioux reservation to locate and establish the site for the new fort."

Custer nodded. "All right. I'll be glad to do that."

"Good." Huston then looked at Grant. "General Sheridan also suggested that the president's son should be on this team."

Grant smiled and said, "Great! I'd love to be in on this project."

Custer turned, looked at Grant, and smiled past his droopy handlebar mustache. "I'll be glad to have you on the team." He then looked back at the commandant. "Just how large a reconnaissance team do you want to send with me?"

Huston leaned forward and placed his elbows on the desktop.

"I'm not sure at this point. We'll discuss it more tomorrow and decide together. You can make your regular patrol tomorrow, Colonel Custer, but I want you back by three o'clock in the afternoon so we can discuss the entire expedition. I'll wire General Sheridan first thing in the morning and let him know that we're working on it."

Over supper, George told Libbie about President Grant's orders to have a large reconnaissance team go into the Black Hills to locate the site for a new army fort and the reason why. He then explained to Libbie that General Sheridan had named him to lead the expedition and that he and Colonel Huston would be planning the expedition the following afternoon.

A frown weighed heavily on Libbie's brow.

George noted it and said, "What's bothering you, honey?"

She bit her lower lip. "The Sioux aren't going to take this invasion of their property without fighting back. By having railroad men laying track and building bridges through their reservation and unceded land, the Laramie Treaty will be broken."

George shrugged his narrow shoulders. "Libbie, certainly President Grant and General Sheridan have taken this into consideration. I'm sure they believe that building the railroad is the right thing to do and will be worth the risk of angering the Indians."

Libbie's eyes misted with tears. "But you and your men will be subject to Indian attack. They will be very angry at seeing the Laramie Treaty broken."

George patted her hand. "We'll be all right. I'm sure that Colonel Huston will send a large number of men—large enough to keep the Sioux from attacking us."

The tears spilled down Libbie's cheeks. "I—I certainly hope so."

Seeing the fear in her eyes, George left his chair and put an arm around her shoulders. "I shouldn't be gone too long, sweetheart. I've been in far greater danger than this appears to be. I'll be just fine. Now, stop your fretting, and let's enjoy the evening together."

Taking her hand, George lifted Libbie out of her chair and drew her close. "It'll be okay, my love. I'll be back before you know it." He kissed her forehead.

She wiped the tears from her cheeks with the palm of her free hand and forced a smile to grace her lips, but it failed to reach her eyes.

༄

The next day at precisely three o'clock in the afternoon, Lieutenant Colonel George Armstrong Custer sat down with Colonel Daniel Huston in the commandant's office. Huston's first comment was about the telegram he had just received from General Philip Sheridan in response to the telegram that he had sent to the general that morning. Sheridan had received a wire from President Grant yesterday about the reconnaissance expedition that Custer was going to lead into the Black Hills.

Custer adjusted his position on the chair in front of Huston's desk and asked, "So what was the president's message, sir?"

Huston cleared his throat gently. "Well, the president said that he had heard recently that gold had been discovered in the Black Hills a few years ago, but that it had not been confirmed. He wants you to see if there is any gold there while you're on your expedition. If you should learn that there is, the president will want to lay claim to the gold to help the nation's economy."

Custer's brow furrowed, and he chewed on his lower lip.

Huston bent his face downward slightly. "What's bothering you?"

"Well, sir, if this expedition did in fact verify that there is gold in the Black Hills, and the news got out…there would be an uncontrollable rush of gold seekers to the Black Hills like happened in California in the late '40s and early '50s. This would break the Laramie Treaty and would without a doubt bring war with the Sioux."

Huston eased back in his chair, drew a deep breath, and said, "Colonel Custer, let's face it. Sooner or later the government of the United States will have to fight the Indians in this country, and the Indians will eventually be wiped out."

While Custer stared at the commandant in silence, Huston picked up that day's edition of the *Bismarck Tribune* from his desktop and handed it to him. "Colonel Custer, I want you to read that article on the left side of the front page by the *Tribune's* chief editor."

As Custer took the paper from him, Huston said, "There have been rumors in Dakota Territory for a long time that there is gold in the Black Hills."

Custer nodded. "I've heard that a couple of times since I came to Dakota Territory, sir." He then read the article silently.

Is there gold in the Black Hills? This is God's country. He peopled it with red men and planted it with wild grasses; then He permitted the white man to gain a foothold in the Dakotas. As the wild grasses slowly disappear, so the Indian disappears before the advance of the white man. This nation is in a financial depression. The American people need the land that the Indians now occupy, especially the Black Hills, if there is gold in those hills. And I believe that there is.

Though the Laramie Treaty of 1868 forbids white men to trespass on Black Hills land, those forbidden hills—if the rumors are true—hold the answer to America's financial difficulties. The American people need this land that the Sioux now occupy. Many of our people are out of employment; the masses need what lies in the rich soil of the Black Hills.

Some say that to invade those forbidden hills would bring an Indian war. We need the gold that is buried in the Black Hills. An Indian war is inevitable, anyhow. For the sake of the American people, let's get it over with and lay hold on the gold that will get us out of the depression.

Custer handed the newspaper back to the commandant. "Colonel Huston, do you believe that there is gold in those 'forbidden hills'?"

Huston nodded. "I do. Now, let me show you something."

Opening a folder that contained a collection of newspaper clippings from many newspapers, Huston read them to Custer one by one, giving instances of white men who had found small amounts of gold in the Black Hills before the land was set aside for the Sioux.

When Huston had read the last clipping to Custer, he said, "When you and your men go into the Black Hills, you will not be breaking the Laramie Treaty. You will recall that though it states, 'No white person or persons shall be permitted to settle upon or occupy any portion of the reservation for any reason,' it also states that authorized United States government officers, agents, and employees may enter the lands set aside for the Sioux nation. As soldiers of the United States Army, you qualify as agents of the government.

"I have in mind to send along a couple of experienced gold miners so that if you find anything that appears to be gold, they can determine whether it's the real thing. Since they will be sent by me, they will also be considered government employees."

Custer eased back in his chair and smiled. "Looks like you've got it all figured out, sir. I hope you plan to give me a large enough number of men to ward off any attacks by Indians who might decide we're violating the treaty."

Huston smiled back and nodded. "I told you last evening that we would talk about that number today and that together we would decide how many men will be in the expedition."

"Yes, sir."

"I figure it will take us a couple of weeks or so to get everything ready."

"Of course."

"I'll have my adjutant corporal get us each a hot cup of coffee, and then I'll go into the details of my plan."

THREE

On Saturday afternoon, June 20, the sun was shining down brightly on Cheyenne, Wyoming, as farmer Newt Bannon and his wife, Sarah, came out of the general store, carrying grocery bags while talking to another couple about the recent sale of Cheyenne's largest bank, the Bank of Wyoming.

The Bannons, who were in their mid-forties, placed the grocery bags in the bed of their wagon as Ben and Esther Stacy told them that banker Frank McGuire and his son, Monty, had arrived in town by train yesterday and were staying at the Beaumont Hotel.

At that moment another couple who were crossing the wide, dusty street drew up to the Bannon wagon. Chet and Marianne Williams were new in town and were attending the church where the Bannons and the Stacys were members. The Williamses greeted their new friends, and then Chet asked, "Did I hear right? The new owner of the Bank of Wyoming is now in town?"

"Yes," said Ben. "He and his son came in from Chicago yesterday."

"I see," said Chet. "Where do you folks do your banking?"

"We and the Bannons do our banking at the Bank of Wyoming," said Ben.

Chet nodded. "We haven't opened a bank account here yet,

but we've been checking all three banks out. We had been told that the Bank of Wyoming had recently been purchased because the previous owner had died. So what can you tell us about the new owner of the Bank of Wyoming?"

"Well, according to the *Cheyenne Sentinel,* Frank McGuire owns three banks in Illinois," said Newt. "When Louise Paulsen put the Bank of Wyoming up for sale after her husband died, McGuire bought it at her asking price, so now he's here to take it over. Mrs. Paulsen is planning to move back east where she has family. Word is that McGuire also bought the Paulsen house just outside of town and has also purchased land next to it, where he's going to have a new and even bigger house built."

Chet rubbed his chin. "Do you know if Mr. McGuire is planning to sell his three banks in Illinois?"

"He's going to keep them, according to one article that we read. He must be quite wealthy."

"I'd say so. Well," Chet said to the others, "we'll be moving along. We'll see you at church tomorrow."

When the Williamses had stepped up on the boardwalk and entered the general store, Ben Stacy said to the Bannons, "I suppose you read in yesterday's *Sentinel* that those Indian attacks on the farmers and ranchers north and east of here last week weren't done by Cheyennes as the army had thought, but by Sioux."

"Yeah, we read it," Newt said. "And you saw in the article that those same Sioux raiders are killing cattle, stealing horses, and frightening farm and ranch families south of here a few miles, too." He glanced at Sarah and then said to the Stacys, "I talked to a unit of cavalrymen from Fort Laramie who I met on the road yesterday, and they told me that the Sioux killed three people on a ranch over in Orchard Valley on Thursday. The rancher and his family fired on the Sioux when they were stealing their horses. The savages shot them down and scalped their dead bodies."

Ben noticed the fear that filled Sarah Bannon's eyes. "Have

there been any hostile Sioux in your area?" he asked, running his gaze between Sarah and Newt.

"We had a couple of neighbors who lost horses to them two weeks ago, but no blood was shed. Of course, at that time our neighbors thought that they were Cheyenne."

Esther sighed. "Well, I'm glad, at least, that no blood was shed."

Ben wiped a palm across his mouth. "I sure hope the army gets those Sioux raiders under control."

Sarah was trembling. "I just don't understand why the Sioux leave their own reservations and unceded land to make trouble for the white farmers and ranchers."

Newt chuckled. "*Because* they're white, honey. The Sioux have a burning hatred toward white people."

Sarah's face paled and fear twisted her features. "We're farmers, too, Newt. Those savages might come on our place next."

Newt put a strong arm around her shoulders. "Now, honey, don't borrow trouble. It'll be all right. The army is working on this problem. And more than that, you know that we are in God's hands, and those Indians can't get to us and do us harm unless He allows it. He takes care of His born-again children."

Esther took hold of Sarah's hand, looking her in the eye. "Newt's right, Sarah."

Sarah held Esther's gaze for a brief moment and then looked up at her husband. The fear left her face, and her cheeks took on some color as she let a smile curve her lips. "You're right, sweetheart. I—I just forget sometimes that the Lord controls every facet of our lives."

"I'm afraid all of God's children do that at times," said Esther, giving Sarah's cheek a tender pat.

Ben smiled. "We'll get through this Indian problem soon. Well, Esther dear, we'd best be getting home."

The Bannons told the Stacys that they would see them at

church the next day, climbed into their wagon, and headed north out of town.

The Bannon farm was a sixty-acre place situated on the Lodgepole River some ten miles north of Cheyenne. Thirty acres of it was used for wheat, and the rest was for alfalfa, except for some two acres where the farmhouse, barn, corral, and a few outbuildings were situated. There was also a small pasture for their saddle and draft horses and two Guernsey milk cows.

The afternoon was brilliant and as clear as crystal under the beautiful, blue Wyoming sky as twenty-two-year-old Jim Bannon worked in the alfalfa field, putting up the season's first cutting of hay. He and his father had mowed the alfalfa two days before and raked it into windrows yesterday, and now Jim was pitching hay from the windrows onto a hay wagon so that he could haul it close to the barn and put it in neat stacks.

As he was about to take the full wagon toward the barn area, movement across the hayfield caught the corner of his eye. He swung his gaze that way and saw an army patrol of at least a dozen men riding toward him. He waited till they were within fifty yards of him and then waved at them. The leader of the patrol waved back.

Jim stuck the pitchfork into the load of hay and then moved close to the wagon seat. Both draft horses bobbed their heads and nickered at the sight of the oncoming horses and riders.

Moments later when the patrol drew up, the leader said, "Howdy, sir. I'm Lieutenant Brent Hinshaw. We're from Fort Laramie."

Jim smiled. "I figured you were from Fort Laramie, Lieutenant. My name is Jim Bannon."

"Glad to meet you, Mr. Bannon. We're one of the patrols policing the area to protect the farmers and ranchers from the

Sioux raiders who are moving about. Have you seen any sign of the raiders?"

"No, sir, for which I'm very glad. But I have been keeping an eye out for them."

Jim turned and lifted a Winchester .44-caliber repeater rifle off the wagon seat, brandished it in a flamboyant manner, and said, "I'm ready for them."

Lieutenant Hinshaw's brow furrowed. "Be careful, Mr. Bannon. Don't try to take on the Sioux raiders by yourself. They're experienced warriors, mean as teased rattlesnakes, and they love to kill white men. Even if you're a crack shot, they ride in bands of anywhere from six to ten men each. You wouldn't have a chance against that many."

Jim let a slight smile curve his lips. "Well, Lieutenant, I am indeed a good shot, but I'll use my head if they ever show up. However, I won't hesitate to use this rifle if either of my parents is in danger."

Hinshaw adjusted his position in the saddle, its leather creaking, and said, "I understand your attitude, Mr. Bannon, and I appreciate your willingness to protect your parents. But if you face such a situation, be careful."

Jim watched the uniformed men ride away, and as they neared the road, he prayed, "Please, dear Lord, don't let those hostile Indians ever threaten my parents or ever ride onto this place and steal our horses or kill our cows."

He placed the rifle back on the seat, climbed up, and put the team of horses in motion.

Lieutenant Brent Hinshaw and his patrol trotted their horses northward toward Fort Laramie. Some twenty minutes after leaving the Bannon farm, they topped a rise on the dusty road and headed down the gentle slope toward a bridge that covered a bubbling creek. Off to their right was a small farm with the usual frame house, barn, corral, and outbuildings.

Suddenly they heard gunfire coming from that direction and caught sight of a band of Sioux Indians off their horses exchanging shots with two white men at the corral from behind trees and bushes. The two farmers were hunkering down behind a water trough in the corral as frightened draft and saddle horses whinnied and ran in circles inside the corral's split-rail fence.

The lieutenant whipped out his revolver. "Let's go, men!"

The cavalry carbines were quickly in hand, and as the patrol galloped toward the scene at the corral, they began firing at the Sioux, though they were still out of range.

Hearing the volley of shots, the Indians turned to see the cavalry patrol thundering toward them and quickly dashed toward their mounts. As Lieutenant Hinshaw and his men fired, the Sioux's horses galloped away at full speed, their hooves tossing up clots of earth.

Drawing near the corral, the patrol kept firing at the Indians as they fled, and just as they reached the bridge over the creek, one Indian peeled off his horse and fell in the creek. The others kept on riding, with the riderless horse following them.

Lieutenant Hinshaw led his men up to the corral gate, where the two white men were just coming out of the corral, carrying their rifles.

"Anybody hurt?" asked Hinshaw, pulling rein.

"No, sir," said the older of the two men. "Our wives are safe in the house. I'm Cliff Campbell, and this is my son, Craig."

The lieutenant introduced himself, explaining that the patrol was from Fort Laramie and they were heading back to the fort when they heard the gunfire.

Cliff smiled and said, "Well, Lieutenant Hinshaw, if you and your men hadn't come along when you did, those Indians would have killed us when we ran out of bullets."

Hinshaw smiled. "Fort Laramie is putting a number of cavalry patrols all over this area. We're going to do our best to protect the farmers and ranchers from those hostile Sioux."

Craig Campbell smiled. "We appreciate that, sir."

Hinshaw looked around at his men and said, "Well, let's go see if that Indian who fell into the creek is dead or alive. Then we've got to get back to the fort."

At the Bannon farm some thirty minutes after the cavalry patrol had ridden away, Jim was almost finished unloading the hay wagon onto the stack that he had just enlarged when he saw his parents coming from the road toward the house in their wagon. He left the hay wagon momentarily to go to his parents.

Newt Bannon pulled the wagon up to the back porch of the house. As Jim was drawing near, Newt climbed down from the seat and smiled. "Looks like you're making progress on getting the hay in, son."

Jim chuckled. "Wouldn't want you to cut my salary, Dad!"

Both Newt and Sarah laughed. Jim helped his mother down from the wagon seat and said, "I'll help you and Dad carry the groceries in."

While the Bannons were carrying the grocery sacks into the kitchen, Jim told his parents about the army patrol that had come onto the place and of his conversation with Lieutenant Brent Hinshaw about the hostile Sioux and their attacks on white ranchers and farmers.

A strong shiver overtook Sarah as she placed a sack on the kitchen cupboard. She drew in a deep breath, released it slowly, and squared her shoulders.

Jim placed a gentle hand on his mother's arm. "Please don't worry, Mom. Lieutenant Hinshaw assured me that Fort Laramie has a good number of cavalry patrols all over this area to protect us."

Sarah removed her bonnet and sighed. "I'm glad for that. We

need protecting. I'll take care of putting the groceries away. You two go on with your haying."

Jim looked at her with compassion. "Are you sure that you want to be here in the house alone, Mom? I mean, with this hostile Indian situation?"

"You go on about your work," she said. "I'll be fine. You can't hang around the house babysitting me. Now, off with you. I've got work to do."

Newt and Jim exchanged glances, sharing a smile between them.

"Well, I guess we've got our orders, son," said Newt.

"Looks like it."

Both men kissed Sarah's cheek and moved out the back door, heading for the hay wagon.

Sarah stood at the open kitchen window and watched them walking together. She released a tiny sigh when they reached the hay wagon; then she turned from the window and began emptying the paper bags. While doing so, she glanced around her clean blue and white kitchen. A gentle breeze ruffled the white eyelet curtains at the window, bringing a coolness into the warm room.

When Sarah had finished placing the groceries in the pantry and in the cupboards, she sat down at the table, which was covered with a blue and white gingham tablecloth, and bowed her head. "Lord, I'm sorry that I let my fear of the Indians get to me like I do. I know that Your Word says that perfect love casts out fear. It also tells me that when I'm afraid I am to trust in You. I'm doing that right now, Lord Jesus. I'm putting my fear of those hostile Sioux into Your nail-pierced hands and trusting You to take care of this whole family."

A tear slid down Sarah's cheek. She wiped it away, and a smile graced her features. She stood up and said to herself, "Now, Sarah Bannon, you'd better get busy. Those two men out there pitching hay will be coming in for supper soon, hungry as grizzly bears."

Sarah built a fire in the cookstove and hummed a lilting tune as she began to prepare supper in her bright, sunny kitchen.

The next morning, beneath an azure sky decorated with scattered puffy clouds, Jim Bannon drove the family wagon into Cheyenne with his parents beside him. When they arrived in the parking lot at their church, they greeted other members and visitors warmly, and when they approached the door, they were greeted by Pastor Dave Ballert and his wife, Tammy. The Ballerts were in their early thirties.

During offering and announcement time in the morning preaching service, Pastor Ballert had the visitors stand and introduced them to the congregation. The last two he introduced were Frank McGuire and his son, Monty.

While Frank and Monty were on their feet, the pastor said, "It is my pleasure to tell all of you that Frank McGuire is the new owner and president of Cheyenne's Bank of Wyoming and that his twenty-four-year-old son, here, will be the bank's vice-president."

People were smiling and nodding.

The pastor said, "Folks, when Mr. McGuire and his son introduced themselves to Mrs. Ballert and me at the door this morning, they both gave clear and shining testimonies of having been born again. They belong to a strong, Bible-believing, Christ-honoring, soul-winning church of like faith and practice as ours, in Chicago. They also told us that Mrs. McGuire and their daughter, Alyssa Rose, will be coming to Cheyenne in early August and that both of them are also born-again children of God. When Mrs. McGuire and Alyssa Rose arrive in August, the entire family will join the church at the same time."

There were many smiles and *amen*s.

The choir sang a special song just before the pastor preached a powerful sermon on the crucifixion, death, burial, and resurrection of the Lord Jesus Christ, and when the invitation was given, several adults and young people came forward to receive Him as their Saviour. Many Christians also came forward to kneel at the altar and simply thank the Lord for what He had done for them on the cross.

After the service the Bannons, along with many other members, moved about the auditorium welcoming visitors. When the Bannons approached Frank and Monty McGuire, they told them that they were farmers and customers of the Bank of Wyoming and welcomed them.

Frank, who was slender and balding, smiled and said, "Thank you for your warm welcome. I'm glad to meet some of our customers."

Monty smiled. "Dad and I will do our best to keep the bank as good as it has been in the past."

"We have no doubt of that," Newt said.

Sarah flashed the bankers a bright smile. "I'm looking forward to meeting Mrs. McGuire and Alyssa Rose."

Frank grinned at her. "They will be glad to meet you, too, Mrs. Bannon."

"We were so glad when Pastor Ballert told us this morning that all of you are born-again Christians," said Newt.

"Born again, redeemed by the blood of the Lamb, and bound for heaven," said Monty.

In a friendly gesture, Jim extended his right hand. "Put 'er there, Monty! That makes us *blood* brothers, doesn't it?"

Monty laughed and grasped Jim's hand. "Well, I never thought of it that way, but it sure does!"

As they shook hands, Monty winced, looked down at their clasped hands, and said, "Boy, you've got quite a grip!"

Jim released Monty's hand and chuckled. "Comes from milking cows."

"Well, you've got the edge on me there. In the banking business, we don't have any kind of work that develops a powerful grip like yours."

"Tell you what. Come out to our farm at milking time, and

I'll let you milk the cows so you can develop a good grip."

Monty looked at his father. "How about that, Dad?"

"Sorry, son," said Frank. "Bankers just don't have time for milking cows."

"Well, we've got to be going," said Newt. "Will we see you in the evening service?"

"Sure will," said Frank.

On Tuesday of that week, Jim Bannon drove the family wagon into town to do some shopping for his mother at the general store and for his father at the hardware store and also to make the family's mortgage payment at the bank.

When Jim stepped into the bank, he noted Monty seated at his desk in the officers' area. He was talking to a man and woman and did not notice his new friend.

Jim went to one of the teller's cages, chatted warmly with the young man behind the counter while making the mortgage payment, and then turned and walked toward the officers' area, which was enclosed by a waist-high railing. Monty was alone now, doing some paperwork at his desk.

Jim pushed his way through the swinging gate nearest Monty's desk and said, "Good morning, Mr. Vice President."

Monty looked up, smiled, and rose to his feet. "Good morning, Jim. Nice to see you." As he spoke, he extended his right hand and said, "Try not to break it, okay?"

They laughed together as they shook hands, and then Monty said, "Anything I can do for you?"

Jim eased into one of the two straight-backed chairs in front of the desk and said, "Why, yes, there is. I'd like to borrow a trillion dollars."

Monty shook his head. "You have the collateral to secure a trillion-dollar loan, I presume."

"If I had that kind of collateral, I wouldn't need the loan!"

They laughed together. Jim noticed a picture frame sitting on Monty's desktop. It was angled so that Jim could see that it was a family photograph. Eyeing it, he said, "I recognize you and your dad. Who are those pretty ladies?"

Monty picked up the frame, turned it toward Jim, and pointed to the lady next to his father. "This is my mom. And this one standing by me is my little sister, Alyssa Rose."

"Your mother is very pretty. She looks so young."

"She'd love to hear you say that."

Jim then focused on the young lady next to Monty. "Wow, Monty, Alyssa Rose is beautiful! What color are her eyes?"

"They're a soft green."

"And quite expressive, I might say. And what color is her hair?"

"Dark brown."

"This photograph seems to be quite recent. How old is your sister?"

"She's eighteen in the picture, but she's nineteen now." Monty extended the frame to Jim. "Here, take a good look."

Jim took the frame in hand, held it close, and studied the photograph for a long moment, fixing his gaze on Alyssa Rose. Not only was she captivating, but he felt such a sharp tug in his heart toward her that it took his breath away. *I wonder if she is as nice as she is beautiful,* he thought. *Sometimes beauty can be deceiving. But her eyes show a sincerity in them.*

He studied her face some more, and finally Monty said, "Hey, Jim, remember me? Where did you go? You're off in your own little world somewhere!"

Jim grinned at his new friend. "Yeah, I guess I did drift off there for a moment. Sorry, but your sister… I'll tell you, Monty, I don't know that I've ever seen such a beautiful young lady."

"Well, Alyssa Rose is even more beautiful, actually. The picture doesn't do her justice. You'll agree with me when you see her.

When she and Mom arrive in Cheyenne, I'll see that you get to meet her as soon as possible."

"I can't wait. Early August, Pastor Ballert said."

"Yes, I hope. Mom and Alyssa will have to stay there until the house is sold. With the market as it is in Chicago right now, it should sell by then."

Jim handed the frame back to Monty and rose to his feet. "Well, I've got to head back to the farm. I've got groceries for Mom and new tools for Dad."

"Okay," said Monty, rising. "See you soon."

There was a silly grin on Jim's face as he turned and pushed his way through the gate. Monty smiled to himself, sat down, and went back to his paperwork.

Outside, Jim crossed the boardwalk and climbed into the wagon. As he headed back toward home, he couldn't get Alyssa Rose McGuire out of his mind. He wondered if she was spoken for by some young man in Chicago, but he told himself that if that were the case, she would probably be staying there.

Probably.

Or maybe the young man would eventually come to Cheyenne.

The next day, Jim drove back into Cheyenne to pick up a wagonload of grain for their livestock, and it was nearing noon when he was ready to head for home. He decided to stop by the bank to see if he could take Monty to lunch.

When Jim entered the bank, he saw Monty behind the counter talking to one of the tellers. Monty saw him, stepped around the counter, and said, "Well, hello, Jim! You do come into town often, don't you?"

"Sure do. I was wondering if I could take you to lunch."

"Well, it *is* time for me to go to lunch. I'd love to eat lunch with you, but I'll pay for it."

"You can pay next time, my friend. I'm paying this time."

While the two friends were eating in a nearby café, Jim said, "I have a question for you."

Monty swallowed the food in his mouth. "Sure."

"Ah…well, is your sister engaged or at least promised to some young man in Chicago?"

"No, she's not."

Jim felt relief wash over him. "Beautiful as she is, I'm surprised."

"Well, you'd have to know my sis. She's had plenty of guys who wanted to get serious with her, but she walks very close to the Lord, Jim. She's waiting for Him to bring the right young man into her life, and I've heard her say many a time that she will know when that right young man comes along."

"Bless her heart. She's got to be some kind of gal."

Monty grinned. "Oh, she is. Just wait. You'll see."

Soon Monty returned to the bank, and Jim was in his loaded wagon, heading north out of town.

When Jim was almost halfway home, he noticed two farm wagons stopped on the side of the road up ahead. He recognized two families who had farms near the Bannon place. They were obviously traveling together toward town. Dave Payne had his wife, teenage son, and two smaller sons with him, and Russ Fender had his wife, two teenage sons, and younger daughter with him. The farmers and their teenage sons were examining a rear wheel on the Payne wagon.

Jim's body jerked when suddenly, from a ravine that ran parallel with the road for a stretch, he saw a band of eight Indians galloping their horses up the steep slope toward the wagons, whooping and firing their rifles.

Quickly, the farmers and their teenage sons had rifles in hand and were shooting back while the women and smaller children scampered to get underneath the wagons.

Jim grabbed the Winchester rifle from the seat beside him and worked the lever to insert a cartridge in the chamber. He put his team to a gallop and headed toward the scene, his teeth clenched and his jaw squared.

FOUR

As Jim Bannon closed in on the scene in his bounding, fishtailing wagon, his heart was beating in his throat. Nola Payne and Leanne Fender had their younger children underneath the wagons, lying flat on the ground, while sixteen-year-old Wally Payne, seventeen-year-old Ervin Fender, and his fifteen-year-old brother, Doug, hunkered down by the wagons with their fathers. All five were firing their rifles at the mounted barking, whooping Indians, who were firing fiercely in return.

The rapid gunshots sent echoes rolling across the surrounding plains, and little puffs of gun smoke filled the air, riding the breeze.

As Jim pulled rein, drawing the wagon to a halt, he saw that one of the Indians was on the ground with a slug in his leg, gripping his rifle and struggling to get to his feet. Another one lay unmoving on the ground a few feet away, face down.

Another Sioux came riding Jim's way, whooping at the top of his voice. In a flash, Jim shouldered his Winchester, took aim, and squeezed the trigger. The Indian was hit in the chest and peeled off his horse.

Even as the Indian hit the ground, the Sioux with the wounded leg fired at Jim. The bullet whizzed by Jim's left ear, and with another cartridge already in the chamber, Jim took aim and fired back. The slug plowed into the Indian's chest, and he fell flat.

Jim's attention was drawn to movement on the plains toward the north, where he saw a cavalry patrol some three hundred yards away, galloping toward them at full speed. The mounted men in uniform held their guns ready for action.

Guns were still roaring at the scene around the wagons, and bullets were still flying.

Wally Payne fired his rifle at a galloping, barking Sioux but missed him. Suddenly Wally felt like someone had hit him in the chest with a sledgehammer. The breath gushed out of him as he fell backward to the ground, and he became aware of a white-hot pain where the blow had hit his chest. Nola's scream from beneath the wagon pierced everybody's ears.

Jim took aim at the Indian who had shot Wally and fired. The Indian went off his horse with a bullet in his heart.

The four Indians still on their horses saw the cavalry patrol thundering toward them. Their leader shouted loudly in the Sioux language, and they wheeled around and rode hard toward the ravine from which they had launched their attack on the farmers.

Russ Fender drew a bead on the fleeing Sioux and squeezed the trigger. One of the warriors fell off his horse, and the cavalry patrol veered toward the remaining three, guns blazing.

Within seconds, all three of the fleeing Indians were cut down by army bullets.

While the men in uniform gathered around the three fallen Sioux some fifty yards away, Dave Payne knelt beside Nola, who was sitting on the ground and holding the lifeless body of Wally in her arms, sobbing.

Jim Bannon stood close by, his face drawn and his heart heavy.

Dave had a strong arm around Nola. Nine-year-old Donnie Payne and seven-year-old Randy Payne were holding onto each other, pressing up against their father, wailing and saying over and over that Wally was dead.

As the Fenders stood sadly over the grief-stricken Payne family, Ervin and Doug clung to their father, and eleven-year-old Susie had a hold on her mother with both arms. Leanne's eyes were on Nola, and her heart was broken for her.

Tears streamed down Nola's cheeks, and anguish shook her hunched shoulders as she caressed the ashen face of her firstborn son, who had been so dear to her heart for sixteen years.

By the time the breeze had cleared the air of the gun smoke, the cavalry patrol drew up, leading their horses. They also led two pintos, each carrying one of the two wounded Sioux warriors who had been shot down by cavalry guns as they tried to escape. Both were bent over, clinging to bleeding wounds. The third Indian, who had been their leader, lay dead at the edge of the ravine.

The patrol leader dropped the reins of his horse and stepped up to where Jim Bannon and the grieving families were gathered. Compassion showed on the leader's face as he looked down at the mother holding her son. He then ran his soft gaze over the others and said, "Folks, I'm Captain John Kirk. My men and I are from Fort Laramie."

The group looked at him but did not move.

Jim turned to face him and said, "Captain Kirk, I'm Jim Bannon. My parents and I are farmers near here, and these two families—the Paynes and the Fenders—are our neighbors. I came along in my wagon just as the Indians were beginning their attack. The Indians killed Mr. and Mrs. Payne's son Wally."

The captain nodded solemnly, looking at the dead boy. "I'm so sorry. I wish we had been closer when they attacked you."

Dave Payne rose to his feet and moved up to the captain, the grief he was feeling deeply etched into his features. He put a hand on Jim's shoulder and said, "Captain Kirk, if Jim hadn't come along and joined with us in fighting the Indians, they might have killed us all. Jim brought down three Indians himself."

Russ Fender nodded, setting appreciative eyes on the gallant young man. "Jim, you put your life on the line when you jumped in and helped us. We'll never forget it."

"You're right about that, Russ," Dave said, looking at Jim. "We will never forget what you did here today."

Jim nodded. "I only wish I could have done something to keep this from happening to Wally."

Nola sniffled and said with a quavering voice, "There was nothing you or the rest of us could do."

Dave turned back to Nola and said, "Honey, we need to take Wally to the undertaker in town." Even as he spoke, he bent down and took Wally's body from Nola's arms.

Russ stepped up quickly, offered a hand to Nola, and helped her to her feet.

At the same instant, Leanne moved up to Nola with tears in her eyes and said softly, "Nola, Russ and I will take Donnie and Randy home with us. You and Dave just take your time with the funeral arrangements. Whenever you're ready, you can come by our place and pick them up. They'll be fine with us, I promise."

Nola wiped her tears and replied with quivering lips, "Thank you, Leanne."

"If there's anything else we can do, you just let us know," spoke up Russ.

Dave and Nola both spoke to their younger boys lovingly, saying that they would come to the Fenders' to get them as soon as they could. As they were walking toward their wagon, they saw a buggy coming along the road, heading south toward Cheyenne. There were two men in the buggy, and they pulled up and stopped.

The Paynes and the Fenders recognized the men in the buggy. The one holding the reins was Edgar Simpson, who was employed at the *Cheyenne Sentinel*, and the man next to him was Ralph Evans, the owner and editor of the newspaper.

When Simpson pulled the buggy to a halt, Evans ran his gaze

over the faces in the group, letting it settle on Dave Payne, who was placing the body of his dead son in the bed of the wagon, and said, "Dave, what happened here?"

"Indians attacked us, Ralph. Killed Wally. Nola and I are taking him to the undertaker in town. I'll let the others tell you all about it."

Evans nodded slowly. "Sure. Sorry about Wally."

Dave helped Nola onto the wagon seat, and as they drove away, Russ introduced Ralph Evans and Edgar Simpson to Captain John Kirk. Together, Russ, Nola, and the captain told the newspapermen the whole story.

Captain Kirk then turned to Jim Bannon and said, "Jim, I commend you for your courage and sharpshooting. I think I know where these Indians are from."

"Oh?"

"Let's see if I'm right."

Evans and Simpson observed with interest as the captain stepped up to the Indians, who were still gripping their wounds to stay the flow of blood. Jim was beside him.

"Are you two from the Black Hills Sioux reservation?" Captain Kirk asked.

The bleeding warriors looked at each other, and then one of them said, "We do not have to tell you."

Kirk shrugged his shoulders. "I can find out another way if I have to. You will make it easier on yourselves if you simply answer my question."

The Indians exchanged glances again, and then the one closest to Kirk said, "We are from the Black Hills reservation."

"Who is your chief?"

The Indians looked at each other again, stubbornness showing in their dark eyes.

"I can find that out another way, too," said Kirk. "Might as well save me some time and yourselves some trouble."

Again, the Indians looked at each other, and after a few seconds they nodded, and the one who had spoken before said, "Our chief is Red Cloud."

Kirk nodded. "All right. Now what are your names?"

The one closest to Kirk showed his reluctance to reply, but he said through tight lips, "I am Black Crow."

Kirk looked to the other one, who also showed his hesitance but said, "I am Spotted Buffalo."

"All right, Black Crow and Spotted Buffalo, we will take you to Fort Laramie. I will report to our commandant, Colonel Jack Taylor, what you and your warrior friends did to these white people, and in spite of it, I am sure that Colonel Taylor will have the fort physician patch up your wounds. I'm sure he will also have my men and me take you to Chief Red Cloud in the Black Hills. Chief Red Cloud must answer for what you and the rest of your band of warriors just did."

Black Crow tried to swallow the lump of fear that suddenly blocked his throat. Kirk saw it but said nothing.

Spotted Buffalo tried to remain stoic, but when his cheeks paled and a film of sweat appeared on his upper lip, Kirk knew that he was afraid.

Ralph Evans observed it all and spoke from his buggy. "Well, folks, Edgar and I need to get back to town. I'm going to write this story up in my newspaper." He swung his gaze to Bannon and said, "And, Jim, I want to commend you also for your courage in jumping in to help your neighbors fight off the Indians."

Jim made a thin smile. "Just did what had to be done, Mr. Evans."

Evans shook his head. "A lot of men would have run the other way to save their own skins, son."

Jim shrugged silently.

Moments later, the cavalry patrol rode away, leading the pintos that carried the two wounded Indians.

The Fenders drove away, heading for home. Donnie and Randy Payne rode in the rear of the wagon with Ervin, Doug, and Susie, who were attempting to comfort their friends in the loss of their brother.

The newspapermen headed their buggy toward Cheyenne.

Jim Bannon drove the wagon full of grain home and told his parents about the incident on the road. He left out the details of his part in bringing down three Indians.

When Newt and Sarah learned of Wally Payne's death, they gave thanks to the Lord that Jim was still alive.

The next day, Jim and his father were working inside the barn just after lunch, spreading new straw on the floor with pitchforks. Newt was telling Jim again how glad he was that the Lord had spared Jim's life when he looked up through the open double doors to see a rider coming into the yard.

Jim noticed his father concentrating on something outside and turned to see what it was. "Look's like we've got company, Dad." He squinted. "Oh, it's Monty!"

Sarah was on the back porch of the house, shaking dust out of a small rug. Newt and Jim saw Monty McGuire draw rein at the porch, tip his hat to Sarah, and speak to her. Sarah smiled and pointed toward the barn.

Monty smiled in return and guided his horse in that direction.

Pitchforks in hand, Newt and Jim stepped out into the sunshine, and as Monty drew up and pulled rein, they noticed that he had a folded newspaper in his hand.

Jim said, "Howdy, my friend. What brings you out here? Did you want to milk some cows and develop a powerful grip?"

Monty laughed as he dismounted. "Ah…no. I'm here for a different reason. Howdy, Mr. Bannon."

"Howdy to *you*, Monty. Glad to see you."

Monty stepped close and waved the folded newspaper. "I have a copy of this morning's edition of the *Cheyenne Sentinel*. Have you gentlemen seen it?"

When father and son both told him that they had not, Monty took a step closer to Jim and said with a lilt in his voice, "Jim, from now on I'm going to call you *Daniel Boone, Indian fighter*! According to Mr. Evans's article, you really distinguished yourself yesterday!"

Jim blushed, glanced at his father, and looked at the newspaper in Monty's hand.

Brow furrowed, Newt set quizzical eyes on Monty. "What do you mean Jim distinguished himself?"

Monty gave him a blank look. "Why, by the way he came upon the scene when the Sioux warriors were attacking the Paynes and the Fenders there on the road. Jim opened fire on the Indians. Didn't he tell you? There were eight of them, and he killed three himself. In the article, Ralph Evans says that if Jim hadn't jumped in and helped his neighbors, the Indians might have killed all of them. Jim's a hero!"

Newt shook his head. "No, Jim didn't tell his mother and me about killing three Indians in the gun battle." He extended his hand. "May I see it?"

"Sure." Monty handed him the newspaper.

Newt unfolded it and found the article on the front page under bold headlines that read: HOSTILE SIOUX ATTACK FARMERS!

Jim rubbed the back of his neck, grinned at Monty, and shook his head.

When Newt finished reading the story, he smiled at Jim. "Son, you didn't tell your mother and me about your heroics yesterday. She'll be as proud of you as I am!"

At that instant, Sarah Bannon drew up, cocked her head sideways, and said, "Newt, what did Jim do that would make me proud of him?"

Jim blushed again.

Newt smiled at his wife and handed her the newspaper. "Here, darlin', read it for yourself."

When Sarah finished reading the article, tears filled her eyes. She embraced her son, saying, "Jimmy, I'm so very, very proud of you. Why didn't you tell your father and me the full extent of your deed in helping the Paynes and the Fenders fight off the Indians?"

Blushing once more, Jim said, "Mom, I was only doing what any man would have done."

Monty patted his friend on the back. "Jim, many men would have stayed out of it, not wanting to risk their own lives. You are a hero, my friend."

Jim wiped the back of a hand across his mouth. "I—well, I just wish this 'hero' could have prevented Wally from being killed."

At ten o'clock in the morning on Thursday, the Paynes' pastor conducted the funeral for Wally. The Paynes were members of a different church than that of the Bannons.

Later, at the burial in the Cheyenne cemetery, the Paynes and the Fenders expressed their deep appreciation to Jim Bannon once again. Dave Payne repeated his words that he had spoken to Captain John Kirk that day, saying that if Jim hadn't come along and joined with them in fighting the Indians, they might have all been killed.

On Friday morning, June 26, Captain John Kirk led his unit of 125 mounted men out of Fort Laramie and headed north toward the Black Hills of Dakota Territory. They would ride until sundown, make camp, and proceed on Saturday morning, with plans to arrive in the village where Chief Red Cloud dwelt at midafternoon. Riding in an army wagon, with their bandages showing, were the solemn-faced Sioux warriors Black Crow and Spotted Buffalo.

Captain Kirk had often told his men that travel on the prairie was like sailing on the ocean, with an unbroken horizon and no steady drift of landmarks past the eyes.

They pulled away from their camping spot at sunrise on Saturday morning and reached the Black Hills region just after one o'clock in the afternoon.

Riding on the captain's right side was Lieutenant Brent Hinshaw, and on his left rode a corporal who carried a white flag on a long stick, holding it high so that any Indians who saw the cavalry unit riding in their territory would know that they were there peaceably.

When the Black Hills region stretched out before them, Lieutenant Hinshaw ran his gaze over the scenery and said, "Now I know why they call them the Black Hills. Those dense pine and cedar trees are so thick, they *look* black!"

Both the rolling hills and the numerous valleys before them were heavy with trees. In the distance a series of distinct mountain peaks rose up above the tree-studded hills. The shapes and angles of the mountains added to the breathtaking scenery. And in addition to the majestic mountains were the towering masses of white cumulus piled to magnificent heights above them, dwarfing the mountains to insignificance. The crests of the clouds were resplendent with golden sunlight.

It was just past three o'clock in the afternoon when the army unit approached the Sioux village. Countless tepees were visible, some in open areas and others in the deep shade of the trees. The corporal held the white flag high. The wagon carrying Black Crow and Spotted Buffalo was right behind Captain Kirk and the two men who rode beside him. The two Sioux warriors were noticeably nervous.

At the edge of the village a pair of stern-faced warriors stepped in front of the mounted unit, noting the white flag flapping in the breeze on the long stick in the corporal's hands. They raised their hands for them to stop. Their eyes widened when they noted the two wounded Indians in the wagon.

"What you want?" grunted one of the warriors.

Captain Kirk introduced himself, explaining that he and his men were from Fort Laramie, and said, "I would like to speak to Chief Red Cloud."

The same warrior who had asked what the soldiers wanted stepped up close to Kirk's horse, his jaw set. He had wide shoulders and a narrow waist and was well muscled. "I am White Eagle. I will take you to chief Red Cloud, Captain John Kirk."

The rest of the unit remained behind as White Eagle led the captain into the village. Black Crow and Spotted Buffalo watched from their place in the rear of the wagon, fear showing on their dark faces.

As Captain Kirk and his guide moved past the tepees, men, women, and children looked on. When they drew up to the village's largest tepee, Chief Red Cloud was standing in front of it in conversation with a young Sioux woman. Captain Kirk recognized Red Cloud from pictures that he had seen of the chief. Seeing the uniformed white man with White Eagle, the chief stopped in the middle of a sentence and glanced at the army unit at the edge of the village.

Red Cloud then set his dark eyes on the captain. White Eagle stepped up to him and told him that Captain John Kirk and his men had brought Black Crow and Spotted Buffalo, who had been wounded, in their wagon. He told Red Cloud that the captain wished to speak to him.

Red Cloud offered his hand to the captain, calling him by name, and they shook hands Indian-style.

The chief motioned toward the young woman and said, "Captain John Kirk, this is my daughter, Quiet Dove."

Kirk noted the young Sioux maiden's smooth, dark skin, her expressive black eyes, and the way that the sun shone on her long, black hair. She set her gentle eyes on him and said, "Quiet Dove is pleased to meet you, Captain John Kirk." She then turned to her father. "Quiet Dove will enter the tepee now and join her mother so that her father and Captain John Kirk may talk."

When his daughter had moved inside the tepee, Chief Red Cloud looked at Kirk and said, "You want to talk to me about Black Crow and Spotted Buffalo."

Kirk nodded. "Yes."

Kirk then told Red Cloud of the attack that the eight warriors had made on the white farmers on the road north of Cheyenne and of the sixteen-year-old farm boy they had killed. He explained that the farmers had fought back, shooting and killing five of the attackers before he and his men arrived on the scene and that his cavalry unit had killed the leader and wounded Black Crow and Spotted Buffalo when they tried to escape. He said that he and his men had taken the wounded pair to Fort Laramie, where the fort physician had treated their wounds and bandaged them up.

Captain Kirk saw a thread of anger begin to grow in Chief Red Cloud's countenance, and the chief looked past him, his dark eyes fixed on the two wounded warriors in the bed of the army wagon.

When no words came from the chief, Kirk said, "Chief Red Cloud, you signed the Laramie Treaty six years ago. I am here to ask you why your warriors were off the reservation and why they attacked those white people. We have had other Sioux warriors stealing horses from ranches and farms, killing their cattle, and killing the ranchers and farmers who have resisted them. We have not been able to identify which Sioux tribe they are part of, but when we took the wounded Black Crow and Spotted Buffalo into custody, they admitted that they were from this reservation and that you are their chief."

Red Cloud took his eyes from the two wounded warriors and

looked at the captain. Drawing his lips into a thin line, he said, "The eight warriors who attacked the white farmers and killed the sixteen-year-old boy have rebelled against Chief Red Cloud's signing the Laramie Treaty, and along with several others they have become renegades. I am very sorry for what they have done, Captain John Kirk. But I assure you that the other renegades have been punished by my orders, as will Black Crow and Spotted Buffalo. I also assure you that these attacks against the white farmers and ranchers by warriors under my authority will never happen again. However, I cannot speak for the warriors of other Sioux tribes."

Kirk nodded. "I understand that, Chief Red Cloud. I want to thank you for the apology and for the promise that you just made. I will report this to my army superiors, and they will report it to the proper government officials in Washington."

Red Cloud nodded in return. "I will now deal with Black Crow and Spotted Buffalo."

The chief wheeled about and loudly commanded his men to remove the two warriors from the wagon. Even as he did so, terror etched itself on the faces of Black Crow and Spotted Buffalo.

Moments later, Captain Kirk rode in the lead of the cavalry unit as they moved away from the village and headed south through the thick forest of the Black Hills. As before, Lieutenant Brent Hinshaw rode beside him.

Hinshaw looked at his superior officer and said, "Captain, you saw how frightened those two wounded warriors were."

"Yes. *Very* frightened."

"I've heard, sir, that some of the Sioux chiefs who signed the Laramie Treaty have actually executed their warriors who became renegades."

Keeping his eyes straight ahead through the dark, shaded forest ahead of them, Kirk said, "Yes. I've heard that, too. And by the way Black Crow and Spotted Buffalo were acting, they might very well know that a similar fate awaits them."

FIVE

In Cheyenne on a partly cloudy morning on Sunday, June 28, Pastor David Ballert stood behind his pulpit and ran his gaze over the crowd. The auditorium was comfortably full. Every window was open, and many of the women were fanning their faces with small fans.

"We have a serious situation developing, folks," Pastor Ballert said, "and we need to be praying about it. I'm sure that most of you have been keeping up with the articles in the *Cheyenne Sentinel* the last several days about what's happening at Fort Abraham Lincoln. Under orders from President Grant and Congress, the army is about to send a reconnaissance team into the Black Hills to choose a piece of land on which to build a new fort. This fort will be there to protect the railroad workers who are laying track through the northern part of the Black Hills from Indian attack."

All over the congregation people were nodding their heads.

The pastor went on. "I remind you of the 1868 Laramie Treaty, which placed the Black Hills region in the hands of the Sioux Indians, along with the guarantee that no white men could occupy the land for any time or any purpose. This is sacred land to the Sioux, and with hundreds of railroad men laying tracks and constructing bridges, the Indians, I am sure, are going to be upset.

"Most of you know that Chief Sitting Bull is regarded as the spiritual leader of the entire Sioux nation. He was quoted in the *Sentinel* last week as having said recently, 'We are an island of Indians in a lake of whites.' Sitting Bull is obviously antagonistic toward white people and our government. This intrusion into sacred Sioux land could just be enough to stir him to push the whole Sioux nation into war against the whites. I'm asking all of you to please pray that this intrusion into the Black Hills will not cause an all-out war with the Sioux nation as well as with their Indian friends, the Cheyenne and the Shoshoni nations."

Again, heads nodded in agreement with what the pastor was saying. Pastor Ballert then led the congregation in prayer, asking God to keep the situation from causing a war between the Indians and the white men.

The offering was taken, and then the choir sang a rousing gospel song, which was followed by a stirring sermon by the pastor.

When the service was over, Jim Bannon and Monty McGuire stepped outside, and Monty said, "Jim, do you realize it's almost July?"

"Well, yes, I'm aware of that. Why?"

"Well, according to Mom's letters, they have several people interested in buying the house, and she thinks that it will sell soon so that she and Sis can be here in August."

A broad grin spread over Jim's face. "Praise the Lord!"

"You know, I detect that you very much want to meet Alyssa Rose."

Jim shrugged and thrust his hands in his pockets. "Well, yes, I guess you could say that."

Later, Jim drove the Bannon family wagon with his mother sitting between him and his father on the wagon seat. As they headed out of town under an azure sky flecked with small white clouds, Jim's thoughts went to Alyssa Rose McGuire. There was a strange feeling in his heart about her.

While the rhythmic thumping of the wagon team's hooves on the road filled the air, Jim asked himself, *Is it possible to fall in love with someone simply by seeing her in a photograph?*

On Wednesday, July 1, at Fort Abraham Lincoln, Lieutenant Colonel George Armstrong Custer stood at the main gate, which was wide open. He ran his gaze over the large number of covered wagons gathered in a circle some fifty yards away. Several men moved about the wagons, while others watered and fed the horses that made up the wagon teams. They were kept in a rope corral nearby.

The sun was a burning brand flung down from the brassy sky. A stiff, hot breeze blew across the prairie, causing the canvas covers of the wagons to billow in and out against the frames that held them.

Custer's petite spouse stood beside him, the breeze toying with her long, black hair. An uncomfortable expression settled on Libbie's features as she observed the wagons and the activity around them. She was aware that the expedition to the Black Hills would pull out of the fort the next morning.

Libbie turned to her husband. "My, so many wagons! How many are there?"

"A hundred and ten. They will carry food, water, and supplies for the journey. Colonel Huston has planned a large number of men to make up the reconnaissance team. There will be close to a thousand of us."

"I'm surprised that there will be that many, but I'm also very pleased. I want my husband to be as safe as possible."

George grinned. "Well, honey, all ten companies of my Seventh Cavalry will be going, as well as two companies of the Seventeenth and Twentieth Infantries, who will be on horseback.

There will be six army engineers, a photographer, a geologist, a topographer, a naturalist, four newspaper reporters, and two experienced gold miners."

Libbie shook her head. "Colonel Huston is really going all out, isn't he?"

"There will also be a few Arikara Indians to serve as scouts and guides. Bloody Knife brought them to talk to Colonel Huston about it, when the colonel asked him to do so."

Libbie scrubbed a shaky palm across her mouth.

"What's wrong, honey?" George asked.

She turned and looked him in the eye. "George, I'm afraid that if you *do* find gold in the Black Hills, it will bring on a gold rush…and *that* would bring on an all-out war with the Sioux."

George sighed. "If there is gold in those Black Hills, people from all over the country will definitely rush to get a share of it. I hope it won't come to an all-out war, though. But for sure, President Grant is hoping to hear that there is gold in those hills so that it can be used to get the country out of this depression."

It was Libbie's turn to sigh. "It will be bad enough in the eyes of the Indians to have government men on their sacred land digging for gold—but when gold seekers from all over the country come by the hundreds or maybe the thousands into those forbidden hills, the Sioux will declare war."

George pulled at one corner of his mustache. "Like I said, I hope it won't come to that."

Libbie turned and looked him in the eye once more. "You know I had tea yesterday afternoon with Colonel Huston's wife."

"Uh-huh."

"Well, Laura and I were discussing the expedition, and she told me that she had read in the *Bismarck Tribune* of a trapper named Hercule Levasseur who went into the Black Hills before the Sioux held legal title to the land as they do today. Laura said that the Sioux considered Hercule a trespasser, and they chopped off both of his hands and cut out his tongue."

George's head bobbed. While he was digesting what he had just heard, Libbie said, "This invasion of the Black Hills is going to infuriate the Sioux. They may not attack the reconnaissance team because of its size and military might, but it wouldn't surprise me if it incites Sitting Bull to lead the Sioux and even the Cheyenne and Shoshoni into a bloody, full-scale war against us."

George shook his head. "You could be right, Libbie, but I have my orders from Washington and Colonel Huston, and that's to find a site for a new fort…and to look for any sign of gold while we're there."

Libbie took a short breath and put her hand to her mouth, her face a deathly white. "Don't President Grant and the men in Congress realize what kind of chances they're taking? As leader of the expedition, you will be the one the Indians—" She choked and tears filled her eyes. "You'll be the one the Indians target first and foremost. I—I just can't stand the thought of you facing those savages as their number-one target. Any man who is part of the expedition will be in danger, yes, but those Indians know that their victory is much more assured if they take out the leader. Oh, George, I—" She burst into sobs.

George took her into his arms and held her close. "Sweetheart, I've been through many a battle in my time. I'm still here, aren't I?"

Libbie took a deep, shaky breath. "Yes. Thank God, yes."

"You've been an army wife for many years now. You should be getting used to the fact that your husband is in danger, no matter who he's fighting."

She shook her head. "I'll never get used to it, George. I don't think that any soldier's wife can ever get used to it."

"We talked about this before we got married, remember?"

She sniffed. "I know. I—just didn't think it would be so hard. I'm sorry, darling, I don't mean to make it harder for you. You're a born soldier, and I could never ask you to give it up simply because

I have a difficult time when you are risking your life day after day for your country. I'll miss you terribly when you're gone on this expedition."

George squeezed her tight and kissed her forehead. "You will have plenty of other soldiers' wives to keep you company and help make the days go by swiftly."

Libbie sniffed again, looking him in the eye. "Yes, but it's the nights that are so long and frightening. From dusk until dawn seems like an eternity when you're gone and facing enemy weapons. When I don't know exactly where you are, or even if you're still alive, that's the hardest part." She snuggled even closer in his arms.

"It won't last forever, honey. Try to stay busy, and maybe you could have one of the other officers' wives stay with you each night. No doubt that would help both of you. And…and maybe you could get involved in some project. Like making quilts. You're good at that. And before you know it, I'll be back all safe and sound."

She stroked his cheek. "I'll be living for that moment. But even when you get back, this gold rush situation will just be getting started."

"Well, maybe it won't be as bad as we're thinking."

"I hope you're right." She glanced at the circle of wagons. "How long will it take you to get to the Black Hills?"

"I figure it will take about twenty-three or twenty-four days. The Black Hills region is about 275 miles from Fort Lincoln, and with the great number of wagons and men on horseback, we'll be able to cover only about twelve miles a day. We'll have to watch for Indian attacks along the way, too. Most of it will be uncharted territory where few white men have ever been. That's why we need the Arikara scouts to guide us."

"I just wish that this whole thing was over," Libbie said. "Even the large number of soldiers in the expedition may not keep some angry Sioux from launching an attack on you. And you'll be gone for at least a couple of months, won't you?"

"I would say so. But I'll be back, sweetheart. And if by finding gold in those Black Hills I can help get the country's economy turned around, it will be worth it."

"Colonel Custer," came a voice from behind them. "Excuse me, sir."

Both of them turned around to see one of Colonel Daniel Huston's adjutant corporals drawing up to them.

"Yes, Corporal Watson?"

The corporal smiled at Libbie, touched his hat brim, and said, "Hello, Mrs. Custer. Sorry to interrupt, but Colonel Huston sent me to get your husband."

"It's all right, Corporal," Libbie said.

Watson set his eyes on the lieutenant colonel. "Sir, Colonel Huston wants to see you in his office immediately. He said that there are some last-minute details concerning the expedition that the two of you need to discuss."

Custer nodded and said, "Libbie, I need to go. I'll see you at the apartment after a while."

She managed a smile. "All right, darling."

Libbie watched her husband hurry away with the corporal; then she turned and headed for the officers' apartment building. She was almost there when she saw Victoria Grant coming from another direction toward the apartment building. Victoria was the wife of President Grant's son, Lieutenant Colonel Frederick D. Grant. There was a look of despair on her face.

When the two women met up, Libbie said, "Hello, Vickie. You look upset. What's wrong?"

Victoria put a palm to her mouth. "Oh, Libbie, this expedition that our husbands are going on is about to tear me apart. Who knows how many hostile Indians will be waiting to wipe them out? Once that long train of wagons and those cavalrymen get close to those Black Hills, there could be a vast army of Sioux, and even Cheyenne and Shoshoni, waiting in the hills to attack them."

Libbie took hold of Victoria's hand. "I have the same fears that you do. I was just talking to my husband about them. How about you come to my apartment and we'll have some tea? Maybe some good, hot tea will help settle our nerves."

"Sounds good to me," said Victoria, trying to form a smile.

Moments later, the two officers' wives sat at the Custer kitchen table over steaming cups of tea. They shared their fears about how the Sioux would react when the railroad workers invaded their sacred territory and over what would happen if gold should be discovered in the Black Hills and those hills swarmed with trespassing gold seekers.

Victoria took a sip of tea, swallowed, and said, "Libbie, sooner or later this breaking of the Laramie Treaty is going to result in a bloody war."

Libbie set her cup in its saucer and sighed. "I know. Ol' Sitting Bull is not going to sit still for this."

That night, George Custer was sleeping peacefully when he was jolted from his slumber by a wild, piercing scream. He blinked his eyes and jerked again when a second scream stabbed his ears. Libbie sat bolt upright on the bed. This time, he realized that she was screaming his name. Then, suddenly, she was whimpering and gasping for breath.

George sat up in the lambent moonlight that streamed through the bedroom window and gathered her into his arms. "It's okay, honey. It was only a nightmare. You were screaming my name."

Sniffling and wiping away tears, Libbie's voice trembled as she said, "I dreamed that you and your Seventh Cavalry were attacked by a large number of Indians and your men were being cut down by bullets and arrows. Suddenly I saw you off your horse, firing at the Indians with your revolver. There was a wild-eyed Indian sneaking up behind you with a tomahawk in his hand. You didn't know that he was there. I—I screamed as loud as I could to warn you…and woke myself up with my screams."

George brushed the hair from her eyes and kissed her cheek. "It was only a dream, sweetheart. Nothing more."

She clung to him, sobbing and trembling all over, and dug her fingernails into his back.

George talked to her in soft tones for several minutes, working at calming her down. Finally, though her voice was weak, her trembling ceased. "Oh George, I'm so fearful over this expedition to the Black Hills."

"Honey, please don't be. Do you remember how, on the night that I proposed and you said that you would marry me, I warned you that there would be times like this?"

She nodded. "Yes. But I—"

"Listen to me. Let me remind you that I fought in that bloody Civil War and that I made it through so many horrible, fierce battles. I'll make it through whatever happens on this expedition to the Black Hills, too."

Libbie hugged her husband close and lay quietly in his arms. After nearly an hour she fell asleep.

SIX

The next morning, Thursday, July 2, 1874, the sun was just lifting above the eastern horizon as the expedition team prepared to leave Fort Abraham Lincoln and head southwest across the rolling Dakota Territory prairie toward the Black Hills.

At the stables near the back side of the fort the cavalrymen, the infantrymen, and the civilians who were going on the journey bridled and saddled their horses. Lieutenant Colonel Grant was bridling and saddling Colonel Custer's horse for him, since Custer and the fort's commandant were having a final talk before the expedition headed out.

In the tower at the main gate, Corporal Justin Scott and Private Neal Kline watched the scene just outside the fort where the men who were to drive the 110 wagons were making last-minute preparations to leave.

Inside the fort, just below the tower, Colonel Daniel Huston and Colonel George Custer were talking when Huston smiled and said, "Sounds to me like you're ready for the task ahead of you, Colonel Custer."

"I believe so, sir."

Huston's smile broadened. "Except for one thing."

Custer's brow furrowed. "What's that, sir?"

"The music."

Puzzlement showed in Custer's pale blue eyes. "Excuse me, sir? What music?"

"This is a military journey, isn't it?"

"Yes, sir."

"Well, you can't go without the brass band."

"Don't tell me you—"

"Yes, I did. When you've been out on your patrols the last couple of weeks, I have secretly been preparing the band to go along with you."

"You mean all the way to the Black Hills?"

"Exactly. This will give you music when you leave, while you're on the trip, and on your way back."

Custer shook his head in wonderment. "Sir, I had no idea that you were going to do this."

"I know. Everybody here has been keeping it a secret, so I could surprise you."

"Even Libbie has known about it?"

"She has."

"Well, what do you know? My wife's keeping secrets from me."

Huston laughed. "I'm sure that's the only one." As he spoke, he moved back a few steps so that he could see the men in the tower and said, "Corporal Scott…"

Justin Scott leaned over the railing. "Yes, sir?"

"Signal the band to come."

Custer watched as Scott took his hat off, looked toward the stables, and waved it.

Seconds later, the sixteen-piece military brass band appeared from the back side of the barns, riding their horses and carrying their instruments. People in the fort began to applaud them.

Custer noted that the men in the band wore sidearms and there were rifles in their saddle scabbards. They were soldiers, ready for battle just like the other men. He grinned at the commandant. "Colonel Huston, you are something else!"

Up in the tower, Private Neal Kline elbowed Corporal Scott, who was watching the band, and said, "We've got company."

Scott wheeled around and followed the finger that Kline pointed at a lone Sioux Indian drawing up from the south on his horse. His jaw slacked. "What's that Indian doing here?"

"Beats me, but he's sure got nerve riding in here all by himself."

Scott moved to the outside edge of the tower, looked down at the Indian as he pulled rein, and said, "Is there something I can do for you? Or do you speak English?"

The Sioux fixed his dark eyes on the corporal and said, "I wish to speak to Bloody Knife."

"Well, he's about to leave on a trip. You know him, do you?"

"Yes. I must speak to him."

"Wait here. I'll see if he wants to talk to you. What's your name?"

The Indian's features were solemn. "Bad Dog."

Scott and Kline exchanged glances and Scott shrugged. "I'll be right back, Neal."

Colonel Huston and Lieutenant Colonel Custer were still in conversation when they saw Scott coming down the stairs. He stopped and said to the commandant, "Colonel Huston, we've got a lone Sioux warrior at the gate. He's asking to see Bloody Knife."

Huston frowned. "He's all by himself?"

"Yes, sir."

"What does he want to see my chief scout about?" Custer asked.

"I don't know, sir. He didn't say."

Custer wiped a hand over his mustache. "Well, I'll go get Bloody Knife. Did you find out this Sioux's name?"

"Yes, sir. He said his name is Bad Dog."

"Bad Dog?"

"That's what he said."

"Okay. Colonel Huston, anything else we need to talk over?"

"Not that I can think of. Go ahead and get Bloody Knife."

Custer saw that most of the officers' wives and the wives of the Arikara scouts were gathered a few yards away, watching the brass band guide their horses toward the main gate. He caught sight of Bloody Knife and Summer Wind standing with Howling Wolf and Little Flower. He hurried toward them and said, "Bloody Knife, there is a Sioux warrior at the main gate who wants to see you. Says his name is Bad Dog."

Bloody Knife's lips pulled into a thin line. "Bad Dog," he said with sand in his voice.

"Who is he? How do you know him?"

Bloody Knife set his gaze on Custer's face. "Colonel Custer, Bad Dog and I did hand-to-hand battle several grasses ago. I wounded him but let him live. He swore that one day he would find me and we would do battle again—only next time, he would kill me."

Custer sighed. "Guess you should've killed him, then."

"I will go to him."

Summer Wind grasped her husband's arm. "I know that you must go face Bad Dog. Please be careful."

Bloody Knife nodded, patted her arm, and headed toward the gate.

Moments later, with Custer at his side, Bloody Knife drew near to the front gate, where Corporal Scott had Bad Dog standing just outside the gate, which was wide open.

When the Sioux warrior saw Bloody Knife approaching, his dark features grew hard. Custer remained back a few steps and watched. Other soldiers were gathering around.

Bad Dog looked Bloody Knife in the eye and said, "You

remember me. Bad Dog. On the bank of the Missouri River at Yankton."

"I remember."

"You let me live when you could have killed me. By letting me live you made me have to feel the shame before my people that I had been conquered. I begged you to go ahead and kill me so that I would not have to live in shame, but you refused. I told you then that I would find you and kill you for it. I have not been able to face the shame all of these grasses. We will do battle now."

There was a glint of steel in Bloody Knife's eyes. "You speak as a foolish man. I still do not want to kill you, Bad Dog. Go, and do not force me to do it."

Bad Dog shook his head. "It is *you* who are going to die, Bloody Knife." As he spoke, Bad Dog whipped his long-bladed knife from its sheath and lunged at Bloody Knife.

Bloody Knife dodged the blade but did not pull his own knife. Instead, he hooked a right to Bad Dog's jaw that slammed Bad Dog to the ground. As Bad Dog rolled onto his knees, Bloody Knife bent over and snatched the knife out of his opponent's hand. He tossed it handle-first to Colonel Custer and then stood over Bad Dog. "Bad Dog will leave now."

Bad Dog's nostrils flared, his jaw jutted, and wrath danced in his flashing black eyes. He rose to his feet and growled, "Since I now have no knife, I will kill you with my bare hands."

Bad Dog lunged at Bloody Knife, reaching for his throat. Bloody Knife grabbed Bad Dog's wrist, twisted it, and flung his opponent to the ground. Bad Dog howled in pain and looked at his wrist. He looked up at Bloody Knife and hissed, "You broke my wrist!"

Bloody Knife nodded. "Because I do not want to kill you. Get on your horse and ride. I never want to see you again."

Bad Dog held the broken wrist with his good hand and glared at Bloody Knife. He was breathing hard. He started to say something but then shook his head and walked out the open gate. The crowd looked on, and Summer Wind eased up to her husband's side as Bad Dog swung onto his horse with difficulty and rode away without looking back.

One of the soldiers in the crowd said, "You should have killed him, Bloody Knife."

The muscular Arikara warrior set steady eyes on the soldier. "I only kill a man when I have to. I feel better for allowing him to live."

"We could all learn from you!" another soldier called out.

An hour later, the 110 wagons were lined up in four rows with the cavalrymen and mounted infantrymen flanking the outside rows. The civilians were on their horses, positioned between the rows of wagons.

At the front of the wagon rows was the sixteen-piece brass band, mounted on white horses, instruments in hand.

At the fort's main gate the officers were saying parting words to their wives, as were the Arikara scouts to their squaws.

Summer Wind held Bloody Knife's hand, telling him how proud she was that he had chosen to spare Bad Dog's life. Howling Wolf and Little Flower stood close by. Howling Wolf said, "Bloody Knife, I am glad that you are my brother. I wish I could go with you on this expedition, but my body is still too weak from my bullet wound."

Bloody Knife smiled. "I am sure that is true, my brother."

A short distance away, Victoria Grant gripped both of her husband's hands and said, "I wish you didn't have to go on this dangerous mission, but I know that you have no choice."

"I chose to be a soldier like my father once was, and soldiers must do their duty. But, sweetheart, I promise…I will come back to you."

A few feet from the Grants, Libbie Custer clung to her husband, and her voice quaked as she said, "I will be waiting for your return."

George held her close and said, "I will return indeed, my love—and in one piece." He then turned to Grant. "Well, Colonel, we must be going."

Libbie and Victoria held each other's hands, as did some of the officers' wives, as they watched their husbands mount up and ride to the front of the line.

In the lead, just in front of the brass band, was Lieutenant Colonel George Armstrong Custer. On his right was his faithful scout, Bloody Knife. On his left was Lieutenant Colonel Frederick D. Grant. Just behind them were the five Arikara scouts.

The officers' wives and the Arikara squaws all gathered near the gate as Colonel Custer led the riders and wagons away slowly, heading southwest. The women and children waved as the riders and wagons moved out and the brass band played "Garry Owen."

Each wife and squaw was battling her own emotions, fully aware that throughout the centuries that mankind has been on the earth, women have watched their men go off to war. In each heart lay the same deep-seated fear: *Will he come back alive? And if not, what then?*

The women watched until the last of the riders and wagons had disappeared among the low hills in the distant haze, and a collective sigh was heard as those who had children gathered them close and all of them reluctantly turned from the scene.

Libbie Custer was the last to turn around. When she did, she found Victoria Grant standing a few feet away with a tender look in her eyes. "Libbie," Victoria said softly, "how about coming to my apartment with me? I'm sure the kettle is still hot. A nice cup of tea might help settle our nerves."

Libbie smiled. "Vickie, I'd love it. I really would rather not be alone right now."

Victoria linked her arm with Libbie's. "Good. Me either. Come on…a bracing cup of tea always works wonders for me."

When the thousand-man reconnaissance team had traveled for over three hours, one of the men at the rear of the wagons was watching a flock of geese flying up ahead of them and coming their way. When the honking birds passed overhead, the soldier hipped around in his saddle to study their amazing *V* formation some more, and when he did he noticed a lone rider following the team at a fast trot.

Straightening in the saddle, the soldier called to an officer a few yards ahead of him, "Lieutenant Warfield, we've got somebody following us. Look back there."

Lieutenant Cecil Warfield twisted around and saw the lone rider. "I'll ride up and tell Colonel Custer."

Warfield galloped to the front of the procession and swung in between Custer and Bloody Knife. "Colonel, sir, we have a lone rider following us. Do you want me to go ask him what his purpose is?"

Custer frowned. "I'll go with you." Then to Colonel Grant he said, "Keep things moving. I'll be back as soon as I talk to the man who's following us."

Custer swung his horse out of line, followed by Warfield, and together they headed toward the rear of the line. As they rode past the last of the wagons, the rider was about fifty yards away, still coming on at a fast trot.

Custer and Warfield could see that he was dressed shabbily, wearing a tattered old hat, trousers with patches on the knees, and scuffed-up boots.

Custer raised a hand, signaling for the rider to stop. The rider obeyed, pulling rein. Both officers looked at each other when they focused on the rider's face.

It was a woman.

Custer halted his horse and said, "Ma'am, I am Lieutenant Colonel George Custer. I'm in charge of this expedition. Who are you?"

The woman started to answer when suddenly Lieutenant Warfield said, "I know who you are! You're Martha Jane Canary, better known as Calamity Jane! I met you once in Abilene, Kansas, which is where I'm from. That must've been about five years ago. Yes, in '69 when James Hickok was still marshal there. You were only seventeen or eighteen years old at the time, if I recall."

Calamity Jane grinned and nodded. "Something like that."

"You and Hickok are friends, aren't you?"

"We are," said Calamity Jane, squinting and studying his face. "Oh, now I remember you. Your name's War—uh, something with 'War' in it."

The young officer smiled. "Yes, ma'am. I had just graduated from West Point and was about to enlist in the army. My name's Cecil Warfield."

Custer said, "I've heard of you, Miss Canary. I'm interested in this nickname, Calamity Jane. How did you get that name?"

She adjusted the wide-brimmed hat on her head. "It's a long story, Colonel. I'd better not get into it right now."

"Do you know where Hickok is at present, ma'am?" Warfield asked.

"Well, for the past four years he's been back east, working in Buffalo Bill Cody's Wild West Show. And he isn't called by his real name anymore. Somebody dubbed him Wild Bill Hickok. He liked it, and so that's what he goes by now. He recently left the show, and I saw him in Abilene about a month ago."

Custer said, "Would you mind telling us what you're doing here, Miss Canary?"

She smiled. "Colonel Custer, the reason I'm following the reconnaissance team is that I've been in Bismarck for the past two weeks, and there I learned that this expedition was headed to the Black Hills to find a site for a new fort and to see if they could find any gold.

"I've heard stories on several occasions that there quite possibly is gold there, and I'd like to get my hands on some of it. I was following the team with the intention of asking you, Colonel Custer, if I could tag along. I could really use the money. I'm willing to do washing, cooking, or anything else to become a part of the expedition."

Custer adjusted his position in the saddle. "Ma'am, I'm sorry to disappoint you, but there simply is no place for a woman in the expedition. I cannot allow it. This journey could become very dangerous, and I'm in no position to take you in. I would have to have permission from Colonel Daniel Huston, commandant of Fort Lincoln, to do so, and there's no way to contact the colonel. I'm sorry, but I cannot let you join the team."

Disappointment showed on Calamity Jane's face. She nodded solemnly. "Well, Colonel Custer, it's things like this that have happened in my life that have caused me to be known as Calamity." She wheeled her horse around and looked over her shoulder at the two officers. "Good-bye."

Custer and Warfield watched her gallop away and then trotted back toward the long lines of horses, riders, and wagons. Custer said, "Cecil, I would like to have granted Calamity Jane's request, but if things got rough on this journey and she got hurt or killed, I would not only feel bad, but I would be in deep trouble with my superiors."

Warfield nodded. "I understand, Colonel. You did the right thing. You had no choice but to turn her away."

As they caught up to the team, the lieutenant slipped back into his place, and the colonel returned to his spot in the lead.

Some two hours later, when the team stopped to eat lunch beside a creek and to feed and water the horses, the brass band played a couple of snappy marches. Then they continued on their southwestwardly trek and soon entered a floral valley.

"The birds are singing sweetly here on the prairie, my friends," Custer said to Colonel Grant and Bloody Knife. "All of nature seems to smile on our expedition. Everything here seems to encourage us onward. I feel certain that we'll see that railroad extended to California, and maybe we will also have supreme success in finding gold."

"I hope so, sir," Grant said. "Not only will it help the country to have that railroad to the west coast, but I feel as my dad feels: There have been enough rumors over the years about gold being in the Black Hills to warrant a search for it. If a substantial amount can be mined, the country's national debt can be paid off, and the depression will be over."

Custer nodded. "I sure would like to see us get out of the depression."

Bloody Knife did not comment. He was worried that invading the Black Hills could exact a cost that would far outweigh any financial benefit.

SEVEN

The expedition out of Fort Abraham Lincoln moved on through the afternoon. Word of Calamity Jane's approach to their leader, asking to join the team, spread quickly along the lines of men on horseback and in the wagons. As they talked about it, it was clear that all of them understood why Colonel Custer had to turn her down.

When the sun was at last dropping near the edge of the western horizon, one of the Arikara scouts rode up beside Colonel Custer and told him of a creek that flowed through a large patch of trees about a mile ahead. He suggested that it would be a good place to make camp for the night. Custer thanked him and told him to ride along the lines of horsemen and wagons and tell them that they would soon be stopping for the night.

When the expedition reached the area, all were glad for the gurgling creek and that the stand of trees was large enough that the wagons could make a circle within the trees. There was also plenty of room to make a rope corral to hold all the horses for the night.

After all the men had eaten their supper, several campfires were lit, and Colonel Custer had the brass band play a half-hour concert. When the concert was over, they all sat around talking in small groups by the flickering light of the fires. Mostly they talked of what might lie ahead for them when they entered the Black Hills.

Custer and a few of his Seventh Cavalry officers sat around a campfire near the rope corral, talking about the stories that had been told for years about gold in the Black Hills.

A lieutenant named Patrick Ryan ran his gaze around the fire and said, "Speaking of stories about gold in the Black Hills, let me tell you one I heard one time. About twenty years ago, an Oglala Sioux warrior was hunting eagles alone in the Black Hills and happened to come upon a badger digging a hole in a stream bank. He shot the badger, and when he went to pick up the carcass, he saw the upturned earth covered with gold nuggets.

"The Oglala dug more nuggets out of the ground and was able to fill a buckskin pouch with them. He rode out of the Black Hills and headed for Laramie, where he intended to buy a horse that he had seen in a stable there. He had been riding for a couple of hours when he came upon a band of Hunkpapa Sioux warriors. He told them about the gold that he had found in the Black Hills and showed them the buckskin pouch, saying that he was going to use some of it to buy the horse that he had seen in the stable at Laramie.

"The Hunkpapas got angry. They told the Oglala that the whites must never learn about this gold or they would invade the Black Hills to get all the gold they could. The Oglala told the Hunkpapas that he had to have a new horse. The one he was riding was very old, and one day soon it would collapse and die. His mind was made up to go to Laramie and buy the horse that he had seen at the stable. The Hunkpapas snatched the pouch of gold from him, threatened to kill him if he ever took any gold to white men, and then beat him and left him lying on the ground half-conscious and bleeding."

With the fire crackling and smoke lifting toward the black sky, Custer nodded and ran his fingers across his mustache. "I don't have a problem believing that story, Lieutenant Ryan. Every word of it is probably true. And I'm sure that if this expedition verifies that there is gold in the Black Hills, there will be an uncontrollable rush into those hills by thousands of gold seekers. I heard just a couple of days ago that people in and around Bismarck are waiting for one positive sign. If they get it, they will stampede into the Black Hills, and that will bring gold seekers from all over the country."

"That's the way it was when gold was discovered in the Sacramento area in California in 1849," one of the lieutenants said. "Thousands upon thousands of gold seekers rushed westward."

Colonel Grant said, "Tell them the Colorado story that you told me about yesterday, Colonel."

Custer grinned. "All right. Not long after the California gold strike became big news, in Colorado the story went out that a group of gold seekers slid down Pikes Peak's east side from its summit on a large harrow. It was said that each tooth of the harrow gouged out a curl of gold. People believed the story, and soon the Front Range of the Rocky Mountains around Pikes Peak crawled with eighty thousand gold prospectors. I can tell you for sure that if word gets out that there is gold in the Black Hills, the same kind of rush will happen there."

There was silence as the men thought about what could lie ahead if gold was indeed found in the Black Hills.

The quietness was split by the cry of a coyote. The men around Custer's fire looked out into the darkness in the direction that the cry had come from.

The cry came again and rose strange, wild, and mournful—not the howl of a prowling beast baying at the campfires or at the men in plain view around them, but a wolf-like wail, full-voiced, crying out the meaning of the vast rolling Dakota plains and the depth of the night.

When the lonely howl ceased, Colonel Custer ran his gaze over the faces of the men around the fire and said, "Sounds like he's a bit forlorn."

One of the captains smiled. "I'd say he sounds *very* forlorn, sir."

"Well, back to the subject. Certainly, a stampede of whites through Dakota Territory would bring war. Though Sitting Bull is in Wyoming, he definitely would get involved. The Sioux at first would defend the land by massacring isolated miners; then they would concentrate on the wagon trains bringing the miners to the Black Hills."

"Knowing what I do about Sitting Bull, Colonel Custer," said Grant, "he would get in on it, all right. He hates white people with a passion. There would most certainly be attacks on the gold seekers."

Custer pulled at a corner of his mustache. "Of course, the United States government would retaliate, but white men would shed much blood in a war with the Indians." He paused and sighed. "Since what we're doing right now could light the fuse for that war, it makes us an integral part of it. And I'm the appointed leader. But…there's nothing I can do about it. I do not formulate policy. I'm merely following orders that started with President Grant and came down through army authority to me."

Colonel Grant met Custer's gaze and nodded.

"Even if I refused to lead this expedition," said Custer, "someone else would do it. The Black Hills are going to be searched for signs of gold by the United States Army. So I might as well carry on." Custer rose to his feet. "Well, gentlemen, it's time for all of us to turn in for the night."

All over the camp, men made their bedrolls ready for the night. Soon only those who were appointed to serve as sentries on the first watch were moving about.

The day had closed, and the lonely prairie night set in with its dead silence.

⚬⚬⚬

Dawn's early light seemed to touch Colonel Custer's eyelids shortly after he had fallen asleep. He left his bedroll, stood to his feet, and stretched and yawned. Several men were already moving about. Some were lighting cook fires.

The men ate a hearty breakfast, and soon they were moving further southwest.

As the next several days passed, the air was fragrant with wildflowers all around. Blueberries, cherries, and gooseberries grew in abundance, to the delight of the thousand-man team.

Each evening, the brass band entertained the large crowd.

On the eighteenth day since leaving Fort Abraham Lincoln the expedition entered a green valley. It was yet early morning, and they were skirting the edge of some rolling hills heavy with trees. The morning was bright, still, and as clear as crystal. The day's heat had not yet begun.

Custer was talking to his chief scout about the Sioux nation's supreme leader, Chief Sitting Bull, when he suddenly stopped, his eyes wide.

Bloody Knife twisted around to see what had caught Custer's attention, and at the same time Colonel Grant said, "Well, look at that, will you?"

An enormous cinnamon-colored male grizzly bear had emerged from the shadowed timber on all fours and watched the riders and wagons passing by. A deep roar came from his wide-open mouth. A pair of ravens squawked and flew away from a nearby tree.

Custer said to Grant and Bloody Knife, "I've got to bag me that bear." He moved his horse out where he could be seen by the long lines behind him and waved his hat to signal the procession to come to a halt.

"Are you sure you want to do this?" Grant asked.

"Yeah." Custer dismounted and yanked his rifle from its saddle scabbard. At the same time, Bloody Knife slid from his horse's back, grasping his own rifle, and followed on Custer's heels.

The others in the expedition watched with interest as the huge grizzly rose to his hind feet, growled, and shook his head at the oncoming humans.

"I will not fire unless it is necessary, sir," said Bloody Knife, now walking at Custer's side, his gun cocked and ready. "I know that you would like to kill the bear by yourself."

"I appreciate your understanding that," Custer said, still moving toward the grizzly, his rifle cocked as he gripped it tightly in his right hand.

The grizzly's mouth was slavering, and his muscles bunched as he lumbered toward them, still in a standing position.

Face to face with eight to nine hundred pounds of teeth, claws, fur, muscle, and snarling meanness, Custer stopped some sixty feet from the oncoming brute, shouldered his rifle, drew a bead, and fired. The bullet hit the grizzly square between the eyes. The bear stopped and roared, shook his great head, pawed at the air frantically, and slumped to the ground in a heap.

Bloody Knife stayed at Custer's side as the lieutenant colonel cocked his rifle again and cautiously moved up to the massive ball of fur.

Easing up slowly, Custer nudged the grizzly's head with the muzzle of his rifle. The eyes were closed, and there was no movement.

"Go get Alf Hoover for me, will you, Bloody Knife?" Custer said with elation in his voice. "I want him to take a picture of this."

Frederick Grant and several other men left their horses and walked to where Custer stood over the dead grizzly, while the rest looked on from horseback and wagon seats. Moments later, the team photographer rushed up, camera in hand, with Bloody Knife at his side.

Custer said, "Alf, I want you to take a picture of Bloody Knife and me standing over this dead grizzly."

Hoover smiled. "Happy to oblige, Colonel."

The next morning, the dead grizzly was left for the other prairie animals and carnivorous birds to feast on as the riders and wagons pulled away from the site.

As the days passed and they drew nearer to the Black Hills region, Colonel Custer warned all of his men to keep an extra sharp lookout for Indians.

On Wednesday afternoon, July 22, at Abilene, Kansas, James Butler "Wild Bill" Hickok stepped out of the Rusty Gun Saloon into the heat and brilliant sunlight.

Riders on horseback, as well as wagons and buggies, passed by on the wide, dusty street. People strolled along the boardwalks going to stores and shops, often stopping to talk with friends and acquaintances.

Hickok pocketed a wad of currency that he had just won in a poker game. His long, stringy hair rested on his shoulders, and he ran his fingers through his droopy mustache as he looked around on the sunlit Main Street. Holstered on his wide belt were two silver-plated Colt .45 revolvers.

Suddenly, above the sounds of the busy street and the shuffle of feet on the boardwalks, Hickok heard a female voice calling his name. He turned in that direction and saw a woman on horseback and dressed in men's clothing riding toward him. He smiled, stepped to the edge of the boardwalk, and said, "Well, Calamity Jane! Where've you been? I haven't seen you around town for a month or better."

Martha Jane Canary pulled rein and dismounted. While she

was tying her horse's reins to the hitch rail, she said, "I made a trip to Bismarck in Dakota Territory just over five weeks ago, James. Or should I say Wild Bill?"

He chuckled. "Either one is okay."

"All right, James. I made a few stops on the return trip and just got back into town." She pointed a thumb over her shoulder. "A couple of elderly men sitting on a bench up the street a ways told me they saw Wild Bill Hickok go into the Rusty Gun Saloon about two hours ago but hadn't seen him come out. So I was coming to find you."

Hickok smiled. "Anything special you wanted to see me about?"

"I wanted to tell you about the army sending Lieutenant Colonel Custer and a large number of men into Dakota Territory's Black Hills to look for gold. I figured you just might be interested if it turns out that they do find gold up there."

Hickok rubbed his chin. "I heard something about that, but I wasn't sure it was true."

"Well, believe me, it is. I saw Custer and his massive expedition with my own two eyes."

"Really?"

"Really. He's got a thousand men, all on horseback or in covered wagons. Custer has to find a piece of ground where the army can build a new fort so that the railroad workers who are laying track through Indian territory can be protected. But President Grant is even more interested in finding gold in the Black Hills to pay off the national debt and get the country out of its financial depression."

"I did hear about the Northern Pacific Railroad wanting to lay that stretch of track. And I've known about the rumors of gold in the Black Hills, too. I'm glad to learn from you that Custer really is leading an expedition into the Black Hills in search of gold."

Calamity Jane looked him square in the eye. "So, are you interested?"

"I just might be. But if there is a gold rush, then I'll go and make my fortune taking gold from miners at the gambling tables. It's much more fun that way than panning for gold in the streams and digging it out of the ground."

She shrugged. "Whatever makes you happy. Ah…you ever going to become a lawman again?"

"I just might. Right now, I'm resting up from my four years of working with Bill Cody in his Wild West Show."

At that moment two riders came along the dusty street and hauled up to the hitch rail in front of the Rusty Gun Saloon. When they were about to dismount, Hickok recognized one of them as Duff McCall, whom he had arrested some five years ago when he was marshal of Abilene.

Suddenly McCall's attention went to Hickok, and his features turned to stone.

Calamity Jane noticed the rider's anger as he looked at Hickok, and she frowned as Hickok snapped, "Don't look at me like that, McCall!"

People moving along the boardwalk came to a halt. Their eyes bulged at the sight of Duff McCall.

McCall snapped back, "I can look at you any way I want to, Hickok! You framed me for a robbery I didn't commit when you were marshal of this town. You did it to make yourself look good. I just got out of prison two weeks ago."

McCall and his companion dismounted and stepped up on the boardwalk.

Calamity Jane moved away from Hickok, figuring bullets were about to fly.

The crowd back-stepped, expecting the same thing. They watched intently as Hickok let his hands dangle over his holstered guns. He took a couple of steps closer to the two men, ran his gaze between them, and asked, "Who's this with you, Duff?"

"He's my younger brother, Jack."

"Well, you and Jack get back on your horses and get outta town. Right now."

Jack's features reddened. "You ain't got no authority to order us to leave town, Hickok. Abilene's been our home since we were boys."

"I'm gonna make you sorry for what you did to me, Hickok," Duff said. "Because of your dirty lies, you cost me five years of my life and ruined my reputation."

"Don't you threaten me, McCall!" Hickok said. "I did not tell any lies about you, and I didn't frame you! You committed that robbery, and the jury found you guilty!"

"Hah! Only on your testimony, you *liar!*"

Hickok bristled like an angry wolf and shook his head. His long hair swirled about as he snarled, "That's garbage! You did it and you know it!"

Duff McCall stiffened and let his right hand drop near the handle of his holstered revolver.

Jack grabbed his brother's right arm. "Don't be a fool, Duff! You can't outdraw him! He's killed many a man who tried to beat him to the draw! Let's just go on into the saloon."

Duff lanced Hickok with steely eyes and said, "All right."

Jack looked at Hickok. "And don't you try to stop us. We have every right to be in Abilene and to go anywhere in this town we want to. And you have no authority to tell us to do otherwise."

Hickok gave him a blank stare.

The McCall brothers crossed the boardwalk and entered the saloon. The people in the crowd released sighs of relief.

Calamity Jane rushed to Hickok, took hold of his arm, and said, "O James, I was so afraid there was going to be a shootout!"

The ex-marshal of Abilene patted her hand. "You needn't worry, Martha Jane. Duff's brother was right. He can't outdraw me."

A man standing close by said, "I don't think he can outdraw you either, Wild Bill, but I sure don't want to see any bloodshed."

Hickok chuckled, a wide grin on his mouth. "I don't either. Especially mine." He let his eyes roam over the faces of the crowd. "I guarantee you, folks, the McCall brothers are lying about my framing Duff. But I'm glad that Jack talked Duff out of drawing against me."

One of the town marshal's deputies pushed his way through the crowd. People were excitedly telling Deputy Will Lamont what had just happened as he moved toward Hickok.

Lamont drew up and said, "Sorry the marshal isn't here, James. He's in Topeka on business."

Hickok nodded. "You know I didn't frame Duff McCall for that robbery, Will."

Lamont nodded. "I'm sure glad you didn't have to gun him down just now."

"I didn't want to kill him. I don't hold anything against Duff. The man did his time, and he just needs to get on with his life, now that he's out. Sure, I could've outdrawn him, but I certainly don't want to kill him."

Deputy Lamont looked around at the crowd and said, "Okay, folks. Excitement's over. Might as well get back to your business."

The crowd broke up, and Deputy Lamont headed back to the marshal's office.

Hickok turned to Calamity Jane and said, "Well, sweet gal, I've got things to do. See you around."

She smiled up at him. "Okay."

"And thanks for telling me about the possible gold rush in Dakota Territory. Like I told you, if it happens, I'll go and collect my gold at the gambling tables."

EIGHT

As Deputy Will Lamont walked back toward the marshal's office, he was just about to pass the Western Union office when he saw the silver-haired messenger, Abe Wilson, coming out the door.

Abe was about to head up the boardwalk when he happened to glance in the other direction and his eyes fell on the deputy. He grinned and said, "Well, howdy, Will!" He held up a yellow envelope. "I was headin' to the marshal's office to bring you and the other deputy this telegram from Marshal Atwood."

Will hastened to him and took the envelope. "Thanks, Abe. I wonder what he wants?"

"Well, I can save you readin' it. He's comin' home from Topeka a day early. He's arrivin' this evenin' on the 6:15 train. Says he got his business taken care of quicker than he thought."

Will smiled. "Well, that's good. Did he send Mrs. Atwood a telegram, too?"

"Nope. Says in there that he'd like one of you to pick him up in his buggy at the railroad station, and since whichever of you is going to pick him up has to go to his house to hitch the buggy to his horse, he can tell Loretta that the marshal will be home for supper."

Will looked down at the envelope in his hand. "Anything else in here I need to know?"

Abe chuckled. "Nope. That's it. But you can read it anyways."

"Guess I'd better do that."

At 6:10 that evening, Deputy Will Lamont stood on the platform at the Abilene depot, chatting with a man, his wife, and his two children who had come to pick up the wife's parents, who were coming for a visit. Will thought that it was marvelous that the two children showed such excitement about seeing their grandparents.

A train whistle interrupted their conversation, and soon they heard the chugging of the steam engine as the train pulled into the station. Will watched the children dash to their grandparents when they stepped off the train and then spotted his boss coming out of another coach and hurried to meet him.

"I'm glad that you could come home a day early, Marshal. For two reasons," Will said as they shook hands.

Marshal Dale Atwood smiled as they moved along the platform toward the baggage coach. "All right, I'll bite. What's reason number one?"

"Number one is that when I went to your house to get your horse and buggy, Loretta invited me for supper. So I get to eat supper with the Atwoods tonight."

"Okay. What's number two?"

"Number two, sir, is just because I like having you right here in town."

Atwood shook his head and smiled again. "Well, now, that's mighty good to know."

They picked up the marshal's luggage, and as they climbed into the buggy, Will said, "Something happened here today, Marshal, that you need to know about."

The marshal took the reins in hand and put the horse in motion. As they drove toward the Atwood home, Will told him of the incident between Hickok and the McCall brothers that had happened in front of the Rusty Gun Saloon.

That evening after eating supper at one of Abilene's cafés, the McCall brothers swung into their saddles and rode to their house, which they had inherited from their parents. It was located at the west edge of Abilene on a two-acre plot. Jack had lived there alone during the five years that Duff was in prison.

When Duff and Jack entered the house, they lit a couple of lanterns in the parlor, where Duff was going to read the day's edition of the *Abilene Post*.

Jack said, "Well, big brother, you enjoy the paper. I'm going to heat up some water on the kitchen stove and take a bath."

Duff grinned, sniffed a couple of times, and said, "It's about time!"

After Jack headed for the kitchen, Duff took a pair of his boots from a hall closet and sat down in the parlor to polish them. When he finished, he returned the boots to the hall closet and made his way back to the parlor, where he picked up the newspaper.

He was about to sit down in one of the overstuffed chairs when the sharp roar of a gun cut through the night. The parlor window shattered as the slug hit Duff in the back of the head. He stiffened and fell facedown on the floor.

In the kitchen, Jack was about to remove the steaming kettle from the stove and pour the hot water into the galvanized tub that he had brought into the kitchen from the back porch when he heard the gun fire and the parlor window shatter.

He dashed down the hall and into the parlor. He stopped in stunned disbelief when he saw his brother lying facedown on the floor with a bullet hole in the back of his head. He was not breathing.

"Hickok!" Jack hissed as he dashed into the hall, grabbed a rifle that leaned against the wall in a corner, and headed for the front door. He eared back the hammer, turned the knob on the door, and cautiously opened it. He heard the fading hoofbeats of a galloping horse.

He dashed onto the front porch, and though he could not see the fleeing horse and rider, he fired a shot in that direction. The fading hoofbeats could still be heard.

Jack went back into the parlor, picked up the body of his dead brother, and carried it into Duff's bedroom. He placed the body on the bed, covered it with a sheet, and then hurried to the kitchen. He grabbed the burning lantern that was on the cupboard and ran outside to the barn. He quickly bridled and saddled his horse and rode hard toward the other end of town.

Supper was over at the Atwood residence, and the marshal and Deputy Lamont were sitting in the parlor talking about the incident in front of the Rusty Gun Saloon that day when they heard pounding hooves skid to a stop at the front of the house, then hasty footsteps on the front porch.

The marshal hurried from the parlor with the deputy on his heels and opened the front door in response to the rapid knock. He was surprised to see Jack McCall standing there, his face livid.

"Duff was just shot, Marshal!" Jack said. "The bullet came through the parlor window. I was in the kitchen and ran in to find Duff with a bullet in the back of his head. He's dead!"

Before Atwood could speak, Jack said, "You remember that I told you when you became marshal that James Hickok had framed Duff for a robbery that he didn't commit."

Atwood nodded. "Yes, but—"

"Will, did you tell the marshal what happened today on the street?"

Will nodded. "Yes, I told him."

"Did you tell him how Duff said that he was going to make Hickok sorry for framing him with his dirty lies?"

Will nodded. "I did."

"Well, it had to have been Hickok who shot Duff to keep him from whatever he was going to do to make him sorry." Jack looked at the marshal, his face hard and his lips compressed. "I want Hickok arrested, Marshal!"

Atwood frowned. "Did you see Hickok?"

"No. I told you that I was in the kitchen when the shot was fired. When I got to the parlor and found Duff dead, I did hear somebody riding away on a horse. I went out on the porch, but it was too dark to see the horse and rider."

"So you can't prove it was Hickok."

"No. But I'm sure it was him."

The marshal shook his head. "Jack, I know that Hickok has been accused of murder before, but there was never enough evidence to prove that he had done it. He was never convicted."

"But Will heard what Duff said about making Hickok sorry. It *had* to have been him who shot Duff!"

"There's no way to prove it, Jack. Tell you what. I'll go find Hickok right now and talk to him."

Jack nodded. "Can I go along?"

Atwood rubbed his jaw. "All right. But you have to promise me that you're going to keep cool and let me handle any situation that arises."

Jack took a deep breath. "Okay. I promise."

"Do you want me to go along too, Marshal?" Lamont asked.

"There's no need, Will. You go on home."

"Okay, but if you need your deputies, just holler."

After Will had gone out the door, Atwood turned to Jack. "Before we look for Hickok, I want to go to your house and look it over."

"Let's go."

Moments later, the marshal stood over the bed where Duff McCall's body lay and shook his head. "I hate this, Jack, and I promise that I'll do everything possible to bring your brother's killer to justice. The first thing I want to do is examine the ground where the killer had to have been when he fired the shot."

Jack pulled the sheet back up over his brother's lifeless form. "All right. Let me grab a lantern."

As Jack held a lantern, the marshal carefully examined the ground in an extended area outside the parlor window. They could see many footprints, as well as hoof prints. After a while, Marshal Atwood said, "Jack, there's nothing here that could identify the killer or his horse. Most of these prints have to be yours and Duff's. And I don't find any shell casings."

"I see what you mean, Marshal. What next?"

"There are three different saloons in town where Hickok is known to spend his evenings gambling. He's probably at one of them right now. I suggest we go find him."

By the lantern light, Marshal Atwood could see the hatred in Jack McCall's eyes. "Remember what you promised. You'll keep cool and let me handle this."

Jack nodded. "All right."

When the marshal and Jack came out of the third saloon, Atwood said, "All right, so nobody's seen Hickok tonight. Let's go on over to the house he's renting."

A few minutes later, when the two men drew up in front of the house, no lantern light showed in any of the windows.

"Doesn't look like he's here, Marshal," Jack said.

"We'll see." Atwood stepped up on the porch and pounded on the door.

The marshal waited several seconds and then pounded harder

and called out, "James Hickok, It's Marshal Atwood! I need to talk to you! If you're in there, come to the door!"

Even as the marshal spoke, lantern light danced on the curtains at the front window.

When Hickok opened the door, he was clad in a robe, and his long, straggly hair dangled on his shoulders. He yawned sleepily and rubbed his eyes. "Whaddya want, Marshal?"

"Duff McCall was shot through a window in his house an hour and a half ago, James. He's dead. The killer galloped away on a horse."

Hickok blinked. "Sorry to hear it. Why come to me?"

"Where were you an hour and a half ago?"

"Right here in this house. I was having some stomach problems this evening so I went to bed early. Almost three hours ago."

Jack McCall's eyes flashed. "Can you prove it?"

Hickok looked at the marshal and then back at Jack. "No, I can't prove it. I live here alone."

"James," said the marshal, "Jack told me about Duff's confrontation with you in front of the Rusty Gun Saloon today and of Duff's threat to make you sorry for framing him. Duff's murder would make those who heard the threat think that it was you, gunning him down so that he couldn't carry out his threat."

"Marshal, I acknowledge that the confrontation took place, but I certainly did not kill Duff." Hickok then set his dark eyes on Jack. "I'm sorry that somebody took your brother from you. But it wasn't me."

Jack met Hickok's level gaze but said nothing.

"Sorry for waking you up, James," Marshal Atwood said. "I hope your stomach gets better."

Hickok yawned again, nodded, and said, "Good night, Marshal. You too, Jack."

As the marshal and Jack walked away, Atwood said, "Jack,

even if Hickok did kill Duff, I have no way to prove it. I'll come out to your house tomorrow and look at the ground again in the daylight, but as far as Hickok is concerned, there's nothing else I can do unless I find incriminating evidence against him."

"I understand, Marshal," said Jack, but in his mind he said to himself, *Someday Mr. Wild Bill Hickok will pay!*

It was a bright, sunny morning in Chicago on Thursday, July 23. In the city's affluent Seward Park section, Kathleen McGuire and her daughter stepped out of their mansion—each with a happy look on her face—and were helped aboard the McGuire carriage by their silver-haired chauffeur and gardener, Wilson Reeves. Both women were clad in flowery summer dresses, fancy wide-brimmed hats, and white gloves.

As Wilson climbed onto the driver's seat and took the reins in his hand, he looked over his shoulder and said, "Mrs. McGuire, do you want to go to the Western Union office first?"

"No, Wilson. Alyssa Rose and I want to go to the railroad station first so that we can purchase the tickets for our trip to Cheyenne. We'll go to the Western Union office after that. We want to wire Frank about the good news of the sale of the house and let him know the date when we'll arrive in Cheyenne. After that we'll do our shopping downtown."

"Yes, ma'am." And with that, Wilson put the carriage in motion.

As they moved away from the mansion, Alyssa Rose turned on the seat next to her mother and cast a nostalgic look back at the beautiful red-brick, three-story mansion. The windows gleamed in the morning sunshine, and the white trim and black shutters reflected the sun's glow.

Alyssa took hold of her mother's gloved hand. "Mama, I know that it's going to be difficult to leave our home. You and Papa have lived here since just after you married. Of course, this is the only home I've ever known, and—and it's hard to imagine living any-where else."

Kathleen sighed and shrugged her shoulders. "Yes, my dear, it's hard for me to imagine, too. But since the days of old, women have followed their husbands wherever their wanderlust led them." She looked back toward the mansion and then set her eyes on Alyssa. "It's only a house, after all. It's the people who live in it that make it a home. So now our home will just be in a different part of this great country."

Alyssa Rose squeezed her mother's delicate hand and smiled. "You are so right, Mama. Though Cheyenne will take some get-ting used to, I'm sure, we will make our house there a wonderful home, because that's where you and Papa and Monty and I will be. I'll just have to get used to the new surroundings and make new friends. But from what Papa and Monty have told us about the people there, that should come easily."

Kathleen smiled at her daughter, who looked so much like Kathleen had at that age. "That's my girl. After all, it's going to be exciting to be a part of the wild and woolly West. Maybe someday they'll write the McGuires into the history books as those bankers who helped settle the West."

Alyssa's eyes brightened. "Oh, yes! That would be great, wouldn't it?"

Wilson spoke over his shoulder. "Mrs. McGuire, the rest of your servants and I are going to miss being employed by the McGuire family. We've been talking about it a lot, and we are so thankful that you were able to talk the new owners into keeping all five of us on staff."

Kathleen said, "I'm glad it worked out this way, Wilson. And believe me, the McGuire family will miss all of you very much."

Alyssa became quiet as the carriage continued its journey down LaSalle Street.

After a few minutes, Kathleen sensed her daughter's thoughtful mood. She patted Alyssa's hand. "Alyssa, what is it? You are so deep in thought."

"Oh, I was just thinking of how our lifestyle is going to change so drastically out West. Here in Chicago we have exquisite restaurants, beautiful parks, the opera house, and so many magnificent stores. I have a feeling that Cheyenne will be lacking in these areas. It's going to take some getting used to!"

"That it will, honey. But I'm sure that you and I are up to the challenge. Who knows? We may come to love Cheyenne and the surrounding area as much or even more than we love Chicago."

"Well, from what Papa and Monty say, they sure love Cheyenne. I'm so glad that they love the church, and Pastor Ballert and his wife, too."

"Yes, that makes me very happy. And it seems from your brother's letters that he already has that friend of his, Jim Bannon, eager to make your acquaintance. Now, that must be exciting!"

Alyssa giggled and shook her head. "Oh, Mama, I'm nervous about meeting Jim. If he is all that Monty says he is, he must be quite the young man. I—I'll just have to see about him when we meet."

Kathleen patted her hand once more. "Of course."

"Mama, I'll never forget the people in our church here. I mean Pastor Johnson, his family, and all the wonderful people. They mean so much to me."

"Of course we will never forget them," Kathleen said. "I hope that we'll be able to stay in contact with those we are closest to by mail."

"I'm sure that we will, Mama. And as for Cheyenne, I'm looking forward to living in the new house that Papa is having built. From his letters, it sounds like it is going to be beautiful—especially with the view of the Rocky Mountains from the balcony!"

Wilson Reeves swung off of LaSalle Street and headed the carriage toward the railroad station.

❧

It was almost closing time at the Bank of Wyoming that Thursday afternoon when Frank McGuire's secretary, Gail Conlon, entered his office with a yellow envelope in her hand. As Frank looked up from his desk, she smiled and said, "Mr. McGuire, a Western Union messenger just delivered this telegram. It's from Mrs. McGuire."

Frank's eyes lit up as he took the envelope from her. "Good!"

Monty came into his father's office, having heard Gail's words as he was passing through her office. He was holding some official-looking papers. He laid them on his father's desk and said, "Open it quick, Dad. Maybe Mom sold the house."

Gail smiled at Monty. "I sure hope that's what it's about." She headed for the door. "Let me know, won't you, Mr. McGuire?"

Frank grinned. "I will."

Gail closed the boss's door as she entered her own office and sat down at her desk.

Frank opened the envelope and read the telegram to his son. They both rejoiced in the news about the sale of the mansion. When Frank read the train schedule that Kathleen and Alyssa Rose were able to obtain, Monty said, "Great! That means that they'll be here in just eighteen days, Dad!"

"Can't come soon enough for me, son!"

"Me, either!" Monty pointed to the papers that he had laid on his father's desk. "You'll find those all in order, Dad."

"Good. Thank you."

When Monty returned to the open area where his desk was located, he was surprised to see Jim Bannon standing there. "Well, howdy, Jim. To what do I owe the pleasure of your presence?"

"Since it's almost closing time, I came by to see if I could take you out for supper."

"I'd love to eat supper with you," Monty said, "but there's one stipulation."

"And what might that be?"

"No matter where we choose to have our evening repast, I'm paying for it."

Jim shook his head. "Well, Mr. Banker, I know better than to argue. How soon can you get away?"

Monty glanced at the clock on a nearby wall. "No reason I can't go right now. Bank closes in four minutes."

"Good! Let's go."

As the two friends walked along the boardwalk toward the restaurant that they had chosen, Monty told Jim about the telegram that had come from his mother and that the mansion had been sold.

"Hey, praise the Lord!" Jim said. "That's good news. When will your mother and sister be coming to Cheyenne?"

"Well, Mom and Sis will leave Chicago on Saturday, August eighth, and arrive in Cheyenne on Monday, the tenth."

"I'm sure looking forward to meeting them."

Monty laughed. "Especially Alyssa Rose, right?"

Jim smiled and shrugged. "Well...what can I say?"

NINE

On Friday, July 24, the expedition team was moving southwest, and as they came over a rise on the rolling prairie, Bloody Knife pointed ahead and said, "That river ahead, Colonel Custer, is the Belle Fourche. It is shallow enough that the wagons will have no problem getting across."

"Good," Custer said. "I saw it on the map that I'm carrying, but I had no idea how deep it might be."

From Custer's other side, Colonel Grant said, "We're fortunate to have you along, as well as the other Arikara scouts, Bloody Knife. You Arikaras really know this country, don't you?"

"Yes, sir," Bloody Knife responded. "We have traveled it many times."

Suddenly one of the Arikara scouts who was riding just behind Custer and his two companions shouted, "Colonel Custer, look! A wagon train! And there's a band of Sioux riding down on them!"

The small train of wagons was easily seen about a mile off to their left and a bit south. The Sioux warriors were galloping toward them, whooping loudly. Custer pulled his horse out of line so that everyone behind could see him and waved his hat for them to stop. Raising up in the stirrups, he shouted, "Wagon train being attacked by Sioux to the south! I want all of the men of the

Seventh Cavalry to go with me! The other cavalry units stay here in case there are more Indians around!"

Bloody Knife stayed at Custer's side as the lieutenant colonel put his horse to a gallop.

As the men of the Seventh Cavalry rode toward the wagon train, which was now forming a circle, the Sioux opened fire on the wagons from horseback. The men of the wagon train began firing back.

Custer whipped his revolver from its holster and began firing at the Indians, and every man behind him spread out and opened up with their rifles.

When two of the Indians fell from their horses, having been struck by army bullets, the Sioux leader jerked his head around and saw the great number of uniformed riders coming on fast, rifles spitting fire. He shouted to his fourteen remaining warriors, all of whom had now caught sight of the oncoming cavalry. As they galloped away at full speed, another Sioux was struck with a bullet and fell from his horse.

The three riderless horses followed the band of warriors as they rode away due south in a cloud of dust. Within seconds, they disappeared over a gentle rise.

When the Seventh Cavalry drew up to the wagon train, the white travelers came out from inside the circle of wagons, waving at the cavalrymen and smiling.

Custer looked down at a group of six men and said, "Anyone in the wagon train get shot?"

"No, sir," said a middle-aged man. "I'm Jess Toomey, the wagonmaster. If you and your men hadn't shown up when you did, there would have been blood shed in this wagon train. What fort are you from?"

"We're from Fort Abraham Lincoln, Mr. Toomey. I'm Lieutenant Colonel George Custer, and these men are of the Seventh Cavalry."

Toomey's smile broadened. "Well, we sure are glad you came to our rescue, sir. Are you going to chase those hostiles down?"

Custer shook his head. "Don't have time. We're on assignment from President Grant, and we must keep moving. I doubt those hostiles will be back to bother you."

"Probably not. Well, Colonel Custer, we'll not detain you. Thanks again for coming to our rescue."

"Our pleasure, Mr. Toomey. Where are you headed?"

"Montana."

"I hope that you make it safely."

Custer touched the brim of his hat and led his men back to where the long train of wagons waited to continue toward the Black Hills. He put the expedition in motion once again, and when they reached the Belle Fourche River, they had no problem getting across.

Soon they were following a creek that flowed from the river, as one of the Arikara scouts suggested. At noon they stopped for lunch on the bank of the creek. In the distance to the south they could now see great rolling, forested hills in the bright light of the sun. Bloody Knife spoke softly to Custer, whose eyes lit up at his words.

Quickly Custer called for everyone to assemble for a moment.

When the entire team had gathered, Custer said, "Gentlemen, take a good look at those tree-laden hills due south. Bloody Knife tells me that we are nearing the very tip of the Black Hills, and you are looking at them! Tomorrow, we will enter the Sioux's sacred land."

Everyone cheered. Then the men broke up into their usual groups, built cook fires, and soon were sitting on the creek bank eating their lunch.

At one spot on the creek bank the team's two experienced miners, Horatio Ross and William McKay, were sitting together with three of the Arikara scouts. As Ross was eating a slice of beef jerky, a flash of sunlight reflected from something in the sand. Curious, he picked up a handful of the sand, examined it closely, and turned to McKay, who was in conversation with one of the scouts. "William, take a look at this."

McKay glanced at the sand in Ross's hand. "Mm-hmm. I've seen sand before."

Ross tipped his hand right and left. "With this kind of shiny stuff in it?"

Suddenly the sun's reflection hit McKay's eyes. "Hey, that's gold! Those shiny particles in the sand are gold nuggets!"

McKay's exclamation was loud enough to gain the attention of every man. All along the creek, they jumped to their feet and hurried to where the miners and their Arikara friends were sitting.

Custer drew up and pushed his way through the crowd. "Let me see!"

Ross rose to his feet and placed his open handful of sand close to the lieutenant colonel's face, tipping it from side to side so the tiny nuggets would catch the sun's rays. "Take a look."

Custer's mouth dropped open. He ran his gaze between the two miners and said, "It really looks like gold, but are you sure that's what it is?"

"Looks like the real thing to me, sir," Ross said.

"Look down here, Colonel," McKay said. "There's plenty more in the sand right under our feet. Tell you what. We'll gather up some more nuggets and test them, just so we'll know for sure."

Ross looked at McKay. "You get started, William. I'll run back to our wagon and get the stuff that we need to make the test."

The crowd of men strained to see as William McKay gathered more of the shiny nuggets. Only two or three minutes had elapsed when Horatio Ross returned, carrying two small bottles and a small, shallow metal pan. Ross helped his partner gather up a sufficient supply of the nuggets. Then those who were up close watched as Ross and McKay washed the nuggets with acid in the pan and then mixed them with mercury.

"Acid and mercury, eh?" said one of the men close by.

Ross nodded. "It's the only way to know for sure. We'll be able to tell in just a minute here."

Less than a minute had passed when Ross looked at McKay and said, "You want to tell 'em?"

McKay smiled broadly, looked at Custer, and said so that all could hear, "Colonel, we have real, genuine gold here!"

The crowd whooped it up, shouting and waving their hats in the air.

When the noise subsided, Ross said, "Colonel Custer, I can guarantee you that, as close as we are to the Black Hills, there will be plenty more of the real thing when we get in there. Gold, sir! Gold! President Grant and Congress are going to be very happy when they hear about this."

The men cheered and shouted once more, and when they quieted down, Custer said, "Well, men, let's get things cleaned up here and push on toward those Black Hills!"

Soon they had the wagons and all the mounted men moving south, following the same creek toward their destination.

By midafternoon they pulled into the shade of the tall evergreens just inside the northern tip of the Black Hills. Horatio Ross and William McKay had suggested that once they were actually in the Black Hills, they should see if they could find more nuggets on the bank of the creek.

With the help of several men who were using shovels, picks, axes, and tent pins to dig shiny nuggets from the creek bank, Ross and McKay filled kettles, cups, and platters with the nuggets. They then did the test on the nuggets and pronounced them pure gold.

Colonel Grant looked at Custer. "Well, sir, the insistent rumors of half a century have been verified. We are actually in the Black Hills, and here's proof!"

Again, the crowd of a thousand men waved their hats in the air and cheered.

When the cheering subsided, Custer called for them to make

camp and told the men whose turn it was to be on watch to keep an extra sharp lookout.

Later, after supper, they built fires as dusk settled in, and the flames burned against the shadows. When the weary men began to slip into their bedrolls for the night, the light of twinkling stars broke through the enamel black of the sky. Most of them quickly fell asleep, and the sentries moved about, listening for any strange sounds and peering carefully into the surrounding shadows.

The next morning, they rose at dawn and had their usual hearty breakfast. Then the riders mounted up, the drivers climbed onto the wagon seats, and the team slowly moved deeper into the forest. In less than twenty minutes they came to a level, open area that Custer judged covered seven or eight acres. A creek ran along one side of the area. He had the team stop and pointed it out to the men as a very good spot for the fort. Everyone agreed.

Custer had a rough map of the Black Hills in his saddlebag. He took it out, found the line for the railroad tracks running east and west, and marked the open area on the map to show Colonel Huston when they returned to Fort Lincoln.

They moved on, with a corporal riding beside Colonel Grant, holding a stick with a white flag in plain sight. Riding just ahead of Grant and the corporal were Custer and his chief scout. Bloody Knife led the expedition along a trail that would take them to the village where Chief Red Cloud and his Oglalas lived.

Soon they came upon a small group of teenage Indian boys who had just shot two hawks out of a tree with their bows and arrows. The boys' eyes filled with fear when they saw the train of wagons and the uniformed men on horseback.

Colonel Custer said to Bloody Knife in a low voice, "Tell them that we are here peaceably and mean them no harm. We are here to talk to Chief Red Cloud."

Bloody Knife nodded as he pulled rein, looked down at the

boys, and spoke to them in the Lakota tongue. The fear immediately left their eyes.

The wagon occupied by William McKay and Horatio Ross was at the head of one of the long lines. Suddenly McKay hopped out of the wagon and ran up beside Custer's horse. "Colonel, look at the tips of those arrows that the boys are holding!"

"My goodness, those arrowheads look like gold!" Custer said, eyes twinkling.

Ross was now beside his partner. He looked up at the colonel's chief scout. "Bloody Knife, ask the boys if I can take a look at one of the arrows."

Bloody Knife spoke again to the boys in their language. One of them stepped up and handed Ross an arrow.

Ross thanked him in English and examined the shiny arrowhead carefully. After a moment a smile spread over his face as he looked up at Custer. "Colonel, there's no doubt about it. These arrows have genuine gold tips. There has to be gold aplenty around here!"

One of the cavalrymen sitting on his horse close by said, "Colonel Custer, when word gets out about what we've found, white people will be coming into these hills by the thousands."

Custer looked at him and shrugged his shoulders. "Nothing I can do about that. My orders are to report to General Sheridan and Colonel Huston if we find gold in here. I will do as ordered."

Soon the expedition came upon Red Cloud's village. They noted that the tepees—some made of buffalo hide and the others of cowhide—spread out in three directions, with many set back in the forest. A narrow, bubbling stream ran along one side of the village.

Indians of all ages moved about among the tepees. Several dogs of various breeds could be seen, some following children while others lay in the sun. The people stared impassively at the large number of uniformed men on horses and the long lines of covered wagons.

Four warriors saw them coming and alerted more warriors, who came on the run.

The corporal still rode beside Grant, holding the stick bearing the white flag as high as he could.

As better than a dozen warriors hurried up to meet the white men, Custer signaled for the expedition to come to a halt and spoke to the solemn-faced warriors. "Do any of you understand English?"

The majority of them nodded, and one warrior who appeared to have some authority stepped up close. "I am sub-chief Eagle Claw. What is it that you want?"

Custer nudged his horse a couple of steps ahead of the others and looked down at the warrior. "I am Lieutenant Colonel George Custer. We are from Fort Abraham Lincoln. I would like to speak to Chief Red Cloud."

Eagle Claw looked past Custer at Bloody Knife and then at the other Arikara scouts just behind him. A shadow fell across his eyes as he returned his gaze to Custer. "I must tell you, Lieutenant Colonel George Custer, that Chief Red Cloud will not like it when he learns that you have our enemies, the Arikaras, with you."

Custer met Eagle Claw's dark gaze and said, "These Arikaras are employees of the United States Army and are allowed here on your land under the Laramie Treaty. The white men you see back there who are not in uniform are employed by the United States government for this expedition, and they also are allowed here by the treaty."

Eagle Claw licked his lips, glanced toward the rest of the team, and said, "I will go tell Chief Red Cloud that you and all these men are here. I will explain to him what you just told me. I will return shortly."

Custer thanked him and let his gaze roam over the faces of the other warriors who stood close by, looking the wagons and the mounted men over with suspicious eyes.

Colonel Grant eased his horse up beside Custer's horse. They talked in low tones about the situation for a few minutes and then cut off the conversation when they saw Eagle Claw hurrying toward them.

When the sub-chief drew up to Custer, he said, "Chief Red Cloud will see Lieutenant Colonel George Custer and one other soldier of his choice at his tepee."

Custer nodded. "All right. This soldier next to me is Lieutenant Colonel Frederick Grant. He will come with me."

Eagle Claw gestured toward the ground. "Please dismount, and we will go."

Both men left their saddles and followed the sub-chief into the village. The great crowd of Oglala Sioux looked on the two uniformed men with distrust.

When the trio drew up to Red Cloud's tepee, the chief was not in sight. A young woman with long, black hair stood there smiling at Custer and Grant. Eagle Claw told her the names of the two soldiers. She set her bright eyes on them, and her words fell softer than snowflakes on a horse's winter coat. "Gentlemen, I am Quiet Dove, daughter of Chief Red Cloud. My father will be out in just a moment."

Both men were returning her greeting when the stalwart chief emerged from the tepee. Red Cloud had prominent cheekbones and expressive black eyes. His hair was braided with raven feathers. His mouth was set in a thin line as he looked at the two army officers.

Eagle Claw pointed to Custer. "Chief Red Cloud, this is Lieutenant Colonel George Custer."

When the chief did not offer his hand in a gesture of friendliness, Eagle Claw then pointed to Grant. "And this is Lieutenant Colonel Frederick Grant."

Red Cloud set his eyes on Custer but remained silent.

"Chief Red Cloud," Custer said, "we have a large number of cavalrymen and many white men in covered wagons. And we have some Arikara Indians, also."

At the mention of the Arikaras, Red Cloud's features took on a stony look. "Eagle Claw explained this," he said. "The Laramie Treaty."

"Yes, the United States government sent us here to look the Black Hills over for gold," Custer said. "Since you and your people use very little gold, the government leaders want us to take much with us if we can find it. The country is having money problems, and if we can find enough gold, it will solve those problems."

"The Laramie Treaty allows you to make your search. I hope that you find enough gold quickly."

"Thank you, Chief. We will work hard to do so as soon as possible."

Without another word, Red Cloud went back into his tepee. Quiet Dove smiled at the two cavalry officers and then moved inside with her father.

Eagle Claw said, "You may now return to your horses and begin your search for gold."

As Custer and Grant walked away, Eagle Claw folded his arms and remained in front of Red Cloud's tepee, watching them.

"You didn't say anything to the chief about the fort site that you were sent to locate," Grant said in a low voice.

Custer shook his head. "No. He can learn about that when the army comes in and builds the fort, and he can learn about the railroad coming through at the same time. No sense getting him and his warriors riled up right now."

Grant nodded. "You also didn't tell him that gold seekers will swarm the Black Hills if a sufficient amount of gold is reported found by this expedition."

"I didn't see any need to do that right now, either. No reason to stir things up with the Sioux beforehand. They will learn about them when they show up and after a fort full of soldiers is in place. It's best right now if all that Red Cloud knows is that only government employees will be in the Black Hills to dig for gold."

In the weeks that followed, Custer and his men found sufficient deposits of gold to convince them that the Black Hills were full of it. Taking samples with them, they left the Black Hills on Thursday, August 6, and headed back to Fort Abraham Lincoln.

TEN

At the Bank of Wyoming in Cheyenne, on Thursday morning, August 6, bank owner and president Frank McGuire was going over a loan application in his office when there was a familiar light tap on the door. Looking up, he called, "Yes, Gail?"

McGuire's secretary, Gail Conlon, entered the office with a yellow envelope in hand and approached his desk. "A Western Union messenger just delivered this telegram, Mr. McGuire. It's from Mrs. McGuire."

A smile lit up Frank's countenance as he reached toward her with an open hand. "All right."

Frank quickly opened the envelope and took out the telegram. He read it quickly, looked up at Gail, and said, "Kathleen sent this wire from North Platte, Nebraska, when the train stopped there two hours ago. She and Alyssa Rose were able to get on an earlier train in Chicago than they had planned. They will arrive in Cheyenne at five-thirty this afternoon."

"Wonderful!" exclaimed Gail. "Shall I go tell Monty?"

Frank rose from his desk chair. "Thank you, but I'll go tell him myself."

Gail grinned. "I understand, Mr. McGuire."

Leaving his secretary in her own office, Frank hurried down

the hall and found Monty's office door open. When he stepped in, Monty looked up from some papers that he was working on and said, "Yes, sir?" At that point he saw the telegram in his father's hand. "Who's that from, Dad?"

Frank's face was beaming. "Your mother! She and Alyssa got an earlier train than planned, and when the train stopped in North Platte, Nebraska, your sweet mother sent this wire. They are arriving in Cheyenne this afternoon at five-thirty!"

Monty popped his hands together. "Well, praise the Lord!"

"Yes, son! Praise the Lord! It sure will be great to have your mother and sister with us again."

"Yes, it will, Dad. I miss Mom's cheerfulness and the peace and contentment that she always brings to our home. And, of course, I miss teasing that little sister of mine! Life just hasn't been the same since you and I left them behind."

Frank grinned and nodded. "That's for sure."

"However," said Monty, "I sure hope that Mom and Alyssa are prepared for a very different lifestyle than what they're used to."

Frank chuckled. "Son, I have no doubt that those two beautiful ladies can adapt to whatever they need to. They are very special human beings, and I know that they will allow the Lord to give them the grace to fit right in here in the wild West!"

"Can't argue with you on that, father of mine! Oh, it will be so good to have them here with us!"

Ever since crossing the Nebraska-Wyoming border just after 4:30 that afternoon, Kathleen and Alyssa Rose McGuire had been staring through the smudged windows of the westbound train, taking in the rugged country and the breathtaking beauty of the rolling grassy hills and open fields.

When the engineer cut the speed of the train, Alyssa Rose pulled her face away from the window and smiled. "We're almost to Cheyenne, Mama! We're slowing down!"

Kathleen smiled back. "Sure enough, honey! We're almost there!"

At that moment the conductor entered the coach, calling out as he hurried toward the rear, "Cheyenne! Ten minutes! Cheyenne! Ten minutes!" Seconds later he moved out the rear door.

Alyssa bounced up and down on the seat. "Oh, Mama," she said breathlessly, "I can hardly sit still. I'm so eager to see Papa and Monty! And I'm so excited about seeing our property and the new house that Papa is having built!"

"I know what you mean, dear. This is a new and different experience for both of us. It will be so good to have my family under one roof again!"

Soon the train was slowing even more, and they could see the uneven rooftops of Cheyenne's business district, as well as a few houses. The eyes of mother and daughter were sparkling as they took in their first view of the frontier town under a wide blue sky.

Hurriedly they both smoothed their hair and placed attractive bonnets on their heads. Other female passengers were doing the same thing.

The bell on the engine was clanging as the train chugged to a halt in the depot. Immediately the passengers left their seats, as did Kathleen and Alyssa Rose. They took their small pieces of hand luggage down from the rack above them and slipped into the line that was heading for the front of the coach.

When mother and daughter finally reached the door and were ready to move down the steps behind a man and woman just ahead of them, they caught sight of Frank and Monty standing back a few feet on the platform, smiling at them. Mother and daughter smiled in return and waved.

Seconds later, their feet touched the platform, and as mother and daughter darted toward father and son, Monty rushed ahead of his father and wrapped his arms around his mother, kissing her cheek and telling her how much he had missed her.

At the same time, Frank folded his daughter into his arms, kissed her cheek, and told her how good it was to see her again.

Then the inevitable exchange took place. Frank folded his wife into his arms and kissed her warmly.

Monty gave his smiling sister a bear hug.

Easing back after kissing Kathleen, Frank took hold of both her hands and squeezed them. "Darlin', I'm so happy to see you! I'm so glad you got to come earlier than expected!"

Kathleen squeezed back. "Me, too!"

When brother and sister let go of each other, Alyssa Rose turned round and round with a wide grin on her face, trying to see as much of the town as possible. "Well, this is really something! Papa, I feel at home, already! I can hardly wait to see our new house!"

Frank chuckled. "Well, come along, then. The carriage is parked on the street right next to the depot's main building. Monty and I will pick up your bags at the baggage coach, and we'll soon be on our way! We'll take you to the carriage first."

"All right," said Kathleen. "We brought two trunks and four large bags. You will need to have one of the baggage handlers bring them on a cart."

"That we'll do," said Frank. "Let's go."

Frank and Monty walked the ladies to the carriage, helped them in, and then headed for the baggage coach.

Kathleen and Alyssa Rose sat in the carriage, their eyes roaming up and down the dusty street.

"Well, Mama," said the lovely girl, her soft green eyes shining, "it's certainly different, but it's home now, and I'm so happy to be here!"

"Me, too, sweetheart," replied Kathleen. "Me, too."

Presently, father and son were seen coming from the depot, along with a baggage handler pushing a cart. The trunks and luggage were placed in the rear of the carriage, and with Frank sitting on the back seat with his wife and daughter, Monty sat in the driver's seat and guided the team up the street.

"Tell you what," Frank said to the ladies, "we'll take you to the new house first so that you can see it. Of course, it's still under construction, but it's coming along well. You already know that both houses are on the same property. Then we'll take you to our present house and unload the baggage. You can freshen up, and then we'll take you to Cheyenne's nicest restaurant. The restaurant is just a half-block from the bank, so you'll get to see the outside of the bank, too. Tomorrow we'll take you to the bank so that you can see it inside and meet all of our employees."

"I'm looking forward to that, Papa," said Alyssa Rose. "And I'm looking forward to meeting Pastor and Mrs. Ballert and all the other people of the church. From your letters, it sure sounds like a good church."

"It's marvelous," said Monty over his shoulder as he turned the carriage onto Main Street. "You and Mama will love them all, just like Papa and I do. Pastor Ballert is an excellent preacher. He really has a marvelous way of exalting the Lord Jesus in his preaching. Just wait till you hear him. Sunday is only a couple of days away, you know."

Alyssa leaned up closer to the driver's seat. "Someone else I'm looking forward to meeting, big brother, is your friend Jim Bannon, and of course, his parents, too."

Monty continued to face forward but nodded and said, "You'll get to meet them on Sunday, too, baby sister."

The ladies continued to look the town over as the carriage moved along the streets. Soon they pulled up to the property, and when Kathleen saw the house under construction, she gasped and said, "Oh, Frank! I can't believe this! Why, it's a red brick mansion very much like our house in Seward Park!"

"Sure is!" said Alyssa Rose. "I never dreamed you'd do this, Papa!"

Monty laughed as he pulled the carriage to a stop in front of the mansion, which was obviously in the final stage of construction. "That's our Papa! First class all the way!"

Frank looked into Kathleen's eyes. "I know how much you loved our Seward Park house. So…"

"Oh, darling," said Kathleen, gripping Frank's arm. "I love it! I love it! Thank you for remembering how much I loved our Chicago home! I'll have great delight in decorating this beautiful new house!"

Monty jumped down from the driver's seat and offered his hand to his sister. Alyssa let him help her out of the carriage.

Frank smiled as he stepped out of the carriage and offered Kathleen his hand. As she took it and stepped down, he said, "I'm so thrilled that you approve of your new house, sweetheart. It's very important to me that you are happy here. It will be finished in another three or four weeks. Cheyenne has a brand-new furniture store, and it's well-stocked with nice furniture. By then we can buy all the furniture you want, and you and Alyssa can enjoy decorating the place to your hearts' content."

"We'll have fun, Mama," spoke up Alyssa Rose.

Kathleen smiled at her husband. "I didn't tell you, but I did keep some of my most treasured pieces of furniture, along with the rest of our household goods. They'll be arriving here in Cheyenne by rail in a couple of weeks."

Frank smiled. "Well, all right."

Kathleen looked at her daughter. "I'm sure glad now that I sold most of the furniture, even though I had a hard time parting with some of it."

Even as she spoke, Kathleen ran her gaze to the much smaller, white frame house nearby. "So that's our home for now?" she said to Frank.

"Mm-hmm. It's not terribly spacious, but hopefully we can make do for a little while."

"Oh, honey," said Kathleen, "it's a pretty house. I think it's very quaint. We'll do just fine in it for as long as we need to. I—I'm just so thankful to be here at last. Besides, precious husband of mine, wherever *you* are is home to me."

Frank smiled at her and said, "Well, tomorrow we'll give you a grand tour of your unfinished mansion. As for now, let's take you and Alyssa over to the little white house so you can freshen up. Then we'll treat you to a good meal in town."

The next day was a busy one, with Kathleen and Alyssa Rose being given the grand tour of their new mansion by Frank while the construction workers were busy inside and out. Monty had gone to work at the bank.

Later in the morning, Frank took his wife and daughter to the bank, where they met all the employees and were warmly welcomed.

Frank then drove the carriage up and down Main Street so that Kathleen and Alyssa Rose could look the business section over. They were pleasantly surprised at the array of shops to be found in this frontier town. One stop was made at the general store so that the McGuire women could pick up a few groceries. They made plans to come back to the business section the next day and do some shopping.

When this was said in Frank's presence, he laughed, saying that he had known that it wouldn't take them long to jump into their favorite hobby.

It was late on Saturday morning as Jim Bannon drove the family wagon toward town to purchase some new tools for his father at the hardware store. Since the bank stayed open till noon on Saturdays, Jim planned to stop at the bank first to see Monty for a few minutes and then go on to the hardware store.

At the same time that Jim was driving along the dusty road, waving at neighboring farmers who were working in their fields, Kathleen and Alyssa Rose were doing the shopping that they had planned. Monty had driven them to the business section of Cheyenne in the family carriage at ten o'clock, saying that he would pick them up at the general store, since they needed to stock up on more groceries. He would meet them there just after the bank closed at noon.

Kathleen and her daughter were having a happy time going from shop to shop and store to store, purchasing and ordering items for themselves and for their new home. As they came out of a small variety store, Alyssa Rose said, "Mama, remember that Papa told us that if we can't find everything we want here, we can always make a trip to Denver."

Kathleen smiled as she adjusted the packages in her arms. "I know, honey, but I really think that I can buy or order most everything right here in Cheyenne. And when our belongings arrive from Chicago, we should be all set."

As they moved on, stopping at almost every shop or store, mother and daughter were having a happy, productive morning together.

When it was nearing 11:30, Kathleen said, "Alyssa, we'd better head for the general store now so that we can get those groceries we need and be ready by the time Monty comes to pick us up."

As they were moving along the boardwalk, their arms loaded with packages, they came upon Padgett's Clothing Store. They both stopped when they saw some pretty dresses on display in the window.

"Oh, Mama, aren't they beautiful? I'm surprised to find dresses this exquisite out here in the West."

Kathleen nodded, smiling. "They certainly are exquisite, indeed, honey."

Alyssa pointed out a blue dress with white collar and cuffs. "I really like that one!"

"It is quite lovely," said Kathleen, "but we don't have time for you to try one on right now. We've got to get the groceries and be ready for Monty when he comes."

Alyssa Rose shrugged, smiling. "You're right. I'll come back and buy one some other time."

They moved on up the boardwalk, crossed the street at the next intersection, and entered the general store on the corner. A clerk allowed them to place their packages behind one of the counters for safekeeping, and as they were picking out food items and placing them in a basket, they were greeted in a friendly manner by four women who were also shopping. When the four women learned that Kathleen and Alyssa Rose were the wife and daughter of the new owner and president of the Bank of Wyoming, they were full of questions.

Since the questions were all being directed to her mother, Alyssa leaned close and whispered, "Mama, since you and these ladies are chatting, how about if I run down to Padgett's Clothing Store and buy that blue dress?"

Kathleen paused in the conversation that she was enjoying with the women. "Go ahead, honey, but hurry, okay?"

"Won't take me long. I'll be back in a jiffy."

As Alyssa Rose was moving hastily down the boardwalk, threading between people in her path, she noticed two unkempt young men coming out of a saloon just ahead of her, and they spotted her immediately. The taller one said to the other one, "Hey, Lanny, watch me charm that pretty lass." Lanny grinned and nodded, and the taller one stepped in front of her, blocking her path.

Alyssa came to a stop, giving him a frown. His foul odor almost gagged her. "Excuse me," she said coldly.

He grinned, exposing a mouthful of yellow teeth, touched his hat brim, and said, "My name is Jed Harris, little lass. What's your name?"

Finding him very repugnant, Alyssa did not reply. She tried to sidestep him, but he quickly blocked her way.

Lanny looked on, his lips curled in a gruesome grin.

People walked by, going both ways, but paid no mind to what was happening. Frustrated, Alyssa scowled at Jed and said loudly, "Leave me alone! Get out of my way!"

At the same time, Jim Bannon was driving the wagon along the street, nearing the spot where Alyssa was being accosted, and his ears picked up the sound of her perturbed voice. Alyssa's back was toward him. He slowed the wagon as he heard Jed Harris say to the young lady, "I don't want to leave you alone, girlie! You would like me if you got to know me!" As he spoke, he laid a hand on Alyssa's shoulder.

She cringed at his touch, jumped back, and shouted loudly, "Get your hands off me! I told you to leave me alone!"

People were now stopping and looking on.

Having heard the young woman whose back was still toward him, Jim guided the wagon over to the side of the street and pulled rein. He jumped out of the wagon intending to rescue the young lady from the obnoxious man.

Harris laughed fiendishly and reached for Alyssa again, causing her to jump back another step to avoid him.

At the same instant the muscular Jim Bannon moved up behind the young woman he intended to rescue, stepped between her and the foul-smelling Jed Harris, facing him angrily, and snapped, "She told you to leave her alone. Now do it!"

Alyssa looked at the back of the broad-shouldered young man who faced the unkempt ruffian and breathed a silent prayer of thanks.

Anger reddened Harris's face as he met Jim's flashing eyes and growled, "Mind your own business, bud!"

Jim set his jaw and glared balefully at Harris. His voice rasped as he bellowed, "When a rude, foul-smelling brute accosts a lady, I *make* it my business to protect her!"

Harris's right fist shot out, but Jim dodged the blow, and with a jarring uppercut he caught Harris with his mouth open. Harris's teeth clicked together like a steel trap, and he staggered backward, shaking his head. When he was able to balance himself, he came back at Jim, swinging both fists.

Again Jim avoided being hit and countered with a wicked right hook that whipped Harris's head back. Then he slammed a left into Harris's belly that knocked the wind from him and doubled him over. One more uppercut smashed him square on the nose, and he fell flat on his back, out cold.

The crowd looked on wide-eyed, many with their mouths gaping.

Jim was about to turn and speak to the young lady when, suddenly, he was jumped by Lanny, who grabbed him from behind, attempting to pin his arms to his sides and throw him down.

The powerful young farmer shook Lanny loose and, pivoting speedily, hit him with one solid punch that put him down and out.

The crowd watched in mute silence as Jim quickly removed the revolvers from the holsters of both unconscious men.

At that moment, Alyssa stepped up behind her rescuer, wanting to thank him, just as Jim turned around to face her, holding a revolver in each hand. When his eyes focused on her lovely features, his jaw slacked. "I—I know you! You're Alyssa Rose McGuire!"

Puzzled, Alyssa fluttered her eyelids as she took in the muscular, six-foot-one-inch, 210-pound man who had rescued her and thought, *My, oh, my! They sure grow them tall and handsome in this part of the country!* Her cheeks took on a tinge of pink as she said, "Have we met before?"

Jim started to reply when he noticed that Jed Harris was

regaining consciousness. He looked back at Alyssa. "I'll explain in just a moment. Please excuse me." He wheeled about and walked to a nearby water trough that was filled to the brim with water. Quickly he emptied the cartridges from the cylinders of both guns and dropped the guns and cartridges into the water.

He then went to Harris, who was rising to his feet unsteadily, and said in a harsh tone, "Take your friend and get out of town. Right now!"

Fury flamed Harris's rough features, and he tried again to punch Jim, who adeptly dodged the blow and pounded Harris with a powerful three-punch combination that put him down and out.

The crowd cheered him.

At the same instant, Jim saw Laramie County Sheriff Harley Carter riding up, curious as to why the crowd was gathered on the street.

People in the crowd began telling the sheriff how Jim Bannon had come to the rescue of the young lady, whom they pointed out.

Sheriff Carter drew up to where Jim stood close to Alyssa, glanced at the two unconscious drifters, and said, "Jim, tell me about it."

Jim explained that Alyssa was the daughter of Frank McGuire, the new owner and president of the Bank of Wyoming and then gave the sherriff the details of how the drifters were bothering her and he was forced to put them both down and out.

The sheriff commended Jim for his deed and asked four men in the crowd to help him carry the unconscious drifters to the jail.

When the drifters were being carried away, the crowd began to disperse while Jim turned to Alyssa.

She smiled brightly. "The sheriff called you Jim. Are you Jim Bannon?"

The handsome young farmer smiled and nodded. "Yes, ma'am. I recognized you from the recent family photograph that your brother Monty showed me."

"I figured that had to be the case, since your name is Jim and you knew I was Frank McGuire's daughter."

Jim cleared his throat gently. "I…ah…asked Monty what color your hair is and what color your eyes are. I'll say the dark brown of your hair and the soft green of your eyes sure go good together."

Alyssa blushed, and tears filmed her lovely green eyes. "You're very kind, Jim. I don't know how to properly and fully thank you for coming to my rescue, but please know that it is deeply appreciated."

Jim grinned. "My pleasure, Miss McGuire. I…ah…I'm surprised to see you in Cheyenne. You weren't supposed to be here till Monday."

She thumbed the tears from her cheeks and said, "Mama and I were able to get seats on an earlier train. We got here on Thursday."

At that moment, up the street, Monty was pulling up in front of the general store and found his mother just coming out the door, pushing a cart full of packages and grocery sacks.

Kathleen smiled when she saw him and pushed the cart toward the wagon, saying, "Perfect timing, wouldn't you say, son?"

"Sure enough," replied Monty, jumping down from the wagon seat. He looked around. "Where's Sis?"

"She went down the street to Padgett's Clothing Store while I was getting these groceries. She saw a dress in the window that she wanted to buy when we passed it on our way here to the general store."

As Kathleen was speaking, both she and Monty looked down the street and caught sight of Alyssa Rose standing in front of Padgett's Clothing Store talking to the tall, muscular, handsome young man on the boardwalk.

Monty chuckled. "Well, whattya know? That fellow she's talking to is Jim Bannon, Mom."

Kathleen's eyebrows arched. "Really? How do you suppose that happened?"

"I don't know, but we'll soon find out."

Monty piled the packages and groceries in the rear of the wagon and helped his mother onto the wagon seat. He quickly took the cart back inside the store, returned, climbed up beside her, and put the wagon in motion.

A moment later when he guided the team up to the hitch rail near Padgett's Clothing Store, Jim and Alyssa both saw the wagon and moved toward them.

Monty grinned at the pair and said, "It sure didn't take you two long to get together. How did this happen?"

"Introduce me to this lovely lady beside you, Monty, and then we'll tell you."

Monty said, "Jim Bannon, this is my mother—*and* Alyssa's mother—Kathleen."

Alyssa Rose stayed at Jim's side as he stepped around the hitch rail and up to the wagon seat. "Mrs. McGuire, I am honored to meet you."

Kathleen extended her hand. "And I am honored to meet you, Jim."

Jim took her hand gently, bowed, clicked his heels, and planted a soft kiss on her hand.

As Kathleen was smiling at him, Alyssa said, "Mama, Monty, I will explain how Jim and I met." She then told them of being accosted by the repugnant drifter and how Jim had rescued her by knocking both the drifter and his equally repugnant friend unconscious. She added that the sheriff had hauled them both off to jail.

Touched deeply by Jim's chivalrous deed on behalf of Alyssa Rose, both Kathleen and Monty thanked him.

Jim smiled. "My pleasure. You see, after I had put the drifters down, I recognized Alyssa Rose from the picture you had shown me, Monty. I was surprised to see her in Cheyenne today when I knew that she and her mother weren't supposed to be here until Monday. She explained it to me."

Kathleen said, "Jim, I'm looking forward to getting to know you better." Then to Monty she said, "Son, we need to be getting home."

Kathleen scooted closer to Monty on the seat, and Jim helped Alyssa Rose onto the seat beside her.

Jim smiled at mother and daughter. "I'm so glad that I finally got to meet both of you. I'll see you at church in the morning."

Alyssa set her soft green eyes on him. "Thank you again, Jim, for coming to my rescue."

His heart thumped in his chest. "It was my pleasure, Miss McGuire."

Alyssa giggled. "You can call me Alyssa."

His heart thumped even harder. He smiled warmly. "Thank you, *Alyssa*."

ELEVEN

Jim Bannon drove north out of Cheyenne, his mind fixed on Alyssa Rose McGuire. He took a deep breath and said aloud, "No question about it. It is possible to fall in love with a young lady simply by seeing her photograph. Something happened when I first laid eyes on that picture, and now that I've met Alyssa in person, she has captured my heart."

As the wagon bounced along the dusty road, Jim recalled his conversation with Monty that day in the café while they were eating lunch together.

Jim looked at Monty across the table. "I have a question for you."

Monty swallowed the food in his mouth. "Sure."

"Ah…well, is your sister engaged or at least promised to some young man in Chicago?"

"No, she's not."

Jim felt relief wash over him. "Beautiful as she is, I'm surprised."

"Well, you'd have to know my sis. She's had plenty of guys who wanted to get serious with her, but she walks very close to the Lord, Jim. She's waiting for Him to bring the right young man into her life,

and I've heard her say many a time that she will know when that right young man comes along."

"Bless her heart. She's got to be some kind of gal."

Monty grinned. "Oh, she is. Just wait. You'll see."

The wagon hit a bump. Jim bounced on the seat and said, "Well, Monty was right. I *have* seen. Alyssa *is* some kind of gal."

He took a deep breath and said, "Dear Lord, You know how Alyssa's picture affected me when Monty showed me that family photograph. And You know how she affected me when I met her in person today. I realize, Lord, that I must go slow in letting Alyssa know how I feel toward her. Please lead me and guide me, won't You? And if I'm right and You have chosen us for each other, please speak to her heart and let her know. And, Lord…real *soon,* please."

Soon Jim reached the gate of the Bannon farm, guided the team down the tree-lined lane, and pulled rein at the tool shed, which was near the barn and the corral.

He placed the new tools that he had purchased in the shed and led the horses to where the wagon was always parked near the barn. He removed the harnesses, led the horses into the corral, and took the harnesses inside the barn and hung them up in their places.

When Jim entered the house, he found his parents sitting together on the sofa in the parlor, looking at an old photograph album that had been in Sarah's family since she was a child.

Newt and Sarah looked up from the album, smiling. "Get the tools all right, son?" Newt asked.

"Sure did, Dad. I put them in the tool shed."

"So, did you and Monty have lunch together?" Sarah asked.

"Ah…no. Come to think of it, I didn't even eat any lunch."

Newt frowned. "'Come to think of it?' What do you mean? You didn't get any lunch, and you just now realize it?"

"Well, I guess you could put it like that. I…ah…" He pulled a straight-backed wooden chair in front of them and sat down. "Mom, Dad, I met Alyssa Rose McGuire in town."

"I thought that she and her mother weren't going to arrive till Monday," Sarah said.

"Let me explain, and tell you a story."

Newt and Sarah listened as Jim told them of the incident with the drifters and how he had met Alyssa Rose by rescuing her from them. He also told of meeting Kathleen McGuire.

When Jim finished telling them the story, Newt said, "Well, I'm glad that Sheriff Carter put them in jail. I hope they're behind bars for a long time. Poor Alyssa Rose."

"Is she all right after that horrible experience?" Sarah asked.

"She's fine, Mom. And just wait till you meet her. I'm telling you, Alyssa is a sweet young lady and every bit as charming as she is sweet. And gorgeous, too! I told you that Monty said she has dark brown hair and soft green eyes. Well, her picture and Monty's words still couldn't tell it fully. Just wait till you see her!"

Newt and Sarah looked at each other, and a knowing smile passed between them. Sarah held Newt's gaze and said, "I'm most anxious to meet this sweet, charming, gorgeous young lady who seems to have taken possession of our boy's heart."

"Me, too," Newt said. "Well, Jim, you'd better grab yourself some lunch. You and I have work to do in the barn, remember?"

Jim chuckled. "Oh, yes. How could I forget?"

That evening after supper was over and the dishes were done, the Bannons were sitting on the front porch of the farmhouse. The sun had already set over the mountains several miles to the west, and the fading light left in the sky cast soft shadows from the cottonwood and pine trees around the house. It had been a hot, tiring day, but a gentle breeze picked up and offered some cool relief across the porch.

Newt, Sarah, and Jim each held a large glass of cool tea, and all three sighed as the breeze swept over them.

Jim thought about the incident in town that had brought him and Alyssa together. A tender smile formed on his tanned face, and he gazed toward the sky above as the evening stars were making their appearance.

Suddenly the Bannons heard the sound of hoofbeats, along with the rattle of a vehicle. They looked toward the tree-lined lane and saw a carriage coming toward the house in the shadows. When it pulled up and stopped in front of the porch, there was still enough light for the Bannons to recognize Frank McGuire.

As the wealthy banker stepped out of the carriage, all three Bannons rose from their chairs and welcomed him.

Frank smiled at Newt and Sarah. "Nice evening, eh?"

"Sure enough," Newt said.

"The cool breeze feels plenty good," Sarah said.

Frank stepped up to Jim and extended his right hand. When Jim grasped it, Frank said, "I want to thank you for what you did to protect my daughter from that drifter and his pal."

Jim squeezed Frank's hand and smiled. "It was my pleasure, Mr. McGuire. And let me say that you sure have a beautiful daughter."

As they let go of each other's hands, Frank said, "Tell you what, Jim, Alyssa Rose is as beautiful on the inside as she is on the outside."

"That's the same thing that Monty told me after I had admired her picture, sir. And I don't doubt that at all. I'm looking forward to getting to know her better."

"Well, Jim, because you're a fine Christian young man, you have my permission to get well acquainted with her. You're a hero, not only in Alyssa's eyes, but in the eyes of her mother and me, too."

"Thank you, sir."

Moments later, the Bannons stood on the porch and watched the McGuire carriage move toward the road. When it was swallowed by the gathering darkness, Newt put his arm around Sarah and said, "Well, my dear, I guess we'd better take our hero here and head inside."

"Do you suppose the door is large enough to accommodate his head?"

Jim laughed. "Don't worry, Mom. I can still get through the door."

The next morning when the McGuires arrived at church, Monty McGuire introduced Kathleen and Alyssa Rose to Newt and Sarah Bannon in the parking lot.

Alyssa said, "Mr. and Mrs. Bannon, I want to commend you for raising such a fine son. I shudder to think what might have happened to me yesterday if he hadn't rescued me from that drifter."

"Well, young lady, I have to say that Sarah and I are very proud of Jim," Newt said.

"You have reason to be *very* proud, sir."

The two families walked together toward the church building and found Pastor David Ballert and Tammy on the porch, greeting people as they arrived.

Jim took it upon himself to introduce Kathleen and Alyssa Rose to the pastor and his wife. Frank McGuire reminded the pastor that he and his family would be joining the church today, as he and Monty had discussed with him when they first came to Cheyenne.

Pastor Ballert's face beamed. "No need to remind me, Frank. I've been looking forward to this ever since we talked about it."

Kathleen and Alyssa Rose were led into the auditorium, and members of the church gathered around and warmly welcomed them.

By the time the McGuires and the Bannons sat down together on a pew, Alyssa turned to her parents and said, "What a wonderful place! This is the friendliest church I've ever been in."

"That's how I've felt ever since the first day here," Frank said.

Alyssa and her mother found Sunday school inspiring as Pastor Ballert taught on how Christians are told in the Bible to love one another, reflecting the love of Jesus.

In the morning service, Pastor Ballert had Kathleen and Alyssa Rose stand up, and he introduced them to the congregation. Then after the choir had sung a special number, he preached a powerful sermon on salvation, and when he gave the invitation, two adults and two teenagers came forward to receive Christ as Saviour. The McGuire family also came forward to formally announce that they wanted to join the church.

After the four new converts were baptized, Pastor Ballert had all four McGuires give their testimonies. He then explained that they were coming from a Bible-believing church in Chicago and recommended that the congregation welcome them into the membership, which they did.

After the service the Bannons and the McGuires were talking, and Alyssa took advantage of a break in the conversation to turn to Jim and say, "Papa and Monty told Mama and me last night about your heroic deed back in June when the Indians attacked your neighbors on the road."

Jim blushed. "I just did what any other man would have done."

Admiration showed in Alyssa's eyes as she met Jim's gaze. "You're a very brave man, Jim. I admire you for it."

Later, as Jim drove the family wagon toward the farm, his parents talked about what a fine girl Alyssa was, and Jim smiled to himself. His heart throbbed as he thought of Alyssa Rose McGuire and how right her father and brother had been when they said that she was as beautiful on the inside as she was on the outside.

When Jim Bannon was putting on his work clothes on Monday morning, he knew that, with all the work that had to be done that week on the farm, he would have to be satisfied with seeing Alyssa just at the church's midweek service. He wanted to ask her for a date when he saw her on Wednesday night but realized that he would have to move slowly. He didn't want to lose out by being too aggressive.

Monday, Tuesday, and Wednesday were long, hot, hard days as Newt and Jim went to work on the summer's second cutting of alfalfa. On Wednesday they quit early and headed for the house. They paused at the water pump near the back porch to wash up before going in for supper.

Jim's body was tired, but there was joy in his heart. He would get to see Alyssa at the service in a little more than two hours.

When father and son entered the kitchen, it was quite warm but full of delicious aromas. Sarah stood at the stove and turned to smile at her husband and son. Her cheeks were red from the heat. "Sit down, boys. Supper is ready."

She carried one last bowl of steaming food to the table and sat down at her place. Newt and Jim were ravenous, and as soon as Jim had prayed, they began to pass around the succulent fried chicken, mashed potatoes, and gravy, plus fresh tomatoes, green onions, and sliced cucumbers from Sarah's garden.

"Mm-mm, this is good, Mom!" Jim declared between mouthfuls. "I wonder if Alyssa is a good cook. If she's not, I'll have her take lessons from you."

"That'd do it, son!" Newt said.

Sarah chuckled. "Okay, boys, I'm flattered. But you'd better hurry and get your meal down. We need to leave for church soon."

At church that evening the Bannons made sure that they sat on the same pew with the McGuires so that their son could sit near Alyssa Rose. When the service was over, Jim and Alyssa stood alone near the front of the auditorium and chatted. Her very presence, her warmth toward him, and her sweet smile kept Jim's heart pounding. Again he thought of asking her for a date but refrained, telling himself that they would have to get better acquainted first.

Thursday it was back to work. The hot August sun was relentless as Newt and Jim toiled in the fields. Jim, however, hardly noticed it. His mind was so full of Alyssa and his plans for the future.

Occasionally Newt had to smile to himself as his son hummed one happy tune after another.

At the McGuire house, Alyssa was busy helping her mother prepare for the move to the new mansion, as well as keeping up with the day's normal tasks.

Kathleen frequently noticed the dreamy look in her daughter's eyes and often heard her humming happily.

At midafternoon, while Alyssa was ironing clothes in the kitchen and humming another lighthearted tune, Kathleen was tidying up the back porch. Holding a broom in her hand and listening to her daughter's humming, she smiled. *Looks like love is in the air*, she thought, a sweet contentment filling her own heart. "Lord," she whispered, "You knew what You were doing when You led Frank to move us here to Cheyenne. Thank You for always keeping Your wonderful hand on our lives."

On the following Sunday morning the Bannons were just getting out of their wagon when they saw the McGuire carriage pulling into the church parking lot and heading in their direction. The two families greeted each other, and Jim rushed up to the carriage and offered Alyssa his hand. "May I help you out, Alyssa?"

She flashed him a warm smile. "Of course."

As he was helping her down, Jim noted the beautiful blue dress that she was wearing. "I like your dress."

"This was the dress that I was on my way to buy at Padgett's when that drifter accosted me. I went back and bought it last Thursday."

"I'm glad that you did."

The two families walked toward the church building together, Jim and Alyssa following a few steps behind the others.

Jim worked up enough courage to look down at her and say, "Would you sit with me in both services this morning?"

She flashed him a warm smile. "Of course. I'll tell my parents. They won't mind, I assure you."

After being greeted by Pastor David and Tammy Ballert at the door, the Bannons and the McGuires stepped inside and went to their favorite pew. Alyssa informed her parents that she and Jim were going to sit together. They both smiled and nodded. Monty winked at Jim, who gave him a crooked grin.

In the evening service, Jim and Alyssa sat together again.

As the weeks passed, Jim saw Alyssa only at church, but he was thrilled that she sat with him in every service.

On Saturday afternoon, August 29, beneath a clear sky and the blazing sun, the wagons and riders of the army reconnaissance expedition led by Lieutenant Colonel George Armstrong Custer took a slightly different route to Fort Abraham Lincoln than they had used when traveling to the Black Hills. They all knew that by Sunday afternoon, the journey would be over.

As they drew up to the Cannonball River, Colonel Frederick Grant pointed across the wide stream and said, "Colonel, look there!"

Custer saw evidence among the trees on the far bank of what had been a Sioux camp. Several tattered and torn tepees lay on the ground, and the area was speckled with what had been cook fires.

He could also make out the spot where the Indians' horses had been kept.

On Custer's other side, Bloody Knife grunted, "Sioux camp has been abandoned."

"It was a big one, too," Grant said. "I'm glad that those Indians moved somewhere else. At least we won't have to fight them."

"With this rough and rugged Seventh Cavalry," Custer said, "I could whip all the Indians in the Northwest."

Grant smiled to himself but did not comment. He knew that Custer had a tendency to get a little cocky at times.

Custer raised his hat, waved it toward the long lines of riders and wagons, and called out, "We'll camp here!"

On Sunday morning everyone was eager to pull out and head for the fort. At one o'clock that afternoon, Custer had them stop beside the Heart River some ten miles south of Fort Abraham Lincoln to water and rest the horses and eat their lunch.

While the large crowd of men was enjoying lunch, Custer stood before them and said, "Men, I want us to enter the fort in a particular way. Listen close as I give instructions on our entrance. I will ride in the lead as usual. Lieutenant Colonel Grant will flank me on my left, and Bloody Knife will flank me on my right. Our Arikara scouts will follow directly behind us."

Custer then pointed at the men who made up the brass band. "You men will follow the scouts. When you are passing through the fort's gate, I want you to strike up 'Garry Owen' just like you did when we left the fort. Next will be the officers on horseback, and they will be followed by the other cavalrymen and infantrymen on their horses."

Custer then looked toward the men who manned the wagons. "The wagons will form a circle outside the fort as before, and those of you in the wagons will go in on foot. Some of you will be carrying the gold samples.

"Once everyone is inside the fort, I will make the announcement to Colonel Huston and everyone else that there is definitely gold in the Black Hills. Then I'll call for those men carrying gold samples to step forward and show them to Colonel Huston and all the occupants of the fort."

A couple of infantrymen waved their hats in the air and ejected a happy shout. The rest of the crowd joined with them, showing their excitement.

TWELVE

The sun was setting as Libbie Custer stood at the parlor window of her apartment in the officers' quarters at Fort Abraham Lincoln. She noted the clouds that hung low over the western horizon. They were coloring into deeper gold as the sun slowly lowered behind them.

Libbie's eyes were misty as she kept looking westward, and her voice quavered through trembling lips. "Oh George, where are you? Are you all right? Why haven't you and your expedition come back by now?"

Her body knotted with tension as memories of the horrible nightmare that she had experienced the night before persisted in marching through her mind. She had dreamed that her husband and a small number of his Seventh Cavalry had been surrounded by hundreds of whooping, wild-eyed Indians with painted faces and had been cut down in a bloody battle.

In the nightmare her eyes had focused on the lifeless, bloody body of her husband lying on the ground, and she had awakened suddenly, gasping and weeping in the darkness of her room.

As she stood at the window looking at the sunset, the horror, the revulsion, and the terror that kept her upset all day had her trembling.

In the tower at the fort's main gate, Corporal Justin Scott was sitting on a small bench cleaning his carbine while Private Jake Barth slowly walked around the tower platform, letting his eyes roam over the rolling plains made golden by the setting sun.

Suddenly Jake stopped and said, "Justin, look! It's the Black Hills expedition!"

Scott jumped to his feet and focused on the approaching lines of riders and covered wagons that were coming from the south. "I'll go tell Colonel Huston! He's probably still in his office." He placed the carbine on the bench and darted down the stairs.

People moving about inside the fort noticed the corporal hurrying from the tower toward the commandant's office and wondered what was going on.

Scott found the commandant's office door open, and seeing Colonel Daniel Huston at his desk, he tapped on the door frame. Huston looked up to see the tower guard breathing hard. "Something wrong, Corporal Scott?"

"Oh, no, sir! Something's right! The Black Hills expedition is back! They're about a mile away!"

Huston smiled. "Great! I want to see Colonel Custer as soon as he's inside the fort."

"I'll tell him, sir."

As Scott ran back toward the tower, he waved at the people who were staring at him and shouted, "The Black Hills expedition is coming in from the south! They'll be here in a few minutes!"

Instantly, men were running about, shouting in every direction that the expedition had returned and would soon be at the main gate. Men, women, and children were coming from buildings all over the fort, hurrying toward the main gate.

Libbie Custer had gone into her kitchen and was about to build a fire in the cookstove to prepare her supper when she heard the shouting. The kitchen window was open, and she was able to hear what was being announced.

She ran toward the front door of the apartment. This was the sound that she had been waiting for since her husband rode out of sight so many weeks ago. She had kept herself busy, finding things to do for other people in the fort, and the days had passed quickly…but the nights had been long and lonely. Even before her nightmare last night, menacing thoughts of bloodthirsty Sioux warriors attacking the expedition had invaded her mind.

Libbie paused at the door and looked into the small mirror that hung on the wall beside it. She patted a few loose strands of hair into place and then rushed out the door.

When she stepped off the porch, she heard Vickie Grant's voice behind her. "Hey, Libbie! Wait up!"

The two women clasped hands and ran together toward the main gate, where a large crowd was gathering.

By the time the expedition team reached the main gate, everyone in the fort—except for Colonel Huston and his wife, who were waiting in front of his office—had gathered to greet them.

Colonel Custer rode through the wide-open gate first, with Grant and Bloody Knife flanking him. Directly behind them were the Arikara scouts, followed by the brass band, who instantly struck up "Garry Owen."

The crowd was ecstatic with excitement.

Everyone saw tower guard Justin Scott dash up to Colonel Custer and tell him something. Custer nodded, and Scott quickly moved back toward the tower.

As the officers rode past the cheering crowd, they stopped their horses long enough to dismount and embrace their wives and children. The other riders waited patiently so that all of them could move on together.

Libbie Custer, Vickie Grant, and Summer Wind each dashed up to her husband's horse, and the crowd cheered the scene as all three husbands dismounted to greet their wives.

A gloss of wetness was in Libbie's eyes, and her heart was beating so hard that she almost thought that she could hear it. George folded her into his arms, and they held on to each other for a long moment. Finally, as they separated, Libbie looked him up and down. "You're all right, darling?"

"I'm fine."

"How did it go?"

"I'm about to announce it to Colonel Huston so that everybody else can hear it, too. He's waiting in front of his office. Come on."

By this time the men from the wagons had entered the fort on foot, and the entire crowd followed Custer and his wife as they moved toward the commandant's office. Libbie happily held her husband's hand and squeezed it repeatedly.

Colonel Daniel Huston and his wife stood just in front of his office door, looking on with pleasure.

With Libbie at his side, Custer stepped up to Colonel and Mrs. Huston and said loudly so that all could hear, "Colonel Huston, sir, we indeed found gold in the Black Hills!"

A smile spread over Huston's face. "Wonderful!"

Custer looked back toward the eight men who were carrying the gold samples. They hurried through the crowd, and as they drew up, Custer said loudly, "Men, open those sacks and show the gold to Colonel Huston!"

After the men had allowed Huston to look in their sacks, they waved them at the crowd. Horatio Ross and William McKay threaded their way through the press and stepped up to the commandant.

Ross said, "Colonel Huston, may I speak to the crowd?"

Huston nodded. "Certainly."

When the cheering had died down, Ross said, "Ladies and

gentlemen, you all know that Colonel Huston sent my partner, William McKay, and me to do the necessary tests if we should find what appeared to be gold in the Black Hills. I am happy to tell you that what we found was real gold. And there is plenty more of it in those Black Hills!"

A roar went up from the crowd, and some of the men gleefully waved their hats.

When once again the cheering had died down, Custer faced the crowd and said, "Folks, I am sure that there is gold aplenty in the Black Hills and that the country's financial depression will soon be over!"

The roar from the crowd this time was louder than before.

Custer then reached into his shirt pocket, took out the map of the Black Hills, and held it for Colonel Huston to see. He pointed to the spot that he had marked on the map where the new fort should be built and then told Huston that it was about seven or eight acres of open land surrounded by a forest.

"Perfect!" Huston exclaimed. "It's very close to the northern tip of the Black Hills, where the Northern Pacific Railroad will be laying tracks."

Huston lifted up his voice, explained it to the crowd, and then said to Custer, "I commend you and all the men of the expedition for a job well done!"

The people of the fort cheered loudly again.

Colonel Huston then said to Custer in a normal voice, "I will wire President Grant and General Sheridan first thing in the morning and tell them the good news."

At midafternoon the next day, Colonel Custer was talking with Bloody Knife and the other Arikara scouts near the fort's stables when one of Colonel Huston's adjutant corporals, Hector Nelson, approached, saluted, and said, "Colonel Custer, sir, Colonel

Huston would like to see you in his office immediately."

Custer looked around at the Arikaras. "Please excuse me, my friends. This sounds important."

"It is, sir," Nelson assured him.

Custer and Nelson hurried away together. When they neared the log building that contained the commandant's office, Nelson told Custer that he had another errand to run and veered off in another direction.

The commandant was standing in the open door of his office as Custer drew up. "Come in, please."

When the two men entered the office, the commandant sat behind his desk and Custer sat facing him. Huston smiled and said, "I wired the president and General Sheridan first thing this morning. I just heard back from both of them. General Sheridan's wire came first by about half an hour. He said that upon receiving my wire, in which I stated that I had also wired the president with the good news, he immediately wired President Grant to get his reaction."

"Yes, sir?"

Huston's smile spread from ear to ear. "General Sheridan said that the president was ecstatic, saying that the depression would soon be over. And General Sheridan told me to congratulate you for doing such an excellent job."

Custer grinned. "I'm glad that he feels that way. And what about President Grant's wire to you?"

"He also wants you to be congratulated for an excellent job."

"I'm honored by that, Colonel."

Huston's eyes sparkled. "You deserve it."

"Thank you. So, what else did President Grant say, sir?"

"He told me that, upon receiving my wire, he sent for three men at the Capitol Building to come to his office at the White House. They were Secretary of the Interior Zachariah Chandler, Indian Affairs Commissioner Edward Smith, and Secretary of War William Belknap. When he gave them the news, they agreed with the president that the construction of the fort on the land that you chose should begin immediately and that government-employed miners must be sent to the Black Hills right away.

"President Grant also said in his lengthy wire that an army corps of engineers will be sent right away, along with carpenters, to begin construction of the fort. Also, four hundred cavalrymen and two hundred infantrymen equipped with Gatling guns will be sent there from various forts to keep the Indians in line. They will dwell in tents until the fort is finished."

"Sounds like things are hopping, sir," Custer said.

"For sure. The president is calling it Fort Lookout, naming it after the Fort Lookout in another part of Dakota Territory that the army abandoned in 1857."

"I recall hearing about some fort being abandoned in Dakota Territory about that time, but I'd forgotten what it was called."

"The president said that he would advise Northern Pacific Railroad authorities right away that they could begin their construction through the northern tip of the Black Hills and that they will have the protection of the United States Army."

"I'm sure that the Northern Pacific people will be glad to hear that."

"Exceedingly so, Colonel. President Grant also stated that he is sure that once word gets out about the gold that your expedition discovered, a multitude of prospectors will head for those hills from coast to coast and border to border. In spite of the Laramie Treaty the president and the Department of the Interior will allow it. Grant's reasoning is that the more gold Americans extract, the more money will flow into the economy."

Custer nodded. "I don't doubt that, sir. But in spite of our army being in the Black Hills, we're going to have trouble with the Indians."

Huston sighed. "I can't argue with that."

On Thursday morning, September 10, Monty McGuire was at his desk at the Bank of Wyoming in Cheyenne when he saw Jim Bannon come in and go to one of the tellers' cages. Monty saw Jim turn and look in his direction while the teller was taking his deposit. Jim smiled and waved a folded newspaper at him.

After the teller handed Jim his receipt, Jim headed toward Monty's desk. As he drew up, he held the day's issue of the *Cheyenne Sentinel* open so that Monty could see the headline on the front page. "Have you seen this?"

Monty shook his head. "No, I haven't." His eyes were fixed on the bold headline that declared in large print:

GOLD DISCOVERED IN THE BLACK HILLS!
DEPRESSION WILL SOON BE OVER!

"What do you think of that?" Jim asked.

"Wow! Have you read the article?"

"I have."

Monty eased back in his chair. "Well, sit down and tell me about it."

Jim sat in one of the two chairs in front of the desk. "Well, I won't go into details. I know you're busy. The article says that they found genuine gold in the Black Hills...lots of it. Lieutenant Colonel Custer says he is sure that there is plenty enough gold in there to get this country out of its depression, so President Grant is going to send government-employed miners in there right away."

Monty rubbed his chin. "What about the Laramie Treaty?"

"Well, the article says that Custer found a good location to build a fort, and they're going to build it right away. They'll be sending six hundred soldiers equipped with Gatling guns to protect the men who build the fort, plus the Northern Pacific railroad workers who now will be laying track through the Black Hills. President Grant is sure that they will find enough gold to eliminate the national debt. So he figures that even though the Indians won't like the treaty being violated, with the army in those Black Hills bearing Gatling guns, there won't be much that they can do about it.

"The article says that President Grant has conferred with the secretary of the interior, the Indian affairs commissioner, and the secretary of war, and they are in complete agreement with his plan."

Monty nodded. "Does the article say anything about the fact that once this news gets out, gold seekers will swarm into the Black Hills like they did in California in 1849?"

"Yes. President Grant said that since the Sioux do very little with the gold in the Black Hills, it's best that the people of the United States and its Territories be allowed to go in there and make their fortunes if they're willing to put forth the effort."

Monty rubbed his chin again but did not comment.

Jim said, "There's a quote in here from a recent editorial in the *Chicago Inter Ocean*. Let me read it to you. 'It would be a sin against this great country if the Black Hills region were not opened up to both government and private individuals to go in there and take the gold from the hills and streams.'"

Monty nodded. "Let me ask you—"

Abruptly his secretary stepped up and said, "Excuse me, Mr. McGuire."

"Yes, Carrie?"

"I have a couple at my desk who want to talk to you about a mortgage loan. They're planning to buy a new home here in town."

Jim stood up. "Monty, we can discuss this some more later."

Monty rose to his feet. "All right."

"You started to ask me something. Do you want to ask me real quick now or when we get together later?"

Monty looked at his secretary. "Carrie, bring the couple on over. I'll ask Jim my question while you're doing so."

"Yes, sir," said Carrie, and she headed back toward her desk.

Monty said, "You told me that the article declared that key cabinet members are in agreement with all that the president is planning for the Black Hills. How about Congress? Does it mention how Congress feels about this?"

"Congress is backing President Grant 100 percent."

"Well, that's reassuring. All right, Jim, I'll see you later."

Jim headed toward the bank's entrance, and he saw Frank McGuire come in, carrying a copy of the day's paper.

As Jim drew up to him, he said, "Hello, Mr. McGuire. I was just at Monty's desk, telling him about the article about Custer's expedition finding gold in the Black Hills. Have you read it?"

"Just a moment ago."

"What do you think?"

"Well, I have to tell you, Jim, I'm a bit worried that in spite of the army being at Fort Lookout, there may still be some serious Indian trouble."

Jim sighed. "I'm worried about that, too, sir. I just hope that somehow it won't come to that."

Frank scratched behind his ear. "If it was left up to Chief Red Cloud, he probably would just tolerate it, but I fear that when Chief Sitting Bull gets wind of it, he'll try to get Red Cloud to lead his warriors against the whites. No matter how you look at it, the Laramie Treaty is being broken."

"Yes, sir, it is. There could be a lot of blood shed over this. I can understand why President Grant and the authorities in Washington want the gold and to see the railroad go through. Something has to be done to get this country out of financial trouble. I just wish that there was another way. I'm sure that Pastor Ballert will ask the church to pray that war with the Sioux won't come as a result."

"I'm already praying that way. And I'm sure that Pastor Ballert will be asking us to pray about it."

Jim glanced at the door. "Well, sir, I'm sure that you've got work to do. Nice to talk with you."

Jim stepped outside and went to his horse, which was tied to the hitch rail. As he swung into the saddle, he decided to go by the McGuire house and see Alyssa Rose for a few minutes. He was finding it harder and harder to go without seeing her except at church on Sundays and Wednesdays.

THIRTEEN

While riding toward the McGuire place, Jim determined that it was time to tell Alyssa Rose that he was in love with her. He believed that when he confessed his love for her, she would reveal that she was in love with him, too. He would ask her if he could take her out for dinner one night soon.

"And on that night," he told himself audibly, "I will declare my love for her."

When Jim rode into the yard at the McGuire place, he noted that the construction of the new mansion was coming along well. A crew of men was working on it at the moment.

As he pointed his horse toward the old white frame house, he saw Alyssa and her mother at the side of the house weeding the flower garden.

Alyssa looked up at the sound of hoofbeats. When she saw that it was Jim, she straightened her skirt and brushed away the garden dirt clinging to it. "Mama, Jim's here."

Kathleen was on her knees digging weeds loose from around the geraniums. She looked up at the rider drawing close and said, "Sure enough." As she spoke she rose to her feet.

Jim he smiled and lifted his hat, exposing his sand-colored hair to the bright light of the sun. "Good morning, ladies."

"Hello, Jim," Kathleen said.

"Nice to see you, Jim," Alyssa said, happily adjusting her sunbonnet so that she could get a better look at him.

"I hope it's all right that I just stopped by like this. I don't mean to impose on you."

Kathleen smiled. "Of course it's all right, Jim. You are always welcome here. Of course, Alyssa and I don't look our best right now."

"Ma'am, you both look mighty fine to me." Jim dismounted and ran his gaze over the flower garden. "Your flowers are sure beautiful." He wanted to add that Alyssa was even more beautiful than the flowers, but he refrained.

"The previous owners did a good job with them," Kathleen said. "All Alyssa and I have had to do is take over from where they left off."

"Well, you're doing a great job."

"We appreciate the encouragement," Alyssa said. "We had a gardener in Chicago, and he did most of the work on our flowers."

Kathleen moved a little closer to him. "It's almost noon. Is your mother expecting you home for lunch?"

"No, ma'am. When I ride into town in the morning, Mom never holds lunch for me, especially since Monty and I have become close friends. You probably know that Monty and I often have lunch together."

"Yes, and he always talks about your time together. Could you stay and have lunch with Alyssa and me?"

"Why, thank you. I'd love to."

The McGuire women guided Jim inside the house and to the kitchen. Alyssa pulled a chair from the table. "Here, Jim, sit down. We'll have lunch ready in a jiffy."

Jim thanked her, hung his hat on a nearby wall peg, and sat down.

The stove still had smoking embers from breakfast. Kathleen

stirred the embers and placed fresh logs on the fire, and the women went to work to prepare the meal.

While mother and daughter were busily performing their task, Alyssa teased her mother, saying, "You never had to cook when we lived in Chicago, Mama. But now, here in the wild West, you have to do it."

Kathleen flashed her daughter a smile. "I enjoy cooking, Alyssa Rose. Sure, I miss our two cooks and the other servants we had in Chicago, but I like living in Cheyenne much better than living in Chicago. And I also enjoy doing housework. Cooking and housework remind me of the days when your father and I were first married," Kathleen said, a reflective look in her eyes. "I love being a housewife. And you know, daughter dear, that even though we had servants in Chicago, my hand was very much at the helm of all the housekeeping."

Alyssa looked at Jim and then turned back to her mother. "I know you were. I just thought I'd tease you a little bit."

Kathleen met Alyssa's gaze. "I'm just so happy being in this place they call the wild West. I feel—how should I say it?—*rejuvenated*. The air is so clean, and the sky is like an endless blue canopy. Why, you can almost see forever. No, I don't miss having servants. I'm sure that your father would hire whatever help I needed here, but at least for now, I'm fine and enjoying every day!"

"I'm glad, Mama. I want you to always be happy."

Mother and daughter quickly had a simple lunch put together. When it was on the table, they sat down with Jim, and Kathleen asked him to pray over the food.

The three of them had a pleasant time eating together. Jim especially enjoyed being with both of them in their own surroundings. Observing Alyssa helping her mother prepare lunch, as well as working with her in the flower garden, gave him some insight into the kind of wife she would be. He could tell that her mother had trained her well.

He loved watching Alyssa's graceful movements while lunch was being prepared, and in his mind's eye he pictured the two of them in their own home.

While they were eating, Jim could hardly keep his eyes off the lovely young lady. At one point he was thinking what a beautiful bride she would be, and a small sigh escaped his lips.

Alyssa looked at him quizzically, and he tried to disguise it by turning it into a slight cough while covering his mouth with his hand. But Alyssa Rose was quite aware of what had just happened and flashed him a bright smile. Jim blushed.

When they were about to finish lunch, Jim said, "I don't suppose you've heard about this morning's edition of the *Cheyenne Sentinel.*"

Kathleen shook her head. "No. We never know what was in the day's paper until Frank and Monty come home with it in the evening. Something special?"

"Very," he said, pushing his chair back. "I think you should see it. I have it in my saddlebag. Be right back."

Mother and daughter hurried to clean off the table and at least get the dirty dishes on the cupboard next to the stove.

They were just sitting down at the table again when Jim returned. Flashing the front page at them, with the bold headline declaring that gold had been discovered in the Black Hills and that the depression would soon be over, Jim said, "Let me read you the article that goes with this headline."

Kathleen and Alyssa listened intently as Jim read the article to them.

When he had finished, Kathleen said, "I am glad to know that the country's economic depression will be coming to an end."

"Mama, Jim has told me about the price of hay and wheat being down since the depression hit almost two years ago. That's what they raise, hay and wheat. He told me that his family has been selling both commodities at a very small profit. I sure hope that things will look better for them now."

Kathleen set her eyes on Jim. "I agree with Alyssa Rose, but I also have to say that the possibility of war with the Sioux over the government breaking the Laramie Treaty has me worried. When gold seekers from all over the country begin swarming into the Black Hills, the Indians are likely to do their best to kill them."

"I see your point, ma'am, but the one factor that could keep the Indians from going after them will be all those Gatling guns that the army is taking in there with them. I've heard that the Indians have a genuine fear of the Gatling gun, so maybe they will remain peaceable."

"I sure hope so, Jim. I sure hope so." Kathleen rose from her chair. "Alyssa, I'm sure that Jim came here to spend some time with you. I'll take care of the dishes and cleaning up the kitchen. Why don't you take him out onto the back porch where there's some shade and sit down and talk for awhile?"

Jim stood up. "I'd like to do that, Mrs. McGuire, but I really need to get home. Dad needs me to help him do some repairs on the chicken coop."

Alyssa rose from her chair. "I'd like that, too, but I understand, Jim."

"Thank you. I…ah…I *would* like to ask you a question, though."

"Of course."

"Would you go out to dinner with me one night real soon?"

"Why, I'd love to! My calendar is wide open. Do you have a particular night in mind?"

"I'd like to take you tonight. I may not be able to afford Cheyenne's fanciest restaurant, but I'll take you to a nice one."

"I don't need a fancy restaurant. Any one of them will do."

"I'm honored that you will let me take you out. Dad and I have chores to do before suppertime every day. Would it be all right if I picked you up at six o'clock?"

"Of course."

"All right. I'll be here at six. Do you mind riding in our family wagon?"

"Of course not. That'll be fine."

"Okay." He picked up his copy of the *Cheyenne Sentinel* off the table. "Well, ladies, I enjoyed having lunch with you. It was delicious. Thank you very much."

"It was our pleasure, Jim," Kathleen said, patting his arm.

"I'll walk you to your to horse," Alyssa said.

Moments later, Alyssa stood on the front porch of the house and watched Jim ride away. Just as he was about to pass from view, she heard the door open and glanced over her shoulder at her mother.

Kathleen moved up beside Alyssa, looking in the direction that Jim had gone. "He's one nice young man, honey."

Alyssa wrapped her arms around her mother. "Oh, Mama, I'm so happy! Jim has had a special place in my heart ever since the day he rescued me from that obnoxious drifter."

Kathleen eased back in her daughter's arms and smiled.

"Mm-hmm. I've seen it written all over you. I like Jim very much. Not only is he strong and brave, but he's also a Christian gentleman."

"I agree, Mama. And he's also very handsome, which doesn't hurt anything, either."

Kathleen giggled. "You're right about that!"

As soon as Jim Bannon was out of sight—and safely out of earshot—from the McGuire house, he looked toward the sky and shouted, "I've done it! I've got my first date with the love of my life!"

Unused to such exuberance coming from his master, Jim's horse twisted his head around, eyes bulging, and snorted. Jim laughed.

"Just keep going, ol' buddy. We've got to get home."

The gray gelding snorted again, looked ahead, and kept up his pace.

Jim looked toward heaven. "Thank You, Lord. I just know that Alyssa feels the same way about me that I feel about her. Please prepare both of our hearts for what You have planned for our lives."

Soon Jim was riding along the bank of the Lodgepole River with the Bannon place in sight. When he turned onto the place and rode down the tree-lined lane toward the house, he could see his father carrying tools from the tool shed toward the chicken coop.

He put the gelding to a gallop, and as he drew near the house he saw his mother coming out the front door carrying a small throw rug. She went to the railing and shook the rug free of dust. She looked up just as her son drew close to the porch. "Hi, honey. Did you have lunch with Monty?"

Jim drew rein and shook his head. "No. I talked to him for a while at the bank, but he had customers come in who wanted to borrow money, so I left."

Sarah frowned. "So you didn't have lunch?"

"Oh, yes, I had lunch, all right. I dropped by the McGuire house after leaving the bank. I wanted to see Alyssa for a few minutes."

A smile crept over Sarah's face. "Are you telling me that you—"

"I sure did! Mrs. McGuire asked me to stay for lunch."

"I imagine you enjoyed that a thousand percent."

"You've got that right. And guess what?"

"What?"

"Well, my plan when I headed for the McGuire house was to get my first date with Alyssa."

Sarah's eyes lit up. "And?"

"I'm picking her up in our wagon at six o'clock this evening. We're going out to dinner together!"

She shook the small rug joyfully. "Oh, Jimmy, I'm so glad! I've been expecting something like this to happen pretty soon. I'm so glad that it did!"

"Thanks, Mom. Well, I see Dad's getting things ready for fixing up the chicken coop. I'd better get out there and help him before I get fired!"

Sarah laughed. "I wouldn't want that to happen!"

Jim started to put the gelding in motion and then halted. "Oh, I have something for you to read." He slid from the saddle, took the newspaper from the saddlebag, and handed it to her. "This is today's issue of the *Sentinel*. It tells all about the gold that George Custer and his expedition found in the Black Hills and what President Grant is doing about it. You can read it whenever you have time this afternoon. I'll tell Dad about it, and he can read it this evening."

Sarah looked at the headlines. "Mmm. Sounds interesting."

As Jim rode around the corner of the house, Sarah sighed and said, "Thank You, dear Lord. You know that I've been praying about Jim and Alyssa getting together. Thank You!"

It was twenty minutes after six o'clock that evening as Kathleen McGuire was working at the kitchen stove, doing her best to keep the food hot but not to burn it. Frank and Monty were usually prompt in leaving the bank a few minutes after five o'clock, which always brought them home around five-thirty. Kathleen told herself that something must have happened to delay their departure.

After a few more minutes at the stove, Kathleen looked up at the clock on the wall, noting that it was now almost six-thirty. She took a deep breath, and just as she let it out, she heard the rattle of the family carriage and the pounding of hooves. She rushed to the kitchen window and saw the tail end of the carriage as it passed by.

Monty always took the bridle and harness off the horse and

put the horse in the small corral and the carriage in the shed.

She expected Frank to come through the kitchen door first, and she was not disappointed. She rushed up to him. He folded her in his arms and kissed her soundly, and then he said, "I'm sorry we're late getting home, sweetheart. The Rocky Mountain Printing Company in Denver is opening up a printing office here in Cheyenne, and the two executives from Denver needed to open an account and take out a loan to purchase the empty building where the Smith and Johnson law office used to be. They didn't come in till late afternoon. Monty and I had to work up the papers on the spot because the two men had to catch the six o'clock train to Denver."

Kathleen smiled. "I understand, darling. I've kept supper hot on the stove. Get washed up."

Frank looked around. "Where's Alyssa?"

A beam glowed on Kathleen's face. "She is on her first date with Jim Bannon. He took her out for dinner."

Frank frowned. "Did you give her a time to be home?"

"Well, no, I didn't. Alyssa Rose is almost twenty years old, Frank. She's not a little girl anymore. She's a young woman and needs some freedom. Besides, since she's with Jim there certainly is nothing to worry about."

Frank turned and went to the wash bowl at the kitchen cupboard and began washing his hands.

Kathleen gave the back of his head a quizzical look and returned to the stove.

Frank was drying his hands when Monty's footsteps were heard on the back porch; then the kitchen door opened. He headed for his mother, who was pouring gravy from a skillet, and hugged her. "How's my sweet mom?"

She smiled at him. "I'm fine."

He glanced toward his father and then looked back at his mother. "Did Dad tell you why we're late?"

"Yes. He explained it to me."

Monty hurried to the wash bowl, and while he was washing his hands, he looked around the kitchen. "Mom, where's Sis?"

"Well, Monty, your sister is on her first date with Jim Bannon."

Monty's eyes lit up and a smile spread over his face. "I'm glad to hear that. It's about time!"

"That's exactly how I feel," Kathleen said.

As Monty was drying his hands, he said, "I know that Jim has been interested in Alyssa Rose since I first showed him the family photograph. And it sure hasn't been hard to tell that she thinks a lot of him."

"You should have seen how elated she was after Jim had been here and asked for the date. And for the rest of the day, until Jim came and picked her up, she was like a cat on a hot tin roof. She was so excited, she couldn't sit still."

When they sat down to eat, Frank asked Monty to pray over the food. Kathleen could tell that her husband was upset that Alyssa and Jim were on a date together but could not understand why.

As they began to eat, Frank looked at Kathleen. "Honey, I've got to tell you about today's issue of the *Cheyenne Sentinel*. The headlines were massive. They said—"

"'Gold discovered in the Black Hills,'" cut in Kathleen. "'Depression will soon be over!'"

Frank blinked. "How did you know?"

"When Jim came by the house today, he showed Alyssa and me the paper and read us the article."

"I didn't realize that he was here long enough to do that."

Kathleen smiled. "Jim came by just before lunch time, so he ate with Alyssa and me at my invitation."

"Oh. Well, that was nice of you."

Kathleen nodded and said, "I'm very concerned about what might happen over this Black Hills crisis. You know…the breaking of the Laramie Treaty and just how the Indians are going to react to it."

Frank sighed. "Me, too."

The three of them discussed the Black Hills situation for a while. Frank's concern over Alyssa's date with Jim Bannon had him under a strain, and though he did not mention it, his being upset was obvious even as they discussed the Black Hills.

When there was a slight lull in the conversation, Monty frowned at his father. "Dad, is something bothering you?"

Kathleen was drinking from a coffee cup and averted her eyes as Frank looked at her and then at Monty. "I'm just tired, son. It was an extra long day, you know."

FOURTEEN

At 6:15 that evening, Jim Bannon—with butterflies in his stomach and his heart racing—pulled the wagon up to the hitch rail in front of Callie's Cottage Restaurant, which was small but elegant. The front of the place actually looked like a cottage, with a small peaked roof over what would be the porch and several cottage-style windows, each with small square panes.

Alyssa Rose McGuire was having a problem with her own heart racing. She turned and smiled at Jim. "I first noticed this restaurant just about two weeks ago. Quaint, isn't it?"

"Yes. That's one of the reasons I like it. Although, I have to tell you...I've never eaten here before. Many people have told me how good the food is, but I just never had a reason to go to a place as pleasingly unique as this." He took a deep breath and smiled at her. "That is, until *now*."

Alyssa blushed. "Thank you."

He patted her arm. "I mean it. This is a very special occasion for me." Jim jumped out of the wagon, tied the team to a post at one end of the hitch rail, and helped Alyssa down.

The inside of the place definitely looked like someone's cottage. White linen cloths covered the tables, the dishes that customers were using were painted in a rose garden design, and matching curtains were pulled back at each window to let in the cool evening breeze.

Alyssa looked around with a smile on her lips. "Jim, this place is enchanting. I love it!"

"I'm glad. It is nice, isn't it?" *I should have checked about the prices here. I hope they aren't too high.*

Alyssa looked up into his eyes. "Is anything wrong?"

"Oh, no, everything's perfect! Come on. Let's pick out a table."

He took hold of her elbow and escorted her to a table for two in a front corner, which had windows on both sides. He pulled out a chair, assisted her as she sat down, and then eased onto a chair facing her.

"I like this spot," Alyssa said. "That breeze is nice."

"I ordered it just for you."

At that moment a waitress walked up to the table bearing menus. "Good evening, folks, and welcome to Callie's Cottage."

Alyssa smiled up at her. "Thank you. This is really a nice place. I'm fairly new in Cheyenne, and I've never been here before."

"Well, you're in for a treat. The food here is first-rate." The waitress handed each of them a menu and asked what they would like to drink. Both ordered cool tea.

When Jim opened the menu, he was relieved to find that the prices were quite reasonable. After they ordered their meals, Jim asked Alyssa what it was like to be a banker's daughter. They were already deep in conversation when their meals arrived. They were so engrossed in each other that neither took much notice of the other customers coming and going.

Soon it was time for dessert, and both of them ordered apple pie. They lingered over it, talking about the blessings of the Lord on their church with people being reached for Christ and how much they liked Pastor Ballert's preaching.

Suddenly Jim noticed that all the other tables were empty. He and Alyssa were the only two customers left.

She noticed the strange look on his face. "What's wrong?"

Jim leaned toward her and whispered, "We're the only ones left in here. All the other patrons are gone. Guess we should go so these tired people can go home."

Alyssa looked around the room, noting all the empty tables and their waitress talking to the cook at the large open window at the kitchen. Another waitress was at the counter talking with the cashier. Both were looking their way. She giggled and put a hand to her mouth, her eyes sparkling. "Hmm, I guess you're right. They do look a little tired and are probably waiting for us to pay our bill and leave."

Jim rose to his feet and offered her his hand. She took it, and he helped her from her chair. Jim paid the bill at the counter, and they left Callie's Cottage hand in hand.

As they headed for the wagon, a silver moon was rising into a star-spangled sky.

Jim helped Alyssa Rose into the driver's seat, climbed up beside her, and said, "Alyssa, could we go for a moonlight ride before I take you home?"

"Oh, I would love it!"

Soon Jim was driving the wagon along the bank of the Crow River. He silently asked the Lord to help him handle it just right when he told Alyssa that he was in love with her.

They came to a spot along the bank where a fallen tree lay parallel with the river. Jim pulled rein and stopped the wagon. He hopped to the ground, rounded the rear of the wagon, and helped Alyssa down. He then guided her to the fallen tree. "All right if we sit here?"

She looked at him and smiled. "Of course."

They sat together beside the gurgling stream, and Alyssa said, "Look, Jim. See how beautifully the moonlight reflects off the surface of the water?"

He glanced down at the river and then turned to her. "Yes, it is beautiful. But the moonlight reflects even more beautifully from your eyes."

Alyssa blushed. "Really?"

"Yes. Really."

For a few minutes they sat in silence, listening to the music of the running water and enjoying the moonlight.

Alyssa looked up at the twinkling stars, the silver moon, and the dark sky above. "Jim, it's awesome out here. It's almost as if we were the only two people in the world."

"Maybe we are," he said softly, looking admiringly at her.

She met his gaze and then looked down at the river and said, "I loved living in Chicago, but that was before we moved here and I saw how special it is here in the West. It's so quiet. Chicago is always bustling and noisy. It seems like people never sleep. There's a cacophony of sound in the city even in the middle of the night."

"I don't think I would like living there," Jim said as he stared up at the night sky. "I'm sure that it would be very hard to adapt to any of the eastern cities after having lived in this place."

Abruptly, from somewhere in the night, they heard a high-pitched howl.

Alyssa blinked and looked around. "Was that a wolf?"

"No, a coyote. He's calling for his mate."

"Oh."

A more distant howl came from another direction.

Jim looked at Alyssa. "That was her answering him."

"I see."

"He will find her soon, I guarantee you."

She smiled. "Back to what you were saying a moment ago about how hard it would be for you to adapt to city life."

"Mm-hmm."

"I'm not having any problem adapting to Cheyenne and its surroundings. You are fortunate to have been born and raised here.

I know it's where I want to live and make my own home some day."

Those words were music to Jim's ears. His heart was beating against his ribs as he took both of her hands in his own and looked into her soft green eyes.

"Alyssa, I want to ask you something. Have...have you ever heard of a man falling in love with a woman he saw in a photograph?"

She let a slight frown furrow her brow. "No, I can't say that I have."

"Well, you have *now,* because I fell in love with you when Monty showed me that family picture. And that love has grown deeper and stronger since I've met you. Alyssa, I am very much in love with you. I can't keep it inside any longer. I just *had* to tell you."

Tears misted Alyssa's eyes. It took her a moment to find her voice. She choked a bit and cleared her throat gently. "Jim, you've had a very special place in my heart since the day you protected me from that drifter...but since I've gotten to know you, that special place has now spread throughout my heart. I am desperately in love with you, and it's wonderful to hear you say that you feel the same about me."

Jim's smile seemed to light up the night beyond the glow of the moon and the twinkling of the stars. He took Alyssa in his arms and looked into her misty eyes. "Oh, Alyssa, this makes me the happiest man in the whole world! May I...may I kiss you?"

She smiled and nodded.

The kiss was sweet but brief. Then, as they clung to each other, Jim said, "Thank You, Lord, for bringing this wonderful lady into my life. Thank You that she is in love with me, too!"

Alyssa squeezed him hard. "And thank You, Lord, that Jim is in love with me!"

He looked into her eyes again. He wanted to say something about them one day marrying but decided not to push things too fast. "Well, my sweet Alyssa, I had best take you home."

⁕

It was almost nine-thirty when Jim pulled the wagon into the yard at the McGuire home, hopped out, and helped Alyssa to the ground. Jim held her hand as they climbed the porch steps.

When they were at the door she said, "I know that you have to be up early in the morning to do the chores, but could you come in for a few minutes?"

"I'd be happy to."

They moved inside, and Alyssa led him by the hand to the parlor, where her parents and Monty were sitting in overstuffed chairs, reading books by lantern light.

Monty laid his book on a small table next to his chair and jumped up, smiling broadly. "Hey, you two! I'm so glad that you finally had a date. I figured that this would've happened a long time ago."

"Well, it wasn't that I didn't *want* a date a long time ago," Jim said, "but I didn't want to upset the applecart by moving too fast. Besides, it took a while to get up the nerve to ask the most beautiful young lady in all the world to go to dinner with me."

Alyssa's features flushed and a smile curved her lips as she shook her head.

Kathleen was out of her chair and headed toward them.

Jim noticed that Frank was looking at him from his chair with what appeared to be a perturbed look in his eyes.

Kathleen drew up to the couple and asked, "Did you have a good time?"

"Oh, yes, Mama," Alyssa said. "It was wonderful!"

"Well, tell us about it!" Monty said.

While Alyssa was telling her mother and brother about the meal at Callie's Cottage Restaurant and the moonlight ride along the Crow River, Frank stayed in his chair, looking on and listening.

When Alyssa finished her story, Frank left his chair and moved up to the four who stood in the middle of the room. His voice was level as he said, "Alyssa, Jim, I'm glad that you had a good time. And Jim, I appreciate your having Alyssa home before nine-thirty."

Jim smiled and nodded at him.

Kathleen turned to Jim and asked, "Would you like to sit down and have a cup of coffee? It's still hot on the stove."

"Thank you, Mrs. McGuire, but I really must be heading for home. Dad and I start our day at four-thirty every morning."

"Well, I sure am glad that you and Sis finally had a date," Monty said, his face beaming. "I hope that there'll be many more."

Jim grinned, glancing at Alyssa and then back at Monty. "Yes, sir. There will be lots of them."

Jim bid Alyssa's parents and her brother good night, and Alyssa said, "I'll walk you to the door."

When Jim and Alyssa moved into the foyer and up to the door, Alyssa kept her voice low as she said, "Don't let Papa's tone of voice and that stony look on his face bother you. With us having our first date, he's having to face the fact that his little girl is growing up and one day will no longer live under his roof. I think that most fathers struggle with that."

Jim released a sigh. "Yes, you're probably right. I wasn't sure what to think, but what you say makes sense."

Alyssa smiled. "It'll all work out. The Lord has His hand in this."

"Yes, He does. He put this love in my heart for you, Alyssa. I love you more than words could ever tell."

Her eyes grew misty once more. "And I love you more than words could ever tell, too, Jim."

Jim smiled from ear to ear. "I'm sure glad. Well, I'll see you at church on Sunday."

"Yes, and thank you again for such a wonderful evening."

"My pleasure. Good night, Alyssa."

Alyssa read in Jim's blue eyes that he wanted to kiss her, but she saw him glance uneasily down the hall toward the parlor door.

"Good night," she said softly.

Alyssa watched him climb into the wagon and put the team in motion. He looked back over his shoulder, saw her standing in the open door, and waved.

She waved back and watched the wagon until it passed from view, but she stayed on the spot until she could no longer hear the muted *clip-clop* of the horses' hooves.

Alyssa hugged herself, whirled about, and stepped inside. She took a deep breath and said in a whisper, "He loves me! He loves me! Oh, thank You, dear Lord, for this most special and wonderful night!"

She took one more long look at the starry sky and then closed the door.

At the sound of the door closing, Kathleen and Monty came out of the parlor and moved toward her.

"Well, it's bedtime," Alyssa said.

Kathleen nodded. "Your papa already went upstairs to get ready for bed."

"I'll douse the lanterns down here, Mom," Monty said. "You and Sis go on upstairs."

"We can help you, Monty," Alyssa said.

The three of them spread out to douse the lanterns in various rooms and then met at the foot of the stairs, where light from a lantern at the top of the stairs glowed down on them.

They climbed the stairs together, and as they headed down the hall, they bid each other good night.

Alyssa entered her room, still in a dreamy state of mind.

Monty went into his room, closed the door, and thanked the Lord that Jim Bannon and his sister were showing such great interest in each other.

When Kathleen entered the master bedroom, Frank was in his nightshirt and about to climb into bed. "I'll be with you shortly," she said. "You can go ahead and get our Bibles out."

In her room, Alyssa was soon ready for bed. She put out the lantern, picked her hairbrush up from the dresser, and sat down at the window. She began to brush her long, luxuriant hair. The moonlight streamed through the window, making a pattern on the polished wood floor.

Slowly drawing the brush through her hair, Alyssa Rose McGuire relived every single moment with Jim and every word spoken between them on this remarkable, life-changing evening.

A smile spread over her features as she thought of the flame of love that burned deep inside of her heart.

In the master bedroom, Frank was sitting up, ready for their Bible reading and prayer time. He had already braced Kathleen's pillow against the back of the bedstead and laid her Bible next to it. His own Bible was in his hand.

Kathleen came out of the washroom in her nightgown, picked up her Bible, and moved in beside him.

"Well, dear, we finished First Peter last night," Frank said, "so let's read Second Peter chapter one tonight."

Kathleen leaned against her pillow and opened her Bible to Second Peter.

When Frank had finished reading the chapter, he noticed that Kathleen seemed pensive. "Is something bothering you, honey?"

Kathleen replied softly, "Read verses five through seven to me again."

Frank's brow furrowed. "Why do you want me to repeat those verses?"

"Because we need to talk about something before we pray and go to sleep. And what I want to say is covered in those verses."

FIFTEEN

A puzzled look filled Frank's eyes. He shrugged his shoulders and dropped his gaze back onto the page. "Verses five through seven, you said?"

Kathleen nodded. "Yes, please."

"You want to say something to me that's covered in these verses?"

"Yes."

He cleared his throat and read the verses aloud again: "And beside this, giving all diligence, add to your faith virtue; and to virtue knowledge; and to knowledge temperance; and to temperance patience; and to patience godliness; and to godliness brotherly kindness; and to brotherly kindness charity."

Frank kept his Bible open to the passage and looked at his wife. "All right, my dear, what is it that you want to talk about?"

Kathleen smiled at him. "Frank, darling, I am proud that you are a man of diligence. I am also proud that you are a man of faith and virtue. I am also proud to say that you are a man of knowledge, temperance, patience, and godliness."

He smiled at her. "Thank you."

"But, darling, tonight you did not display brotherly kindness nor charity to Jim Bannon. You came very close to being unkind to him, and there certainly was a lack of charity in your demeanor."

Frank's smile vanished. By the way he stared at her and chewed on his lower lip, Kathleen knew that she had struck a sensitive spot.

"Monty and Alyssa both saw it, and I could tell that Jim did, too. Why did you treat him that way?"

His eyes went cold and his mouth tightened as he said, "We'll talk about it later. I need to get to sleep."

"How could you treat Jim like that after what he did to protect Alyssa from those drifters? And he has been a good friend to her ever since."

Frank sighed deeply. "Honey, I appreciate what Jim did to rescue her from those drifters, and I had no problem with Alyssa's friendship with him. But when I came home and found out that they had gone on a date this evening, it was—well, it was more than I could take. You and I both know that every young woman eventually marries somebody she dates."

Kathleen looked at him incredulously. "Frank, Jim Bannon would make a wonderful husband for Alyssa. He's a fine young man…a dedicated Christian, a genuine gentleman, and a hard worker."

"He is that, all right, honey, but he's also just a poor dirt farmer. I don't want our daughter to marry someone on that level. I want her to marry a Christian, of course, but she needs to marry a young man on her own social scale—a young man with plenty of money who knows how to handle it and provide a life of luxury for her like she's used to."

Kathleen studied his eyes. She was thinking of saying that God's choice of a husband for Alyssa may not be a wealthy man, but she did not want to get into an argument. She licked her lips. "Frank…are you going to forbid Alyssa to date Jim anymore?"

He scrubbed a palm over his face. "I won't forbid it because I don't want to upset Alyssa, nor do I want to hurt Jim. I'll talk to her about it and let her handle how to keep things with Jim on a 'just friends' basis and not let it develop into a romance."

Kathleen drew a deep breath and let it out slowly. "You may be asking too much of her. I can tell that Alyssa already admires Jim a great deal. Her feelings may go even deeper than admiration."

"You really think so?"

"That you could be asking too much of her?"

"No, that her feelings might go deeper than admiration. That she might be in love with him."

"It's possible. She really thinks a lot of him and talks about him a great deal. I think she just might have her heart set on him."

Frank rubbed his jaw. "I'll have a talk with Alyssa tomorrow night after supper. I'm sure that I can make her understand that she would be miserable living a life on the edge of poverty when all she has ever known is luxury and plenty. I don't think that I told you, honey, that several weeks ago Jim and I were talking together at church between services. He told me that he wants to be a farmer like his father, and he plans to have his own farm someday soon."

"No, you didn't tell me. But I think that's admirable. Jim knows what hard work is. He will do well with his own farm, especially if this Black Hills gold thing works out and frees the country of its financial depression."

"Well, let me put it like this: Even if the country's economy is vastly improved by the government's digging millions of dollar's worth of gold out of the Black Hills and the price of wheat and alfalfa goes up, farmers, Kathleen, are still farmers. None of them ever gets rich."

"Frank, may I sit in on your conversation with Alyssa tomorrow night?"

"Why, of course. After all, you're her mother."

She managed a smile. "Thank you."

He smiled back. "You're welcome. Now, let's pray so we can get to sleep."

❧

In her room, Alyssa Rose found sleep elusive. Her mind was fixed on the way her father had treated Jim that evening and on the knowledge that Jim was upset over her father's attitude toward him.

She flipped from one side to the other and then finally lay on her back and looked up toward the ceiling. She thought of what she had said to Jim just before he left. Now, lying there in her bed, Alyssa wondered if there was more to it than a father struggling with his daughter growing up. Was there some other reason that her papa didn't like Jim? Would he stand in the way of her marrying him if Jim proposed?

Alyssa's mind slid into panic. She sat up in the bed and put her hands to her face. "Lord, You wouldn't let Papa keep Jim and me apart, would You? I—I just *know* that I'm in love with him. And he certainly is in love with me." Her voice grew shaky. "Oh, this can't happen! Lord, I need You to help me! You brought Jim and me together. I just know it. Papa can be awfully stubborn when he sets his mind to something. By the way he treated Jim tonight, it makes me think that he just might try to keep us apart. I—I'm afraid, Lord."

Abruptly words from the Bible came to her: *I will trust, and not be afraid.* Last Sunday evening Pastor Ballert had used those very words as the title for his sermon. Alyssa got out of bed and lit the lantern on the small table next to the bed. She picked up her Bible, opened it to Isaiah chapter twelve, and focused on verse two: "Behold, God is my salvation; I will trust, and not be afraid: for the LORD JEHOVAH is my strength and my song; he also is become my salvation."

She recalled Pastor Ballert saying that there are certain things that come into our lives that tend to darken us with fear. When our hopes seem threatened by another person or circumstance, we shrink back and give in to fear.

Alyssa clearly remembered Pastor Ballert's next words in the sermon: "When we find ourselves frozen with fear in such a case, what is the remedy? *I will trust, and not be afraid.* Christian, you trusted the Lord to save you when you came to Him as a lost sinner, in need of salvation. If you could trust Him to save you from an eternity in hell, certainly you can trust Him to overcome those menacing things that bring fear in your everyday life. Jesus is the Lord Jehovah, and He personally has become your salvation. Then ask Him to give you the same faith that Isaiah spoke of when he wrote under the inspiration of the Holy Spirit, 'I will trust, and not be afraid.'"

Those seven words emblazoned themselves on Alyssa's mind. She closed the Bible and laid it back on the small table. She put out the lantern light, slid back under the covers, and wiped away her tears as she looked toward heaven and said, "Thank You, Lord Jesus, for giving my pastor that sermon. I'm placing this whole matter into Your mighty hands. I will trust and not be afraid."

Kathleen McGuire kissed her husband goodnight after they prayed together and the lantern light had been put out. He was asleep in a matter of minutes. Kathleen lay wide awake, staring at the ceiling with her heart aching.

"Lord," she whispered, "I just don't understand Frank's attitude about Jim, just because he wants to be a farmer for the rest of his life like his father. Frank has never been a snob. He has never projected outwardly that he thought that he was better than someone else. What has come over him? It is only by Your grace that we have the income and wealth that we do. Surely he hasn't forgotten that."

An hour passed with Kathleen's thoughts in turmoil. She feared that Frank's attitude toward Jim Bannon would create a hurtful separation between father and daughter. She wiped away tears as she lay next to her sleeping husband, and her mind flashed to a Scripture verse that she and Frank had discussed at length a few nights before.

"First Peter 5:7," she breathed, barely moving her lips. "'Casting all your care upon him; for he careth for you.'"

Quoting that verse to the Lord, she claimed it by faith and prayed herself to sleep.

The next day at the Bannon farm, while working with his father around the barn, Jim's thoughts kept going to Alyssa Rose and the wonderful knowledge that she was in love with him.

However, a dark cloud seemed to hover in his mind as he thought of Frank McGuire's attitude toward him, and Alyssa's explanation of it. Having lain awake until quite late thinking about it, Jim sensed that there was more to it than just that Alyssa's father was facing the fact that his little girl was growing up and would one day marry and leave home.

While pitching fresh hay from the hayloft into the feed trough at the milking stanchions, Jim whispered to his heavenly Father, "Lord, I'm asking You to please work this problem out for Alyssa and me so that one day I can marry her with the blessing of both her father and mother. I love her with all my heart, Father. You know that. I can't imagine going on in life without her. I know that You brought us together. I can't imagine why Mr. McGuire objects to my dating his daughter. Please work in his heart and change his attitude toward me."

That evening as the McGuire family was finishing supper, Frank said to Alyssa Rose, "When the dishes are done and the kitchen has been cleaned up, I want to talk to you in the parlor about something very important."

Alyssa's heart seemed to turn over in her chest at the flat sound of her father's voice. Her mind rushed to those seven stabilizing words: *I will trust, and not be afraid.* As she held her father's gaze, she said deep within, *Lord, I am trusting You to take care of this.*

To her father she said, "May I ask what it's about, Papa?"

"It's about Jim Bannon. Your mother is going to sit in on the conversation, also."

Leaving what food was left on her plate untouched, Alyssa laid her fork down and nodded. "All right, Papa."

Monty looked at his father. "Dad, can I be in on it, too?"

Frank gave him a dull look.

"Well, it *does* involve my sister and my best friend."

Frank shoved his chair back and stood up. "I guess you might as well. You and I will go on into the parlor."

While Alyssa was helping her mother do the dishes and clean up the kitchen, she continually said to herself, "I will trust, and not be afraid."

A half hour after Frank and Monty had left the kitchen, Kathleen and Alyssa Rose entered the parlor, where both men were sitting on the sofa reading portions of the *Cheyenne Sentinel.* The papers were laid aside when the women sat down next to each other in overstuffed chairs, facing them.

"All right, Papa," Alyssa said. "I'm listening."

Frank told Alyssa the same things that he had said to Kathleen the night before about Jim Bannon. He made it plain that he wanted her to marry a Christian man but that he wanted that man to be wealthy and a good manager of his money.

Alyssa prayed in her heart for God's strength, with the words *I will trust, and not be afraid* echoing in her mind. She felt her throat swell and a lump form. She told herself that a single tear would loose a flood. *Help me, Lord,* she pled silently.

Frank said, "Alyssa, you would be miserable as the wife of a poor dirt farmer."

"I wouldn't be miserable married to Jim, Papa," Alyssa said, struggling not to cry, "if the Lord had led us to each other, show-ing us that it was His will that we spend the rest of our lives together as husband and wife. I know in my heart that the Lord has brought us together."

Frank sighed. "Alyssa Rose, since you were born and raised in a wealthy home, you have no idea how difficult it is to always be pinching pennies to survive. I want you to marry a man who can provide the kind of life that you've had since you were born."

Alyssa was fighting to keep from breaking into tears. Kathleen saw it and reached over and took hold of Alyssa's hand. "Honey, keep a grip on yourself. Everything will work out all right."

Monty left the sofa, knelt in front of his sister, and took hold of the other hand. "Sis, Mom's right. Don't worry. The Lord will work everything out just perfect for you."

In her heart, Alyssa prayed, *Help me, dear Lord. I will trust, and not be afraid.* She looked at Monty and then at her mother and nodded. "Thank you both."

Frank looked into Alyssa's eyes, smiled, and said, "Honey, I am simply looking out for your best interests. I'm your papa, and I want the best life possible for you. Understand?"

Alyssa bit her lower lip and nodded in tiny, jerky movements.

Frank took a deep breath. "Alyssa, I don't want to hurt you by insisting that you and Jim never date anymore, nor do I want to hurt Jim. He is a fine Christian young man, and I like him very much. But, honey, he is just a poor dirt farmer. Even when he gets his own farm, that's still what he will always be. My daughter must have a better life than Jim Bannon can ever provide. Since I'm not going to stop you and Jim from dating, I'm going to trust you to keep your relationship on a 'just friends' basis and not let it develop into a romance. Can you do that?"

Alyssa Rose met her father's gaze and nodded. "I will work at it, Papa."

Frank grinned. "Good! Then when that right Christian young

man comes along, you'll be free to marry him."

Monty swung his eyes to his mother and shook his head.

"What's wrong, Monty?" Frank asked.

Monty was still holding his sister's hand. "Dad, Alyssa will never meet a young man like Jim. How many rich, young Christian men do you know who would have gone to her rescue like Jim did and take on two rowdy drifters by himself?"

Frank cleared his throat. "Son, there's a whole lot more to life than being tough and fearless. Jim's a fine young man, yes, but he can't provide the kind of life that your sister has known since she was born."

Monty stared unflinchingly at his father. "I still say that my sister will never meet a young man like him. Sure, Jim Bannon might never be rich, but he would be a better husband to her than anyone else could ever be."

Frank rubbed the back of his neck. "Son, you have a right to express your opinion, but since Alyssa has told me that she will work at keeping her relationship with Jim on a 'just friends' basis, I am satisfied that she will do just that." He looked at Alyssa. "Has Jim ever said anything to you about wanting to marry you?"

Alyssa shook her head. "No, Papa, he hasn't."

Trying to help, Kathleen said, "Then, honey, it will be much easier for you to keep things from developing romantically between the two of you."

Heavy of heart, Alyssa covered her feelings and said, "Yes, it will, Mama."

Frank clapped his palms together and rose to his feet. "Good! End of discussion. Well, family, let's read till bedtime as usual."

Monty patted Alyssa's hand and stood up.

Kathleen reached for the book that she was presently reading, which lay on the table next to the overstuffed chair where she was sitting.

Alyssa arose from her chair and ran her gaze over the rest of the family. "If you will excuse me, I'll go on up to my room."

After Alyssa entered her room and closed the door, she ran to her bed, threw herself on it facedown, and muffled her sobs in a pillow.

After a few minutes her sobs turned into sniffles. She sat up on the edge of the bed, drying her face with a corner of the spread. She then went to the dresser, which held a wash bowl and a pitcher of water.

She poured water into the bowl, washed her face, and began blotting it dry with a soft towel. Looking at her reflection in the mirror, she also dabbed at the tears that once again spilled from her eyes.

Alyssa returned to her bed and knelt beside it. "Dear Lord, I'm trying so hard to trust and not be afraid, but this has me all torn up. I need Your help. You know that I love Jim and that he loves me. Both of us are sure that You brought us together. You know that we are mature adults, not just silly children experiencing puppy love."

She drew a shaky breath. "But Father, You also know what my papa is requiring of me. I know that You say in Your Word, 'Children, obey your parents in the Lord: for this is right.' Since I still live with my parents and am under their authority, Lord, I know that I'm still supposed to obey Papa. I never want to disobey my parents. I want to honor my father and mother. I just ask, Lord Jesus, that You help me to be submissive to Papa and do as he has told me. But I also ask that if Jim is the one You have for me—which I believe he is—that Papa will have a change of heart. Help me to always walk faithful to Your leading in my life, and may this uncomfortable situation someday glorify You. I thank You, Lord, that Your Word says, 'Be careful for nothing; but in every thing by prayer and supplication with thanksgiving let your requests be made known unto God. And the peace of God, which passeth all understanding, shall keep your hearts and minds through Christ Jesus.' I love You, my heavenly Father, and may Your will be done. In Jesus' precious name I pray. Amen."

Alyssa rose to her feet and once again sat on the edge of the bed. She decided that for the time being she would not tell Jim what her father had said. She and Jim were in love, and she was positive that the day would come when he would bring up marriage, or even propose. In the meantime, she would pray about it and would do as the Lord directed her.

Peace now flooded Alyssa's soul. Rising from the bed, she went back downstairs to the parlor. Her parents and Monty looked up from their books as she entered the room. They saw her red and swollen eyes as she said, "I just wanted to tell all three of you good night and that I love you."

She bent down and kissed her father's cheek. "Good night, Papa. I love you."

Frank smiled. "I love you, too, sweetheart. Sleep tight."

She turned to her mother, who was now on her feet. "'Night, Mama. I love you."

Kathleen hugged her close. "I love you, too, dear. Pleasant dreams."

Monty left his chair, and when Alyssa turned to him, he folded her in his arms. "I love you, Sis. Sweet dreams."

She kissed his cheek. "I love you, too, big brother. Good night."

Alyssa walked to the door, waved with a smile, and passed from view.

As Kathleen and Monty sat down once again, Frank smiled at them and said, "She'll do the right thing."

SIXTEEN

On Sunday morning when the Bannon family arrived at church, the McGuire carriage was not yet in the parking lot.

Jim drew the wagon to a halt, hopped down, and tied the horses to a hitching post while his father was helping his mother. He then turned to them and said, "I'll wait out here. You two go on inside."

Newt grinned. "Oh, of course. You're wanting to see Monty when the McGuires arrive."

Jim cuffed his father playfully on the chin. "Dad, I really like Monty...but, well, there'll be someone else in that carriage who I'm really eager to see."

"Who do you suppose he's talking about?" Newt said to Sarah.

Sarah shook her head. "I have no idea."

Jim smiled at them and then turned his attention toward the street. The McGuire carriage was just turning into the parking lot. When Monty McGuire swung the carriage up to a hitching post, Jim headed toward it and stepped up beside the carriage. "Good morning! Beautiful day, isn't it?" he said.

All the McGuires agreed.

Jim then stepped up to where Alyssa was seated, offered his hand, and said, "Miss McGuire, may I help you down and escort you into the house of God?"

Alyssa smiled. "Why, of course, *Mister* Bannon."

As he took her hand, he said, "You don't have to call me mister."

She giggled. "And you don't have to call me miss."

As they all headed toward the building, Bibles in hand, Frank said, "So how are things at the farm, Jim?"

"Just fine, sir. Lots of work, of course, but that goes with farming."

"Banking is the same way, pal," Monty said. "Only the work is different."

Jim laughed. "That's putting it mildly."

Pastor David and Tammy greeted them on the porch, and when they stepped inside, Jim leaned close to Alyssa. "May I take you out for dinner tomorrow evening?"

"I would like that very much."

"Where would you like to go?" Jim asked, smiling broadly.

"How about Callie's Cottage?"

"You really like the place, don't you?"

"I think it's charming."

"Okay. Callie's Cottage it is. Pick you up at six?"

Alyssa noticed her father looking her way. There was suddenly a cold, sinking feeling in her stomach. *Papa, why couldn't you have left well enough alone?*

Jim lowered his face closer to hers. "Okay?"

Alyssa blinked. "What was that, Jim?"

"Will six o'clock be all right for me to pick you up?"

"Oh. Yes, of course."

As Jim and Alyssa walked toward their pew, she glanced at her father, who was talking to his secretary's husband, his eyes following her. Alyssa felt as if her world would shatter into fragments if she lost Jim because of her father. In her heart she said, *Lord, help me to trust and not be afraid.*

꙳

Later that evening after the McGuire family had returned home from the evening service, Monty and his mother happened to meet up in the hall on the second floor while Frank and Alyssa were downstairs. Kathleen was headed for the staircase.

When Monty stopped in front of her, she said, "Aren't you coming down for the snack before bedtime, dear?"

"Sure, Mom. I just need to go to my room for a couple of minutes. But since we're alone, I want to talk to you about this thing with Dad taking control of Alyssa's relationship with Jim."

Monty could see worry in his mother's eyes. "Mom, I don't think that Sis will be able to keep things between Jim and herself as 'just friends.' I can tell that she is head-over-heels in love with him, and to me it's obvious that Jim is in love with her. It's written all over both of them, especially when they're looking at each other."

Kathleen glanced down at the floor before raising her head and looking into Monty's eyes. Her lips quivered as she said, "Honey, I see it exactly as you do. I think that the only reason Jim hasn't proposed marriage yet is because he isn't financially able to take on a wife. But when he works out buying his own farm and has it producing a reasonable income, he will ask your sister to marry him."

Monty nodded. "You're right, Mom. Jim is just that kind of man. He would want to know that he was able to provide for Alyssa before he asked her to marry him. But I sure don't want to see anything happen between them because of Dad's obsession with wanting her to marry some rich guy."

"Me, either. The only thing we can do is pray about the situation, Monty, and let the Lord work it out. Contrary to your father's opinion, I believe that Jim would make an excellent husband for your sister, even if he remains a farmer."

"I do, too, Mom. Jim has real character, which some rich guy Dad would want her to marry might not have. He's also a dedicated Christian. That kind is hard to come by, too. I will most certainly be praying that the Lord will work it out so that those two can marry and have Dad's blessing at the same time."

Tears filled Kathleen's eyes. "We'll both be praying that way, son."

On Monday morning, Jim and his father were up on the roof of the barn in a flood of golden September sunshine, nailing some new shingles on worn spots in preparation for the winter snows. When the last shingle had been nailed in place, they both sat down on the slanted roof to take a breath.

Birds twittered in a nearby cottonwood tree as Newt said, "Jim, I've noticed that you and Alyssa seem to be getting closer as time by goes by."

Jim gave him a crooked grin. "You've observed that, eh?"

"Mm-hmm. And, son, I want to tell you that I really like that girl."

"I'm glad."

Newt looked him straight in the eye. "It's not just friendship. You're in love with her, aren't you?"

Jim's face flushed slightly. "When she and I went on that date last Thursday evening and we sat on the bank of the Crow River in the moonlight, I told her that I was in love with her. And you know what?"

Newt's features brightened. "What?"

"She told me that she's in love with me, too!"

"Great! Your mother and I have been talking about it, and we decided that it was a mutual thing. Whenever you and Alyssa are together, it's obvious that you are in love with each other. I'm just glad to hear you say it. Your mother and I both agree that you and Alyssa make a terrific couple. We would love to see you marry someday. We'd just love to have her for our daughter-in-law."

Jim smiled. "I'd love for you to have her for your daughter-in-law!"

Newt laughed and then asked, "How do her parents feel toward you? Are they glad to see you and Alyssa dating?"

"Well, Dad, her mother is. And I know that Monty is. But…but Frank—"

"Frank isn't glad about it?"

Newt listened intently as Jim told him about Frank McGuire's attitude toward him after his date with Alyssa and of her explanation of it just before he left the McGuire house.

"I don't understand, son," Newt said. "Frank has had almost twenty years to accustom himself to the fact that when his little girl grew up she would get married. It's only natural."

Jim pulled at an ear. "I know that Alyssa wouldn't lie to me. I'm sure she thinks that the reason she gave for the way her father treated me is exactly as she sees it. But I really think that maybe Mr. McGuire wants Alyssa to marry a man on her level of the social scale."

Newt nodded. "That would make sense, son. I know that wealthy people often oppose their sons and daughters marrying below their social level."

"Dad, I want to marry that wonderful girl one day. But I don't want my marrying her to cause a problem between Alyssa and her father."

"Of course not."

"Which brings up an important subject. I think it's time for me to get a good job and make enough money to buy my own farm. Then I can work toward providing well enough for Alyssa that her father will approve of her marrying me. With the government about to dig gold out of the Black Hills in order to get the country out of this depression, prices on farm products will go up. And if I work hard enough at it, I can do well. I know I can."

"I don't doubt that for a minute, son. Let's you and me talk about all this with your mother at lunch so that she'll understand what's going on."

"I'd like to propose to Alyssa soon," Jim said, "but that'll have to wait until I can prove myself financially so that there will be no problem in Frank McGuire's mind with his daughter's marrying me."

"Well, if you're right that the real reason that Frank doesn't approve of you courting his daughter is that you're not rich, you've got a big job proving yourself worthy of her in his mind. Even if you own your own farm and make a decent living, you still won't be what he considers wealthy."

Jim rubbed his chin. "But if he sees me prospering at least to a degree, it might be enough to change his mind about me."

"Can't fault you for trying, Jim. I hope it works."

During lunch, Jim explained to his mother what he had told his father while they were on the roof of the barn.

Sarah smiled across the table at her son. "Jimmy boy, I admire you for loving Alyssa so much that you're willing to do whatever it takes to make her your bride and stay in her father's good graces. We'd love to have that sweet girl for our daughter-in-law."

"That makes me so happy, Mom," Jim said. "She truly is a wonderful girl, and no matter what I have to do in order to marry her without causing a problem between her and her father, I will do it."

Sarah sighed. "You are such a good boy. Now, tell me…what kind of job are you hoping to get in order to make enough money so that you can qualify for a loan to buy a farm?"

"I don't know yet, Mom. I'm going to start looking at what might be available in Cheyenne. I really don't want to have to go elsewhere, like Denver or Colorado Springs. And I certainly don't want to be away from Alyssa…or from you two, either. I want to stay right here so that even though I'm working a job, I can continue to help Dad out on the farm as much as possible. I can't go off and leave my parents. Yes, it's important to get things rolling so that I'll be in a position to provide well for Alyssa and so that I can ask her to marry me. I'm seeking the Lord's guidance in it all."

As Jim was speaking, he ran his gaze between his mother and father and saw understanding on their faces.

Newt broke into a wide smile. "You know, son, I'm not so ancient and decrepit that I can't take care of this farm by myself. If the job you find takes up all your time, that'll be all right. Of course, I'll miss not having you by my side, and I'll miss your help, but your mom and I will make it all right."

"Jimmy boy, you have your own life to live," Sarah said, "and we sure don't want to stand in your way. We want that sweet Alyssa Rose to be our daughter-in-law."

Jim's eyes misted. "The Lord has blessed me with the best parents in the whole world."

Newt and Sarah exchanged glances and smiled at each other.

"I mean it. All my life, you two have always been there for me. It means more than I could ever tell you."

Sarah reached across the table and patted Jim's hand. "We always want what's best for you, son, but more importantly, so does the Lord."

Jim blinked at the mist in his eyes. "I know He does. Please pray for Alyssa and me, won't you?"

Sarah was now holding the hand that she had patted a moment before. "Your dad and I will be praying about it every day, sweet boy. Let's just trust Him and do as the Bible says and wait upon the Lord."

Jim smiled and gave his mother's hand a gentle squeeze.

That evening at six o'clock sharp, Jim knocked on the door of the McGuire house and was greeted by Alyssa. Her parents were both standing in the hallway, just outside the parlor door, and spoke to him in a friendly manner.

During the meal at Callie's Cottage Restaurant, Jim and Alyssa chatted happily, enjoying each other's company. Alyssa never let on about what her father expected. She was warm toward Jim and knew that she was falling deeper and deeper in love with him. In her heart she was asking the Lord to work the situation out in His own wonderful way. Her deepest desire was to become Mrs. Jim Bannon.

Later, when they took their moonlight ride to the bank of the Crow River, they sat together on the old fallen tree, held hands, and shared words of love. After a sweet kiss, Jim helped her back into the wagon and drove her home.

Once again Alyssa stood on the porch as Jim drove away, and she watched him until the darkness swallowed up wagon, team, and driver.

As time passed, Jim and Alyssa had dates at least once a week and sat together in the church services on Sunday morning and evening and on Wednesday evenings.

With only his parents aware of it, Jim earnestly looked for a well-paying job but could find nothing that would pay what he knew he would need in order to make a down payment on a farm anytime soon.

On Wednesday morning, September 30, Jim walked out of Cheyenne's hardware store and gun shop. The proprietor had told Jim that he wished he could hire him, but there was just no place for him.

Jim felt dejected as he left the hardware store, but as he swung into the saddle, he said, "Lord, please forgive me for my lack of faith. I know that You have a plan in all of this. You have given Alyssa and me a powerful love for each other, and I know that You're going to work this out in Your own way and in Your own time. Just lead me as I seek to buy my own farm."

Jim's next stop before heading for home was the Bank of Wyoming. His father had sent him with a deposit from the sale of a stack of hay, purchased by a neighboring dairy farmer. He reminded himself to pick up the day's edition of the *Cheyenne Sentinel* to take home. He would do that after leaving the bank.

As he rode along Main Street, Jim spoke to people he knew as he headed toward the bank. He hauled up at the hitch rail in front of the bank and dismounted.

When he entered the bank and headed toward the tellers' cages, he saw Monty McGuire sitting at his desk. A man was just walking away from the desk, and Monty spotted Jim. He waved and called out, "Hey, Jim, come on over as soon as you make your deposit."

Jim nodded and waved back.

A few minutes later, Monty looked up from his desk and smiled as Jim passed through the nearest gate and headed toward him. He rose to his feet when Jim drew up and said, "Good to see you, pal. Have you seen today's edition of the *Sentinel*?"

Jim noticed a copy of the newspaper lying open on Monty's desk. "No. I was going to buy one before I headed for home. Something special in today's edition?"

"Oh, yes! Sit down and let me tell you about it."

"You have time?"

"Sure. Sit down."

Jim eased onto one of the two chairs in front of the desk. "Okay, I'm all ears. This doesn't happen to be about the Black Hills, does it?"

"Sure does. It's official now. Fort Lookout has been established in the northern part of the Black Hills." He picked up the newspaper and turned the front page toward Jim. "Look at this."

Jim read the bold headlines:

U.S. ARMY FULLY INSTALLED IN FORBIDDEN HILLS

"Tell me more."

"Well, the article says that all four hundred cavalrymen and two hundred infantrymen are in the fort now, equipped with their regular firearms as well as a large number of Gatling guns. Their commander is Colonel Martin Lowry, who proved himself as a combat leader in the Union Army during the Civil War."

"Sounds like they're in business," Jim said.

"The soldiers are living in tents while the army corps of engineers builds the fort. The article also says that government prospectors are in the Black Hills, and already they're finding large deposits of gold."

Jim's eyes brightened. "Really?"

"Really. And President Grant is warning any prospective gold seekers to wait until the Indians are convinced that they must accept what's happening and that they are not to cause trouble. He says that there have been several incidents already where Sioux warriors have threatened the lives of railroad workers and government miners. The president insists that no private citizens should enter the Black Hills to dig for gold until he says it's safe to do so."

Jim grinned. "From the sound of it, I think that day will come in the near future, though, don't you?"

"I sure do," Monty replied. "I sure do."

On Tuesday, November 3, the country's newspapers—including the *Cheyenne Sentinel*—reported that Fort Lookout's buildings were finished, complete with housing for enlisted men and officers, office space for the commandant, a stable, and a stockade with guard towers.

President Ulysses S. Grant was quoted as saying that some private gold seekers had tried to enter the Black Hills in spite of his warnings to wait for his announcement that it was safe to do so. Some had been turned away by the army, but a few had slipped past the soldiers' notice and had been killed by unidentified Sioux warriors. The president solemnly warned again that no one was to attempt entering the Black Hills until permission came from him. He added that he expected to grant that permission possibly by next spring.

Jim Bannon had not yet found a good-paying job in Cheyenne. He had picked up some part-time work, but he could not bring himself to leave the Cheyenne area to find a full-time job.

On Wednesday, November 11, Jim arrived home at the farm with that day's issue of the *Cheyenne Sentinel*. He found his parents in the parlor and stood over them with the newspaper in his hand.

"Well, Mom, Dad, President Grant is now saying that if all goes well, he will authorize the military forces at Fort Lookout to allow private citizens to enter the Black Hills as gold prospectors in early March."

"I figured that President Grant would get around to it pretty soon," Newt said, "since there hasn't been any sign of trouble from Chief Red Cloud and his warriors lately."

"Now, Mom, Dad, you know that I'm eager to propose to Alyssa, but I've been unable to find a job so I can make that down payment on a farm of my own."

Both parents nodded, a look of expectancy in their eyes.

"I've been praying about this, though I've said nothing to you, Alyssa, or anyone else. I'm convinced that the Lord is leading me to go to the Black Hills as soon as President Grant gives the okay. I will work hard, and with the Lord's help I'll become wealthy enough to marry Alyssa with her father's blessing."

Newt rose from his chair. "Well, son, maybe this *is* the Lord's way of providing you with enough money to satisfy Frank and have him put his blessing on the marriage."

"I don't like the thought of you being gone from us, Jimmy boy," said Sarah, also rising to her feet, "but I know that your dad is right. It could be the quickest way to come up with a fortune."

"Well, even if what gold I find can be termed a fortune, Mom, I still want to be a farmer. It's in my blood. But with enough gold I can buy a farm outright and not have mortgage payments."

"That would be great, son," Newt said.

Jim looked at both parents. "Since it looks like the president will open up the Black Hills to private citizens in March, do you think that I should wait till February to tell Alyssa my plan?"

Sarah and Newt looked at each other; then Sarah set her eyes on Jim. "I think that you should tell her now so she'll know why you haven't proposed marriage. I know how we women think. Alyssa is no doubt wondering why you haven't yet asked her to marry you."

Newt nodded. "I'm not a woman, Jim, but I know that your mother is right. Alyssa has to be wondering why you haven't brought up the subject of marriage by now. And I'm sure that it will help her to know that you're willing to go to the Black Hills and dig for gold in order to have her father's blessing on your marriage. Most young men would say that if a young woman loves him enough to marry him, she should marry him in spite of what her father says, even if her father disowns her and never speaks to her again."

"Dad, I love Alyssa too much to ever put that kind of pressure on her. She and I both want to do this God's way, and asking her to comply with an ultimatum like that is not God's way."

"You're right, Jimmy boy," Sarah said. "I so much appreciate your sweet attitude about that. It certainly would not be a good way to start a marriage. Family relationships are far too important to let bad feelings get in the way."

Newt laid a hand on his son's shoulder. "You have been gallant in this situation, and Alyssa will appreciate the attitude that you've had all this time about her father's feelings when she learns your plan."

"I'm sure she will, Dad," Jim said. "When we're at church tonight, I'll ask her to go out to dinner with me tomorrow night, and I'll explain the whole thing to her then."

SEVENTEEN

On Thursday evening the cold air hugged the hard November night, low to the ground, and filled it with frost. As Jim Bannon and Alyssa Rose McGuire rode together in the farm wagon from the McGuire home toward Cheyenne's business district, they saw smoke rising from hundreds of chimneys. A full moon lit the smoke plumes as a stiff breeze caused the plumes to coalesce into broad bands, coursing across the rolling plains of southeastern Wyoming.

Clad in one of her favorite fur coats, Alyssa sat close to Jim, holding onto his arm. "I'm glad we're going to Callie's Cottage again. I just love the food and the atmosphere."

Jim looked at her in the silver light of the moon and smiled. "I'm glad that you chose Callie's again when I gave you your choice of eating places. It's my favorite, too, especially since we've gotten to know Callie so well."

"She is a nice lady."

Soon Jim swung the wagon up to the hitch rail as close to the restaurant's door as possible. He hopped out, rounded the back side of the wagon, and helped Alyssa down. When her feet touched the ground, Jim looked around to see if anyone was watching them. Since no one was, he bent down, planted a tender kiss on her lips, and then offered her his arm as they crossed the boardwalk and entered the restaurant.

Callie Carson, a widow in her mid-fifties, happened to be standing with the cashier at the counter. Jim and Alyssa both spoke to the restaurant owner and the cashier before threading their way among the tables. When they found an empty table, Jim took Alyssa's coat, hung it on a nearby wall peg, and seated her.

Jim took off his own coat and hat, hung them up, and looked down at Alyssa. "Excuse me for a moment. I'll be right back. If a waitress comes while I'm gone, order me the chicken and dumplings and coffee, okay?"

"All right."

Alyssa watched Jim as he made his way to the counter.

When Jim drew up to the counter, he smiled at the owner and said, "Callie, could I talk to you privately for a moment?"

"Of course." She led Jim to a spot near the kitchen door and said, "What is it, Jim?"

"I need a favor."

"Name it."

"Could I borrow your office after Alyssa and I have our meal so that I can talk to her in private? It's too cold outside to talk to her in the wagon."

"Why, of course. If I happen to be in there when you're ready to use it, just tap on the door. If I'm not in the office, I'll either be in the kitchen or out here where you can see me. Either way, just whistle, and the office is yours."

"Thanks, Callie. I appreciate it very much."

When Jim returned to the table, Alyssa was curious about his conversation with the restaurant owner but did not ask any questions. A waitress delivered their food shortly thereafter, and after they prayed over the food, they chatted while they enjoyed the meal.

During the meal, Alyssa could tell that Jim was excited about something, but she decided to see if he would tell her what it was first before asking any questions.

After they finished their dessert of apple pie, Jim looked at Alyssa across the table and said, "I need to have a private conversation with you, sweetheart. Callie has given permission for us to talk in her office."

Alyssa grinned. "Oh, so that's what you were talking to her about."

Callie was once again at the counter. Jim looked at her, and as she saw him helping Alyssa from her chair, she smiled, nodded, and pointed toward the office at the rear of the building.

Jim carried Alyssa's fur coat and scarf, as well as his own hat and coat, as they made their way toward the office, speaking to people they knew at some of the tables along the way.

They entered the office, and Jim closed the door. There was a sofa on one side of the office, opposite Callie's desk. Jim hung their wraps and his hat on the clothes tree that stood nearby and said, "Sit down here on the sofa, sweetheart."

Alyssa sat down on the sofa, and she was surprised to see Jim kneel in front of her. He took both of her hands in his and said, "I won't beat around the bush, sweetheart. I just want to ask you a very important question."

Alyssa smiled. "All right."

"Will you marry me?"

Her face beamed as she said quickly, "Yes, I will!"

After a tight embrace and a sweet kiss, Jim sat down beside her, took hold of her hand, and said, "Do you think that your father will give us his blessing?"

Alyssa cleared her throat gently and explained her father's demand that she remain "just friends" with Jim so that she would be free when that right rich, young man came along wanting to marry her.

Jim nodded slowly. "I see. Let me ask you something. If *I*

became rich, do you think that your father would approve of our marriage?"

"Oh, I know he would! He really likes you. It's just that in his mind you don't qualify to be my husband and his son-in-law because you're not on the McGuires' social level. But my mother would gladly have you for her son-in-law right now."

Jim grinned. "I figured that she would. She's so sweet."

Alyssa squeezed Jim's hand. "Darling, listen to me now."

"Yes?"

"In spite of the fact that you are not rich, I love you with all of my heart, and I will marry you even if Papa turns against me. It won't be easy, of course, because he's so dear to me, but I cannot allow him to keep me from marrying the man I love."

He pulled her close and kissed her cheek. "You're so wonderful."

Tears now misted Alyssa's soft green eyes. "Jim, I have prayed ever since Papa made this 'just friends' demand of me that the Lord would work it out so that when you did ask me to marry you, we could marry without causing a problem with him. But if it comes to that, I will marry you anyhow."

"Alyssa, I deeply appreciate your willingness to marry me just as I am, but I don't want to ever come between you and your father. I want and need his blessing on our marriage. Hopefully when we marry the Lord will give us children. What a sad thing it would be if our children couldn't have a good relationship with their maternal grandparents! I love you for freely giving me your heart, and I will cherish and keep it in sacred trust."

Now the tears were streaming down Alyssa's cheeks. "There will never be anyone for me but you, darling. Thank you for your attitude toward Papa and your desire to have everything just right for me and our children. I just know that the Lord is going to work it all out so that Papa will accept you."

Jim adjusted himself so that he could look her in the eye. "I'm so glad that you're willing to marry me, even if the Lord chooses not to make it so that your father will accept me…but I want to tell you that the Lord indeed *is* working it out."

Alyssa wiped tears from her cheeks and batted her eyelids. "What do you mean?"

"Well, I have a plan that I have no doubt will make me wealthy enough that Mr. Frank McGuire will approve of my marrying his daughter."

She looked at him quizzically. "Really?"

"Yes."

"Tell me."

"I'm going to go to the Black Hills in Dakota Territory when President Grant opens them up next spring for any private citizens to go in and dig for gold. You're aware of all that's going on about this, aren't you?"

"Yes. Papa and Monty have been talking about it a lot."

"I'm sure that with some hard work on my part, and with the Lord's help, I can come up with enough gold to buy a farm outright, provide well for you, and be considered wealthy, even in the eyes of your father. There won't have to be a wedge between him and me."

More tears filled Alyssa's eyes and streamed down her cheeks. "Oh, Jim, that's so sweet of you."

Jim wrapped an arm around her, wiped the tears from her cheeks, kissed her tenderly, and said, "I appreciate your being willing to marry me no matter what. It means more than I can tell you. We're going to have a wonderful life together."

Alyssa sniffed. "Yes, we are."

"And I want you to know that my parents are in full agreement with my plan to go to the Black Hills. They very much want you to be their daughter-in-law."

She sniffed again and rubbed more tears from her eyes. "Bless their hearts. I'm so glad."

Jim smiled. "Then we'll go on right now as 'friends,' even though we are secretly engaged."

"Yes."

"When I come back from the Black Hills, I'll buy you an engagement ring. Then we'll be officially engaged."

"Sounds good to me."

"I'll talk to your father just before I head for the Black Hills next spring, explain my goal, and ask him whether, if I find enough gold, I will have his blessing to marry you."

Alyssa smiled. "I know what he will say."

"Good." Jim took hold of both her hands. "Sweetheart, in Genesis chapter twenty-nine, we learn that Jacob loved Rachel so much that he agreed to work for her father Laban for seven years so that she could be his wife. Do you remember that when he had served the agreed time, the Bible says that those seven years seemed to Jacob but a few days because of the love he had for Rachel?"

She smiled. "Yes, I remember."

"Well, I believe that I can mine out enough gold to be considered wealthy in a much shorter time than seven years, but if it took that long so that I could marry you without a black cloud hanging over us, I would still do it. I love you more than mere words could ever tell."

Alyssa choked back the tears and said, "Oh, Jim darling, I love you so much!"

He folded her in his arms. "I love you so much, too."

After another kiss, Jim said, "Let's talk to the Lord together."

They bowed their heads, and Jim led in prayer, thanking the Lord for bringing them together and filling their hearts full of love for each other. He then asked the Lord to bless his efforts in the Black Hills so that everything could work out for them.

Time passed with Jim and Alyssa dating regularly twice a week, as well as sitting together in the church services.

In late December, Alyssa turned twenty, and Jim gave her a

pretty silver bracelet, telling her that he wished it could be an engagement ring. She thanked him, saying that day would come, too.

In February 1875, Jim turned twenty-three, and on Tuesday, March 2, the newspapers carried the story that government miners had dug out enough gold from the Black Hills to make the depression a thing of the past. The nation's economy was now on the grow.

On Thursday evening, March 4, when Jim and Alyssa were sitting at a table in Callie's Cottage Restaurant waiting for their meal, Jim took a copy of the day's issue of the *Cheyenne Sentinel* from his coat and said, "Sweetheart, let me show you President Grant's message to the country about the Black Hills."

Alyssa smiled. "I think that you're about to show me that the president is opening up the Black Hills to private citizens of this country to go in there and dig for gold."

"You're so right!" Jim opened the paper to page three and laid it before her. "Look right there," he said, placing his finger on the article.

Alyssa read it and then looked up at the man she loved. "It says that the army will allow citizens of the United States and its Territories to come in starting the first of April."

"As soon as I can get everything ready for the 170-mile trip from Cheyenne to the south entrance of the Black Hills, I'll figure out the day for my departure so that I can arrive there on April first."

Alyssa looked into his eyes. "I'll miss you terribly, but the result will be worth it."

"My thought exactly," he said, flipping to another page in the newspaper. "Let me read another article to you; it was written by Lieutenant Colonel George Armstrong Custer. He's the one who led the army's reconnaissance expedition into the Black Hills last summer. Custer says, 'I was extremely impressed by the Black Hills in Dakota Territory. The climate is healthful and temperate; the water in the streams is pure; and the mountains are covered heavily with pine timber. It is my solid belief that gold can be mined there with great profit, even though the government miners extracted a great deal of gold to pay off the nation's debts. There is plenty more. My best wishes go with the men who go in there to make their fortunes.'"

Alyssa smiled. "Well, darling, it sure sounds good."

"It does, doesn't it? I'll begin making ready right away."

In the days that followed, Jim prepared for the journey to the Black Hills by purchasing from a neighboring farmer a wagon that was in good condition. He bought a team of horses from one of Cheyenne's stables, as well as picks and shovels and other tools, along with a canvas tent, from the hardware store.

On Tuesday, March 9, when he picked up Alyssa at her home for their dinner date, he asked Frank McGuire if he could talk to him in the presence of Mrs. McGuire and Monty when they returned later in the evening. Frank granted his request.

It was almost nine o'clock when Jim and Alyssa came through the door of the house. Kathleen was there to greet them with a wide smile. "Did you have a nice dinner?"

"Sure did, Mama," Alyssa said. "We went to the Sundance Café. It was *almost* as good as Callie's."

Kathleen nodded. "Well, your papa and your little brother are in the parlor."

Kathleen moved ahead of the young couple, and when they entered the parlor both Frank and Monty stood and greeted them. Everyone sat down, and Frank said, "All right, Jim. What was it you wanted to talk to me about?"

"I know, sir, that you are fully aware that the government will soon allow private citizens to enter the Black Hills and dig for gold."

Frank nodded.

Jim then explained his plan to become wealthy by mining gold in the Black Hills.

Monty was the first to speak when Jim finished. "Hey, that's great! I'm sure that you'll do well."

Frank set steady eyes on Jim. "I hope you do well. Is there some particular reason you wanted to explain this to me and my family?"

Jim met his gaze. "Yes, sir. I am very much in love with Alyssa, Mr. McGuire, and I want to marry her. I am asking whether, if I do make it good mining gold and become reasonably wealthy, I will have your blessing to marry Alyssa."

Before Frank could reply, Alyssa spoke up. "Papa, you need to know that I love Jim very, very much. More than anything in this world, I want to become his wife."

Frank's steady gaze softened as he looked at Jim. "I want you to know, young man, that I like you very much. I have already seen in Alyssa's eyes, time and time again, that she is in love with you. I don't doubt for an instant that you love Alyssa as you say. If you become wealthy mining gold…you most certainly will have my blessing to marry Alyssa."

Alyssa dashed to her father and embraced him. "Thank you, Papa! Thank you!"

Jim stood up, and when Alyssa drew back from her father, he offered his hand. When Frank stood up and gripped the hand, Jim said, "Thank you, sir! Thank you!"

On Wednesday evening after the church service, Jim and Alyssa asked Pastor Ballert if they could talk to him in his office. This was happily granted, and when they sat down and the young couple explained to him what was happening in their lives, the preacher told Jim that he was wondering when Jim was going to propose to Alyssa.

He then commended Jim for being willing to delay marrying her in order to keep peace in the family. He added that he and Tammy would be praying for Jim's success in the Black Hills.

Jim thanked him and then said, "It will take me about ten days to make it from Cheyenne to the south entrance of the Black Hills. I have learned that the army frequently patrols the area and that, as with all the other gold seekers, when I enter the Black Hills I will have to be escorted to Fort Lookout and make application with the government official in charge of assigning gold claims. I plan to leave from Cheyenne early on Tuesday morning, March 23, Pastor. That should get me there on April 1."

Pastor Ballert assured him that Jim would be in his and Tammy's prayers. He then prayed with Jim and Alyssa, asking God to make everything work out so that the young couple could marry in the not-too-distant future.

On Monday evening, March 22, Jim took Alyssa to dinner at their favorite restaurant. After dinner he drove her directly home since she and her family were going to be up extra early in order to see him off.

When he walked her to the door, he held her in his arms and said, "Since I won't be able to kiss you in the morning with all those people around, I'm going to kiss you good right now."

After kissing her, Jim held her in his arms, noting the sweet scent of her hair. "Sweetheart, I'm going to work extra hard so I can find the gold that I need as quickly as possible. I'm going to miss you so much. Being apart from you is going to be almost unbearable."

"I know, darling," she said softly, looking up into his face by the light of the porch lantern. "It will be the same for me, too. But we know that God's grace is sufficient, and He will make a way through this for both of us."

"Yes, He will."

"I'll be right here waiting for you." She raised up on her tip-toes and gave him another kiss.

When she eased back, Jim looked down into her eyes. "I'll see you at the bank in the morning, but let me say it here and now: I'll be back as soon as I possibly can."

Reluctantly, he stepped off the porch and climbed into the wagon.

"I love you," he said, looking back over his shoulder.

"And I love you," Alyssa said softly.

She stood on the porch in the chilly March air and watched the man she loved disappear into the night. "Go with God, my love. Go with God."

Tuesday morning, March 23, came with a clear sky. The sun painted the dawn horizon a vermilion hue and then lifted its head over the edge of the earth to send its bright beams across the rolling hills of the prairie around Cheyenne.

Jim's parents had come with their son in their own wagon and found the McGuire family already in front of the Bank of Wyoming, along with Pastor and Mrs. Ballert and several church members. They also found three other young farmers from the Cheyenne area who planned to leave for the Black Hills. Jim knew them well and was glad that they would be traveling to the Black Hills together.

Two of them, Hal and Bob Parris, were brothers. They would be traveling together in the same wagon. Floyd Kitchin, the other young farmer, was traveling in his wagon alone.

Jim hugged his parents, telling them good-bye; then he bid Frank, Kathleen, and Monty McGuire good-bye. Next, Jim told Pastor and Mrs. Ballert, as well as the church members, good-bye, thanking them all for coming to see him off.

He then went to Alyssa, took hold of both her hands, and said in a whisper, "I'm sure glad we had our privacy last night on your porch. I wish I could kiss you good-bye again, but you understand."

"Of course," she whispered.

Jim and Alyssa embraced, whispering that they loved each other. Then Jim wheeled around and climbed onto the driver's seat of his wagon.

As the four wagons pulled out, heading north on Main Street, Alyssa was blinking at the tears that filled her eyes. Her mother slipped up beside her, and Sarah Bannon slipped up on the other side. Each put an arm around Alyssa, and together they assured her that the Lord would take care of Jim.

When the wagons were almost out of town, Jim stood up in the box and waved to the crowd. They all waved back.

Monty McGuire then stepped up to Alyssa and said, "Jim will be back with his fortune and ready to meet you at the altar before you know it."

Alyssa smiled. "Thank you for the encouragement, Monty."

Newt Bannon moved up to Alyssa, smiled, and said, "I can hardly wait till the day you become my daughter-in-law."

Alyssa wiped away tears. "Me, too."

She was especially pleased when her father hugged her and said, "I'll be so proud when Jim comes home a rich man and marries you, sweetheart."

EIGHTEEN

On Wednesday evening, March 31, Jim Bannon and his three friends were camped on Wyoming's Beaver River, some twenty miles south of the entrance to the Black Hills. They were eating at their campfire as the melancholy prairie twilight rapidly succeeded the sunset.

To Jim, the twilight accentuated the loneliness of the winding river in the gathering shadows as his thoughts ran to the beautiful girl he loved.

Twenty-six-year-old Floyd Kitchin interrupted Jim's reverie as he swallowed a mouthful of fried jackrabbit and said, "I'll tell you, Jim, I'm sure glad that you're such a good shot with that rifle of yours. All three of us missed every shot we fired when those rabbits sprang out of that gulch and sprinted away when they saw us. Yet you bagged two of them."

Bob Parris, who at thirty-one was four years older than his brother, chuckled and cocked his head sideways, looking at Jim over the crackling flames. "Where'd you learn to shoot like that, Jim?"

"My dad taught me. We used to go rabbit and squirrel hunting a lot when I was in my teens."

"Well, you're sure a good shot with that there Winchester .44,

Jim," put in Hal Parris. "I'm glad that we haven't run into any Indians since we left Cheyenne, but if we had, I sure would've felt safer with you along."

"I'm so glad that Hal and Bob and I decided to make this trip at the same time you did," Floyd said. "It's been good to get to know you better, but the best thing was you talking to us about being saved on that very first night of this trip when we sat around the fire."

"It took us a few days to see the light," Bob said, "but I'm sure glad we did. What a relief to know that I'm going to heaven when I leave this world. It's so wonderful to know the Lord Jesus as my Saviour."

"I'd heard about Jesus dying on the cross and coming out of the grave many times in my life," Hal said, "but it never really came home to my heart till you opened your Bible and explained it so clearly."

"And who would've believed that you could buy Bibles in that little prairie town of Redbird?" Floyd said.

Jim swallowed the last of his coffee and said, "Well, I'm sure glad they had them in stock. You boys can grow in your Christian life now that you have Bibles to read and study. I would've let you use mine, but it's best to have your own."

"Well, boys, let's get the dishes washed so we can have our little Bible study with Jim and then hit the sack," Bob said.

When the dishes had been washed in the river and the horses fed and watered, more wood was tossed on the fire. The three new Christians sat down together beside the fire so they could take advantage of its light, and Jim sat down facing them.

He had them alternately read aloud verses from the twenty-third chapter of Luke and pointed out some truths about the crucifixion of the Lord Jesus. Happy to have learned more about their Saviour, Bob, Hal, and Floyd thanked Jim for teaching them and stood up.

Hal stretched his arms, yawned, and said, "Well, boys, it's bed-time."

Jim stirred the burning embers with a stick and said, "I'm going to sit here by the fire for a while. You boys get yourselves a good night's sleep. By my calculations we should be at the south entrance of the Black Hills by midafternoon tomorrow."

Floyd sighed. "Sounds good to me. We'll be digging for gold before we know it!"

Soon Jim's friends were in their bedrolls and drifting off to sleep.

Jim sat by the fire, and the lonely prairie night set in with its silence. A face was haunting him as he stared into the smoldering fragments of the dying campfire. The beautiful face of Alyssa Rose McGuire seemed to hover in the shadows that hung over the flickering light.

Jim's mind was filled with memories of treasured moments with Alyssa as a soft breeze flurried the paling embers and blew sparks and thin smoke into the enshrouding darkness.

Soon the fire died out, and Jim slipped into his own bedroll, his heart aching for Alyssa.

It was coming up on three o'clock the next afternoon when the three wagons—moving abreast of each other—topped a gentle rise and the four men beheld the south entrance to the Black Hills. A large number of wagons of every description were gathered there, and several men in army uniforms were moving about them.

"Well, look at that, boys!" Floyd Kitchin said. "The gold rush is on for sure!"

"Let's join 'em!" Hal Parris said.

When the men from Cheyenne drew up, Jim Bannon noted that many of the wagons were carrying women and children. Three soldiers walked up to them, welcoming them, and told them that at the moment there were almost five hundred gold seekers in the wagons. They were just about to escort them to Fort Lookout.

Two soldiers mounted up and led the wagons single file deeper into the timber. The Bannon, Kitchin, and Parris wagons brought up the rear.

It was nearing four o'clock on that first day of April 1875 when the wagons made a circle just outside the main gate of the fort and the soldiers led everyone inside the fort, which was surrounded by a stockade of wooden posts some ten feet high. Each of Fort Lookout's four corners had a guard tower, and each tower was equipped with two Gatling guns.

The newcomers also noted that a large number of army wagons inside the fort carried the deadly guns.

With more soldiers coming from other parts of the fort, the crowd was led to an open area in front of the commandant's office, and when the fort's leader came out the door one of the officers ran his gaze over the crowd and said loudly, "Folks, this is our commandant, Colonel Martin Lowry."

The colonel was a stalwart, straight-backed man of fifty-five with salt-and-pepper hair and a mustache to match. He smiled and said, "Welcome to Fort Lookout. I understand that this crowd has come from many parts of the country. I hope you all do well in your search for gold."

The colonel then called for the soldiers to distribute printed material among the men of the crowd. As this was being done, Lowry explained to the gold seekers that the pamphlets contained the rules for digging and panning for gold, plus a clear explanation of the legality of their claims. In addition to this, the pamphlets stated that the gold seekers were to report immediately to the soldiers who patrolled the Black Hills if they had any trouble with the Indians.

When every man in the crowd had a pamphlet, Lowry went

over it with them. They learned quickly that claim jumping would be treated as a serious offence.

Once the commandant had covered it all and had answered questions, he introduced the fort's assayer, Wayne Clarkson, who the government had hired to assess the quality of the ore and nuggets that they found. Lowry pointed out Clarkson's office, which was near his own.

At that point the men in the crowd were told to get in line to have their claims assigned by army officers. Everyone learned that no one could ask for claims next to friends or family members with separate claims. They would be assigned claims strictly at the discretion of the officers, who would place them among gold seekers already in the Black Hills.

The soldiers then led the new gold seekers to their claims in the heavily timbered hills. The soldiers drove small signs into the ground, announcing that each claim belonged to the person or persons whose names were inscribed on the signs.

The Parris brothers were co-owners of one claim. They and Jim Bannon and Floyd Kitchin were several miles apart from each other.

Those new gold seekers who had tents pitched them on their claims, while those who had come ready to live in their covered wagons picked a spot on their claims to park them.

The next day the newly arrived miners went to work digging and panning gold from the streams that flowed through the land allotted to them.

As the days passed, more gold seekers arrived in the Black Hills.

One week later, on Thursday, April 8, Jim Bannon drove his wagon to the fort. He noticed that several new gold seekers had arrived and were being addressed by Colonel Lowry while several soldiers stood by.

Jim entered the office of assayer Wayne Clarkson, who was standing over a table with several bottles of chemicals lined up along one side. He was using a cloth to wipe up moisture and dust from an assaying job that he had just done for another miner.

Clarkson looked up, smiled, eyed the two cloth bags in his next client's hand, and said, "Hello. I think I saw you in the crowd that came in a week or so ago, didn't I?"

"Yes, sir. Exactly a week ago. My name's Jim Bannon. I'm a farmer from the Cheyenne, Wyoming, area."

Clarkson dried off his right hand, shook hands with Jim, and looked once again at the sagging cloth bags. "Looks like you've done well in just a week."

"Well, we'll see when you check it out. This bag is from my diggings, and this one is from the stream."

Clarkson had Jim sit down at the table and went to work. When Clarkson had finished, he smiled broadly. "Well, Jim Bannon, you've done well in just a week. Your diggings amount to $337 worth of gold, and what you panned from the stream amounts to $97 worth."

"Wow, that's great!" Jim said. "I hope I can continue to do this good."

Clarkson chuckled. "Keep working. You'll do better yet."

Much encouraged, Jim left the office, climbed into his wagon, and headed back into the forest.

When Jim arrived back at his claim, he saw a covered wagon parked on the claim just north of his. It had been unoccupied, as was the claim site on the south side.

A young man and a young woman were putting up a tent. Jim walked toward them, noting that the sign the soldiers had driven into the ground had the name Luke Farrell inscribed on it.

Drawing up, Jim said, "Hello, I'm—"

"James Bannon," the man said.

"You can just call me Jim, Mr. Luke Farrell."

Both Farrells laughed, and Jim shook hands with Luke and

smiled at the young lady, who said, "I'm Anna Farrell. Luke's better half."

Jim glanced at a smiling Luke and touched his hat brim. "Glad to meet you, ma'am."

Anna looked toward Jim's wagon and team. "Is there a Mrs. Jim Bannon?"

"Ah, no, ma'am. I'm the son of a farmer in the Cheyenne, Wyoming, area, and I'm engaged to a wonderful young lady named Alyssa Rose McGuire. When the Lord blesses me with a sufficient amount of gold so that I can buy my own farm, Alyssa and I will get married and live happily ever after."

Luke's brow furrowed. "You say when the Lord blesses you with a sufficient amount of gold…"

"Yes."

"I like the way you put that. Do you know the Lord?"

Jim's face beamed. "Sure do. Jesus saved me when I was just a young boy. I was brought up in a good Christian home."

Luke and Anna looked at each other and smiled. Luke then explained that he had been the assistant pastor of a church in Omaha, Nebraska, and over the past three years had developed a mission ministry for the church with the Santee Sioux Indians. Many of the Indians had come to a saving knowledge of Jesus Christ in those three years.

Jim's eyes sparkled as he said, "That's wonderful!"

Luke went on to say that his parents belonged to the same church. His father, who was in his mid-fifties, had been a blacksmith in Omaha for many years. However, he had developed a serious heart problem several months ago and was now in a Chicago hospital under the care of a heart specialist from Switzerland.

Luke said that the care his father was getting was very expensive. What savings his parents had built up over the years was now gone. The pastor and the people of the church had done what they could to help pay the medical bills, but it was not enough. The doctor was being tolerant about the unpaid bills but soon would have to be paid.

Luke sighed. "The hospital bill is getting quite large, too, Jim. After much prayer about Dad's situation, Anna and I decided that we would come to the Black Hills and stake a claim. We have come with the church's blessing. Another young preacher has taken over the mission. If I can hit it good digging and panning for gold, I believe that we'll have enough money to cover Dad's doctor and hospital care until he recovers, which the heart specialist tells us is very much possible under his care."

"My mother," Luke said, "is at home in Omaha because she can't afford to stay in a hotel in Chicago."

Jim moved his head back and forth slowly. "Bless her heart. Luke, Anna, I want you to know that I will be praying that you will make a good gold strike and that your father will survive."

On the following Sunday morning, Jim brought his friends Hal and Bob Parris and Floyd Kitchin to his claim site, where they had a Bible study with Luke and Anna Farrell. Luke led the Bible study, and they all enjoyed it.

By the end of his third week in the Black Hills, Jim found that he was doing better in mining the gold every day. The assayer said that Jim now had nearly three thousand dollar's worth of gold. He missed Alyssa, his family, and his best friend, Monty McGuire. He found himself wishing that there was mail service in the Black Hills so that he could write to Alyssa and the others.

On the day that Jim started his fourth week as a gold miner, the soldiers brought two men to the claim site on the south and planted a sign with two names on it: Zack Johansen and Will Johansen.

Jim worked at panning gold in the stream until the soldiers

rode away; then he went to the two men. He learned that Zack had recently turned seventy and that his son, Will, was in his early forties. They explained that they had come to the Black Hills to find gold and make better lives for themselves and their wives, who had stayed in their home town of Jefferson City, Missouri.

Both father and son cursed as they told Jim that they had been poor all of their lives and had come after Black Hills gold to get rich. As Jim returned to panning on the bank of the stream, he asked the Lord to help him be an effective witness to them and to help him lead them to Him.

By late May Jim had accumulated some seventeen thousand dollar's worth of gold, for which he thanked the Lord. But he knew that in the eyes of Frank McGuire it was a long way from being wealthy.

The Farrells had come up with a little more than eight thousand dollars in gold. They were discouraged, but Luke kept digging and panning, determined to pay his father's medical bills, which he knew by then had to be well over fifty thousand dollars.

With Colonel Martin Lowry's permission, Luke Farrell started holding Bible preaching services in the mess hall of the fort on Sundays. Word spread all over the mining areas about the services, but only a small number of the miners and their families attended. However, quite often in the services someone came forward to receive Christ as Saviour.

Both Jim and Luke had established a friendship with Zack and Will Johansen, and though Zack and Will refused to come to the preaching services, Jim and Luke had given them the gospel several times. Father and son had been polite but had shown no interest. Jim especially, since his claim was next to theirs, kept witnessing to them in a kind, tactful way.

❧

One day in the first week of June, Jim and Luke were coming out of the assayer's office with loaded cloth sacks in their hands when Colonel Martin Lowry happened to be walking toward them, heading for his office. When the commandant saw them, he smiled and stopped. "Well, gentlemen, how's the mining going by now?"

"Quite well for both of us, sir," Jim said.

Luke said, "I see that almost every day there are new people coming here to mine gold, sir. How many are in these Black Hills, now?"

"Just over eighteen thousand, plus a good number of wives and children." He paused and then asked, "Have you heard about the new town that's going to be established here?"

"No, we haven't, Colonel," Luke said. "Tell us about it."

Lowry explained that it was going to be officially announced to the miners soon that a number of businessmen from towns in Dakota Territory, Nebraska, and Wyoming had formed a coalition for the purpose of establishing a town. The men of the coalition had come the third week of May and staked off several acres of forest on the edge of Deadwood Gulch on the northwestern side of the Black Hills. They were going to use the timber from the forest acreage to build a town on a large open area on the edge of Deadwood Gulch. They had engaged a large number of carpenters to come and do the work. There would be a general store, and a medical doctor was coming to open an office. There would be at least three cafés, a clothing store, and a couple of saloons.

"That's quite an undertaking, Colonel," Jim said. "I could live without the saloons, though."

Lowry shrugged his shoulders. "Guess there's nothing we can do about them." He paused and then said, "Good news, though. The government will send two United States Mint workers to the town to mint gold coins for all of you miners so you can use the gold as money."

"That *is* good news, sir," Jim said. "I'm sure all the miners and their wives will be very pleased to hear about that."

"Has this coalition declared when they will have these businesses ready to open?" Luke asked.

"I believe that the general store is scheduled to open in about three weeks. With so many carpenters working, they say they'll have the doctor's office and the other businesses all operating by the third week in July."

Luke nodded. "That's pretty fast work."

"They may have to work by lantern light," the colonel said. "Oh, I didn't tell you. Because the town will be situated on the edge of Deadwood Gulch, the coalition is going to call it Deadwood."

Jim chuckled. "Deadwood, eh? Sounds exciting."

"And something else. Deadwood will also have a marshal and a deputy to keep the town safe and quiet."

"What about the Indians, Colonel?" Jim asked. "Do you think that they'll be upset about the town being on their land?"

"Some of them might be. There are certain Sioux warriors who have given some of the miners trouble. It's happened about a dozen times since we first established the fort. They want all whites off their land. I've had to meet with Chief Red Cloud on each of these occasions, and he has been very cooperative. He has taken action against the warriors who have done this and disciplined them, telling them that they will only bring bloodshed and death on themselves if the United States Army has to deal with them. He even reminded them about our Gatling guns, warning them of how they spit death like some unearthly beast."

"Well, sir, I'm glad that Chief Red Cloud is trying to keep peace between his people and the whites," Jim said.

The colonel nodded. "Of course, outside the Black Hills many warriors from other tribes within the Sioux nation are continually attacking farms, ranches, wagon trains, and other travelers in Dakota Territory, as well as in the territories of Montana, Wyoming, and Colorado and the states of Nebraska and Kansas. The army forts are working hard to put down these attacks. Here in Dakota Territory, the forts are working hard to protect white people. Especially Fort Abraham Lincoln. Lieutenant Colonel George Custer and his Seventh Cavalry are taking a real toll on the Indians, killing them in great numbers in battle after battle."

Luke pulled at an ear. "It doesn't seem that these Indian attacks are scaring very many people off, Colonel. They just keep coming."

"That's right. Because newspapers across the country carry articles daily about the gold strike here, the gold fever is too powerful to keep them from coming to make their fortunes. Most of them are traveling in wagon trains so as to be better prepared and able to fight off the Indians."

"Speaking of gold fever, sir," Jim said, "Luke and I had better get back to our claim sites. Thanks for letting us know about the new town."

Luke chuckled. "Yeah. *Deadwood.* Some name for a town!"

NINETEEN

On Wednesday, June 23, at Merrillville, Indiana, twenty-five-year-old Seth Hamilton stepped out of his hardware store at closing time with his two clerks, Eddie Anderson and Jake Terrell, after a busy day. Eddie and Jake, who were both in their early forties, had been employed at the store by Seth's father for nearly twenty years. Both of Seth's parents had died of different diseases some six months apart in 1871, leaving the store to him.

Seth had a folded copy of the day's issue of the *Merrillville Dispatch* in his hand.

Jake said, "Well, boss, when you tell Mattie about the article in the paper, she'll be as ready as you are to head for the Black Hills."

Seth grinned. "I'm sure she will. I really appreciate you two being willing to run the store for me while we're gone."

"You won't be gone too awful long, boss," Eddie said. "Knowing you, I'm sure that you'll come up with a fortune in a short time."

"I hope you're right. Well, see you gentlemen in the morning."

It was four blocks from the hardware store to the Hamilton home in the residential section. Walking at a rapid pace as he thought about going to the Black Hills to make a fortune, Seth's heart pounded. After he had done it they would come back to Merrillville. He would keep the hardware store, but things would be different. He was going to buy property just outside of town and have a mansion built for himself and his family. They would know what it was like to really be rich.

When Seth walked into the yard and eyed the house that he and Mattie had inherited from his parents, he could already smell the wonderful cooking aromas coming through the open doors and windows. He smiled when he glanced at his wife's wide variety of colorful flowers that surrounded the front porch. He loved the sweet fragrance that they lent to the already aromatic air.

He bounded up the steps, opened the screen door, and called out, "Hello! Papa's home!"

Seth heard a scurrying of feet on the polished wooden floor of the hallway that led to the rear of the house as his family came from the kitchen. Mattie was carrying their youngest daughter, Josie, who was eighteen months old. She had a head start on the other two children and rushed into Seth's arms. Seth kissed both Mattie and Josie and then Mattie stepped aside to allow the other two to greet their father. Three-year-old Katie sprang ahead of her brother into her father's arms. Seth picked Katie up, hugged and kissed her, and then put her down. Four-year-old Aaron squeezed past her and hugged his father's neck as Seth picked him up, squeezing him hard.

Mattie then noticed the folded newspaper in her husband's hand. "Any more information in today's paper about the Black Hills?"

Seth grinned as he put Aaron down. "There sure is. And you're gonna like it."

"Good. You can tell me all about it later when these hungry children have been fed and put to bed."

"That's fine with me, sweetheart. Supper sure smells good. I could smell it as soon as I turned into the yard."

Seth gathered Katie in one arm and Aaron in the other, and they followed Mattie, still carrying Josie, toward the kitchen.

Well over two hours later, twilight was on the land as Seth sat in a comfortable chair on the front porch of the house, sipping a cup of coffee. The newspaper lay in his lap.

He heard familiar footsteps coming along the hall and looked up to see Mattie pushing the screen door open. She was carrying her own cup of coffee. "Well, the little ones are all in dreamland," she said with a sigh as she lowered herself onto the rocking chair, facing her husband.

A summery breeze wafted across the wide porch, and as Mattie dabbed at her brow with a handkerchief from her dress pocket, she said quietly, "Isn't it a beautiful evening?"

"Sure is. A perfect Indiana June evening. The stars will be showing themselves any minute, and the moon's light is already making a glow on the lower part of the eastern sky."

Mattie took a sip of coffee, glanced at the day's *Merrillville Dispatch,* and said, "Well, tell me about the article."

Seth held the newspaper in his hand and began to tell her about the new town of Deadwood that was rapidly being built and how there were now some twenty-five thousand miners in the Black Hills. Many of them had brought along their wives and children. Seth told her that the white population in the Black Hills now totaled nearly forty thousand, in addition to the soldiers in Fort Lookout. He told her that two hundred more soldiers had been added to the fort, making a total of eight hundred, in order to keep the Indians in and around the Black Hills in check.

"I'm glad to hear that," Mattie said. "When I think about those Indians, I get goosebumps. I'm sure glad that the army is there. Does the article say anything about how the miners are doing?"

"It says that overall they are doing reasonably well. Some are doing better than others, of course, really striking it rich, but nobody has left the Black Hills because they weren't finding enough gold to keep them panning and digging."

"I'm glad to hear that, too."

"The article also says that the Northern Pacific Railroad's tracks have been laid through the northern part of the Black Hills and now are being laid across Montana toward the Pacific coast. The Indian situation is bad there, though. The railroad workers are facing sporadic attacks by Sioux warriors who have been identified with Chief Sitting Bull, whose camp is still in northern Wyoming. Soldiers from Montana forts are having to protect them."

Mattie lowered her coffee cup and said, "From all I've heard about Sitting Bull, he seems to be the most vicious of all the Sioux chiefs."

"I think that's true."

Seth and Mattie then talked about their plans to leave their successful hardware store in the hands of Eddie Anderson and Jake Terrell when they took their journey to the Black Hills. They had been following the story for several months, and though they were making a comfortable living from the hardware store, they were both caught up with gold fever.

Mattie finished her coffee and said, "Well, husband of mine, when are we going to leave for the Black Hills?"

"How about next Saturday?"

"Sounds good to me."

"All right. Tomorrow I'll buy that covered wagon at the wagon works here in town, the one I told you about, and I'll buy that team of horses that I looked over yesterday at the stable."

On Saturday morning, June 26, the Hamilton family pulled away from the front of the Hamilton Hardware Store, heading west out of Merrillville with several close friends, including Eddie

Anderson, Jake Terrell, and their wives, standing on the board-walk, waving at them.

It was a bittersweet moment for Mattie, who was holding little Josie on her lap. She was glad that they were going, but she knew that she would miss her friends.

Sitting between their parents, Katie and Aaron were excited about the new adventure and showed it. Even little Josie was caught up in the excitement.

As the wagon left the outskirts of Merrillville, Seth heard Mattie sniffling and glanced at her. Tears were trickling down her cheeks, and she was chewing on her lower lip.

"Honey, what's wrong?" Seth said.

She sniffed and wiped away tears from her cheeks. "It's—well, it's just hard for me to leave our home here and not know how soon we'll be back."

"I thought that we were in agreement about this venture. Don't you want to go?"

"We *are* in agreement, darling. I want to do this, but Merrillville is the only home I've ever known. I'm just a bit senti-mental about leaving it, even for a while." She smiled at him. "Don't you worry now. I'm looking forward to making a fortune in the Black Hills."

Seth sighed. "Okay, sweetheart."

Mattie reached across the two children between them, patted his hand, and then turned her face toward the west, anticipating what lay ahead.

At the same time that the Hamiltons were leaving Merrillville, a wagon train that had left Huntsville, Alabama, in early May was moving slowly across Dakota Territory on its way to the Black Hills. The sun was shining brightly on the rolling hills as the wagon train drew near the small town of Belvidere.

In the lead wagon, Barney Moe turned to his son, who was driving, and said, "Well, Jason, we are now a hundred and ten miles from the Black Hills. The Lord has taken good care of us, hasn't He?"

Twenty-two-year-old Jason started to say yes when he noticed a covered wagon alongside the road up ahead with a man standing at the rear of it, waving his arms to get their attention. "Look up there, Dad."

Barney set his eyes on the man, who was now joined by a woman who appeared at the opening in the canvas behind him. "We'll stop and see what they want."

As he spoke, Barney stood up on the seat and waved at the wagon behind them, signaling that they were stopping. The signal was then passed on to the other nine wagons in the train.

As Jason drew rein, Barney climbed down and stepped up to the man, who appeared to be in his late thirties or early forties. "Is there something we can do for you, sir?"

"I hope so. Is your train going anywhere near the Black Hills?"

"More than near. We're going *into* the Black Hills to dig for gold."

A smile spread over the man's face. "Good! Could my wife and I join you for the rest of the trip? That's where we're headed."

"I don't see why not. Are you from Belvidere?"

"No, sir. My name is Max Burke, and this lady back here in the wagon is my wife, Loretta. We're from Richton Park, just south of Chicago."

Barney tipped his hat and smiled. "Glad to meet you, ma'am. My name is Barney Moe, and this young man on the wagon seat is my son, Jason."

Both Burkes greeted Jason, and Max shook hands with Barney. "In Chicago we attached to a wagon train that was headed for Oregon, planning to go as far as the Black Hills. But there were men in the wagon train who drank heavily and constantly used foul language. We got this far, and that's all we could take. I don't like profanity, especially when the name of God or Jesus Christ is used in it, but I especially don't want Loretta having to listen to it. Would we have any problem with drunken, cursing men if we traveled with you?"

"No, you wouldn't. You sound like born-again people."

A smile spread over Max's face. "We sure are! You, too?"

"Yes, sir!"

Max and Barney shook hands again and then Barney said, "There are two wagons bearing born-again people in this train. Ours and a family named Stevens. All of us in this train had an agreement when we left Alabama that there would be no drinking on the journey. And so far I haven't heard any bad language. I'll take you back to the Stevens wagon. You can travel right behind them."

"Oh, this is wonderful!" Loretta exclaimed.

Barney walked the couple along the line of wagons, explaining to the occupants in each wagon that the Burkes were joining the train, wanting to go to the Black Hills with them.

When they drew up to the Stevenses' wagon, Barney introduced the Burkes to Micah and Rachel Stevens and their eighteen-year-old daughter, Marylee, and their seven-year-old son, Blake, telling them the Burkes' story. The Stevenses welcomed them, saying that they were glad to learn that they were Christians.

Max hurried back to his covered wagon, drove it up beside the Stevenses' wagon, and helped Loretta climb in. Barney explained to the two miners in the wagon just behind the Stevenses' wagon that the new people joining the train wanted to follow right behind the Stevens family. The miners cooperated gladly and allowed the Burke wagon to move in front of them as the train pulled out.

When the sun was setting, the lead wagon halted alongside a rippling stream, and everyone left their wagons to build fires and prepare their evening meals. The Stevenses invited the Burkes to eat with them, and Max and Loretta gladly accepted the invitation.

As they were eating together, each gave his or her testimony of having received the Lord Jesus as Saviour. Then the Burkes wanted to know more about the Stevens family.

They learned that Micah and Rachel were both born and raised in Macon, Georgia. They had married there, and both Marylee and Blake also had been born in Macon.

Micah had fought in the Civil War and had suffered a wound in his right leg during a battle in February 1864. He was given a medical discharge. Marylee said that her father's leg often gave him severe pain.

Micah tweaked his daughter's nose playfully and then explained that after he had gone home to Macon from the war, he and Rachel had tried to make a living farming, but it was a struggle. Rachel gave birth to a baby girl, who died three weeks later. A year later, she gave birth to a son, but he lived for only two days.

Max and Loretta told them that they were sorry for the loss of those two children.

The Stevenses went on to say that Blake was born in March of 1868, and though he was a healthy baby, something had happened to Rachel when she was giving birth, and now she had a heart problem that kept her quite weak.

Loretta was sitting beside Rachel. With compassion showing in her eyes, she took hold of Rachel's hand and said, "I'm so sorry about your heart condition. If there is anything that I can do to help you on the rest of this trip, or while we're in the Black Hills, I'm at your beck and call."

Rachel squeezed Loretta's hand. "Thank you. I appreciate your kindness."

"Mrs. Burke, I know you mean that," Micah said. "I'm grateful." He took a deep breath and let it out slowly. "Well, to finish our story, because we were having such a hard time making a living at farming, we decided to sell the farm and go to the Black Hills.

We had read so much in the newspapers about the gold strike there that we figured it was quite possibly the Lord's way of getting us out of financial trouble."

Marylee smiled at her father. "Papa, I just know that the Lord is going to bless our efforts when we dig for gold. Everything is going to be all right for us."

Loretta Burke gave the girl a warm look. "That's the spirit, Marylee. You are a ray of sunshine to your family. I can tell."

Blake's features brightened. "She sure is, Mrs. Burke. She's the most wonderful sister in all the world!"

Rachel patted the top of her son's head and then said to the Burkes, "Our Marylee is always so optimistic. Even though this family is poor and at times has had it pretty rough, she has a happiness about her that's contagious. Not only has she done most of the cooking for us on this journey, but she is often found occupying children in the wagon train in the evenings by singing hymns and gospel songs to them and telling them Bible stories."

Max smiled at the girl. "You're quite a young lady, Marylee."

She blushed as Rachel said, "That she is, Mr. Burke. Ever since my heart trouble began, she has tried to make life as comfortable and enjoyable as possible for me. On this trip I've had to lie on a pallet inside the wagon most of each day. And more often than not, she has let her little brother ride next to Micah while she has stayed by my side, singing happy tunes."

At that moment, Barney Moe appeared and said, "Well, Marylee, the children are gathering by the main fire. Are you ready to sing for them and tell them a Bible story?"

Marylee sprang to her feet. "I sure am." She turned to her brother. "Ready to go, Blake?"

At the close of the next day, when the wagon train made a circle for the night beside another stream, Barney Moe—who had traveled across Dakota Territory before—announced that they were now just ninety-six miles from the Black Hills.

At the Stevens wagon, Micah helped Rachel down from the rear of the wagon. Marylee built a cookfire with the help of her little brother and then began to prepare a simple meal. Rachel sat nearby on a small bench that they carried on the side of the wagon, and Micah and Blake watered and fed the horses.

A short time later Marylee called out, "Papa, Blake, are you ready for some supper?"

"Sure am, sweetie," Micah said.

"Yeah!" Blake said. "Seems like a long time since we stopped for lunch."

Father and son sat down on the ground with Rachel between them on the bench. Marylee saw her father wince, and she knew just how difficult this trip was for him. She deeply appreciated his eagerness to dig for gold and make life easier for his family.

Micah led his family in prayer, thanking the Lord for His protection and for the food that He had supplied.

Marylee dished up fried potatoes, beans, and crisp bacon on a plate and then placed a hot biscuit on it. She poured a steaming cup of coffee and added a tiny bit of sugar from her scant supply. She handed her mother the plate and sat the cup on the bench beside her. "There you go, Mama."

Rachel smiled. "Thank you, dear."

Marylee did the same for her father, placing a plate of hot food in his rough, calloused hands. Her little brother dished up his own food and picked up a cup of water that his sister had left for him.

There was room on the small bench for Marylee to sit beside her mother. As the bright-eyed girl sat down beside Rachel, she said, "You look a little better than you did a couple of days ago, Mama."

"I do feel better, honey. You just keep up the good cooking, and I'll keep doing better. And, along with that, please keep up the wonderful singing as you ride in the wagon with me." Tears misted her eyes. "Marylee, I don't know what this family would do without you."

Marylee's eyes twinkled. "Now, that is something that you never have to worry about, 'cause I'm here to stay."

"How about when you get married?" her little brother said.

Marylee squinted at him. "If the Lord has a husband in mind for me, then he and I will have to live next door so I can still take care of Mama."

Micah smiled and shook his head. "Nobody else has ever had a daughter like you, Marylee Stevens."

A little while later, as Micah washed the pots, pans, and dishes, everyone in the wagon train could hear the joyous children's voices singing a gospel song around the main fire. Marylee Stevens had them in her charming spell once again.

On Saturday, July 3, at Fort Lookout, Jim Bannon walked out of assayer Wayne Clarkson's office with two cloth bags bearing gold nuggets. When he climbed into his wagon to head back to his claim site, he said, "Thank You, Lord. You've blessed me with twenty-two thousand dollar's worth of gold. I wish it was enough to satisfy Frank McGuire, but You and I both know that it's going to take a great deal more than that to make me a rich man in his eyes. I'll just have to keep working my claim."

Jim missed Alyssa so much. He wished that he could go home for a few days to spend some time with her, but he knew that he must keep digging and panning.

On Saturday, July 10, a small wagon train came into the Black Hills and reported at Fort Lookout. Jim happened to be at the fort getting an appraisal on more gold that he had dug out of his claim in the past few days. He now had $22,400 worth of gold.

Jim moved among the people who had just come in on the wagon train and invited them to the preaching service at the fort's mess hall the next morning. Some told him that they would attend. Others did not commit themselves.

Noting three men standing beside their covered wagon, Jim stepped up and said, "Welcome to the Black Hills, gentlemen. My name is Jim Bannon. I'm from Cheyenne, Wyoming."

The older man shook his hand, smiling. "Thank you, Jim. I'm Carl Wolfrum and these are my sons, Glenn and Dustin. We're from Franklin, Pennsylvania, just about eight miles from Oil City."

"I've read about Oil City," Jim said. "It's well-known for its oil production."

"The world's first oil well was drilled there in 1859," Carl said.

Jim's eyes widened. "Really? I wasn't aware of that."

"Shipping companies from all over the world have been buying crude oil from the well owners, who now have wells on a sixteen-mile stretch along Oil Creek. The reason we came to the Black Hills is to get enough gold so we can go back home and buy a large piece of that expensive land around Oil City. We want to set up our own oil company. If we do well enough here, we'll all three be multimillionaires within a year after we open our own company back home."

Jim raised his eyebrows. "That's quite a project. I hope you realize your dream." He paused and then said, "I'd like to invite you to the church service at the mess hall here in the fort tomorrow morning. Sunday school is at ten, and the preaching service is at eleven. We've got a fine young preacher from Omaha doing the preaching. His name is Luke Farrell. You'll like him."

Carl looked at his sons and then back at Jim. "Thanks for the invite, but we plan to be digging for gold first thing in the morning."

"Well, I hope you'll come next Sunday, then."

There was no comment. Jim smiled, told them that he needed to get back to his own claim, and walked away.

༄

On Monday, July 12, the wagon train from Huntsville, Alabama, arrived in the Black Hills, and the men left the women and children with the wagons just outside of Fort Lookout.

Along with the other men, Micah Stevens applied for a claim site and was assigned one near where Deadwood was being built. He was told that the general store in Deadwood was in full operation. The other men of the wagon train were assigned sites in areas close by.

Micah climbed into his wagon, and two mounted soldiers led the Stevenses to their claim site, which was on a steep incline in the wooded hills. The soldiers drove a sign into the ground with Micah's name on it and rode away.

"Well, family, let's go to the general store and buy some groceries," Micah said.

It was barely a half-mile from the site to the town. When they pulled up in front of the general store, Micah, Marylee, and Blake left Rachel on her pallet in the back of the wagon and hurried inside.

As they looked at the long rows of well-stocked shelves, Blake's eyes widened. "Wow, Papa! Look at all of this stuff!"

"Looks like everything from pickles to boots and shoes, son!"

Marylee pointed to one section. "They have mining equipment over there, Papa. Do you need to buy any more?"

"No, honey. I brought along everything I'll need."

With his children at his side, Micah moved along the aisles, taking advice from Marylee as they carefully picked out what groceries they could afford.

When she and her father laid their purchases on the counter, the clerk welcomed them to the store and began adding up the prices. Marylee noticed Blake staring at large glass jars filled with candy that were on the counter. The yearning look on his face captured her heart.

She leaned down and whispered in his ear. "You may have a penny's worth, little brother." She dug into her dress pocket, produced a single penny, and placed it in his hand.

"Oh, thank you, Sis!" Blake said. "I'll be glad to share it with you!"

Marylee patted the top of his head. "That's okay, little bud. You just enjoy every piece all by yourself."

Blake stood on the spot, his eyes moving from jar to jar, before he finally made his choice.

When they returned to their claim site, Blake was sent to gather wood for a cook fire, and Marylee began to prepare their meager meal.

Micah helped Rachel out of the wagon, and with his arm around her, they surveyed their property.

TWENTY

In Cheyenne on Sunday morning, July 18, Alyssa Rose McGuire sat with her parents and her brother in the preaching service. Pastor David Ballert stood at the pulpit and said, "I want to remind all of our members to pray daily for our brother Jim Bannon. Since there is no mail service to or from the Black Hills, we are completely out of contact with him. We have no way of knowing how things are going for him, but I trust that the Lord is giving him success."

There were *amens* heard from the congregation.

Alyssa was sitting between her mother and her brother. Monty noticed his sister wiping away tears with a hanky. He slipped his arm around her and whispered, "Sis, you just hang on. One day Jim will come home with plenty of gold, and you'll become Mrs. Jim Bannon."

Alyssa sniffled and gave him a weak smile.

In the mess hall at Fort Lookout that same Sunday morning, some of the newcomers to the Black Hills were in the Sunday school and preaching services. These included several whom Jim Bannon and Luke Farrell had personally invited, such as Barney and Jason Moe, the Parris brothers and Floyd Kitchin, Max and Loretta Burke, and Micah and Rachel Stevens, along with Marylee and Blake.

At the close of the service, Jim talked to the Stevens family. When he asked Micah how the gold digging was going, Micah's features took on a disturbed look. "Well, I started digging on Tuesday, Jim, and so far I've been able to come up with only twenty-nine dollar's worth of gold. After Wayne Clarkson assessed the worth of the nuggets, I took them to the two government mint workers in town and had them made into cold coins. It's just got to get better than this."

"Just stick with it, Micah," Jim said. "It'll get better."

Marylee smiled at Jim and then looked up at her father. "Papa, Mr. Bannon is right. I just know that you'll find more gold as you keep working at it."

Rachel, who was holding onto her husband's arm for support, said, "Micah, since our resident ray of sunshine agrees with Jim, it just *has* to get better."

Micah chuckled. "Okay, it's going to get better."

The next morning after breakfast, Micah Stevens limped up the steep incline from their wagon and began digging for gold once more.

Rachel sat on a straight-backed wooden chair near the wagon, a light blanket covering her thin legs. She watched her daughter and son work together, washing pots, pans, and dishes. When they had finished, Marylee turned to her little brother. "Blake, would you carry some buckets of water from the creek for me, please, and pour the washtub about three-quarters full? I've got quite a bit of laundry to do. As you can see, I've already placed the tub on the rocks so we can build a fire under it."

"Sure, Sis. I'll get right on it," Blake said.

Marylee went to the wagon, gathered up any dirty clothes that were lying about, and placed them with the soiled clothing that was kept in a wooden box near the tailgate. As she slid the box to the rear edge of the wagon and hopped down to the ground, she saw her little brother coming from the nearby creek carrying two full buckets of water.

It was a glorious summer day without a cloud in sight. Marylee marveled at the blue sky that stretched in every direction as far as the eye could see. She picked up the wooden box of laundry, and as she carried it toward the washtub, she looked around at the towering trees, the dark green grass, the babbling, sunlit creek, and the colorful wildflowers that decorated the hills. As she came near her mother, she stopped and said, "Isn't this a gorgeous part of the world, Mama?"

A tiny smile formed on Rachel's lips. "It sure is, honey. Leave it to you to notice the beauty all around us, in spite of how hard you have to work."

Marylee's features tinted as she looked around once again at her surroundings. "No wonder the Indians want to keep it for themselves, Mama."

"Mm-hmm. Can't blame them."

Blake was back with two more buckets of water and then returned to the creek for more. Marylee stuffed broken pieces of tree limbs beneath the tub and lit a fire. When the water was hot enough, she tossed in shavings from a block of soap that they carried in the wagon, dropped the clothes in, and began to wash them.

When she was finished, Blake went with her to the creek to rinse the clean clothing and then helped her hang it on parts of the wagon and on nearby bushes. All the while, Marylee was humming and singing happily.

Rachel marveled at her daughter and thanked the Lord for her cheerful approach to life.

When the wash was done, Marylee and Blake emptied the washtub. Then Marylee added wood to the fire and placed the coffeepot over the flames.

She carried a steaming cup to her mother, and Rachel thanked her and took a sip. "Honey, your papa has most of the gold coins in his pocket, but there are a few in that cloth sack in the wagon…enough to buy some grocery items that we need. Would you mind walking into town and buying some things at the general store? It won't be a lot, but we're low on a few things."

"Of course I wouldn't mind, Mama. I'd be happy to go. Blake can stay here in case you need anything."

Rachel told her daughter what to buy and Marylee climbed into the wagon and placed the gold coins in her dress pocket. She ran a brush through her long, black hair and then hopped from the wagon, whisked the dust from the skirt of her dress, and said to her little brother, "Blake, you stay close around here. No wandering off while I'm gone."

"I'll stay right here by Mama," replied her little brother, giving his sister a lopsided grin.

Marylee bent over and kissed her mother's forehead. "I won't be gone long, Mama. I'll hurry as fast as I can."

As Marylee walked into Deadwood, she noted the sounds of pounding hammers and the rasping of wood saws as so many buildings were under construction. Many were almost finished. She prayed as she moved along the dusty street toward the general store, asking God to help her father find some good gold deposits on their claim. Knowing that it very well could take more time than usual because of his game leg, she prayed that in the meantime the Lord would provide for the family in some other way.

When Marylee entered the Deadwood General Store, she found widower Clyde Akers standing behind the counter doing some paperwork. She had met him on Sunday at the preaching services at the fort's mess hall and found him to be a fine Christian man.

Clyde, who was in his early seventies, smiled at her. "Well, hello, Miss Stevens. Nice to see you."

She stepped up to the counter, matching his smile. "It's nice to see you, too, Mr. Akers. My mother sent me to pick up a few groceries."

"Well, you came to the right place!"

Marylee giggled as two middle-aged women stepped up to the counter, bearing items that they wished to purchase. "I'll only be a moment, Mr. Akers."

Clyde nodded at her and then turned his attention to the two women as Marylee moved toward the long rows of shelves.

"Thank You, Lord," Marylee whispered, "for allowing Papa to find enough gold to get these coins made. At least we'll have food in the wagon for a few days. I know that You will take care of us."

After some ten minutes she carried the few items to the counter and set them down in front of the silver-haired man.

"Find everything you were looking for, Miss Stevens?"

"I did, thank you."

Clyde picked up a pencil and slid a piece of paper in front of him. Marylee noticed that he winced, stiffened, and gritted his teeth. Her brow puckered. "Mr. Akers, are you in pain?"

He was pressing a hand to the small of his back. "It's arthritis in my lower back. It hurts really bad sometimes. This—this is one of those times."

"I'm sorry."

"Just part of life, dear."

Clyde added up the bill, and Marylee paid him, having barely enough to cover the cost of the items. As he was bagging the groceries for her, he asked, "How's it going at the claim site?"

"Not very good so far, Mr. Akers. Papa was able to dig out only twenty-nine dollar's worth of gold from Tuesday through Saturday."

Clyde's head bobbed. "Oh. Only that small bit, eh? I'm sorry. I'd think he could find more gold than that in six days."

"Well, Papa has a problem, Mr. Akers. Did you notice that he limps on his right leg?"

"Come to think of it, I did notice that."

"He was wounded in the Civil War, and his leg has never been the same. Since it bothers him a lot, it's slower going for him than for the average miner."

"I'm sorry to hear this, Miss Stevens," he said, sliding the bag of groceries toward her. "Your mother is not well, either, is she?"

"No, sir." Marylee explained about her mother's heart condition and then said, "I know that the Lord is going to take care of us, Mr. Akers. I've been praying that He will provide for our family in some other way until Papa is able to find some real good deposits of gold on our claim site."

Clyde's brow furrowed. "Some other way?"

"Yes."

He put a hand to his chin. "Miss Stevens, I have an idea."

"Yes, sir?"

"Well, with the rapid growth here in the Black Hills, I'm staying quite busy, and I've been thinking about hiring someone to help me here in the store. Would you be interested?"

Marylee's face brightened and her brown eyes sparkled. "I sure would!"

"I could pay you a dollar and a half a day, Mondays through Saturdays. The store is always closed on Sundays, of course."

Marylee did the arithmetic in her mind. *Nine dollars a week!* She nodded happily. "I'll take the job, Mr. Akers!"

"Wonderful! Could you start tomorrow?"

"I don't see why not. I know that my parents will approve."

"Well, Miss Stevens, it will be good to have you...especially when I have these bad arthritis days."

"Thank you, Mr. Akers. And since I'm now your employee, you can call me Marylee."

He grinned. "All right, Mary Lee."

She shook her head. "No, it's one word, sir. Marylee."

"Oh. All right, Marylee." He opened a jar of licorice sticks that sat on the counter. "I'd like for you to take a stick of this licorice to your little brother. He's such a cute little guy. His name is Blake, if I remember correctly."

"Yes, sir. Blake loves licorice. Well, *any* kind of candy, for that matter. I'll take it to him."

"Good. If you can be here by a quarter to eight in the morning, I can give you some pointers. Then I can train you completely in a day or two. Of course, your pay will begin tomorrow."

She smiled and picked up her bag of groceries, noting that two customers were coming toward the counter with their chosen items.

"I'll be here at 7:45 in the morning."

Toting the bag of groceries, Marylee happily skipped her way out of Deadwood toward the tall timber. "Thank You, Lord! You were answering my prayer before I even entered the store. Won't Mama and Papa be surprised?"

Shortly she drew near the Stevens claim site and saw her mother sitting on her chair and Blake sitting on the small bench beside her.

"Hello! Hello!" she called out, and both of their heads came up as they looked toward her.

Blake jumped off the bench and ran to meet her.

Marylee held the bag in one arm and slipped the licorice stick out of it. When Blake drew up, she handed him the black stick. "This is a present for you from Mr. Akers."

His eyes widened. "Wow, Sis! Thanks!"

As her little brother walked beside her, she said, "You can thank Mr. Akers the next time you see him at church."

"I will," said Blake, taking a healthy bite off the stick and smacking his lips as he chewed.

Rachel noted the licorice stick and the noisy chewing as brother and sister drew up. "I don't recall that being on the grocery list, daughter dear," she said, smiling.

"I didn't buy it, Mama. Mr. Akers sent it as a special gift to Blake."

"I'm gonna thank him real big, Mama!" Blake said past his mouthful of licorice.

"You'd better." Rachel also noticed that Marylee's eyes were sparkling, and her face was aglow. "You look especially happy, sweetie. Did you find your own gold mine?"

"No, Mama, but have I ever got some good news!"

"Well, tell me!"

"Mr. Akers asked me if I wanted a job working for him in the store."

"He did? Why did he do that?"

"He said that with the population growing here in the Black Hills, business is so good he has a hard time handling it by himself, and he offered me the job. I knew that you and Papa would be all right about it, so I accepted it. He's going to pay me a dollar and a half a day, Mama! I'll work Mondays through Saturdays. That's nine dollars a week!"

"Honey, that's wonderful."

"I figured that since it may take Papa some time to find very much gold, the money I make at the general store will help buy groceries and supplies for the family."

Tears welled up in Rachel's eyes, and she lifted her arms toward her daughter. Marylee bent down, and as Rachel hugged her daughter she said, "Thank you, sweetheart, for being willing to help with the family's expenses."

"The only drawback is that I'll have to be gone for most of each day that I work. I'll do all the chores that I can in the mornings before I leave, and then I can do the rest when I get home."

Blake grinned at his sister. "I'm almost a grown man, Sis. I can do a lot of your chores if you'll just tell me what needs to be done and show me how to do it."

Marylee ruffled his hair. "Well, squirt, you're a far piece from being a grown man, but I'm glad that I can depend on you to help out."

She hugged him and ruffled his wiry hair once more.

That evening when Micah came down from the hill where he had been digging, he had a few nuggets, which he told his family he estimated were worth about fifteen or twenty dollars.

Rachel said that this was his best day so far, but she and the children could tell that he was discouraged. She brightened his day, however, by telling him about Clyde Akers hiring Marylee to work at the general store and how he would pay her a dollar and a half a day.

Micah wrapped his arms around his daughter and said, "Honey, I very much appreciate your willingness to help with the family's expenses."

She raised up on her tiptoes and kissed his cheek. "I'm glad to do my part, Papa."

Micah kissed her forehead. "But once I make that big gold strike, you won't have to work anymore."

Marylee was up well before sunrise the next morning, busily making preparations around the wagon for the first day that her mother and brother would be without her. She had breakfast ready on time, and as the family sat down to eat, the pleasant aroma of hot coffee and bacon filled the sunlit air.

When breakfast was over, Marylee had Blake do the dishes while she fixed a midmorning snack for her father. She gave explicit instructions to Blake about work that he needed to do. Then she hugged him and her parents, told them that she would see them at lunchtime, and walked jauntily toward town, a happy smile brightening her features.

The smile was there again when she entered the store right on time and greeted Clyde Akers.

Clyde gave her instructions on needful things, and then as customers came into the store he let her watch him wait on them for the first couple of hours. Then Clyde watched Marylee as she took care of the customers at the counter and handled the money drawer.

By noon, Clyde was amazed at how quickly Marylee had learned her job, and he was pleased with the way that she related to the customers. Before letting her go home for lunch, he smiled at her warmly and said, "You certainly have caught on quickly, young lady. Having you here has really lifted my load. I'm wondering how I ever got along without you. You're a dear girl and already have brought joy to my heart."

Marylee blushed. "I'm so glad you feel that way, Mr. Akers. The Lord tells us to bear one another's burdens, and I believe that means physical burdens as well as mental or spiritual. You certainly have lifted the burdens of my family and me by giving me this job. The money is going to be a real blessing to us."

Clyde squeezed her upper arm and grinned. "That's good to know. And *you*, Marylee, are a blessing to *me*. You are so friendly to my customers. I just love your happy spirit."

"With Jesus in my heart, it's easy to have a happy spirit, Mr. Akers."

Clyde chuckled. "Well, you just have a way of showing it better than a lot of Christians I know."

❧

The Stevens family had lunch together at their covered wagon, and Micah, Rachel, and Blake were glad to hear that Marylee liked her new job so well. Micah told the family that he had found only about five dollar's worth of gold all morning. Marylee tried to cheer him up by saying that it would get better soon.

When lunch was over, Micah started his climb up the steep slope toward the spot near the top of the hill where he was presently digging.

Marylee headed back to town, and Blake helped his mother do the dishes. When they were done, Rachel was very weary. With Blake's help, she climbed into the rear of the covered wagon and lay down.

Up near the top of his claim, Micah used a pick for better than an hour at a place where he had found the gold that morning and the day before. After finding a few more nuggets he decided to go down the slope a ways and try another spot.

Micah picked up his bucket, grasped his pick and shovel, and carefully made his way down the slope. His eye fastened on a spot that looked good, and as he limped down toward it, a sharp pain shot through his bad leg.

Gritting his teeth, he dropped the pick and shovel and grasped his thigh. Another pain lanced through the leg, causing him to slip on the steep grade. His feet went out from under him, and he hit the ground, dropping the bucket and tumbling down the slope.

When he had tumbled head-over-heels some fifty feet, his head struck a sharp rock that protruded out of the ground. Micah Stevens passed out with blood flowing freely from a gash in his head.

A few miles away, Jim Bannon was placing a sack of gold nuggets into his wagon when he saw his neighbors Zack and Will Johansen doing the same thing at their wagon. He smiled at them and walked to their wagon. "Looks like you're doing okay."

"So far, so good," Zack said. "And you?"

"Doing fine." He paused and then said, "Zack, Will, I sure wish you would come to our Sunday preaching services."

Zack shook his head. "We just don't have time, Jim."

"Right," Will said. "Digging for gold is what we came here to do."

Jim put a soft tone in his voice. "Gentlemen, let me remind you that one day you will both have time to die."

Father and son exchanged glances. Then Zack said, "Well, sure, that'll happen. Everybody has to die."

"So where will you go when you die, gentlemen? Heaven or hell?"

Zack shrugged. "I haven't given it much thought."

"Me neither," Will said.

"You haven't given much thought to where you're going to spend eternity?"

"No, not really. We've just been too busy, Jim," Will said.

"The Bible says of the whole human race, 'All have sinned, and come short of the glory of God.' The problem is, if you die without having repented of your sin and having believed and obeyed the gospel of Jesus Christ, you will go to hell forever. God says in His Word that He does not want anyone to perish but for everyone to come to repentance.

"When you believe that Jesus died on the cross, was buried, and rose again and turn to Him in repentance, calling on Him and receiving Him into your heart as your Saviour, He will forgive your sins and save you from hell."

Neither man said anything.

Jim ran his gaze between them. "Does that make sense to you?"

Zack rubbed his stubbled chin. "I'll think about it, Jim."

"So will I," Will said.

"I don't want to try to push salvation down your throats, my friends, but I want you to know that I am available at anytime to talk to you about it again."

"We'll keep that in mind, Jim," Zack said. "Right now, we've got to get back to work."

Jim nodded, and when he turned around to go back to his claim he noticed that Luke Farrell, his neighbor on the other side, was talking to Carl Wolfrum and his sons, Glenn and Dustin, who were off their horses. They apparently had stopped by on their way to their claim site.

Jim hurried that way, and as he was drawing up he heard Carl talking about how rich he and his sons were going to be once they made a good gold strike in the Black Hills and then went home and invested their money in their own oil business.

Dustin laughed and said, "Yeah, Luke! Pa and Glenn and me are gonna be billionaires!"

"Howdy, Jim," Carl said.

Glenn and Dustin also greeted him.

Jim smiled, laid a hand on Luke's shoulder, and said, "So you fellas are going to be billionaires, huh?"

Dustin nodded. "We sure are!"

Jim looked into Luke's eyes and then back at the Wolfrums. "Gentlemen, I sincerely hope you do well, but the most important thing in this world is to become a child of God by being born again."

"That's what I've told them before, Jim," Luke said.

Jim fixed his gaze on them. "You fellas need to listen to Pastor Luke. More than being rich with the things of this world, you need to be rich toward Almighty God. The only way you can do this is to be born again and become God's children and heirs by receiving the Lord Jesus Christ as your personal Saviour."

"Jesus said that we must be born again to go to heaven," Luke said, "and that new birth comes in only one way. You have to repent of your sin, open your heart to Jesus, and receive Him as your Saviour. As Jim just pointed out, you are not rich toward God unless you are His child. All the money in the world won't help you when you die without Jesus in your heart."

"Being rich in this world without knowing Christ as Saviour means that you will lose it all when you die," Jim said. "But if you are saved, you will enter into your real riches when you get to heaven."

Carl's face grew stone-like. "Luke, Jim, I don't mean to be rude, but my boys and I don't have time for all this religious talk. We've got to get back to digging and panning gold." He moved toward his horse, saying, "Let's go, boys."

Luke and Jim watched Carl Wolfrum and his sons ride away.

"All we can do is pray for them, Luke," Jim said.

Luke nodded. "We'll certainly do that."

TWENTY-ONE

At the Stevens claim site, Rachel had pots and pans steaming over the fire beside the covered wagon in preparation for supper when she saw Marylee coming up the gentle slope. She was singing her favorite hymn, "Amazing Grace."

Blake was inside the wagon. His voice came through the canvas as he said, "I hear Miss Merry Sunshine coming, Mama!"

Rachel smiled to herself as she stirred the contents of the pots and pans.

Marylee changed from singing to humming as she drew up, and Rachel said, "Well, honey, how did things go at the store this afternoon?"

Marylee smiled, running her gaze around in search of her little brother. "Just fine, Mama. I really like my job. Ah…Blake should be helping you here."

"I am, Sis!" came her little brother's voice from inside the wagon. "I'm slicing the bread for Mama, and then I'm gonna set the table for her."

"Blake has been a real help, dear," Rachel said.

"I should have known, little brother," Marylee said. "I'm sorry."

Blake appeared at the rear of the wagon, hopped down, picked up the tray of bread slices, and carried it toward the table. He glanced at his sister and said, "It's all right, Sis. I'm just a kid, so I may not be as dependable as I should be."

"Well, you're doing great, little brother," Marylee said. Then to her mother she said, "Mama, I'll get my apron from the wagon and take over for you."

When Marylee returned, tying the apron around her waist, Rachel thanked her and sat down on her chair. She cast a glance at Blake, who was setting the table, and said, "Actually, Marylee, your little brother has been a real trooper this afternoon. You can be proud of him. He did exactly as you instructed him, and because of that, I was able to get a good rest."

Marylee stepped over to her brother and patted him on the back. "Good for you, Blake. I *am* proud of you!"

Blake finished setting the table, and Marylee was pouring the hot food into bowls when Rachel looked up the steep path toward the area where Micah was digging for gold. Her husband was known to be quite punctual. He knew that it was time for supper. *Why is he not here?*

"Honey," Rachel said to her daughter, "I'm getting concerned. Your papa should be here by now."

Marylee set her eyes on her mother, a worried look in them. "That's what I was thinking, Mama."

A sick feeling settled in Rachel's stomach. "Will you two go up there and see what's keeping him?" Her voice was thin and shaky.

"Sure, Mama," Marylee said. "Let's go, Blake."

Rachel watched them as they hurried up the trail that wound through the trees, with Marylee a few steps in the lead. Soon they disappeared from view.

Marylee was still ahead of Blake, hurrying up the path, when the top of the hill came into view. Suddenly she stopped and gasped. "Oh, no! Oh, no!"

Blake bounded up to her side and stopped as well.

Their father was lying on his back, his eyes closed, with blood smeared on his face. His tools lay farther up the path, and his bucket lay against the trunk of a tree.

Marylee moved slowly toward him. She was squeezing her hands together, making her knuckles a shiny white. Blake followed his sister, trying to find his voice.

"Papa," came Marylee's trembling voice as she dropped to her knees and stared into the blood-smeared, ashen face of her father.

Blake knelt down on the other side of his father. Tears were streaming down his face.

Marylee gently patted her father's cheek and whispered, "Papa, can you hear me? Please, Papa, open your eyes!"

There was no response.

Marylee could see no signs that her father was breathing. She sent a fearful glance toward her brother as she bent down and laid her ear against her father's chest.

Blake stood up and swallowed hard, blinking against his tears. "C-can you hear his heart beating?"

Marylee prayed silently for strength, took a quick breath, and raised her head. Her eyes were misty as she rose to her feet and said, "No. His heart isn't beating. Papa's gone, Blake. The Lord has taken him home. He—must have fallen and hit his head on this rock."

Suddenly they were in each other's arms. Blake burst into sobs, and tears rained down Marylee's stricken face. They wept together for several minutes. Then, as the weeping subsided, they both looked down at their father's lifeless form, sniffling and wiping the tears from their cheeks.

Blake's entire body trembled and his voice quavered as he said, "Oh, Marylee, what's gonna happen to us? What will we do now, stuck here in these hills with no way to dig for gold? You and I can't do it."

Marylee sniffed and drew a sharp breath. "I don't know what

we're going to do, little brother. I only know that we must trust our heavenly Father to take care of us. One thing for sure...we must be strong for Mama."

"Poor Mama," Blake said. "We've got to help her."

"In her weakened condition, this blow could break her spirit. She's going to need constant care and attention, and we've got to be strong for her sake. Can I count on you, Blake?"

The boy looked sadly into his sister's own sad eyes and nodded.

Marylee wrapped her arms around him once more. They wept together again. Then, gaining her composure, Marylee said, "We must take Papa's body down to the wagon."

Though they could not carry the body, together they slowly and carefully dragged their father down the slope.

Marylee stopped when they reached a spot that was still out of sight from the wagon. "Let's leave him here for now. We need to tell Mama what's happened before she sees the body."

Blake looked up at her. "That's a good idea, Sis. We need to break it to her as gently as we can. It's gonna be tough enough on her when we tell her."

The body was lying face-up. Marylee untied the apron and used it to cover her father's face.

Brother and sister descended the steep path, and when they rounded the bend of the decline, they saw their mother sitting in her chair.

Rachel had been watching for her family, and when she saw the anguish on the faces of her daughter and son, her heart skipped a beat. "What is it? Where's your father?"

Marylee knelt down at her mother's feet, and Blake moved up beside the chair and put an arm around her shoulders.

Marylee took her mother's hands in her own, choked, cleared her throat, and said, "Mama, we—we found Papa up near the top of the hill. He—he's dead."

Rachel recoiled as if she had been slapped in the face. She drew in a wheezy breath and, with a constricted throat, said, "Dead? Oh, no! Please, Marylee, say it isn't so!"

"I'm sorry, Mama. I wish I could. But it *is* so. He—he fell down the path from near the top of the hill and struck his head on a big rock."

Rachel seemed to shrink within herself. "Oh-h-h, how could this happen? How could—" She burst into tears.

Marylee let go of her mother's hands and wrapped her arms around her. Blake moved up beside his sister and hugged both of them as all three vented their grief.

The next afternoon, Wednesday, July 21, a relentless sun was burning down from the sky as Luke Farrell held a graveside service for Micah, who was being buried at the bottom of the steep slope on the Stevens claim site. Jim Bannon and other Christians were there, trying to comfort Rachel, Marylee, and Blake. Clyde Akers was among them and was positioned close to the grieving family. Rachel stood between her two children beside the open grave and leaned against Marylee.

Many of the miners were also there, including some who had their families with them.

Unnoticed by the crowd, four young Oglala Sioux warriors were off their horses in the shade of the nearby trees, observing the service and listening to Luke Farrell's sermon.

Luke read several passages of Scripture and carefully explained exactly how to be saved. He then told of Micah's testimony and said with conviction that Micah was now in heaven. Luke dwelt on that statement briefly in order to give comfort to Rachel and her children, stating that one day they would be together with Micah in heaven.

When Luke brought his message to a close, he invited those in the crowd who had never received Christ as Saviour and wanted to do so to step forward. Two men and two women came forward. Luke had his wife, Anna, take one of the women aside. He assigned the other woman to Loretta Burke. He had Jim Bannon take one of the men and took the remaining man himself. All four were led to the Lord and rejoiced in their newfound salvation.

When most of the others had left, Luke spent some time with the new converts, instructing them in the Word. Then Luke moved toward the spot where Anna, Jim Bannon, and Clyde Akers were doing what they could to comfort the new widow and her two children.

As Luke drew up, he noticed that Rachel's face was a sickly gray color. He was about to suggest that she go lie down in the family wagon when suddenly Rachel grabbed Marylee's arm and gasped, "Help me, honey. My heart is pounding!"

"Let's get her into the wagon so she can lie down," Luke said.

"I'll carry her, Marylee," Jim Bannon said.

Moments later, when Rachel was lying on her pallet in the rear of the wagon with Marylee, Blake, and Anna at her side, her heartbeat slowed and her color returned. Standing at the rear of the wagon with Jim and Luke, Clyde said, "Mrs. Stevens, I wish that the doctor who's planning to come to Deadwood was already here."

Marylee looked at him and said, "She'll be all right now, Mr. Akers. I just gave her some medicine that our doctor back home prescribed for her. I know that you need to get back and open up the store. Thank you for being here. I'll be back to work tomorrow."

Clyde thanked Marylee for understanding, told Rachel that he would be praying for her, and headed back to town.

Rachel's breathing was almost back to normal. She set her swollen, reddened eyes on her children and said, "I don't know what we're going to do."

Marylee stroked her mother's face. "Don't worry, Mama. The

Lord has blessed me with a good job. We'll be all right." A wee smile graced her lips. "Our heavenly Father has promised to supply all of our needs."

Rachel bit her lower lip, nodded, and wiped fresh tears from her eyes.

Blake pressed close to his sister, saying that he was going to miss his papa so much. Marylee's heart turned over at the sadness on his face. She put an arm around him and squeezed him tight. "Blake, all three of us are going to miss Papa terribly, but we must remember that God said in His Word that He will never leave us nor forsake us."

The boy wiped his tear-filled eyes with his shirt sleeve and gave her a thin smile. "He did, didn't He? Then we'll make it all right. Papa would want us to carry on, to take care of Mama, and to trust the Lord to watch over us."

Marylee smiled, sensing that a new bond had formed between them. "You've got it right, little brother. You're pretty grown up for your seven years!"

Rachel witnessed the scene with pride in her heart, smiled bravely, and said, "Yes, the Lord will take care of us."

Anna Farrell ran her gaze from mother to daughter. "Marylee, how about if, for a while, I come and stay here each day that you work? I can help Blake look after your mother."

Marylee smiled. "Oh, that would be wonderful, Mrs. Farrell."

"And I'll devote some time to digging for gold here on your site," Jim Bannon said. "Every nugget I find will be yours."

"I'll devote some time with Jim," Luke said. "Between the two of us, we should be able to find quite a few nuggets for you."

Rachel's lips quivered as she said, "Oh, thank you both. That will be a real blessing."

Blake fixed his eyes on his mother. "I'd help them dig for gold if I was older and bigger, Mama."

Rachel managed a tiny smile. "I know you would, honey."

Anna said, "Luke, Jim, I know that you both need to get to your own claims. I'll stay with Rachel and the children for the rest of the day."

When Luke and Jim walked away from the Stevens wagon together, they saw four young Oglala Sioux warriors step out from the deep shade of the trees and head toward them, the sun shining brightly on their copper-colored skin. Each wore a breechcloth and a headband with an eagle feather protruding at the back of his head.

One of them raised a hand in a sign of peace and said, "Mr. Preacher, could we talk to you, please?"

"Of course," Luke said as they drew up.

"My name is Little Wolf." He gestured to the other three. "This is Broken Nose, Brown Bear, and Wind Hawk."

Luke nodded. "My name is Luke Farrell, and my friend here is Jim Bannon. What did you want to speak to me about?"

Little Wolf took a half-step closer. "We listened from those trees back there when you preached from the Black Book over the grave of Micah Stevens."

Luke was amazed at how well Little Wolf spoke English. "Yes?"

"When we were under Chief Red Cloud at our village in what you white men call Nebraska, we had a white preacher named Clayton Keller come to us. Chief Red Cloud asked him to teach any people in the village who wanted to learn the English language. Only a few of us sat under his teaching. While he was teaching us English, he told us of God's Son, Jesus Christ, dying for our sins and of heaven and hell. We did not follow what Preacher Clayton Keller taught us of Jesus Christ, but when the four of us heard you preach the same message at the burial, we agreed that we want to hear more about this Jesus Christ, who died for us to give us forgiveness of sins and to take us to His heaven when we die. Will you tell us more?"

Luke's face lit up with a smile. "I sure will. Let's go over there among the trees and sit down so we can talk."

Luke and Jim led them into the forest. They sat down on the ground together, and after reading several Scriptures and answering their questions, Little Wolf, Broken Nose, Brown Bear, and Wind Hawk each received Jesus Christ as his Saviour. The young warriors then asked if Luke and Jim would let them go to the village and bring their squaws back with them so they could hear about Jesus, too.

Luke gladly told them to go bring their squaws.

The next morning Luke and Jim went to the fort and told Colonel Martin Lowry what happened with the four young warriors and their squaws after Micah Stevens's burial service. Luke explained that he wanted to start an Indian mission, but he knew that he could not ask to use government property. Neither could he ask for a spot in Deadwood where they might build a small building for the mission, so he wanted to go to Chief Red Cloud and ask if they might erect a building close by his village. Luke and Jim wanted the colonel's permission to go talk to Chief Red Cloud about it.

Lowry, though not a Christian, told them that he appreciated their desire to work with the Indians and told them that he would accompany them—along with three of his officers—to Red Cloud's village.

Just over an hour later, Lowry, his three officers, and Luke and Jim drew up to the village. The Sioux guards led them to Chief Red Cloud's tepee. The chief came out and welcomed them warmly.

The colonel, who by this time was well-acquainted with the chief, introduced him to Luke and Jim and told him that Preacher

Luke Farrell would like to talk to him.

Red Cloud smiled at Luke. "Preacher Luke Farrell, is this about Little Wolf, Wind Hawk, Brown Bear, and Broken Nose and their squaws? What happened to them yesterday?"

"Yes, Chief Red Cloud. They told you about it, I assume."

"Yes. They have embraced Christianity."

"Has this disturbed you?" As Luke asked the question, he saw the four young warriors and their squaws draw up close and stop. He looked at them and smiled, and they smiled back.

Red Cloud said, "Preacher Luke Farrell, though I remain true to the Oglala gods, I very much respected the white preacher Clayton Keller, and I will not interfere with this decision by these young warriors and their squaws."

"Chief, would you interfere if others of your people became Christians?" Luke asked.

Red Cloud moved his head back and forth slowly. "I would not interfere. I can see that it does something good for them."

Luke met his gaze and smiled. "I appreciate that, Chief Red Cloud. I would like to ask something of you. Would you grant us permission to construct a small building just outside the village so we can carry on a mission work with your people?"

Red Cloud nodded. "You have my permission."

Luke and Jim both expressed their gratitude for his kindness.

Chief Red Cloud went back into his tepee, and as the white men were about to leave, the four young warriors stepped up and told Luke and Jim how happy they were that Chief Red Cloud had granted them permission to erect a mission building.

Jim explained that they would meet outdoors on Sunday afternoons as long as the weather was warm. When fall came, they would erect a building.

Little Wolf's eyes danced with joy as he said, "This is wonderful! I know that many more of our people will become Christians when they hear the gospel message."

≈

Before returning to their claims to resume digging for gold, Luke and Jim went back to the Stevens wagon. They told Anna, Rachel, Marylee, and Blake what had happened with the four young warriors and their squaws and of the permission that Chief Red Cloud had given them to establish a mission just outside the village. All of them rejoiced.

The following Sunday there was a good turnout for the services in the fort's mess hall. And that afternoon the first Sunday service was held at the edge of the Oglala village, with several Indians attending.

Little Wolf stood beside Luke and translated his words into the Lakota language. Everyone listened attentively as Luke read Scripture to them and told them the story of God's love in sending His Son into the world to provide the one and only way of salvation for the sinful human race.

It was the first time that most of the Indians had heard the gospel. There was no response at the invitation, but they did show much interest.

By the fifth Sunday in August six more adult Oglalas had received Christ as Saviour. Luke, Anna, and Jim were thrilled.

On Tuesday, August 31, Jim walked over to the Farrell claim site after eating a quick lunch. Luke and Anna were just finishing their lunch at the small table beside their wagon as Jim drew up.

"Sorry, Jim," Luke said. "We just ate every morsel that Anna had cooked up for lunch."

Jim smiled. "You know that's not what I'm here for."

"I simply figured you'd had enough of your own cooking and

263

wanted some *good* food!" Luke said.

The three of them laughed together and then Anna asked, "To what do we owe this pleasant surprise, Jim?"

"I just wanted to let you know that I'm going to make a trip home to see Alyssa Rose. I'm missing her terribly, as well as my parents, my church, and my friends."

"I can understand that, Jim," Luke said. "When are you leaving?"

"At sunup tomorrow morning. I'll just ride one of my horses and leave the wagon here. I figure I can average about forty-five miles a day. I'll only be able to be there one Sunday, and I plan to be back next Thursday, September 9."

"I'm glad you're going to do this, Jim," Anna said. "Luke and I will be praying for a safe journey for you."

"I appreciate that. And while I'm gone, I'll miss you both."

Just then Carl Wolfrum and his sons drove by in their wagon. Jim and Luke waved, and Glenn, who was at the reins, brought the wagon to a halt.

"Heading for town?" Luke asked.

Carl shook his head. "No, we're on our way to the fort to see the assayer. This past week has been really good, and we want to see what the gold we dug up is worth. I think we'll find out that we've come up with something like sixty-five or seventy thousand dollars in the last seven days."

"We've already got well over fifty thousand dollars in minted gold coins, but this week has been exceptional," Dustin said. "When we get this gold minted, we'll have somewhere close to a hundred and twenty thousand, I'm sure. We're nearly halfway to the point where we can purchase that oil-bearing property that we told you about, establish our own oil company, and make millions."

"Gentlemen, I sincerely hope you do well in the oil business," Luke said. "But I'm concerned that you haven't done anything about eternity. The main thing in this short life on earth is to know Christ and to have the assurance of going to heaven when you die."

"No, the most important thing in this life is to be rich!" Carl said. "We'll worry about eternity later. Let's go, Glenn."

Glenn put the wagon in motion, and none of the three even looked back as they drove away.

With heavy hearts, Jim and Luke watched the wagon until it passed from view.

TWENTY-TWO

In Cheyenne late on Saturday afternoon, September 4, Alyssa Rose McGuire was in the sewing room at the McGuire home, sorting through materials for the dressmaker who would be coming to the house on Monday to make a new dress for her. The sewing room was halfway between the front door and the kitchen along the hallway that ran from the foyer to the rear of the house.

She was having a difficult time concentrating on the task at hand, for her thoughts were many miles away in the Black Hills with a certain young man. She raised her head and looked out the window, picturing that young man's face in her mind, and was only dimly aware of the sound of a knock on the front door of the house and the voice of her mother calling out that she would get it.

Alyssa looked out the window, daydreaming about the man she loved, and then went back to the dress materials, trying to decide which pattern she wanted for her new dress. Suddenly she was aware of someone standing in the sewing room doorway.

When she looked up, a sharp gasp escaped her lips, and a delighted squeal came right behind it as she jumped to her feet and landed in Jim Bannon's open arms.

Kathleen waited in the hall at the parlor door, wanting to give the young couple some privacy.

Jim kissed Alyssa twice, and then, as she eased back in his arms, she said excitedly, "Oh, what a wonderful surprise! How did you manage time off from your gold digging? How long can you stay? Or did you strike it big and you're home for good? When did you leave—"

"Hold on a minute, sweetheart," Jim cut in with a smile. "I can only answer one question at a time."

"Sorry, darling. I'm just so thrilled to see you that I got carried away."

Jim leaned down and kissed the tip of her nose. "That's okay. I'm happy that you're so glad to see me. You asked how I managed time off from my gold digging. Well, I—"

"Hey, Jim!" came Monty's voice from down the hall. Right behind Monty was Frank, who had Kathleen at his side.

Jim shook hands with both Frank and Monty and explained that he had left the Black Hills on horseback at sunrise on Wednesday. He had just gotten so lonely for Alyssa that he took time off to come and see her.

"How long can you stay?" Alyssa asked, clinging to his arm, her eyes shining up at him.

"I have to head back for the Black Hills on Monday morning, but at least I'll have one full day to be here. I'm looking forward to being in church tomorrow."

"Everybody will be thrilled to see you," Alyssa said with a lilt in her voice. "They've all been praying for you."

"Especially me," Monty said.

Jim cuffed him playfully on the chin. "Well, keep it up, pal."

"So how are you doing with your claim, Jim?" Frank asked.

"It's been pretty good, sir. I now have thirty-seven thousand dollars in gold coins."

Frank nodded. "Not too bad."

"No, but I still have a ways to go. When I get back to the Black Hills, I'm going to work harder than ever."

Kathleen smiled at Jim. "You said that you had already been to the farm and talked with your parents. Are you going to eat supper with them?"

"Well, I told them that I was going to take Alyssa out for supper if she could go with me."

Alyssa squeezed his arm. "I sure can!"

Kathleen smiled. "I'm glad you two can spend the time together."

That evening, after spending more time with his parents at the farm, Jim picked Alyssa up in the Bannon family wagon and asked her where she would like to eat. He was sure that she would say Callie's Cottage Restaurant and was pleased when she did.

At the restaurant, Callie Carson gave them a warm welcome.

While they were eating, Jim looked across the table at the woman he loved and said, "I need to ask you a question."

"Of course I will marry you," she said, giggling.

"I've already had the answer to that question, and happily so."

She giggled again. "So what's your new question?"

He gave her a serious look. "Has your father ever said exactly how much money he expects me to have before he will approve our getting married?"

There was a brief silence, and then Alyssa said, "Well, he has used the figure *a half million dollars* several times."

"Wow, that's a lot of money. I hope my claim can produce that much." A worried look creased his brow.

Alyssa reached across the table, took hold of his hand, and gazed into his troubled eyes. "Jim, you know that as far as I'm concerned, your having that kind of money isn't necessary."

"I know that, sweetheart, but I still want your father's blessing on our marriage. Do you suppose he'd settle for less if my claim runs dry before I'm able to come up with that much gold?"

She smiled and squeezed his hand. "You just do the best you

can, my love. The Lord will take care of all the rest."

"I'll work hard and dig out every gold nugget that can be found in my claim. Some miners have done very well, and even a few have done so well that they've already gone back to their homes. Most of them, however, are like me—still digging and panning, their hopes high."

She smiled warmly. "I would marry you if you never dug up another nugget. You know that. No one is going to keep us from marrying and spending the rest of our lives together."

Jim looked deeply into her eyes. "I love you, Alyssa."

"I love you, too, Jim."

Jim and Alyssa had a wonderful time together that evening, and when they returned to the McGuire home, Kathleen told them that she and Frank had driven out to the Bannon farm and invited Jim's parents for dinner the following afternoon. They had stopped at the parsonage on the way back and also invited Pastor and Mrs. Ballert.

Jim thanked the McGuires for doing this, and Kathleen told him that she wanted to put on a real banquet in his honor.

Jim enjoyed the church services the next morning, and when his parents and the Ballerts were at the McGuire home that afternoon for dinner, everyone listened intently while Jim told them what was happening in the Black Hills.

He told them all about Luke and Anna Farrell and the services that were held in the fort mess hall on Sundays. He talked about the new mission work with the Indians and about those who had already been saved and the building that they planned to erect before winter set in. He also explained about Luke's father and the tremendous medical bills that had piled up. He added that because of Luke's ministry in the Black Hills, he had not had time to dig for gold as he should.

"Jim, I like what I'm hearing about Luke Farrell and his ministry," Pastor Ballert said. "I'm going to tell the church about him this evening and take up an offering so we can help Luke with his father's medical bills."

"That won't be necessary, Pastor," Frank McGuire said. "I'm going to send enough money with Jim to pay the entire doctor and hospital bills for Luke's father, plus money to erect a church building in Deadwood and the Indian mission building. I'll also send enough money for Luke and Anna to live on for the next year so Luke can carry on his ministry without having to dig for gold." He set his eyes on Jim. "Can you give me some figures on the medical bills for Luke's father?"

Jim swallowed the lump that had risen in his throat. "Yes, I can. Luke has shared it with me."

"Is there a lumber company in Deadwood?"

"Yes, sir. It opened up about two months ago."

"Good. Then they can get right to work on both the church building and the mission building. Right after dinner, Monty and I will go to the bank and take the cash out of the vault. I'll send enough money with you to cover the cost."

With tears in his eyes, Jim said, "Mr. McGuire, I want to thank you for your generosity."

Frank smiled. "You're welcome, Jim. My family and I want to be a blessing to Luke's family and his ministry."

When Jim arrived at the McGuire house on Monday morning, the eastern sky was giving notice that the sun would soon rise. Alyssa Rose was waiting for him on the front porch.

As he dismounted he glanced toward the new mansion and said, "Looks like it's about finished."

"Just about," Alyssa said. "As you can see, the outside is finished. The builder is saying that he'll have the inside done within three or four weeks."

"It's sure going to be nice." Jim climbed the porch steps and folded Alyssa in his arms. "Well, sweetheart, I've got to get going."

She eased back in his arms and looked up at him. "I'll miss you so much."

"I'll miss you, too."

Tears misted her eyes. "Jim, please remember what I said. I will marry you, no matter what. It makes no difference to me if you have thirty-seven thousand dollars, a half million, or thirty-five cents. I love you. God intends for us to be married. I appreciate your wanting to appease Papa, and I want his blessing, too. But more than anything, I want to be your wife."

The tears were now slipping down her cheeks. Jim wiped them away and kissed her tenderly. "Thank you, sweet Alyssa. The Lord will make everything work out for us. He knows that more than anything we want to be in the center of His will."

Holding her close once more, Jim breathed in the sweet scent of her hair; then he kissed her again, released her, and mounted his horse. "I'll be back as soon as I can. Keep praying for me as I do for you."

Her lips were trembling. "Always, my love. Always. I will be praying that the Lord will help you to strike it big soon so that you can come home and I can become Mrs. Jim Bannon."

He smiled. "What a wonderful thing that will be. I love you."

"I love you, too."

On that same morning, September 6, Seth Hamilton and his family were within two hundred miles of the Black Hills and moving westward in their covered wagon across Dakota Territory. They were some ten miles east of the town of Presho when Seth guided the wagon into a dense forest, drew rein, and said, "Mattie, since we're out of meat and we've seen lots of jackrabbits in this area, I'm going to leave you and the children here and see if I can bag us some rabbit meat."

Mattie was sitting next to him with twenty-month-old Josie on her lap. "All right, honey. Don't be gone too long."

Four-year-old Aaron and three-year-old Katie were right behind the driver's seat inside the wagon at the canvas opening.

"Papa, when I get bigger, I can go huntin' with you, huh?" Aaron said.

"You sure can, son." Seth hopped down from the wagon seat and helped Mattie down as she held onto Josie. By that time, Aaron and Katie had climbed down from the rear of the wagon.

Mattie and her children watched as Seth walked away with his rifle in hand.

Moments later, he went over a hill and moved down a gentle slope into a ravine. Just as he touched bottom, he saw several jackrabbits bounding through the grass, moving swiftly away from him. He ran in that direction for about half a mile.

Suddenly he saw another bunch collected at the edge of a small stream. When they saw him, they started to run, but he was able to bag four of them with his rifle. "Now we'll have some meat," he said, smiling as he picked them up by their hind legs.

He headed back the way he had come, and some twenty minutes later he moved into the shade of the forest and headed for his wagon. Suddenly his eyes fell on the crumpled form of Mattie lying on the ground with two arrows in her back.

His heart pounded against his ribs as he let the dead rabbits fall from his hand and ran to her, dropping to his knees. The hairs on the back of his neck were standing on end, and he felt a shiver pass through him as he touched her.

Mattie was dead.

Seth felt the foundations of his world start to crumble as he stood up, horror frozen in his eyes, looking around for his children.

Suddenly, terrified cries reached Seth's ears from deeper in the woods, as his children called out to him. Gripping his rifle tightly, he dashed in that direction.

He saw them only a short distance away, huddled together at a large cottonwood tree, wailing but untouched. His own eyes bubbling over with tears, Seth bent down and gathered all three in his arms. His tears mingled with theirs as he tried to calm them.

When Seth was finally able to hush his children and take control of his own emotions, he looked at his oldest and said, "Aaron, tell me what happened."

The boy's features were pale as he drew a shaky breath. "When the Indians came, Mama tried to protect us from 'em. Two of 'em put arrows in their bows, and Mama turned away from 'em, tryin' to keep the arrows from hittin' us. They shot Mama in the back, and when she fell down, all of 'em stood there and stared at Katie and Josie and me for a minute. Then they got on their horses and rode away. We were hidin' here in the forest in case they came back."

Seth placed the three little ones on the wagon seat with baby Josie sitting on Aaron's lap. "You stay here," he said in a strained voice. "I have to bury your Mama."

While they watched, he went to their fallen mother, removed the arrows from her body, carried her to a nearby grassy spot, and gently laid her on the ground. He took a shovel from the wagon and dug a grave close by. He then took a multicolored quilt from the wagon and wrapped Mattie in it. He picked her up, kissed her pallid cheek, and lowered her into the grave.

The children wept, calling out to their mother as they watched their father shovel the dirt over her lifeless body. Seth's own heart was breaking as he piled what stones he could find on top of the mound. Then, removing his hat, he stood with his shoulders slumped and wept. After several minutes he wiped away the tears from his face, turned to the wagon, and climbed aboard.

When he sat down on the seat with his three little ones, he folded them in his arms. Aaron and Katie studied his gray features as he said, "We have to go on now."

He took the reins in hand and put the horses in motion. As they headed out of the forest toward open country, Josie turned around on Aaron's lap and leaned toward the side of the wagon, looking back and holding her chubby arms out. "Mama! Mama-a-a!" she wailed.

Seth stopped the wagon and reached for her. "Come to Papa, baby."

Aaron and Katie looked on as their father cuddled their baby sister and talked to her in a soothing tone, trying his best to calm her. Soon Josie's sobbing ceased, and she placed her thumb in her mouth. Exhausted from crying, she fell asleep against her father's chest.

Seth pushed the blond curls from her forehead, kissed her cheek, and handed her back to Aaron, who cuddled her to his own chest.

With an aching heart, Seth guided the wagon onto the plains and started on the trail westward toward an uncertain future.

When the Hamilton wagon pulled into Presho, Seth stopped at the town marshal's office to report his wife's murder by the Indians. The marshal told Seth that he would wire the commandant at nearby Fort Randall and let him know about it. He added, however, that there would be no way to identify the guilty Indians. Seth told him that he understood but felt that the incident should be reported to the authorities.

He climbed back into the wagon and headed west, doing his best to comfort his children in the loss of their mother.

Jim Bannon arrived back in the Black Hills on Thursday, September 9, as planned. When he sat the Farrells down and gave them the money for a church building and a mission building as a gift from Frank McGuire, they were both astonished and pleased.

Jim then handed them a money sack containing the large amount of currency to pay all of the medical bills for Luke's father and to keep the Farrells in sufficient funds for a year so that Luke could have the time that he needed to carry on his ministry. They were stunned but joyful, giving praise to the Lord.

In the few days that Jim had been gone, Deadwood's bank had opened and Western Union had opened an office and established wire service. The Farrells told Jim that next week Wells Fargo would open their office in Deadwood, and stagecoaches would begin operating. Part of their service would be to carry the U.S. mail.

Jim had known that these things were coming but was pleased that they were happening sooner than expected. Luke told Jim that he and Anna would deposit the money in the new bank and would mail a check to his mother to cover all of his father's medical bills as soon as the Wells Fargo stages were operating. He would wire his mother and let her know that it was coming. He would also wire Frank McGuire and thank him for his kindness and generosity.

Jim told Luke that it would mean a lot to Frank to hear from him and then excused himself to go to the general store to get some groceries.

When Jim entered the Deadwood General Store, three miners were just walking away from the counter, carrying bags of groceries. Jim greeted them and then smiled at Marylee Stevens as he neared the counter. "Hello, Marylee."

She flashed him a smile. "Hello, Jim. Welcome home."

"Thank you. How's your mother doing?"

"She still cries a lot over losing Papa, but overall she's doing better."

"I'm glad to hear that," Jim said, running his gaze around the store. "Is Clyde around?"

"He's lying down on the cot in his office. His arthritis is giving him a lot of pain today."

"Oh, I'm sorry. Bless his heart, he's having a rough time of it, isn't he?"

"That he is. It's going to be a blessing for him when the new doctor opens his office here. We learned while you were gone that Dr. Kord Roberts will be here in just about a week. His office has been completed."

Jim nodded. "It will be great to have Dr. Roberts here, that's for sure."

Suddenly there came the muffled sound of pounding hammers from what seemed to be the rear of the store. Jim looked in that direction and then frowned at Marylee. "What's going on back there?"

She flashed him another smile. "Something else new since you've been gone. Mr. Akers is having two large rooms added to the rear of the store where Mama and Blake and I are going to live. The contractor says that the rooms will be ready in two weeks."

"Well, bless Clyde's heart. I'm glad to hear this. Praise the Lord."

Marylee's eyes were shining brightly. "Yes, praise the Lord! It's going to be a real blessing to us."

Jim picked up a hand basket provided for the store's customers. "Well, I'd better pick up my groceries and get on back to my claim."

When Jim returned to his claim site, he immediately began digging for gold. He prayed that the Lord would help him to do well so he could marry Alyssa soon.

Late in the day he saw Zack and Will Johansen coming from where they had been digging near the back side of their claim site.

They saw Jim and both welcomed him back.

Jim laid his pick down and walked over to them. "How goes the gold digging, fellas?"

"Well, sort of mediocre," Zack replied. "We're finding a little gold, but we're disappointed that we're not finding more."

"Yeah, like the Wolfrums," Will said. "They came by here yesterday on their way to have the latest load of gold assayed and then to have more coins minted. They're really getting rich."

Jim shrugged. "Well, all we can do is keep digging, fellas. Guess I'd better get back to work."

Red and gold leaves adorned the trees in and around Deadwood as Seth Hamilton pulled up in front of the general store at midmorning on Friday, October 1. He helped his children out of the wagon, keeping baby Josie in his arms.

For a moment, Seth stood on the boardwalk surveying the bustling town; then he led Aaron and Katie inside. Seth noted the long rows of tall shelves laden with most everything that anyone could want or need, including mining supplies. A few customers were moving among the shelves.

Smiling brightly, Marylee rounded the end of the counter and stepped up to the newcomers. "Good morning. I'm Marylee Stevens. May I help you?"

"Good morning," Seth said. "Is it *Miss* or *Mrs.* Stevens?"

"*Miss* Stevens."

Seth nodded. "Glad to meet you, Miss Stevens. I'm Seth Hamilton, and these are my children, Aaron, Katie, and Josie. We just arrived from Indiana and need some groceries. We're running low on just about everything."

Marylee ran her gaze over the three children, who looked quite bedraggled. Fixing her bright eyes on the boy, she said, "How old are you, Aaron?"

"I'm four, ma'am."

Then Marylee looked at his sister, who stood beside him. "And how old are you, Katie?"

"I'm three years old," replied Katie, giving her a sweet smile. "How old are you?"

Seth frowned down at Katie. "Honey, you're not supposed to ask adults that question."

Marylee patted Katie's head and said, "It's all right, Mr. Hamilton." Then to Katie she said, "I just had my nineteenth birthday a few days ago." She then turned her attention to the baby in her father's arms. "And how old is Josie?"

"Twenty-one months." Seth gave her a lopsided grin. "And just so that all the facts are in, I'm twenty-five."

"Are you here to mine gold, Mr. Hamilton?"

"Yes, I am."

Marylee glanced around the store. "And is there a Mrs. Hamilton nearby somewhere?"

"Unfortunately, my wife, Mattie…was killed by Indians in eastern Dakota Territory while we were traveling this way."

Marylee's smile vanished. "Oh-h-h, I'm so sorry, sir. You have my deepest sympathy."

Seth smiled thinly. "Thank you." He picked up a shopping basket from the stack nearby. "Well, children, we'd better get started with the groceries."

"May I help you find what you need?"

Seth noticed two older women coming from between two rows of shelves, their baskets full.

"Thank you, but we'll manage. I think those ladies will be wanting your attention."

"Well, if you need anything you can't find, don't hesitate to ask."

"I won't. Thank you."

Holding the shopping basket in his free hand while carrying Josie, Seth started along the shelves with Aaron and Katie at his side. He set the basket down from time to time in order to place items in it. At one point he and the children were paused at a shelf while Seth picked out some baking goods, and he heard a male voice coming from a nearby room. Looking in that direction, Seth noticed by the lettering on the open door that it was the proprietor's office and that the proprietor's name was Clyde Akers.

By what the man was saying, Seth picked up that he was a medical doctor giving the store owner bad news about his arthritis. He heard Clyde Akers call the man Dr. Roberts as he referred to the pain he was experiencing.

The doctor said, "Mr. Akers, since I know that you have a son and daughter-in-law back in Ohio, I strongly suggest that you go back there so they can take care of you."

"You're right, Doctor," Clyde said, "but first I'll have to sell the store. This may take some time."

"I understand, but it is best that you put it up for sale right away."

As Seth and his children moved to another row of shelves, he told himself that he really had no reason to return to Merrillville. Since Deadwood was a boomtown, he might as well just purchase the general store and stay. Eddie Anderson and Jake Terrell could send him checks on his profits at the hardware store every month.

Seth still had Josie in his arms as he paid for the four baskets of groceries that he had picked up. Marylee saw that he was going to have a problem carrying the grocery bags with the baby in his arms and said, "Mr. Hamilton, I'm between customers at the moment. I'll be glad to hold Josie while you carry out the groceries."

Seth smiled warmly. "All right. I really appreciate your help."

He placed the baby in Marylee's arms and told Aaron and Katie to wait there while he carried the groceries out to the wagon.

When he came back in the store to pick up the remaining grocery bags, Seth heard Josie giggling as Marylee tickled her. After he had carried the last bags out he returned to the store, and Marylee kissed Josie's chubby cheek, handed her to her father, and then bent down and kissed the cheeks of Katie and Aaron.

Seth thanked Marylee for taking care of the baby for him and then said, "Miss Stevens, I overheard Mr. Akers and Dr. Roberts talking in the office back there. I would like to talk to Mr. Akers. Would you mind telling me where he lives?"

"He lives in the small house right next door to the store," she said, pointing in the direction where the house stood.

He tipped his hat. "Thank you. You've been very kind. Let's go, children."

As Seth turned to leave, with Aaron and Katie beside him, Josie suddenly reached out her arms toward Marylee and cried, "Mama! Mama-a-a!"

"Shush now, Josie," Seth said. "We need to go."

Josie kept crying and reaching toward Marylee.

"I'm sorry, Miss Stevens," Seth said, his voice strained. "Josie misses her mother so very much."

Marylee moved up and opened her arms. "Let me hold her for a moment, Mr. Hamilton."

Seth smiled. "You can call me Seth." He released Josie, and Marylee held her close, patting her back and cooing softly to her. Josie grew quiet and looked at her father. She smiled at him as if everything was now all right in her world.

Three customers entered the store. Marylee kissed Josie's cheek and said, "Sweetie, I have to give you back to your papa now."

It seemed that Josie understood. She smiled at Marylee and reached for her father. Seth took her once more, kissed the top of her downy head, and smiled at Marylee. "Thank you, again, Miss Stevens."

"It's Marylee. Since I can call you Seth, you can call me Marylee."

"All right, *Marylee.* We'll see you again soon."

"Make it *real* soon, won't you? Bye, Josie. Bye, Katie. Bye, Aaron."

Aaron and Katie told her good-bye, and Josie waved a fat little hand at her.

Marylee's cheerfulness warmed Seth's heart as he placed his children on the wagon seat and then climbed up himself.

Seth found a spot for the wagon in a vacant lot used by other new-comers to Deadwood. Then he asked a young man and his wife if they would watch his children while he went to see the owner of the general store. They gladly agreed to do so, and soon Seth knocked on Clyde Akers's door.

When Clyde opened the door, Seth smiled and introduced himself, explaining that he had been in the store that day and hap-pened to overhear Clyde's conversation with Dr. Roberts. He then told Clyde that he would like to buy the store.

Clyde's eyes brightened, and he invited Seth in.

They sat down, and Seth told Clyde that he was the owner of the hardware store in Merrillville, Indiana, and that he and his family had headed for the Black Hills to try to strike gold. He also told Clyde about Mattie being killed by Indians and gave him the names and ages of his children.

Seth complimented Clyde on the fine employee he had in Marylee Stevens and then asked him how much he wanted for the store. When Clyde named the sum, Seth said that he would take it. He explained that he had sufficient funds in the Merrillville bank to cover the price and would give Clyde a check on the spot.

Clyde then told Seth how Marylee, her recently widowed mother, and her seven-year-old brother were living in the rooms at the rear of the store. He told Seth that he could not sell the store to him unless he had a guarantee that they could stay there perma-nently.

Seth told him that the Stevens family could stay there as long as they needed to. They shook hands, and Seth wrote him out a check.

When Seth left the Akers house and walked the dark streets toward his wagon, he had peace in his heart.

The next day he found a house to rent, and he and the children settled into their new surroundings.

TWENTY-THREE

Winter came, and Jim Bannon worked hard even in the snow and freezing weather. With the new mail service, he was able now to correspond with Alyssa Rose, his parents, and Pastor and Mrs. Ballert, keeping them abreast of his diggings.

In addition to his original claim site, he also had applied for the adjacent site previously owned by Luke Farrell, and it had been granted. Jim worked them both, long and hard.

By April 1876, Deadwood was a thriving city, with more businesses going up and more gold seekers coming in. The church building was already packed for Sunday services and well-attended for mid-week services on Wednesday evenings. The Indian mission building was filling up on Sunday afternoons. Over a hundred Sioux adults and young people had now come to the Lord.

The Deadwood General Store was doing well under Seth Hamilton's ownership, and he was thrilled with it. Seth had turned twenty-six in February.

Marylee Stevens had happily accepted Seth as her new employer and landlord, though she missed Clyde Akers.

Seth still grieved over his loss of Mattie but found much solace in Marylee and her bright spirit. She was an excellent worker, her joyful smile and her helpful ways always there to greet every customer who entered the store.

Seth also admired the way that she worked so hard to take care of her ailing mother and her little brother. To top it all off, Marylee showed great love and compassion toward Aaron, Katie, and little Josie. They openly responded to her, and Seth saw that they were becoming quite attached to her.

Marylee had often told Seth how wonderful it was to be a born-again child of God, and she invited him to the church services every week. He attended the services occasionally but had never responded to the evangelistic preaching and received the Lord Jesus Christ as his Saviour.

Seth had not been able to find anyone to take care of his children during the day, so each business day he took them to the store with him. Often the children played quietly in a corner of the store, and at other times, they went to the Stevens apartment at the rear of the building and played with Blake. Now eight years old, Blake enjoyed entertaining Aaron, Katie, and little Josie. Oftentimes, Josie stayed in the store near Marylee. Seth was aware that a special affection was developing between the two of them.

One day in the second week of April, Seth was carrying Josie as usual when he and Aaron and Katie entered the store a few minutes before opening time.

Marylee was behind the counter putting money in the cash drawer. She looked up and flashed a smile. "Good morning!"

"Good morning," responded Seth, closing the door behind him.

Aaron and Katie dashed toward Marylee, who rounded the end of the counter, her arms open wide. She folded brother and sister close, kissed their foreheads, and told them that she loved them. Then she looked up to see Josie extending her chubby arms, saying, "Mama! Mama!"

Marylee took her from Seth, kissed her cheek, and nuzzled her soft neck, telling her that she loved her. The baby giggled and wrapped her arms around Marylee's neck.

I wonder how she always manages to be so cheerful, Seth thought as Marylee set Aaron and Katie to playing a game and then placed Josie in the playpen that he had built. She has a hard life working for me, caring for her mother, and tending to Blake plus my three children most of the time. She does almost all of the household chores and the cooking in the Stevens home, yet I've never seen her in a bad mood. She's always blithe and radiant. She really would make a marvelous wife and mother.

At that moment a miner named Walt Ferguson and his wife, Susan, entered the store. When Seth asked them how the mining was going, they gave him a sad look and said that it was not going well. Marylee spoke words of encouragement to them, and when they made a small purchase and left the store, Marylee had them smiling and speaking optimistically about their future.

Seth wanted to tell Marylee what he had been thinking about, but he knew that it was too soon. However, he moved up to her as she stood behind the counter and said, "Little lady, you sure cheered up the Fergusons. Your parents certainly named you well."

"What do you mean?" she asked.

"The name is so right, but it should be pronounced differently. It should be Merrily. You are such a cheerful person."

She let a smile curve her lips. "Why, thank you, Seth. I'm glad you see me that way."

"I'd have to be blind and deaf not to."

More customers were coming through the door. Marylee turned away from Seth, a pink tinge creeping into her cheeks. She knew that nothing could ever come of her tender feelings toward this lonely man because he was not a Christian. She told herself, however, that God was able to draw Seth to Himself. She had been praying that Seth would come to Christ. She would just pray harder.

Abruptly, from the back of the store, Blake drew up to Marylee and said, "Mama's not feeling well. Can you come and see her?"

Before Marylee could answer, Seth said, "You go tend to her. Give her all the care she needs. I'll handle things here."

"Thank you. I'll be back as soon as I can."

"Take your time, Marylee. Your mother comes first."

Marylee hurried away with Blake at her side and took a deep breath as she followed Blake into their apartment.

On Tuesday, May 9, Jim Bannon was repairing a spoke on one of his wagon's wheels when he looked up to see the Wolfrum wagon drawing near. All three Wolfrums were in the seat. Jim moved to the trail and smiled as Glenn drew the wagon to a halt.

"So how goes it, Jim?" Carl said.

"Not too bad. I'm still finding gold on both sites. How's it going for you?"

Dustin broke into a big grin. "It's been going so good that we're leaving right now for home!"

"Really?"

"Really," Carl said. "We've come up with even more gold than we had expected to. We're going to go back to Pennsylvania, buy some oil-filled land, and become millionaires!"

"Yeah!" Glenn said. "We're gonna get filthy rich!"

A solemn look settled in Jim's blue eyes. "For a time, maybe. But how about for eternity?"

Carl shrugged. "We gotta get going, Jim. It's been nice knowing you."

The wagon was put in motion, and the Wolfrums drove away without looking back.

"It's so sad to see them turn their backs on You, Lord," Jim said. "When I tell Luke that they've headed home still rejecting You, it's going to break his heart. He had so hoped that we could lead them to You."

By June 1, Jim had garnered some ninety-five thousand dollar's worth of gold, for which he was thankful. But he knew that it was a long way from the half-million that Frank McGuire would want to see before he would give in to Alyssa Rose marrying him.

In private letters to Alyssa, Jim had kept her apprised of his total each week. In response to each letter, Alyssa wrote back telling him that she was praying hard but was still willing to marry him regardless of his finances.

In early May, Seth Hamilton had purchased a large, well-built house on the outskirts of Deadwood, which had been owned by a miner who had struck it rich and had decided to take his family back to New York, where they had come from.

The Hamiltons had moved into the house on May 8, and the children loved it. There was plenty of room to play inside the house and in the huge yard outside. On the same day, Seth had hired a middle-aged widow whose husband had recently been killed while mining gold to take care of the children and to be his live-in housekeeper. Nora Bonfils had been a regular customer at the general store and had already gotten to know Aaron, Katie, and Josie. She was also well acquainted with Marylee Stevens from church as well as from the store.

One day in late May, Seth drove his wagon toward home after closing time and was thinking of Marylee and how she had captured his heart.

Spring was in full bloom in Dakota Territory. Along Deadwood's streets, light green leaves adorned the trees, and spring flowers bloomed in abundance on the hillsides that surrounded the town.

Soon Seth turned into the yard and drove around to the rear of the house. He pulled rein at the small barn, removed the harnesses from the team, and placed them in the corral.

As he turned to go to the house, he stopped and took a long look at it. The sparkling, clean open windows gleamed in the late afternoon sun, and the curtains fluttered in the soft breeze.

As Seth walked toward the house, he thought of how Mattie would have loved it. He told himself that Mattie would always have a special place in his heart but that his children needed a mother and he needed a wife. The only woman he could picture in that place was Marylee.

When he mounted the steps of the back porch and entered the kitchen, the pleasant aroma of chicken frying—as well as his three little ones and Nora Bonfils—greeted him.

Thursday, June 15, was a cloudless day, and it was quite warm in the general store. Marylee Stevens returned from having lunch with her mother and little brother in the apartment at the rear of the store and found Seth Hamilton stocking shelves near the counter. At the moment there were no customers in the store. "I'm back, Seth," Marylee said. "You can go home and eat lunch now, if you'd like."

Seth put the last item on the bottom shelf and moved toward her. "Marylee, since we're alone right now, I'd like to talk to you."

She smiled. "All right."

Seth surprised her by taking hold of both her hands. Looking deep into her shining eyes, he said, "Marylee, I can't hold it inside any longer. I have to confess that I'm falling in love with you. I know that you would make a wonderful mother for my children. They really love you."

Marylee bit her lower lip and swallowed hard. "Seth, I think an awful lot of you, too, and I dearly love Aaron, Katie, and Josie. But as a Christian, I would never marry a man who doesn't know the Lord."

Seth's stomach churned and he let go of her hands. "I…I guess I need to start coming to church more."

Marylee nodded. "That would be a start. But Seth, only when you repent of your sin and receive Jesus into your heart will you be a genuine Christian."

"Marylee, I know that I'm hearing the truth straight from the Bible whenever I hear Pastor Farrell preach. I've been wrong to only come to church once in a while. And my children need to be there, too."

Marylee smiled. "Yes, they do. I'd love to see your whole family there every Sunday."

On Wednesday morning, June 28, Jim Bannon and Luke Farrell were leaving the general store together. Jim had broken his pick handle and had bought a new pick, and Luke had gone to the store to buy a few groceries for Anna.

As they stepped out on the boardwalk both men noticed that Colonel Martin Lowry and two of his officers from Fort Lookout were standing in the street with a crowd of people gathering in front of them. Jim and Luke drew up close, and one of the officers looked around and said, "That's most of the people on the street, Colonel. I think you can go ahead now."

Lowry nodded and ran his gaze over the faces before him. "I wanted as many of the townspeople as possible to hear the news that I have to report. You can tell the others."

The colonel took a deep breath and said, "I received a telegram early this morning from Colonel Daniel Huston at Fort Abraham Lincoln. Most of you know that it was Lieutenant Colonel George Custer who led that expedition out of Fort Lincoln here to the Black Hills in July of 1874 and found the hills full of gold.

"About seven weeks ago, some of my men were patrolling the

Black Hills, as we do continually, and saw two unfamiliar Sioux warriors ride into Chief Red Cloud's village. They watched as the two warriors were escorted to Red Cloud's tepee. Shortly thereafter Red Cloud went with them into the forest. My men came to me and reported what they had seen.

"I gave it a little time and then went to the village and asked Red Cloud what the two warriors had wanted and why he went into the forest with them. He told me that the two warriors were Chief Sitting Bull's men and that they had come to escort him to a meeting with Chief Sitting Bull and Chief Crazy Horse.

"I asked Chief Red Cloud what they wanted to meet with him about. He told me that both chiefs were very angry at him because he was not fighting the white men—soldiers and miners—who had invaded the forbidden hills. Red Cloud told them that since they have been left to live unmolested in their village and are free to hunt all they want to, he found it better to get along with the white men than to have trouble with them. Red Cloud went on to tell me that both Sitting Bull and Crazy Horse were showing a savage hatred toward the white man's army, especially Colonel George Custer, who had led the expedition into the Black Hills and found gold.

"Red Cloud said that Sitting Bull was breathing hotly when he stated that whenever there has been a potential uprising by the Sioux in Dakota, Wyoming, and Montana Territories, it was Custer and his Seventh Cavalry who were sent from Fort Abraham Lincoln to put it down.

"Red Cloud then told me that Sitting Bull said that he wanted to kill Custer. Crazy Horse had joined with him, saying that it would be a pleasure to shed Custer's blood and the blood of all the men in the Seventh Cavalry."

Colonel Lowry wiped a hand over his mouth. "Now, to my telegram from Colonel Huston. He said that last Sunday, June 25, a bloody battle took place on the Little Big Horn River in Montana Territory. Lieutenant Colonel Custer and his Seventh Cavalry were attacked by Chief Sitting Bull's Hunkpapa warriors, plus a large number of Cheyenne and Arapaho warriors. The whole bunch were led by Chief Crazy Horse. The Seventh Cavalry was completely wiped out. Colonel Custer and all of his men are dead."

There were gasps all through the crowd.

Colonel Lowry and his two officers, looking very sad, then mounted up and rode away.

Time moved on, and Jim Bannon kept working both claims. On Monday, July 31, he went into Deadwood to buy groceries at the general store. When he entered the store, he saw Seth Hamilton and Marylee Stevens behind the counter talking to about a dozen customers who were gathered near the counter.

Jim picked up that the infamous Wild Bill Hickok had come to Deadwood. Most everyone knew that wherever Hickok showed up, there was usually trouble, especially gunfights. Many gunfighters wanted to challenge the ex-lawman and make a name for themselves by outdrawing him and killing him. So far, after several challenges, Hickok had been the one still standing when the gun smoke drifted away on the breeze.

Jim purchased his groceries, and as he drove his wagon back toward his claim site, he told himself that there would probably be bloodshed in Deadwood before Hickok left town.

The next day Martha "Calamity Jane" Canary rode into Deadwood, dressed like a man as usual. Asking around, she soon learned that Wild Bill Hickok was in the Number Ten Saloon. She found him there playing poker with a miner who had just hit it big.

When the game was over and Hickok had taken the miner for several thousand dollars, Calamity Jane sat in the chair where the miner had been sitting. Several patrons of the saloon heard her boast to Hickok that since she had last seen him, she had become a Pony Express rider. She had learned while in Abilene several days previously that he had gone to Deadwood, so she had taken a little time off from her new job to come and see him.

The next day, Wednesday, August 2, Calamity Jane was drinking at the bar of the Number Ten Saloon and watching Wild Bill clean another miner out of his money in a poker game. Men passed in and out of the saloon through swinging doors.

Calamity Jane was talking to the bartender when a man in his late thirties came in. He spotted Hickok, whose back was toward him, at the poker table. Quietly, he moved up behind Hickok, whipped out a cocked revolver, shouted, "This is for my brother!" and fired.

The bullet immediately killed Hickok, and the killer dashed out the door.

Calamity Jane, sobbing, dropped to her knees beside Hickok's body. Marshal Don Ryden and Deputy Ben Willis had been a short distance down the street and heard the shot. They were already running toward the saloon, guns drawn, when they saw the killer come out with a smoking gun in his hand.

Ryden shouted for the killer to stop and drop his gun. He did so, and at the same time men came running out of the saloon and told the lawmen that this man had just shot Wild Bill Hickok in the back of the head and killed him.

The lawmen learned that the man's name was Jack McCall. He told them that when Hickok was marshal of Abilene, Kansas, he had framed Jack's brother, Duff McCall, for a crime that he did not commit and then later murdered Duff.

Jack McCall was put in Deadwood's jail, and the next day the citizens joined together to hold a trial. Two gold miners were there from Abilene. They testified that Hickok had indeed murdered Jack McCall's brother but was never convicted because of the badge he wore. Jack was only getting revenge.

The jury declared Jack McCall innocent and set him free.

McCall immediately left town. The next day, since Deadwood as yet had no cemetery, James Butler Hickok was buried next to Whitewood Creek in the Black Hills with Calamity Jane weeping over his grave.

On Sunday morning, August 6, at the close of Pastor Luke Farrell's sermon, the invitation was given for those who wished to receive Christ as Saviour.

Because of Jim Bannon's tactful and patient witness, Zack and Will Johansen—who had the claim site next to Jim's—were in the service and walked the aisle together. The pastor had Jim come to the front to lead both father and son to the Lord.

The invitation went on.

On a pew halfway between the platform and the back of the auditorium the Stevens family, the Hamilton family, and Nora Bonfils were standing. Marylee had little Josie in her arms, and Nora had Aaron and Katie on each side of her.

Seth was on the aisle, with Marylee standing next to him. She noticed that he had tears in his eyes. He started to move into the aisle, but first he stopped and looked back at her. "I assure you, Marylee, I'm not doing this just so that you will marry me. I sincerely want to be saved."

She patted his arm as tears welled up in her own eyes. "I've been praying for this. Praise God!"

After one of the male counselors led Seth to Christ, he told the pastor and the congregation that it was because of Marylee's earnest and shining Christian testimony that he had come to the Lord.

Seth, Zack, and Will were baptized, and after the service many of the people took time to commend Marylee for being such a faithful witness for Jesus.

TWENTY-FOUR

After a pallid-faced Rachel Stevens had expressed her joy to Seth Hamilton in his newfound salvation, Pastor Luke and Anna took her and Blake in the Farrell wagon to their home for dinner.

Marylee, who had been invited to dinner with the Hamiltons, accompanied Seth, his children, and Nora Bonfils as they walked home from church. Marylee was carrying a sleepy Josie as she walked ahead of the others at Seth's side.

Marylee's joy over Seth's salvation showed in her bright eyes as she kept looking at Seth, who was taking pleasure in the attention that she was giving him. As they neared the house, Seth said, "Marylee, after dinner would you take a walk with me? I need to talk to you alone."

Her heart pounded as she said, "Of course, Seth. Right after dinner."

It was midafternoon when Marylee entered the Stevens apartment at the rear of the general store, her face beaming. Blake was playing a game on the floor in the back room, and Rachel was sitting on her favorite overstuffed chair in the parlor area. When she saw her daughter's radiant features and shining eyes, she said, "You had a nice dinner, I see."

"I did. Nora is an excellent cook. How about you and Blake?"

"Our dinner was excellent. Anna is an excellent cook, too. Almost as good as you."

Marylee giggled. "You're so kind."

"Oh, honey, I'm so happy about Seth and those miners getting saved," Rachel said. "Three more precious souls snatched from Satan's clutches."

"Yes, Mama. Praise the Lord." She took a deep breath, let it out slowly, and said, "I have something else to tell you, Mama."

Rachel smiled. "You mean about you and Seth?"

Marylee's face tinted slightly. "Why, yes. How did you know?"

"Honey, your mother may be sickly, but she isn't blind. You think I don't know what's been going on between you two?"

"I hope that when I become a mother, I'll have the kind of insight you have."

"Well, you'll be a stepmother before you have your own children. I'm sure you will gain insight quickly with Aaron, Katie, and Josie."

Marylee's eyes widened. "You...you know that Seth just asked me to marry him?"

"I figured so. I knew that the one thing that was holding this whole thing back was that Seth wasn't a Christian. I so much appreciate your faithfulness to the Lord in not letting things develop between you and Seth until he came to the Lord. Otherwise, there would have been an unequal yoke."

Marylee leaned over and hugged her mother's neck. "The Lord knew that I wouldn't violate His command, Mama."

"But He does answer prayer, doesn't He?"

"That He does!"

"Have you set a date for the wedding?"

"We need to talk to Pastor Luke about it first. I think it'll be about the middle of September. Well, Mama, it's time for you to lie down and take your nap."

When Rachel lay on her bed, Marylee placed a soft, light spread over her. She was happy to see that her mother was losing some of the pallor from her cheeks and that the sorrowful, pinched look around her mouth was gone. There was even a tinge of healthy pink in her cheeks now.

Rachel closed her eyes and quickly fell asleep. Marylee lifted praise to the Lord in her heart and then quietly slipped away.

The next day Jim Bannon was working the claim that had been Luke Farrell's when he looked up to see Luke coming toward him from his wagon, which stood at the edge of the trail that passed by the site.

Jim dropped his pick and said, "Hello, preacher man!"

"Hello, gold-digging man!" Luke said. "I just had to come by and tell you the good news."

"What's that?"

"I received a letter from Mom. She says that Dad is now home from the hospital and doing well."

"Praise the Lord."

"Amen. And praise Him for your future father-in-law's generosity, which has relieved so much pressure on my parents by paying off those huge medical bills. And we also got a letter today from Frank McGuire. There was a check with it for ten thousand dollars to help Anna and me with our living expenses, but part of it is to be used to enlarge the Indian mission building. You must have informed the McGuires that the building is packed out every service."

Jim grinned. "Guess I did mention that in one of my letters to Alyssa Rose."

"So how goes the 'Please Frank McGuire Fund'?"

"Well, I'm still a long way from a half million, but my total worth is now just over a hundred and four thousand dollars."

"That's good," Luke said, "but I know that you desperately want to marry that sweet Alyssa Rose."

"That's for sure."

"Well, let's get on our knees right now and ask the Lord to take care of this whole matter."

In Cheyenne on Wednesday evening, September 13, people were filing out of the church building after the service. Pastor David Ballert and Tammy were at the door shaking hands with people as they were leaving. When the McGuires drew up, the pastor gripped Frank's hand and said, "Frank, could I set up a time for you and me to talk privately?"

"Of course," Frank said. "How about I take you to lunch tomorrow?"

"Sounds good. I'll come by the bank at noon."

Frank smiled. "I'll look forward to it."

On Saturday, September 16, Seth Hamilton and Marylee Stevens were married in a small, quiet ceremony at the church in Deadwood by Pastor Luke Farrell. It was a simple wedding with only their families and closest friends in attendance.

Katie and Aaron sat in the front row in the auditorium next to Nora Bonfils, who held Josie on her lap. The children's faces were shiny, not only from the scrubbing Nora had given them, but from sheer happiness as well.

Marylee wore a white dress, trimmed around the high collar with dainty white lace. A sprig of pink wildflower adorned her upswept dark brown hair, and as she stood with Seth before the pastor in the ceremony, a smile as brilliant as the autumn sunshine flooded her face.

Seth had made arrangements before the wedding to replace Marylee as clerk at the general store with Nora Bonfils. Marylee would stay home with the children and keep her own house. The newlyweds were superbly happy.

On Friday, September 22, Jim Bannon had four sacks of gold nuggets in his wagon as he left the two claim sites and headed for town. Assayer Wayne Clarkson had recently moved his office from the fort into Deadwood.

When Jim came out of Clarkson's office, he was glad for the additional amount added to his small fortune, but he was wishing it had been much larger. He had the gold made into coins and took them to the bank and made a deposit to his account. As he walked out of the bank, he now had a total of $119,575 in his account.

"Lord," he said as he headed toward the post office in hopes that there would be a letter from Alyssa Rose and possibly one from his parents, "I very much appreciate the gold that You've allowed me to find, but I'm still short more than three hundred and eighty thousand. I miss Alyssa so much and want so desperately to make her my wife. Please help me."

Jim entered the post office and asked the clerk for his mail. There was only one letter, and when he saw the return address, his eyes widened. It was from Frank McGuire.

When he settled on his wagon seat, Jim nervously opened the envelope, unfolded the letter, and began to read.

Pastor Luke Farrell was in his office at the church, working on a sermon for Sunday, when he looked through the window and saw Jim Bannon driving his wagon into the parking lot. He laid aside his Bible and notes and went to the door.

As Jim moved up the steps of the porch, Luke said, "You sure look excited! Did you finally hit it big at the claim sites?"

Jim shook his head. "No, I didn't hit it big with gold, but I sure hit it big with Frank McGuire! I just picked up this letter from him at the post office, and I had to come and share the good news with you! After all, you and I have prayed together about my fortune in gold many a time."

"Well, come sit down and tell me what the letter says."

The two of them sat down on a small sofa next to a window in the office. Eyes dancing, Jim said, "Pastor Luke, Frank says that Pastor Dave Ballert had a private talk with him and asked him why, since he could be so generous toward you, the church here, and the Indian mission...why couldn't he be generous with Jim Bannon? Pastor Ballert shamed him for standing in the way of Alyssa and me getting married just because I'm not yet worth a half million dollars. Frank says that the pastor pointed out how generous the Lord had been to Frank, saying that he should show the same kind of generosity to me. Frank says that he suddenly realized how foolish he had been to put this restriction on me before he would give his consent for Alyssa to marry me, since the two of us are obviously so much in love. He asked that I come home immediately and set a wedding date with Alyssa."

"Well, praise God! He really does answer prayer!"

"Yes, He sure does! Frank says that he won't tell Alyssa or anyone else that I'm coming home and now have his blessing to marry his daughter. It will be a complete surprise for them when I get home."

Two days later, with other miners working the claim sites that Jim had owned, he said good-byes to all his friends in Deadwood, including Luke and Anna Farrell, and drove away in his wagon.

At midmorning on Wednesday, October 4, Jim pulled into Cheyenne and hauled to a stop at the hitch rail in front of the

Bank of Wyoming. His heart pounded as he headed for the door. He wanted to see Frank McGuire first and thank him for his change of mind.

It was almost noon when Kathleen McGuire was doing some dusting in the parlor of their new mansion. Her eye caught motion outside the large window, and she saw her husband and Monty climbing the porch steps with a smiling Jim Bannon between them.

Kathleen's heart leaped in her chest. She dashed into the hall and hurried to the winding staircase. Stopping at the bottom of the stairs, she called out to her daughter, who was on the second floor in her room. "Alyssa! Alyssa! Come downstairs! Jim is here!"

When the three men came through the front door, they found Kathleen standing in the foyer and an excited Alyssa Rose bounding down the spiral staircase. She squealed Jim's name and rushed into his open arms. "Darling, why didn't you let me know you were coming?"

"Sweetheart, I have a big surprise for you, but I'll let your father tell you."

Kathleen's eyes were wide. She went to Jim and hugged him and then looked at her husband. "Frank, you knew that Jim was coming?"

Frank chewed his lower lip and nodded. "Yes." Then to Jim he said, "Give Kathleen the letter that I sent you and let her read it aloud so Alyssa can hear it."

Jim took the envelope from his shirt pocket, slipped the letter out, and placed it in Kathleen's hand.

While Jim and Alyssa held on to each other, Kathleen read the letter aloud, pausing from time to time to catch her breath. When she finished, she was crying, as was Alyssa, who went to her father, kissed his cheek, and poured out her appreciation.

Frank was also blinking at tears. Smiling at his daughter, he said, "Thank the Lord first, honey, and then thank Pastor Ballert. As you heard from the letter, God used him to help me see what a fool I've been."

"I've already thanked the Lord at least a thousand times," Jim said. "And I'll be thanking Pastor Ballert when Alyssa and I go to him to make arrangements for the wedding later today." He turned to Alyssa. "How about Saturday, November twenty-fifth for our wedding date?"

Alyssa took hold of his hands, her face beaming. "November twenty-fifth it is!"

"Praise the Lord!" Monty shouted, his cheeks shiny with tears.

"Now, Alyssa, Kathleen, let me tell you what I told Jim and Monty at the bank," Frank said. "You'll recall that a few weeks ago we talked about the ad that the Harvey Jensen family had placed in the *Cheyenne Sentinel* to sell their two-hundred-acre wheat and alfalfa farm."

Kathleen and Alyssa both nodded.

"Well, right after I mailed this letter to Jim, I went out to talk to Harvey. I bought the farm from him, and it's already in the name of Mr. and Mrs. James Bannon. The house, barn, and out-buildings are only seven years old, and they're in beautiful condition. The Jensens have already moved to Denver, where Harvey has opened up a farmers' feed and supply store."

Alyssa squealed and leaped at her father, arms open wide. She embraced him, with tears flowing, and thanked him for his generosity. She stepped back, jumping up and down with excitement, her face flushed a rosy pink, her wide, expressive eyes aglow with joy.

Jim took hold of her hand. "Sweetheart, my parents don't even know I'm back yet. Will you go with me so we can tell them the good news?"

"I sure will!"

"Then we'll go see Pastor Ballert."

"Yes!"

Jim ran his gaze to Frank and then said to Alyssa, "Your father asked me this morning how much money I have from the gold mining. I told him that I have $119,575 in the Deadwood Bank, which I will transfer to my account at the Bank of Wyoming. Of course, it will soon be *our* account. I told your father that I would use twenty-four thousand of it to pay off my parents' mortgage so they wouldn't be strapped so tightly with their finances. And you know what? This generous father of yours used his own money to pay off the mortgage. My parents will be thrilled when I give them the good news."

Jim and Alyssa hurried out of the mansion and drove away in Jim's wagon with Monty and his parents clinging to each other and wiping away tears.

A short distance out of Cheyenne, Jim pulled the wagon off the road, and it came to rest in a small grove of cottonwood trees. A gurgling stream rippled alongside it.

Jim jumped down from the wagon seat and hurried around to the other side, holding up his arms toward Alyssa.

"What are we doing?" she asked, looking puzzled.

"You'll see."

He guided her across the green grass to a large boulder that was half-buried in the ground. Jim helped her to sit down on a level section of the boulder. Then Alyssa's eyes filled with wonder as she watched the man she loved go down on one knee in front of her. Without hesitation, she placed her small hands in his work-roughened hands and looked into his smiling eyes.

"Sweetheart," he said, "now that Frank McGuire has given his permission for me to marry his daughter, I want to do this properly." Jim spoke huskily, tears filling his eyes. "Alyssa Rose

McGuire, I love you with every fiber of my being. I will love you always and forever. Would you please give me the honor of becoming my wife?"

Happy tears spilled down Alyssa's cheeks. "Jim Bannon, you are the absolute love of my life. Nothing would make me happier than to become your wife."

Jim stood up, cupped her face in his hands, and kissed her tenderly. He then held her close, and their happy tears mingled together.

On Saturday afternoon, November 25, the newlyweds left the church in Jim's highly decorated wagon and headed out of Cheyenne toward their farm. It was cold, and both of them wore coats over their wedding attire.

When they pulled up in front of the house, Jim hopped out of the wagon and helped Alyssa down. He embraced her, kissed her soundly, and then said, "Sweetheart, before I carry you over the threshold, I want to tell you something."

She raised up on her tiptoes and kissed him. "I'm listening."

"You know that I tried with all my might to dig up a half-million dollars in gold."

"Mm-hmm."

"I didn't make it."

She met his gaze. "I know."

"But you know what? I am still the richest man in all the world. You know why?"

Alyssa shook her head. "Huh-uh. Why?"

"I'm the richest man in all the world because I have *you!*"

Five years after Jim Bannon married Alyssa McGuire, an evangelist came to Cheyenne at Pastor David Ballert's invitation to preach a revival meeting.

In the Sunday morning service, the evangelist described how riches had destroyed so many people's lives because their money had become their god. During the sermon, he had the crowd turn to Psalm 62:10 and read the second half of the verse to them: "If riches increase, set not your heart upon them."

He said that he had held a meeting a few months ago in Oil City, Pennsylvania. He had learned upon arriving there of a family named Wolfrum who had come into great wealth during the gold strike in the Black Hills back in 1875–76 and had returned to the Oil City area and opened up their own oil business. Within two years, they were multimillionaires.

The evangelist said that Carl Wolfrum's wife of over forty years had left him because he changed for the worse when he became wealthy. The oldest son, Glenn, found life unbearable and committed suicide. The youngest son, Dustin, lived for only one thing: to gain more money. Because his wealth was not multiplying as quickly as he thought it should, he turned to alcohol and died one night in a drunken stupor. All three had set their hearts on their riches.

Jim Bannon sat in the pew with Alyssa beside him, feeling sick at heart for the Wolfrums, remembering how they had shunned him when he had witnessed to them of Jesus Christ and warned them not to let money become their god.

EPILOGUE

Hunkpapa Chief Sitting Bull, whose warriors, along with some Cheyenne and Arapaho warriors, wiped out Lieutenant Colonel George Armstrong Custer and his Seventh Cavalry at the Little Big Horn River on June 25, 1876, fled into Canada in May 1877. The Canadian government understood that the steady encroachment of white men into Sioux country, killing the buffalo upon which the Indians depended for food, had driven them across the border into Canada.

The Canadian government allowed them to stay for four years; then famine in Canada forced the Hunkpapas back across the border. When they were once again in the United States, the U.S. Army kept a close watch on them, knowing Sitting Bull's hatred for whites and his desire to wipe them out.

In 1889 the Ghost Dance religious movement led by Sitting Bull began to prophesy the advent of an Indian messiah who would destroy the whites and restore former Sioux traditions. This augmented the unrest that was already present.

As a precaution, U.S. Army soldiers were sent to arrest the chief. Seized on the Grand River on December 15, 1890, in what had become the state of South Dakota, Sitting Bull was killed when his warriors attempted to rescue him.

He was buried at Fort Yates, North Dakota. His remains, however, were moved in 1953 to Mobridge, South Dakota, where a granite shaft now marks his grave.

Wild Bill Hickok's killer, Jack McCall, was tried and released in Deadwood on August 3, 1876. However, the next year he was tracked down by lawmen, tried again in Laramie, Wyoming, and finally hanged for his crime on March 1, 1877.

The Orphan Train Trilogy

THE LITTLE SPARROWS, Book #1

Kearney, Cheyenne, Rawlins. Reno, Sacramento, San Francisco. At each train station, a few lucky orphans from the crowded streets of New York City receive the fulfillment of their dreams: a home and family. This orphan train is the vision of Charles Loring Brace, founder of the Children's Aid Society, who cannot bear to see innocent children abandoned in the overpopulated cities of the mid-nineteenth century. Yet it is not just the orphans whose lives need mending. Follow the train along and watch God's hand restore love and laughter to the right family at the right time!

ISBN 1-59052-063-7

ALL MY TOMOROWS, Book #2

When sixty-two orphans and abandoned children leave New York City on a train headed out West, they have no idea what to expect. Will they get separated from their friends and siblings? Will their new families love them? Will a family even pick them at all? Future events are wilder than any of them could imagine—ranging from kidnappings and whippings to stowing away on wagon trains, from starting orphanages of their own to serving as missionaries to the Apache. No matter what, their paths are being watched by Someone who cares about and carefully plans all their tomorrows.

ISBN 1-59052-130-7

WHISPERS IN THE WIND, Book #3

Young Dane Weston's dream is to become a doctor. But it will take more than just determination to realize his goal, once his family is murdered and he ends up in a colony of street waifs begging for food. Then he is mistaken for a murderer himself and sentenced to life in prison. Now what will become of his friendship with the pretty orphan girl, Tharyn, who wanted to enter the medical profession herself? Does she feel he is anything more than a big brother to her? And will she ever write him again?

ISBN 1-59052-169-2

Mail Order Bride Series

Desperate men who settled the West resorted to unconventional measures in their quest for companionship, advertising for and marrying women they'd never even met! Read about a unique and adventurous period in the history of romance.

Frontier Doctor Trilogy

ONE MORE SUNRISE–BOOK ONE

Young frontier doctor Dane Logan is gaining renown as a surgeon. Beyond his wildest hopes, he meets his long-lost love—only to risk losing her to the Tag Moran gang.

ISBN 1-59052-308-3

BELOVED PHYSICIAN–BOOK TWO

While Dr. Dane gains renown by rescuing people from gunfights, Indian attacks, and a mine collapse, Nurse Tharyn mourns the capture of her dear friend Melinda by renegade Utes.

ISBN 1-59052-313-X

THE HEART REMEMBERS–BOOK THREE

In this final book in the Frontier Doctor trilogy, Dane survives an accident, but not without losing his memory. Who is he? Does he have a family somewhere?

ISBN 1-59052-351-2

Hannah of Fort Bridger Series

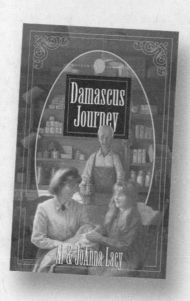

Hannah Cooper's husband dies on the dusty Oregon Trail, leaving her in charge of five children and a general store in Fort Bridger. Dependence on God fortifies her against grueling challenges and bitter tragedies.

Angel of Mercy Series

Post-Civil War nurse Breanna Baylor uses her professional skill to bring healing to the body, and her faith in the Redeemer to bring comfort to thirsty souls, valiantly serving God on the dangerous frontier.

Shadow of Liberty Series

Let Freedom Ring
#1 in the Shadow of Liberty Series

It is January 1886 in Russia. Vladimir Petrovna, a Christian husband and father of three, faces bankruptcy, persecution for his beliefs, and despair. The solutions lie across a perilous sea.

ISBN 1-57673-756-X

The Secret Place
#2 in the Shadow of Liberty Series

Popular authors Al and JoAnna Lacy offer a compelling question: As two young people cope with love's longings on opposite shores, can they find the serenity of God's covering in *The Secret Place?*

ISBN 1-57673-800-0

A Prince Among Them
#3 in the Shadow of Liberty Series

A bitter enemy of Queen Victoria kidnaps her favorite great-grandson. Emigrants Jeremy and Cecelia Barlow book passage on the same ship to America, facing a complex dilemma that only all-knowing God can set right.

ISBN 1-57673-880-9

Undying Love
#4 in the Shadow of Liberty Series

19-year-old Stephan Varda flees his own guilt and his father's rage in Hungary, finding undying love from his heavenly Father—and a beautiful girl—across the ocean in America.

ISBN 1-57673-930-9